Sociology Through Science Fiction

Sociology Through Science Fiction

EDITED BY

John W. Milstead

WINTHROP COLLEGE

Martin Harry Greenberg

FLORIDA INTERNATIONAL UNIVERSITY

Joseph D. Olander

FLORIDA INTERNATIONAL UNIVERSITY

Patricia Warrick

UNIVERSITY OF WISCONSIN, FOX VALLEY CENTER

St. Martin's Press   **New York**

*Since this page cannot accommodate all of the copyright notices,
the page that follows constitutes an extension of the copyright page.*

Acknowledgments

THE CONDÉ NAST PUBLICATIONS, INC.: The following four selections are reprinted
by permission of the authors and their agent, Scott Meredith Literary Agency,
Inc., 580 Fifth Avenue, New York, N.Y. 10036. "Birthright," by Poul
Anderson, copyright © 1970 by The Condé Nast Publications, Inc.; "Gadget
Vs. Trend," by Christopher Anvil, copyright 1962 by The Condé Nast Publications, Inc.; "Positive Feedback," by Christopher Anvil, copyright © 1965
by The Condé Nast Publications, Inc.; "Lost Newton," by Stanley Schmidt,
copyright 1970 by The Condé Nast Publications, Inc. "Integration Module,"
by Daniel B. James, copyright © 1972 by The Condé Nast Publications, Inc.
Reprinted by permission of the author. "Pigeon City," by Jesse Miller, copyright © 1972 by The Condé Nast Publications, Inc. Reprinted by permission
of the author. "Misinformation," by Howard L. Myers, copyright 1972 by
The Condé Nast Publications, Inc. Reprinted by permission of the agents
for the author's estate, Scott Meredith Literary Agency, Inc., 580 Fifth
Avenue, New York, N.Y. 10036. "Generation Gaps," by Clancy O'Brien,
copyright © 1972 by The Condé Nast Publications, Inc. Reprinted by
permission of the author. All the above selections are reprinted from *Analog
Science Fact and Fiction*.

GALAXY PUBLISHING CORPORATION: "Total Environment," by Brian W. Aldiss.
Copyright © 1968 by Galaxy Publishing Corporation. Reprinted by permission of the author and his agent, A. P. Watt & Son. "Primary Education
of the Camiroi," copyright © 1970 by R. A. Lafferty, © 1966 by Galaxy
Publishing Corporation, and "Slow Tuesday Night," copyright © 1970 by
R. A. Lafferty, © 1965 by Galaxy Publishing Corporation, are reprinted by
permission of R. A. Lafferty and his agent, Virginia Kidd.

GERALD JONAS: "The Shaker Revival," copyright © 1970 by Gerald Jonas. Reprinted by permission of Gerald Jonas and the International Famous Agency.

THE HAROLD MATSON COMPANY, INC.: "The Pedestrian," copyright by Ray Bradbury. Reprinted by permission of The Harold Matson Company, Inc. "A
Canticle for Leibowitz," copyright © 1959 by Walter M. Miller, Jr. Reprinted
by permission of The Harold Matson Company, Inc.

MERCURY PRESS, INC.: "Deeper Than the Darkness," by Greg Benford. Copyright 1969 by Mercury Press, Inc. Used by permission of the author. "A Day in the Suburbs," by Evelyn E. Smith. Copyright © by Mercury Press, Inc. Used by permission of the author. Both selections are reprinted from *The Magazine of Fantasy and Science Fiction.*

ARTHUR PORGES: "Guilty As Charged," by Arthur Porges, from *The Best Science Fiction Stories and Novels* (1955), edited by T. E. Dikty. Reprinted by permission of the author and his agent, Scott Meredith Literary Agency, Inc., 580 Fifth Avenue, New York, N.Y. 10036.

JOHN RANKINE: "Two's Company," by John Rankine. Copyright © 1964 by John Carnell for *New Writings in S–F 1.* Reprinted by permission of the author and his agent, E. J. Carnell Literary Agency.

STREET AND SMITH PUBLICATIONS, INC.: "Single Combat," by Robert Abernathy. Copyright 1954 by Street and Smith Publications, Inc. Reprinted by permission of the author. "Of Course," by Chad Oliver. Copyright 1954 by Street and Smith Publications, Inc. Reprinted by permission of the author. Both of these selections are from *Astounding Science Fiction.*

ULTIMATE PUBLISHING COMPANY: "Nobody Lives on Burton Street," by Greg Benford, from *Amazing Stories.* Copyright © 1970 by Ultimate Publishing Company. Reprinted by permission of the author.

The authors would like to extend their thanks to Dorothy Jones and Janet Cox for their valuable criticism of an early draft of the text, and to Betty Simpson, who found time to type the manuscript while she continued to handle her many duties as secretary of the sociology department at Winthrop College.

Contents

Introduction

Although the boundaries between sociology and other social sciences are blurred by the overlap of subject matter and method, each social science offers its own perspective for the study of some aspect of man and society.

Sociology, like the other social sciences, is a relatively new discipline. Auguste Comte (1798-1857), a French social philosopher, is often regarded as the first sociologist. Comte proposed a new field ot study, which he termed "sociology," that would incorporate all other knowledge and therefore sit at the apex of what he saw as a hierarchical arrangement of bodies of knowledge. He assumed that all knowledge must find practical application in society. Sociological knowledge, in particular, would serve as the means through which a "good" social order could be established. In retrospect, contemporary sociologists realize that Comte, in seeing sociology as superior to all other sciences, had excessively lofty aspirations for the fledgling discipline. Few consider the other sciences subordinate to sociology, and many reject the notion that all knowledge must have practical application.

Besides Comte, several other nineteenth-century thinkers are regarded as classic figures in the development of sociology. They too addressed themselves to defining the scope of the new discipline and stating the manner in which social life was to be studied. An important example is Herbert Spencer (1820-1903). Spencer, influenced by Charles Darwin's work in biology, developed a conception of societies as units much like organisms. These social units evolved through time as certain processes operated within them. As Alex Inkeles states, Spencer "stressed the obligation of sociology to deal with the interrelations between the different elements of society, to give an account of how the parts influence the whole and are in turn reacted upon, and in the process may transform or be transformed." [1]

[1] Alex Inkeles, *What Is Sociology?* (Englewood Cliffs, N.J.: Prentice-Hall, Inc., 1964), p. 5.

Like Comte and Spencer, Emile Durkheim (1858-1917) emphasized that sociological study should focus upon societies and their major institutional components. Durkheim gave a good deal of attention to the methods of sociology, stressing the collection and rigorous analysis of empirical data. He felt that social phenomena should be explained by what he called social facts. For example, in his classic work *Suicide*, he demonstrated that the key variable in explaining the incidence of suicide was the degree of integration of the individual into the group. Valid explanations of suicide, Durkheim argued, are constructed in terms of this social variable, and must not be reduced to explanations in which suicide is seen as the consequence of psychological, biological, or geographical factors. In short, social phenomena should be explained in their own terms—by social facts. Thus Durkheim gave sociology a distinctive framework within which to seek its explanations.

A fourth classic figure in early sociology, Max Weber (1864-1920), expounded a method—*verstehen*—through which the sociologist would understand what Weber called social action. Weber held that sociologists must not be content with describing the forms social behavior takes. They must also focus on the subjective meaning of social behavior to the participants in interaction. Only in this way could sociologists understand the forms of social action and thereby comprehend the social relations which comprise social structure. Weber's classic analyses of bureaucracy and his sophisticated comparative study of religion and the social structure remain important examples of both content and method.

Although many others have made important contributions to defining the scope and methods of sociology, Comte, Spencer, Durkheim, and Weber have been particularly influential. Although their lives span 120 years and the four are products of three different cultures, their work reveals common perspectives. They view sociology in large part to be the study of the society as a unit, and they are interested in comparing societies with each other. They also see sociology as the study of the social institutions which constitute a society and the interrelations among these institutions. Finally, they emphasize that sociology should include the study of social interaction and social relationships in a wide variety of social contexts.

All contemporary sociologists owe a debt to these classic early figures. Sociology is now defined in many different ways, but there is probably general agreement that sociology is the social science concerned with patterned, recurrent behavior of human beings in social interaction. Thus, the "sociological question," as William M. Dobriner observes, "centers on the phenomenon of *association* between persons.

Sociology is the *science* which undertakes the study of *relationships* between individuals." [2]

Characteristically, sociology relies heavily on the scientific method to establish a body of verified knowledge about societal life. Assuming that the social universe operates, as does the physical universe, through potentially provable networks of cause and effect relationships, sociologists seek to ask the "right" questions and get the accurate answers that will lead them to fuller understanding of the principles that govern human social behavior.

Controversy still prevails among sociologists over the question of what should be done with the knowledge and understanding they acquire. Those with strong leanings toward empiricism and "pure science" follow the "hard" methods of the physical sciences and argue that values play no part in either their selection of hypotheses or the design of their research. They contend that they have no professional obligation to apply findings directly to solving social problems or to formulating social policy.

In contrast, some sociologists insist that sociology is a humanistic discipline. They are skeptical of the methods of physical science on the grounds that these methods limit the types of questions they can formulate, the types of inquiry they can pursue, and the research methods they can employ. They believe that their own values do, and must, affect their work as sociologists, and they do not hesitate to apply their knowledge to the solution of social problems. They feel a professional responsibility to attempt to affect the formulation of social policy.

Regardless of the value premises from which sociologists approach their work, most of them would agree on certain benefits of the discipline, not only for its professional practitioners but for anyone who undertakes its study. Sociological knowledge can inform, liberate, and provide a perspective for understanding the social worlds in which we will spend our lives. As we understand the nature of the social constraints that patterned recurrent behavior creates, we can understand the social context in which we function. This, in turn, can lead to fuller self-insight and a broader view of the options available to us in any given social situation. As C. Wright Mills puts it, "reading sociology should increase our awareness of the imperial reach of social worlds into the intimacies of our very self." Sociology "helps one to understand what is happening in the world. It also helps

---

2 William M. Dobriner, *Social Structures and Systems* (Pacific Palisades, Calif.: Goodyear Publishing Company, Inc., 1969), p. 1. Emphasis in the original.

to understand what is happening in and to one's self." [3]

Peter Berger's term, the "debunking motif," [4] describes another use of sociology. Sociology provides a way of "going behind" events, of cutting through the facade of common sense and conventional explanations. This is particularly important because we tend to accept common-sense explanations even though they are often false, and we live in a time in which we are subjected to explanations of events by officials and others who have a vested interest in distorting reality or who offer us as facts their own interpretations of the way things are. Sociology helps us to see particular events in a larger context—to understand, for example, how such major social trends as urbanization and modernization are changing the societies in which we live and our own lives as well.

The student of sociology will learn to put the discipline to use in these ways. He or she will develop an ability to see the interrelatedness of things, to juxtapose the apparently unrelated or contradictory. "This very ability to look at a situation from the vantage points of competing systems of interpretation is . . . one of the hallmarks of sociological consciousness." [5] C. Wright Mills has described this ability well and has called it "the sociological imagination." "What social science is properly about," writes Mills, "is the human variety, which consists of all the social worlds in which men have lived, are living and *might live*." [6]

In sum, even for beginning students, sociology can stimulate a consciousness of the world in which they live and an imagination that will provide them greater understanding of that world. Exposure to sociology permits individuals to get outside of themselves, to see their own backgrounds and experience, values, and beliefs as part of one of many possible "schemes of things." This increasing awareness of different social patterns serves well those who live in today's complex world.

To the development of sociological consciousness, or sociological imagination, science fiction is particularly well suited. The questions science fiction writers ask are not about one social world, but about countless possible social worlds. As models, the societies described in science fiction can generate serious inquiry into the

[3] C. Wright Mills (ed.), *Images of Man* (New York: George Braziller, Inc., 1960), pp. 16, 17.

[4] Peter L. Berger, *Invitation to Sociology*, Anchor Books (Garden City, N.Y.: Doubleday & Company, Inc., 1963), p. 38.

[5] *Ibid.*

[6] C. Wright Mills, *The Sociological Imagination* (New York: Oxford University Press, 1959), p. 132. Emphasis added.

nature of contemporary social reality. That is, they provide starting points for constructing hypotheses about the present. As models, they should be judged not in terms of whether they are true or false representations of current reality but, rather, in terms of whether they provide useful insights into social patterns and structures in which we are interested as students of sociology. Grasping the familiar—for all science fiction stories embody elements of the familiar—we can then contrast the unfamiliar with our own experience and thus become more acutely aware of the social world in which we exist and of possible alternatives to it. "The sociologist, at his best," Peter Berger has said, "is a man with a taste for other lands, inwardly open to the measureless richness of human possibilities, eager for new horizons and new worlds of human meaning." [7]

The stories in this book are arranged in six chapters. Chapter 1 deals with some of the concerns of sociologists as they approach their study of human social life. Chapter 2 presents stories about social organization, culture, social and cultural change, collective behavior, and deviance. Chapter 3 is concerned with the relationships between self and society, while Chapter 4 covers social differentiation according to social class, race, and age. Chapter 5 contains a story focusing on each of the five basic social institutions: familial, educational, economic, political, and religious. Chapter 6 is concerned with population and urban life. Introductions to the six chapters provide brief descriptions of major sociological issues and concepts. Each story is preceded by a brief note suggesting the sociological context in which the story can most usefully be seen.

In one sense, science fiction should not be taken too literally. The stories presented here are not offered as *social forecasts*. The science fiction writer describes the *possible* and may even have hit upon the *probable*, but he does not prescribe the inevitable. Who is willing to say, however, that these stories describe the *impossible?*

[7] Peter Berger, *op. cit.*, p. 53.

Sociology Through Science Fiction

I

The Study of Society

The subject matter of sociology is patterned human social interaction. The sociologist is interested in man in all his social relationships—from patterned social interaction between two persons to the social institutional patterns of large, complex societies. In their study of society, some sociologists concentrate on formulating broad, societal questions, such as what is the interrelationship among social institutions and the society of which these institutions are a part? Others focus on analyses more limited in scope—for example, studies of groups or of a particular type of group, such as the peer group or small group. Some study crime or deviance, others collective behavior, still others marriage and the family. The task of comprehending man's varied patterns of behavior is vast and the approaches to making sense of this social reality are varied in scope and specialization.

As social scientists, sociologists attempt to verify knowledge of man's socially patterned behavior. In so doing, they use the scientific method in gathering and utilizing their information. Much sociological research involves the systematic and meticulous collection of observations and the analysis of data. By the method of induction, general statements are then produced from particular data. Detailed attention is often given to the methods through which these data are collected. In the extreme, some sociologists are so insistent on "rigorously" applying a particular method that they ignore important questions and do not consider the context of the questions they do ask. Using the "proper" method the "right" way becomes all important, and minute answers to miniscule questions are celebrated. C. Wright Mills has referred to those who proceed this way as "abstracted empiricists," and he questions their ability to see and develop the theoretical context into which their efforts fall.

Other sociological effort involves the development of propositions combined into highly abstract theory. Some sociologists deduce more concrete hypotheses from abstract theory. Others who engage in this type of effort are content to combine highly abstract propositions into broad theoretical schema, leaving to others the problem of putting these propositions into testable hypotheses. Mills has given the name "grand theorists" to those engaging in this type of effort and has questioned what would be called today the "relevance" of their efforts. For some, these contrasting emphases have reflected a tension between "theory" and "research," but as Robert K. Merton, an influential contemporary American sociologist, has argued, theory and research are not separate and antithetical efforts, but complementary aspects of the development of knowledge.

Not all sociologists agree on what the scientific method entails or how literally it must be applied, but it is the use of this method in the study of human social behavior that classifies sociology as one of the social sciences and separates it from journalism and the humanities. No matter how "hard" or "soft" their methods, sociologists will employ theory, hypotheses, generalizations, and concepts in their search for verified knowledge about man.

The sociologist also uses many research techniques in the study of human social behavior. Examples include approximations of the controlled laboratory experimental setting, computer simulation of mathematical models of social reality, and study and observation of human beings in real-life social settings. In short, the subject matter studied, the specializations chosen, the methods emphasized, and the techniques used by sociologists are richly varied. The understanding of human social behavior is no simple task and commands no less than full use of the sociological enterprise.

Lost Newton

During the early decades of the twentieth century many American sociologists developed full and rich accounts of social behavior in real-life settings by using a technique called "participant-observation." The sociologist participated in real-life situations while recording the behavior patterns that he observed. Although some sociologists feel that true scientific method applied to the study of human behavior is neutral in that those studied are not affected by being studied, more sociologists recognize that the very act of observing human beings has consequences for their behavior. People often will alter their actions when they are being observed.

No sociologist will accept the premise that human beings can be experimented with as "human guinea pigs" for the "good of science." Yet this recognition does not eliminate serious ethical problems the sociologist must confront because his subject matter is the behavior of human beings. What is the proper relationship between the sociologist and those he studies? Should the sociologist try to convert those studied to his own values? Must he urge upon them policy goals that seem desirable in the light of the knowledge he has developed? Some sociologists would answer yes to these questions, but the vast majority of sociologists would reject the idea that they should be militant advocates of their own values or policy goals. The sociologist does not possess the alien "magic" of the research team in "Lost Newton," nor does he find himself at a pivotal point in the history of a culture, when his actions can change the future of a culture. Nevertheless, "Lost Newton" vividly illustrates some of the pitfalls the sociologist must be aware of—if not confront—in his research enterprise. For a participant-observer to violate the confidence of a deviant group being studied by reporting the group's criminal behavior to the police will not change the course of civilization. Yet, the consequences for the group members might be destructively severe. Is it the responsibility of the sociologist—as a sociologist—to bring this about? Wherein does his responsibility—as a scientist and as a human being—lie?

Lost Newton

STANLEY SCHMIDT

● ● ● **H**ave studied the attached documents summarizing the situation on Ymrek—native name—and recommend action as described herein. The essence of the problem is that recent seismic upheavals, resulting in drastic redistribution of land and water areas, have fragmented the budding civilization of Yngmor. Loss of communication among cultural centers, complicated by barbarian raiders frequenting the new waterways, threatens to reverse the growth of a promising humanoid civilization. The attached documents suggest that measures be taken to prevent this regrettable turn of events.

The proposed plan involves the introduction of a small number of Reynolds air-floaters using Type 76CB3 Quasimaterial control elements to provide safe transport among the remaining towns, many of which are now on islands. By skillfully disguising these as imports from a remote region of the planet, it is believed that they can restore an adequate level of communication with a minimum of disturbance and without arousing suspicions of their true nature and origin.

All precautions regarding the dangers of cultural interference must be scrupulously observed. The party sent to introduce the floaters will first conduct thorough field studies to gauge the probable reaction of the natives . . .

Terek uncomfortably eyed the Templeman slinking around the far side of the crowd and then sought a less conspicuous position. He wasn't sure exactly what was wrong, but he felt a vague gnawing of half-certainty that something was. It was not common for those of the Temple to waste their time on itinerant magic shows, and Terek kept imagining that this one was watching *him* . . .

He forced his mind back to the magicians, straining to see over the crowd without attracting the Templeman's notice. There was something odd about *them,* too. Troupes of outlanders giving shows and selling curios from afar were a common sight in the towns—though not as common now as before the Shakes—and Terek had never broken his childhood habit of joining the throngs that gathered around them. Magic was one of their main wares, and Terek still liked to watch their transparent "tricks" and marvel at how easily the peasants and townspeople were taken in by them.

This bunch was different. Already Terek had failed to see how three of their tricks were done. That annoyed him.

He was about to go home to resume his work when he heard the tall male foreigner announcing, "And now, ladies and gentlemen, our grand finale." Terek stopped, hesitated, and turned back toward the hastily improvised platform. He tried again to place the tall foreigner's accent and failed. That bothered him, too.

"Before your very eyes, ladies and gentlemen," the outlander chanted, "this enchanted statue from a far corner of the world will vanish." The crowd—twenty or thirty shabbily clothed men, women, and children—pressed toward the platform for a closer look. Terek decided to stay it out and pressed forward with them, still careful to avoid the Templeman's direct view. Disappearing acts were popular, and he seriously doubted they could fool him on that one.

"On the count of three," the magician warned, "it will begin to vanish, and by ten it will be gone. One . . ." Terek frowned. The statue, a foot high and gleaming metallically, was standing in plain view on the edge of the table. Weren't they going to cover it with a cloth?

". . . two . . ."

Terek found himself staring with an intentness he had not shown since his first magic show. Still the statue stood unprotected in the full light of the Day Star.

". . . three . . ."

Was it imagination, or did the metallic luster begin to dim?

". . . four . . . five . . ."

By six there was no doubt. The once-solid statue had acquired a ghostly pallor. Its form still shimmered unchanged, but was growing harder to make out against the background.

". . . seven . . . eight . . ." Now the background began to be visible *through* the statue. ". . . nine . . ." Only a mere suggestion, a faint, three-dimensional shadow, remained.

"Ten!" It was impossible to say exactly when the last remnant of shadow had passed away, but it was undeniably gone. The onlookers broke into ecstatic applause and even Terek shook with an excitement he had thought long outgrown. That was the most convincing bit of trickery he had ever seen, and he had to find out how it was done!

Muttering hasty apologies, forgetting his uneasiness about the Templeman, he began shoving toward the front of the crowd. On the platform, the performers, all smiles, acknowledged the applause. The smallest one, the only woman of the three, reached into a box and pulled out a double handful of trinkets. Laughing gaily, she threw them out to the crowd, the customary invitation to come and buy more after the show.

And Terek stopped in his tracks, momentarily dumbfounded. It wasn't the sight of the woman's spread hands, which he suddenly realized had only five fingers apiece, but the behavior of the things she had thrown. They flew out over the crowd and fell, but they fell at widely different rates! One drifted slowly down near Terek; a small boy caught it and cried out at its impact. He dropped it—it fell slowly—and Terek picked it up. It felt strangely heavy. *More trickery,* he thought with a grin, recovering quickly from his surprise and moving forward again. *Really first-rate . . .*

Then he saw the Templeman looming in front of him and stopped again, and this time he did not recover. The Templeman threw a handful of the strange trinkets in his face, pointed, and roared with gloating laughter. Nearby heads turned toward Terek and more and more peasants joined the Templeman's coarse mockery. Some began to throw things . . .

And Terek filled with something like horror as he realized what was happening. *No!* he thought in amazement, not heeding the rain of trinkets. *I was so close! Can a few cheap tricks really kill an idea?*

As the derisive hoots closed in around him, he felt for the first time a sinking fear that they could—and a defiant will to prevent it.

He never reached the platform.

Tina led them into the clearing and the boat with her usual amazing confidence—amazing, at least to her husband Chet Barlin, because the boat happened to be invisible from outside. Chet always had to stop and think twice about whether he was following the right landmarks. Tina didn't seem to have to think about it at all —she just pranced deftly through the shrubbery and at just the right moment sang out, "Open sesame!" By carefully following her steps, Chet and Jem Wadkinz, the man from Quasimaterials, Inc., managed to wind up safely inside the familiar cabin.

The inside of the landing boat, being visible, always seemed a good deal more homey than the outside. As soon as he heard the portal seal shut behind Wadkinz, Chet tossed aside the wig he wore to pass as a native and lit up his pipe. Then he noticed Stiv Sandor, copilot of the starship orbiting overhead and the landing party's chauffeur while they were down here in the boat, bending over the communicator with the panel off. 'Trouble?"

"Nah." Sandor reached into the open unit and popped the top off a cylindrical chamber. "Routine overhaul. Have to refresh the vacuum in these things every now and then, and now seemed as good as any." He took a can of Instavac from a cabinet under the console, emptied it into the vacuum chamber so it overflowed, and set the empty can aside. "How'd it go with you? Ready to move on?"

Chet shrugged. "O.K., I guess. Same as everywhere else, anyway." He noticed that Wadkinz had vanished into the galley for his customary post-show beer, while Tina had just as predictably gone straight to her beloved PFSU to read the reviews. The routine was getting a little tiresome. Chet was glad they only had to go through it a few more times before they could get down to their main job and then go home.

Sandor put the cap back on the vacuum chamber and pointed his damping trigger at it briefly. "You sound bored," he chuckled. "I thought you'd be a regular ham by now."

Chet grinned as he watched the quasimaterial liquid fade exponentially from the chamber, leaving an excellent vacuum and heating the surroundings only a few degrees in the process. "It gets to me once in a while," he confessed, "mainly at the end of a show." *Which*, he reflected, *amounts to nothing more than what you just did.* "But it's the same everywhere. They're impressed and intrigued, but not unduly. They've seen so little of the planet for themselves that nothing we claim to bring from another part of it really surprises them. I couldn't see any more evidence here than elsewhere that there's going to be any problem getting them to take a few quasimaterials in stride." He looked across the room. "Could you, Tina?"

Tina, uncharacteristically, was frowning. "Not out there," she said cryptically. "But, Chet, come here and take a look at this."

"Better go," Sandor said, turning back to the communicator. "She sounds worried."

The PFSU—psychocultural field survey unit—was one of the main tools of the modern anthropologist, psychologist, or xenologist. But its use required a formidable complex of highly refined, subtle skills—akin to those demanded by the polygraph of centuries earlier, but orders of magnitude more difficult. Tina Barlin, educated and employed as a xenologist, had those skills. Chet, whose work as a comparative historian brought him into contact with dead cultures more often than living ones, didn't. Consequently his look at the crowded panel of meters, color bars, and chart recorders failed to tell him what had Tina so upset. He wound up staring blankly and asking, "Well, what's it say?"

"This place *isn't* like the others," she explained. "It seemed like it, out there, just watching the audience. But there's a lot we didn't see. Look here." She pointed at some multicolored wiggles and spikes on a roll chart. "This is the time of our show. I can't correlate it down to the minute, but it's in this neighborhood. All through it there's a pattern of unusual activity, highly localized and increasingly intense. I've never seen anything quite like it before, but it looks like a single highly intelligent mind in a state of great agitation. Look at this shock here."

"Can you tell any more?"

"General location—right around that farmyard where we gave our show. It could have been somebody in the audience."

Chet nodded, then brightened. "That little brawl we saw starting up in the audience after the show . . . could it have something to do with that?"

Tina shrugged. "I don't know. I didn't pay much attention at the time. It just looked like typical peasant rowdiness. Didn't seem to have much to do with us."

"That's what I thought, too. But now that I think back . . . Tina, did you notice that there was a Templeman in that brawl?" Unable to pursue the line of thought, Chet bit his lip and looked back at the PFSU traces. Now that they were pointed out to him, he could recognize the highly abnormal character of those patterns. And he could see, faintly, some of the possible implications. But he couldn't follow the interpretation into the present. "Then what?"

Tina motioned at some later charts, and then at screens showing live displays of current monitorings. "It continues. There are a couple more distinct jolts. Then a few other patterns become prominent, too. The locale changes—it seems to be in or near the castle now—but all the unusual activity remains clustered around the one we saw first."

Even with Tina's guidance, Chet could follow only the barest outlines through the PFSU's maze of output. But he thoroughly trusted her interpretation, and it wasn't hard to see what the pattern she was describing might mean. "Some bright boy's onto us?"

Tina nodded. "That's my guess. Somebody who came to our show and recognized that we're not just another band of gypsies from over the hill. He has suspicions about us—powerful suspicions, and a powerful determination to do something about them." She waved a hand at the real-time displays. "Now this. Does this mean that not only does he suspect, but he's already gone straight to the local priest-king and got *him* scared of us?"

"It could," Chet said grimly. "Of course, it could mean something else. You still haven't taught that thing to read actual thought content, have you?"

"Not a chance. That's what's so maddening. All we can see are prevalent attitudes, emotions, mental tones. But when we see a pattern like this we can't resist guessing what's behind it. Our guesses may be all wet, but we worry about them anyway."

"True." Chet couldn't deny that he was worried by these. "It fits together too well, Tina. I don't like it."

"Neither do I. Where do we go from here, Chet?"

"Yjhavet's next on the list," Chet said unnecessarily, "but I see what you mean. I think it's conference time."

Bydron Kel, the Republic's B.E.L. Field Agent who had the ultimate say on whether Project Airfloat would be carried through, chain-smoked. He puffed incessantly and nervously on long thin cigarette after long thin cigarette, and the parts of him that weren't busy smoking found other ways to fidget. He sat impatiently through Tina's exposition of what the PFSU had told her. When she finished, he cleared his throat and complained, "Really, Mrs. Barlin, I hardly see that there's any great problem. If there's a chance we've been discovered here, we move on to the next place without further ado. It's as simple as that. The bulk of the data was typical, wasn't it?"

"Yes," Tina granted, "but you underestimate the possible importance of a sufficiently atypical individual—not to mention the Temple of the Supreme Presence. In case you've been neglecting your brief, let me remind you that the Temple is behind this whole renaissance we're supposed to be protecting. Its *dixar*—priest-king, if you insist on a near translation—directly controls every town in Yngmor. If we get *them* down on us, the project has unequivocally had it. Very probably, so have we."

Kel said nothing. He seemed to ignore her sarcasm, and the face he made seemed to say merely, *Why does life have to be so complicated?*

"Look at it this way," Chet suggested. "If there's a chance we've been discovered, it's especially important that we stay here long enough to make sure. If it *has* happened, we have to *know* about it and see if we can undo any damage the discovery's caused. That means no Project Airfloat—and who knows what else? This started out to be a very small, very cautious intervention justified by special circumstances. They're not special enough to justify any more than that, Agent Kel. You know that . . . don't you?"

Slowly, as if suddenly painfully aware that he didn't really want this responsibility, Kel nodded.

They set out for the monastery at dawn, armed with unusually few traces of their parent civilization and an unusually high level of caution and wariness. The landing boat was hidden a little over a mile from the outskirts of Yldac, isolated by a half-mile barrier of thickets into which natives seldom, if ever, ventured. Chet, Tina, and Jem threaded their way among the grasping thorns with delicate care to avoid damage to the colorful robes which advertised them as travelers from an unnamed far corner of Ymrek. Despite the careful attention to costuming, this morning they felt painfully conspicuous and vulnerable. The PFSU could do little more than raise suspicions and doubts, but it had done that very effectively. And if any trouble arose, they would be able to do little more than contact Sandor and Kel aboard the landing boat.

They paused at the edge of the bush to survey the thousand yards of open plain between them and the town. Then, seeing no danger, they started across.

Yldac rose from the plain directly ahead. The nearest parts, the outermost rim of the town, consisted of low, dingy houses of rough-hewn wood, with thick smoke billowing from tall thin chimneys. Beyond them, surrounded by them, rose the expansive stone terraces of the monastery, surmounted finally by the spires and minarets of the dixar's central castle.

Tiny farmhouses sprinkled the surrounding plain. Far off to the left, one stood abandoned, half-collapsed and rotting, at the very edge of the water that had not been there a few years earlier. Next to it stood a cannon installation, one of many pointing out over the water to remind prowling Ketaxil that they were unwelcome. Chet looked at that and thought involuntarily of how much more complicated things could get before they left this town.

He hadn't wanted to mention it to Kel, but the orbiting starship had seen evidence of Ketaxil raiders approaching Yldac, and another raid seemed imminently possible. So far the island towns had consistently succeeded in repelling the pirates from their shores, although boats sent out from the towns to face them on their own ground—the water—were rarely heard from again. But those cannons were old and primitive, and there was rumor in the towns that the Ketaxil were developing improved weapons and tactics.

If the next attack came today, Chet wondered, *would the old defenses be adequate to repel it?*

All the thousands of eyes along the narrow streets of the periphery and hidden behind chinks in shack walls seemed to be staring at them. Intellectually, Chet knew that was highly unlikely, but the awareness that suspicions had likely been aroused made him unusually wary. He could see something similar in Tina's face, although she hid it so well that anyone not married to her would have missed it. Wadkinz's anxiety, in contrast, was painfully obvious.

The feeling intensified when they reached the gray stone wall of the monastery. Nothing had happened yet, but there would be other eyes behind the small windows high in this wall, and some of those might represent real threats. Yet, precisely for that reason—because the PFSU had said that the recent unusual activity was centered here—this was where they had to come.

They didn't know what they were looking for, and the castle itself was inaccessible atop the sprawling monastery. So they simply started around the monastery, looking for any hint of the disturbance. They completely circled it once—a matter of almost a mile of broad cobblestone street separating the monastery from the town—without noticing anything.

The second time, they saw the Dunce.

Chet didn't recognize the grotesque figure's significance, but that in itself was cause for suspicion. "Look up there!" he whispered, stopping and pointing. "Up on the wall. What's with him?"

Tina and Jen looked. The wall was ten or twelve feet high, and now a native, barely recognizable in garish paint and clothes, stood at the edge some hundred feet ahead. He wore a huge, bizarre helmet and there were chains on his elbows and wrists, but he was standing very erect and looking this way.

"A Dunce," Tina explained. "A minor heretic. The Temple doesn't tolerate ideas too much unlike its own, of course. But the priests know better than to execute anybody, except as an extreme last resort. Martyrs are so awkward—if you kill somebody for his ideas, it strongly suggests you took them seriously. The Temple prefers to nip heresy in the bud by holding the troublemaker up to public ridicule. So they stand him out on the monastery wall in a clown suit and—" She broke off suddenly and Chet could see her mind racing. "Chet!" she squealed. "Could he be it? If we have something to do with his heresy—"

Before Chet could answer, the Dunce called to them.

Startled, Tina looked at Chet. "Maybe I was right. He wants us to come. Should we?"

"Sounds dangerous to me," Wadkinz grunted.

"I think we'd better," Chet said, though he felt no more real enthusiasm than Jem. They went.

❖   ❖   ❖

At close range, they saw that the Dunce was smiling with a surprising air of calm confidence. Looking down from his high perch, he gave an uncomfortable impression of considering himself in command of the situation. He stared at them silently for some seconds and then asked, "Where do you come from?"

Chet suddenly became very apprehensive. He gave the stock answer, but he had a feeling it wouldn't satisfy this customer. "We have traveled far, from a distant land where—"

"Where?" the Dunce interrupted bluntly.

Chet didn't bother to finish the rehearsed answer. And he knew that he was on much more treacherous ground ad-libbing. "You wouldn't know the place," he said. "No one from Yngmor has ever been there."

"I can believe that," the Dunce said. He made it sound as if it had more than surface meaning. "Do you recognize me?"

Evidently Tina's guess had not been too far wrong. "I'm not sure," Chet said. "Should I?"

"I would hope so," the Dunce said wryly. "It's the least you could do after the way you wrecked my life."

Chet blinked. "Wrecked your life? Us? How's that?"

"I was at your show yesterday," the Dunce said. "It was the best I've ever seen. That's the trouble—it was too good. It destroyed everything I had done toward getting the blessing of the Temple for my work. But my work's *right*, your tricks notwithstanding! So I hoped to persuade you to help me unwreck my life—to placate the dixar Kangyr—"

Chet was beginning to see where the Dunce fitted into yesterday's incident—and implications of something possibly much bigger behind that. But before the Dunce finished explaining, they were interrupted by a clatter of rapidly approaching footsteps and a harsh voice. "Hey, you, there! What are you doing?"

Chet turned to see the Templeman running toward them with ceremonial lance raised and instantly recognized potential trouble. He turned quickly back to the Dunce. "For future reference," he said, "what's your name?"

"Terek," said Terek.

The Templeman halted, puffing, a lance length away from Chet. "Why were you talking to the prisoner?" he demanded.

"What difference does it make?" Tina taunted. "He's just a Dunce." She glanced up at Terek and added, "No offense."

"None taken," Terek said. Then, to the Templeman, "These are the so-called magicians who got me in this mess, Xymrok."

Xymrok lifted his lance tip momentarily in a perfunctory threatening gesture. "You know better than to address a Templeman by name," he muttered. Then he looked puzzled—or so Chet thought, although there were enough differences between human and Kemrek facial expressions that he couldn't always be sure. "If that's true," he mused, "why should they be talking to you?"

"He called us," Chet said. "We didn't know—"

Xymrok looked up. "That so?"

"You have the outlander's word," Terek said dryly. "Of course I did. I don't especially like it up here. I thought if they would talk to Kangyr—"

"*The dixar* Kangyr!" Xymrok corrected sharply. He frowned. "None of you are making any sense, but this all smells very funny. I've half a mind to haul you up to the dixar on suspicion, but I'm not sure it's worth his trouble."

"Look at their hands," Terek suggested.

Wadkinz turned white; Chet and Tina just quietly abandoned any remaining hope of evading discovery. The Templeman looked, at first uncomprehendingly, then with widening eyes as he counted only five fingers on hand after hand.

Then he looked up at Chet, all traces of indecision gone from his face. "Come along," he said.

Xymrok led them through musty-smelling torchlit corridors and up long winding staircases. Chet wondered briefly if now was the time to call Sandor with the rudimentary transceiver he carried in a second molar, and decided against it.

They arrived finally in a long room, high above ground level, in which a purple-robed native sat alone at the end of a long table. Alone, that is, except for highly stylized images of himself in niches above all the wall torches—for the dixar was, according to the teachings of the Temple, the literal incarnation of the Supreme Presence in this region. The humans echoed Xymrok's elaborate salute to him, and Kangyr, who looked a good deal like a beardless gnome, returned it.

"These are said to be the magicians whose performance led to Terek's disgrace yesterday, Your Holiness," Xymrok explained. "They were found talking to Terek and could not explain themselves to my satisfaction. I suggest also that Your Holiness examine their hands."

The dixar Kangyr glanced quickly at their hands and his forehead wrinkled almost imperceptibly. "Magnificent and infinitely varied are the ways of the Supreme Presence," he recited indifferently. "Xymrok, you may leave the room."

Xymrok saluted and left, closing the big wood door quietly behind him. Kangyr affected something resembling a very relaxed smile. "I don't suppose you'd like to tell me where you're from?"

"It would be difficult, Your Holiness," Chet said. "It's a very distant land—"

Kangyr dismissed the thought with a wave of his hand before Chet finished. "No matter. There is surely room in the world for a land of people with five fingers, and surely the Supreme Presence would find it no great challenge to create such a people. Is it true that you were talking to Terek?"

"I suppose it is—if that's who the Dunce was."

"You don't know him?"

"No."

"Then why were you talking to him?"

"He called us."

"Why?"

"I'm not sure. He said something about our show having jeopardized his standing with the Temple, but we couldn't understand it. Your Holiness"—and Chet hoped as he said this that he wasn't going too far beyond the bounds of propriety—"could you explain to us any of what's going on and where we fit into it? We meant no harm."

Kangyr nodded slightly. "And you did none." He stared distantly at one of the icons on the wall. "Terek has strange ideas—dangerous ideas. In essence, he tried to condense all the magnificent and infinitely variable complexity of the Supreme Presence into a few simple sayings—some of them clearly and flagrantly wrong, others simply claiming to impose restrictions on the Supreme Presence where there is clearly no need for the Supreme Presence to be restricted at all. There are . . . ah . . . those in the Temple who were tempted to grant some acceptance to his ideas, primarily because he claimed that with some of them he could greatly improve our defense capabilities. With the Ketaxil situation deteriorating as it has been . . . well, I can forgive temptation in the weaker elements of the Temple. Yet I always felt obliged to resist Terek's heresies altogether because of their terrific religious impact. Why, he wanted us to believe Ymrek revolves around the Day Star, when everybody knows that the Day Star and everything else revolves around Ymrek!" He looked at Chet. "So I welcomed the opportunity your show gave to denounce Terek once and for all as a Dunce. After your show it was impossible for anyone to take seriously a madman who thinks all objects must fall at the same speed and—" He broke off. "But I'm boring you. Is there anything else you want to know?"

There was plenty, but Chet was so excited by what he had heard already that he didn't want to risk saying anything else to get them into trouble. The urgent thing now was to get back to the boat and decide what to do about it. "No, Your Holiness. Thank you for clarifying the situation."

"The least I could do," Kangyr said. "I apologize for your inconvenience, but you understand that Xymrok must be suspicious of anyone he finds talking to a dangerous prisoner. Since this wasn't your fault, you may go with my blessing whenever you like."

When they reached the door, Kangyr spoke again. There was a note of something like pleading in his voice now that sounded odd from one in his position. "Your magic," he said. "It is . . . real?"

Chet thought, startled by the question, then said cautiously, "We have learned control of some . . . er . . . spiritual phenomena which seem to be unfamiliar in this land."

"I was just thinking," Kangyr said. "If you have magic which might be effective against the Ketaxil, we could make it worth your while . . ."

"Uh," said Chet, increasingly anxious to get away, "I'd have to consult the spirits on that."

"Please do. And if you find a way, you will let me know?"

Chet nodded uncomfortably.

They returned to the boat as fast as they could.

". . . So it looks to me," Chet finished, "like we've just pulled off the most horrendous piece of cultural interference in history. Now it's up to us to stick around and see if we can undo any of the damage."

Kel, sitting on the far side of the main cabin, looked thoroughly miserable. "What are you talking about, Barlin? I don't see—"

"Don't you see what's happened? We've come at one of the big turning points in their history, and by introducing a few tentative samples of quasimaterials, we've frustrated it."

"We're not all historians, Chet," Wadkinz reminded. "You're not ringing many bells yet."

"Terek," Chet said earnestly, "is this culture's Newton . . . and maybe Copernicus and Galileo, too, all rolled into one. I can't be positive yet, but from what he and Kangyr said I'm almost willing to bet that he's worked out a modern picture of the universe, together with universal gravitation and Newtonian mechanics to back it up. Now we come along and give them a look at some things that don't work that way, and the established church jumps at the chance to laugh his ideas into the ground!"

Kel frowned. "But is it all that important? Sure it is for him, but . . . well, if it doesn't catch on now, somebody else will think of it later."

"Probably," Chet granted, "but who knows when? There are

some times in history when an individual mind *is* of great importance. Just because Newton's laws—Terek's laws?—are now taught in the first week of every kid's science course, we think they're trivial. It's very hard for a modern person to appreciate what a tremendous accomplishment it was to formulate them from scratch, when nobody knew them. It's a huge step which *can* happen when a certain point is reached—but it *doesn't* until some individual comes along capable of taking it. It still doesn't, unless the right things happen to suggest it and encourage him to follow through. That may take centuries.

"If Terek's done it and we let him be stopped, it may be centuries before it happens again. And so much future science and technology depends on that . . . what we may have done to their history is absolutely appalling." He laughed sourly. "We thought quasimaterials were such a timely development—not only for our own use, but just what the doctor ordered for Yngmor's little communication setback. Well, it looks like we've come at just the right time to nip their science in the bud—by showing them just the wrong piece of advanced technology!"

Tina and Jem waited uncomfortably to see if he was going to say more. Then Tina asked softly, "What can we do about it?"

"I don't see that we can do anything," Kel interjected. "The damage is done. They've seen and touched quasimaterials, and we can't undo that. Maybe it'll even turn out better this way—"

"I think," Chet interrupted bluntly, "you're just looking for the easiest way out for yourself, without thinking about the consequences. There are several things we might do. We could remote-trigger all the quasimaterials on the planet to damp out and then hope the natives will forget about them. But there's no guarantee that they will, or that Terek will still be in the humor to push this when the climate improves. I'd write that approach off as too uncertain. There's another one that I'm pretty sure has a better chance. You won't like it."

Kel frowned and started a new cigarette. "Oh?"

"Once," Chet said slowly, "I saw a man poison himself accidentally on a small craft in space. I don't remember what it was, but I remember what the medic did about it. There was no antidote on board, but there was lots more of the poison. The doc poured a whole bottle of the stuff down the patient as fast as he could—and the poor guy reacted so violently that the whole mess came right back up. From that point on, saving him was easy. I think this is a case like that."

Chet saw Tina start to grin knowingly, but Kel just kept frowning and said, "I don't see what you're driving at."

"Simply this: our blunder was showing them quasimaterials that seemed to violate Terek's laws. Well, I think the clergy must have some prejudices of their own about what's reasonable. Let's try to violate a few of those. Let's give them a *real* magic show, on a grand scale!"

"You're crazy!" Kel gasped.

"For instance," said Chet, ignoring him, "I still think some Reynolds air-floaters, introduced to the right people with the right degree of flamboyancy, might shake them up a bit. Kangyr, anyway. And there's a growing market for them—Yldac could have another Ketaxil raid at any time, and they could use some souped-up defense methods to counteract the souped-up offense the Ketaxil have."

"Out of the question," Kel snapped. "A few little quasimaterial trinkets are one thing and a full-scale floater is quite another—"

"Exactly," Chet nodded.

"—And the study is not complete."

"And it won't be! Can't you see yet that we've already messed things up in a big way and we have to try to fix them?"

"But," Kel spluttered, "you're talking about a large-scale cultural interference! Barlin, what are you trying to do to my career?"

Chet turned and stared at the B.E.L. agent with frank disgust for several seconds. "I could care less about your career," he said finally, evenly, "but it wouldn't be easy. I care very much, though, about the fact that we have *already* committed a large-scale cultural interference and it's going to take a comparable one to fix it. We can't guarantee the cure, but we can't leave knowing we've messed things up so thoroughly and made no attempt at one. So, Agent Kel, about your career—if you try to keep us from doing anything, when we get home I'll testify against you as strongly as I can. Think how you'll fare in that."

Kel did, and once more gave his most grudging consent. Chet turned to Jem with a grin. "O.K., quasimaterial man—we're ready to go into production!"

Five fingers, Kangyr thought after the magicians left. *I never met a man with only five fingers before.* The thought lingered all day—that thought and a feeling of almost-shame at the moment of weakness he had had as they left his chamber. It was far from fitting for a dixar to suggest the vulnerability of his own district to that extent. And yet, if it led to help in the form of magic comparable to that which had refuted Terek . . .

Maybe it would be worth it.

At Day's End he went down personally to take Terek off the wall. "I hope," he said as he freed Terek's chains, "that these days have been profitable ones for you. Having seen your error, are you ready to return to the Truth?"

Terek grinned impudently. "I'm not convinced I was wrong, but I won't be preaching any more for a while. But I think one of these days you'll see that you need at least some of what I offered you. And when you do, it's still available."

Kangyr shook his head sadly. "Such arrogance! But time will cure that." His voice dropped, became confidential. "Terek, what do you know about those outlanders? I believe you were the first to notice their hands."

"I know nothing about them," Terek said, "but I suspect there's a lot I'd like to know." He grinned again. "Dixar," he said, gently chiding, "you're not getting ideas about using their parlor tricks instead of my new gunnery methods, are you?"

Kangyr looked away. That was exactly what he had in mind, although he didn't feel completely comfortable about it. From a theological viewpoint, he found the idea of dealing with the foreign magicians less disconcerting than dealing with Terek—at least they didn't try to clamp a tight harness of rules onto the Supreme Presence. Yet there was something which he couldn't quite place which bothered him about them, too . . .

"Because if you are," Terek finished, "I think you'll find you have the same objection to them that you do to me. Good night, Dixar."

Terek strolled off into the dusk toward his shack in the periphery, leaving Kangyr to puzzle over what his last remark meant.

What all quasimaterials have in common is that they are artificial standing wave structures qualitatively similar to ordinary matter—although in general their actual energy content is much lower. And, just as computer-generated sounds can have properties "natural" sounds can't, or hologram images can be made of objects which could never "really" exist, they can have properties wildly unlike those of ordinary matter. Some, like the outer hull of the landing boat, are totally invisible from at least one direction. Some, like some of the trinkets Tina peddled after their exploratory magic shows, have inequivalent gravitational and inertial masses. Most can be induced to damp out and vanish exponentially—like Instavac, or the statues Chet used to finish the magic shows.

The special qualities of the Type 76CB3 control elements used in Reynolds air-floaters are a little harder to describe.

Chet and Tina watched with interest as Jem put the finishing touches on their first floater early the next morning. Mostly it consisted of real matter, a cheap, easily-shaped synthetic that emerged ready-formed from an automatic fabricator. A casual observer would never have guessed that—the fabricator was programmed to imitate minutely skilled handcrafting of wood, even to the extent of providing different minor flaws in each unit. It would have taken sophisticated chemical analysis to prove that the floater was not a boat hand-carved by barbarians in some far-distant region of Ymrek.

Even the control elements were made to resemble carved sticks mounted in crude swivels in the bottom of the boat. But Jem had to mount *them* by hand, and as he worked they often seemed to want to float, or occasionally jump, from his hands. The front one went in without much trouble; the one in back took a little longer. But finally the job was finished and Jem stood up with a look of satisfaction.

"Finished?" Tina asked.

"Almost. But I thought since we're planning to play this magic bit to the hilt, one little finishing touch might be in order." He reached into the pouch of quasimaterials he carried inside his magician's robe and produced something which he attached to the prow of the floater. "Like it?"

Chet looked at the figurehead for a few seconds, then quickly away. It was one of those visual paradoxes that can be drawn in perspective but could never actually be built in three dimensions—with ordinary matter. It made him dizzy to look at it.

"Perfect!" he laughed.

Jem sat in the bow, Tina and Chet behind him in single file, as the landing boat's cargo hatch yawned open to bright clear morning before them. Jem took the front control element in his left hand and the long rod to the rear element in his right. He moved each lever the merest trifle—

And the floater lifted inches off the deck and floated silently out through the hatch. As they cleared, Chet glanced back just in time to see the hatch shut after them, leaving the boat again invisible. Looking over the side he saw the ground several yards below, then falling away as Jem pulled back sharply on his front stick to be sure they would clear the highest parts of the barrier thicket. Tina grabbed Chet's hands tightly and asked, "How does it work, Jem?"

"You never rode one before?" Jem sounded surprised. "Gravity. The strength and direction of the force on each control element depends on its orientation relative to the gravitational field. It's a little like the way the force on an electron in a magnetic field depends on which way it's moving—but not very much. Anyway, I can make gravity move each end of the floater in any direction I like just by moving the control elements around. Like this." Without further warning, he suddenly made the floater twist wildly, stopping just short of pitching the crew overboard, then chuckled at Tina's reaction and settled back to a smooth glide.

He kept climbing as they crossed the barrier thicket, reaching a peak of over a thousand feet and starting downward only after they emerged over the open plain surrounding the town. As they went over the top the entire town came into view sprawled out before them.

The town—and the water around it.

"Look!" Tina gasped suddenly, pointing off to the left. "What are those?"

Chet looked, and didn't like what he saw on the water. "One, two, three, . . . seven," he counted. "I guess today's the day."

"Ketaxil?" Tina asked.

"I'd say so. Wonder what they really do have in the way of weapons? And what kind of defense improvements Terek was trying to peddle to the Temple."

"I doubt that they have antiaircraft guns," Jem said, looking curiously at the boats approaching Yldac. "Want to go over for a closer look?" He veered slightly to the left.

"No!" Tina said instantly. Jem unveered.

"Probably not a good idea, Jem," Chet said. "They might surprise you, and we're not exactly armed to the teeth." They weren't completely unarmed this trip—along with all the other paraphernalia befitting powerful magicians from afar, each had allowed himself the luxury of a compact beamer, just in case. Effective, under the right conditions, but far from limitless in capability. Chet cast one more look at the boats. "This might not be the best possible day for this, but the show must go on. Let's get down to that castle as quick as we can."

As they descended steeply toward the center of town, a few people in the streets below looked up, saw them, and scattered into houses with considerable commotion. Jem ignored them and headed the boat faster and faster down toward the castle at the summit of the monastery. Then, in the last few yards, he slowed them to a gentle landing on the last terrace below the castle proper.

"This must be the place," he said. "Now what?"

"Have to get inside," Chet said. "I'm pretty sure the dixar's chamber is in the extreme top level—that little box right up there in the middle. But it doesn't seem to have any doors or windows on the outside."

"Sure doesn't. Seems odd, but we didn't notice any when they took us up there from inside . . . Hm-m-m. Hang on." He lifted off again, lowered the floater over the edge of the terrace and ran it methodically along the wall in search of an opening.

He found one at the first corner and hovered in front of it to size it up. Then he said, "Duck," and eased the floater through the window, barely clearing the sides. Inside, he hovered again to allow their eyes to adjust to torchlight, then headed along the empty hall until he found a stairway. He tilted the floater's nose upward to match the slope of the stairs and started up, never touching, but occasionally maneuvering delicately past an almost impossibly tight turn.

The stairs rose three levels and then leveled off into a familiar short corridor. At the other end was a big wooden door—and a Templeman. When he saw them float out of the stairwell he let out a gasp clearly audible the length of the hall and then stood frozen— except for some protective religious gestures which he managed to get through in great haste. Jem pulled the floater almost to within a lance length of him and halted.

Chet grinned broadly at the Templeman. "Good morning," he said, his hand resting lightly on the beamer just inside his robe. "We've come to see Kangyr on business. You will please admit us— and I suggest you don't attempt to raise your lance. Right where it is will be fine."

Kangyr's eyebrows rose quite noticeably when they floated through the open door—much more so than when he had counted their fingers. "*What*," he demanded, staring at the bow of the floater, "is *that?*"

"Your Holiness wondered if our magic could help you," Chet said, "and I said I'd have to consult the spirits. This is their answer. And none too soon, I might add."

Kangyr looked at him sharply. "What do you mean by that?"

As if in answer, the faint sound of an explosion, muffled by distance and the indirectness of its path, reached them. Kangyr's expression changed abruptly. "The Ketaxil are back," Chet said quietly.

Kangyr nodded solemnly, then seemed to turn fiercely defiant. "We've stood them off before!" he said hotly. "We can do it again, just as we've done in the past." His gaze returned to the floater suspended two feet above the floor, full of what Chet was pretty sure was suspicion.

"Are you sure you can?" Chet asked. "It is said that the Ketaxil have new weapons and plans of attack. Are you sure the ways you held them off before will work again?"

Kangyr started to say something, but broke the first word off to listen to a particularly violent and rapid volley of gunfire. "I think so," he said finally, but there was a lack of conviction in his voice.

"With the Supreme Presence on our side—"

"It might not hurt to have some of our magic on your side, too," Chet suggested. The distant rumble of battle continued to underline their conversation. "Take this boat, for instance. With the spirit-sticks mounted in bow and stern, it can fly high over the enemy. If nothing else, it could carry a messenger to a neighboring island for help when all other routes are blocked. The mere surprise of seeing such craft could place the enemy off guard. No doubt Your Holiness could even find ways to use them in actual battle. Would you like to go for a ride and see how it works?"

"No," Kangyr replied at once, shrinking slightly away from the floater. "No, thank you. Perhaps later. I can see what it does. But . . ." He stared distantly at an icon of himself, much as Chet had seen him do once before. "From all sides," Kangyr said sullenly, "I'm besieged not only by Ketaxil but by people telling me I must adopt this or that new-fangled contraption to protect my town. First Terek, now you—"

"Might I ask," Chet ventured cautiously, "just what Terek tried to get Your Holiness to adopt?"

"Guns," Kangyr said with a shruglike gesture. "New kinds of guns firing more rapidly, and firing larger balls to larger distances . . . It would be impossible to aim such devices, of course, yet Terek claimed he could aim them better than our old guns—by doing mumbo jumbo with figures on paper!"

Hardly surprising, Chet thought, *that he'd spend some time on trajectory problems—probably complete with fudge factors for air resistance and such.* He asked Kangyr, "Did you ever try Terek's methods?"

"Of course not! A dixar is no fool. And the ideas underlying Terek's wild scheme were so terribly at odds with the Truth . . ." He broke off, and a flurry of cannon filled the pause. With an abrupt change of expression, Kangyr dropped the subject of Terek and looked with renewed interest at the air-floater's figurehead. "These spirits of yours," he said. "They are of the Supreme Presence?"

Chet wasn't sure how to answer that and was relieved to hear Tina, who was somewhat more familiar with the Temple's beliefs and practices, fill in for him. "Of course," she said brightly. "Isn't everything?"

For the moment Kangyr seemed almost satisfied. Then he sank back into his mood of doubt. "Actually," he said slowly, "I hardly see the need of either. I know Terek's a crackpot, and I don't see that your flying boat is any panacea. If it's true that the Ketaxil have better guns, flying boats will hardly counteract them."

"Maybe not," Chet said. "But if you change your mind, we can get you many more such boats on short notice—"

He didn't finish the sentence because suddenly there was an insistent pounding on the door and then a Templeman ran in, panting from exertion. Chet recognized him as Xymrok, the one who had originally brought them before Kangyr.

"Your Holiness!" Xymrok said excitedly. "Our guns are failing to repel them. The periphery is feeling unprecedented destruction—" Then he noticed the floater and broke off in midsentence, staring wide-eyed. "Your Holiness, what *is* that?"

Xymrok's report had had its effect. Kangyr's decision had been made with obvious reluctance, but it had been made. "Salvation," he said curtly, and then added under his breath, "I hope."

Terek moved swiftly through the cobblestone street around the monastery, driven by the pounding of gunfire in his ears. He knew the street well, and he knew exactly what he was looking for.

And he found it.

Xymrok was pacing back and forth near the west entrance, and he was alone. That was good. Terek hurried up to him and slipped him a coin. "Any word?" he asked, glancing significantly up.

Xymrok pocketed the coin and looked around. "The dixar Kangyr has accepted aid from the foreign magicians," he whispered quickly. "They have a strange boat which flies, and say they will sell Kangyr a number of these—"

Terek didn't wait for all the details. He pounded the door until another Templeman opened it from inside, recognized him as one enjoying slight and variable favor with the dixar, and let him in.

Then he started at top speed up the long succession of corridors and stairs.

"Your Holiness," Terek insisted, even more exasperated than he dared show, "you're being taken in. The magicians' boats aren't going to save Yngmor, or even Yldac. Not by themselves, anyway. At best, they'll provide a way to carry word from one town to another. But what good's that if the Ketaxil have destroyed the towns? Face it, Your Holiness—we can't survive without better defense. And no matter what else you use in addition, that means better coast guns. And I can tell you how to make them."

Kangyr stared at him for a long time, his face full of weariness and uncertainty Terek had never seen there until quite recently. "Terek," he said finally, "we've been through all this before. Do you want to spend all your time on the wall?"

"I'll risk it," Terek said tightly, "if the alternative is to watch you throw away a chance to salvage some of what we call civilization." He paused. Then, "Your Holiness, what makes you believe that these so-called magicians are infallible while everything I say is wrong?"

"Do I?" Kangyr snapped. "I don't think so. Why are *you* so suspicious of *them?* 'Magnificent and infinitely varied—'"

"'—Are the ways of the Supreme Presence,'" Terek finished quickly. "Yes. I know. But how is it that with the Supreme Presence everything is possible but what *I* suggest?"

"You're verging on blasphemy," Kangyr warned. "And you miss the point. It's not that way at all. It's just that you try to impose artificial restrictions on—"

"Your Holiness misses *my* point," Terek interrupted. "O.K. Maybe the foreigners' magic is real—*but that doesn't prove my work is wrong!* You preach that the Supreme Presence can act in any way it chooses—and I say that includes the ways I describe. But there's even more than that. Maybe nature can act any way it likes—but there are certain ways it seems to prefer most of the time, and there's strength in learning those. You believe that yourself."

"How dare you tell me what I believe—"

"It's implicit in all your actions. Your discomfort at the thought of the flying boats is obvious. Why do they make you uncomfortable? Because they clash with your built-in ideas of how things naturally act. And you're *very* sure that everything revolves around Ymrek?"

"Yes!"

"O.K., let's leave that to argue about later. But meanwhile, give my guns a try." His voice lowered. "As for your magicians—I don't know how their tricks work. It doesn't matter. But, as dixar, haven't you wondered about the possibility that you're being enticed into a trap?"

Kangyr looked at him sharply, "What do you mean?"

Terek paused, momentarily hesitant to attack a man with his own religion. Then he said it. "You never did find out where they come from, did you? Yet the Temple recognizes sources of power opposed to the Harmony of the Supreme Presence. And these people have hands like no others we've ever seen. I'd think you'd wait to deal with them until you knew . . ."

Kangyr looked startled, then pensive. For several seconds he was silent. Then he said grimly, "On *that* point, I'll have to agree with you. The question bears further examination."

The next time they descended toward the castle, the Barlins and Wadkinz had two more floaters in tow. They also had a considerable assortment of the most outlandishly "magical" objects Jem had been able to concoct. Chet felt that the first visit, in succeeding so easily, had failed in its real purpose. The object had been not to have Kangyr eagerly accept airfloaters, but to confront him with magic that defied his own intuitive ideas of natural law—which he must surely have—as thoroughly as the earlier examples defied Terek's laws.

With the result, hopefully, that he would decide the magic must not be taken too seriously and should be viewed as a thing apart from either the Temple's teachings or Terek's innovations, neither proving nor refuting either.

Unfortunately, it didn't seem to be working that way—anyway not as fast as hoped. Kangyr had balked noticeably at the floaters, but had given in far too easily. A stronger dosage was indicated.

Kangyr had appointed a spot on a lower terrace for delivery of the floaters. He was waiting as they approached, but he was not alone. Chet frowned in puzzlement as they got close enough to recognize the other figures.

Two armed Templemen—and Terek.

Why?

Despite apprehension, they landed as scheduled. As soon as they were down, the armed Templemen flanked the floaters menacingly and Kangyr strode out to meet them. "For religious reasons," he said crisply, "I cannot conclude business with you until I have more definite knowledge of your origins. You will please answer the simple question: Where is your home?"

Chet knew it was up to him to answer, and he felt trapped. Somewhere along the line a new factor had entered the picture—and he wasn't sure what it was.

"*Quit stalling!*" a voice rasped. Chet looked up, surprised. It was Terek who had spoken, and there was an odd expression on his face. "Answer the question," he prodded. "You do have a home, don't you?" After a short pause, he turned to Kangyr. "He refuses to answer, Your Holiness. Our suspicions—"

Kangyr nodded gravely. Chet saw him give an almost imperceptible signal to the Templemen, and their free hands moved to their lances—

"I'll answer," Chet said.

Kangyr's eyebrows shot up, he glanced at the lancers, and they seemed to relax. Terek's expression changed abruptly to a rather bewildered one. He and Kangyr stared attentively at Chet.

Chet's pulse raced. He knew that Bydron Kel would never forgive what he was about to do, but he suddenly thought he understood what was going on.

And that, at this stage, however drastic it might seem, the rest of an answer might be as simple as the truth.

"I'll tell you where we came from," he said evenly. "The place is called Larneg. It is a planet which revolves around a very distant star—much as Ymrek revolves around the Day Star."

He heard Tina and Jem gasp, shocked. Kangyr's face registered first confusion, then disbelief, then anger. Terek's reactions were the most complicated—first, very briefly, he was stunned and incredulous, but then he believed, and with belief came a flood of satisfaction and excitement and humility.

"You're lying!" Kangyr snarled.

"I'm not," Chet said simply. "Terek knows. And we know that Terek is right, because we've seen both your world and ours from outside. Can you think of a more believable way to account for us and the things we do?"

Terek said quietly, "Coming here must have been very difficult—"

"Not for us," Chet said, "but it took our ancestors many centuries to learn how—even after our Terek's work was accepted." He addressed Kangyr. "There's a lot of what you would call magic in it. We have a lot more 'magic' that you haven't seen, and some of it could help you. But those that can help you most are the same ones Terek can show you. *Let him.*"

Kangyr stared at Chet, hard to read, for a long time. During that pause, Chet moved his hand inconspicuously to his beamer. Finally Kangyr said, "You will not leave. You will stay and show us all this magic, and we will select what we want of it." He nodded to the lancers.

But before they could get their lances up, Chet had whipped his beamer out and they backed away from it. "Stay put," he said. "This little piece of magic can be deadly at a distance." They stayed put.

"We're going," Chet announced. "We'll leave these two boats here, but they're the last you'll get from us. Whatever else you want, you'll have to get for yourselves. Terek can get you started—and when we go, he's your only chance. Make the most of him. There aren't many like him." Chet disconnected the two new floaters from the one they were riding. "Let's go, Jem."

Jem lifted their floater off the terrace and started it almost imperceptibly skyward. "And if I don't?" Kangyr asked sullenly.

Chet grinned at him. "I don't think you're that stupid, Kangyr. When you honestly ask yourself if you can afford not to try Terek's suggestions, you won't answer wrong. And one thing will lead to another—"

He waited. When Kangyr said nothing, he nodded to Jem.

This time they lifted off in earnest and rose skyward with appreciable speed. Chet looked back at the dwindling figures on the monastery terrace and tried to foresee the future. There could be no absolute certainties in such things, of course, but—

"I think they'll make it," he told Tina.

Misinformation

The successful sociologist is more than a scientific plodder, diligently applying scientific methods to the study of human social behavior. Sociologists also do more than record and catalog social detail or theoretically speculate about abstract propositions. The purpose of their endeavor is understanding—either for its own sake or for use in solving social problems or establishing social policy. Moreover, although there is a logical pattern to the development of sociological understanding, this understanding requires more than fitting the parts of the puzzle together in their proper arrangement. Often it is the unexpected insight or the surprising result—what Robert K. Merton called serendipity—that makes sense of the effort.

Rof Tosen, in "Misinformation," is neither theorist nor researcher, but one who attempts to gain knowledge so that it may be put to use to his own people's advantage. Tosen encounters some typical difficulties in gathering data (a few sociologists have been "burned" beyond the degree of "the equivalent of a bad case of sunburn"), but he has his own serendipitous finding—this is not a flash of brilliance, but the simple recognition that the Lontastans are copiers not imitators, an insight that undermines Tosen's assumptions about Monte and permits him to make sense of his task.

Misinformation

HOWARD L. MYERS

Rof Tosen entered the outer office of the Bureau of Strategic Information and gazed about with dismay.

There were half a dozen Bureau staffers in the room, and his emo-monitor picked up high enthusiasm from each of them. But it was obvious at a glance that the enthusiasm was not for their work.

Three were huddled in conversation that seemed to concern, from the snatches Tosen overheard, the doings of their various children. Two others were seated at their desks using their communicators. One of these, a man, was close enough for Tosen to gather that he was discussing plants for a hunting trip on the planet Glarsek.

Only one was going through the motions of handling some paperwork, and her main attention was focused on the conversing group.

Tosen sighed. Just like back home in the offices of his Arbemel Systems Corporation on Haverly, he reflected glumly. Anyone would think the econo-war was over—or had never existed—from the actions of these people. And in the Bureau of Strategic Information, of all places! Regardless of the indifference of Commonality citizenry at large, he had expected somehow to find competitive morale still running strong here.

The woman doing paperwork looked at him. "May I help you?" she asked.

"I'm Rof Tosen," he said. "I have an appointment with Stol Jonmun."

"The Bureau chief won't be in this week," she replied. "Dave Mergly will see you instead. This way, please.'

She rose, ignoring the flash of annoyance from Tosen, and led the way up a jumpshaft and along a corridor. Dave Mergly was the one man in the Bureau Tosen had hoped to avoid. He was Stol Jonmun's top assistant in charge of saying "no." But if Jonmun was out gold-bricking like everyone else . . . well, it would have to be Mergly.

The woman guided him into Mergly's office and departed. The two men studied each other for a moment. Dave Mergly was middle-aged, several years Tosen's senior, and was one of those men who remained slender with minimal exercise. He could burn up energy simply sitting at a desk. A high-tension type, Tosen reflected—and clearly that way as a matter of genetics, because psych-releasers made doubly sure, when treating government officials, that every possible source of unsanity was fully lifted.

Tosen's emo-monitor read the bureaucrat's attitude as one of detached curiosity, which gradually shifted into reserved approval, as they studied each other.

Mergly's thin lips bent in a slight smile. "Still competing, Tosen?" he asked.

"Trying to. You, too, I would judge."

"Yes. Not many of us around anymore. Welcome into the shrinking minority. Have a seat."

Tosen lowered into a chair, asking, "You holding the fort alone, here in the Bureau?"

"Not quite. How about your company . . . Arbemel Systems, isn't it?"

Tosen nodded. "I've got two good men. Mike Stebetz in Management and Clarn Rogers in Research. Makes two out of a payroll of sixty-seven hundred."

"Three counting yourself," observed Mergly. "A little better than average, I would say." He studied Tosen for a moment, then asked, "How do you explain the situation, Rof?"

With a shrug Tosen replied, "I don't have any original thoughts on the subject. The obvious answer is that the public at large considers the econo-war to be over, so they're no longer participating in it. The Lontastan Federation, with its telepath Monte, has an over-powering advantage over us. So the average citizen considers it all over but the official surrender and seizure."

Mergly frowned. "The Commonality has been in tight squeezes before, and managed to squirm out, and morale didn't go to pot while we were doing it. Remember old Radge Morimet?"

"No, he predated me by ten years. But, of course, I'm familiar with what he accomplished—and what he didn't accomplish. His motto was 'war in our time,' and let the next generation worry about war in its time. Well, we're the next generation, and the compromises he made to keep the econo-war going have made our position even more difficult. He managed to squirm, but in doing so he left no squirming room for us.

"I think the public realizes that," Tosen continued thoughtfully. "The time is past when we can find a short-term answer by compromising the philosophical foundation of the econo-war. Morimet didn't leave us any compromises to make. Except for a handful of diehards, which includes the two of us, nobody sees any possibility of bringing the war back to life."

"And the public doesn't seem to care," grunted Mergly.

"Oh, the people care, all right," Tosen disagreed. "I have talked to a lot of the people in my company about it. They regret the ending of the war, but without panic or grief. That's the sane way to face a loss, no matter how tremendous it is. We're inclined to misjudge their reaction—and this is something to think about—because this is the first major social crisis humanity has faced since we attained racial sanity, nearly a thousand years ago. We listen for screams of anguish and look for people wringing their hands, or lashing out angrily at everybody and everything, or sinking into the apathy of defeat. But such responses from the Earth-Only days are no longer in character."

Mergly nodded slowly. "A good point. The people write off their loss and fall back on what they have left—their purely personal interests, their love for their families, and what not. Meanwhile, our social structure collapses about us."

"Yes," Tosen agreed. "That's what the econo-war was for, essentially . . . to stimulate the individual's motivation as a functioning member of a racial social structure."

"Then why," demanded Mergly, "are we few diehards still hanging on?"

"Maybe because we're more informed than most on how damaging a social collapse could be. At the best, we would have a stasis civilization. At worst, we could slide back into unsanity. Unless . . . and this is a trillion-to-one shot . . . some sublime genius of a philosopher discovered some presently unsuspected Higher Purpose for humanity to pursue."

Mergly gave a dry chuckle. "Another explanation for us diehard types," he said, "could be that we still see, or imagine, some thin hope to cling to."

"Yes," nodded Tosen, "there's that."

"Which gets us around to the real reason for your visit, doesn't it?"

Tosen hesitated. "I'd rather not have my scheme termed a 'thin hope' before you've even heard it," he said with a grin.

Mergly nodded, and his emo reading was a cold nothing. He was, Tosen guessed, all set to listen analytically—and thoroughly critically

—to the proposal. "Go ahead," he said.

"What I have in mind," Tosen began, "would get us away from damaging compromises, and hit at the basic imbalance in the econo-war. That is, at the fact that the Lontastan Federation has Monte, and the Commonality of Primgran doesn't. Essentially, Monte was the first compromise. The Lontastans should never have allowed a nonhuman to participate in what was a purely human conflict. Do you agree with that?"

"Yes."

"Unless, of course, Monte isn't a nonhuman life form at all," Tosen added, eying the information man closely.

Mergly blinked. "Oh? You think there's room for doubt about that?"

"That's what I'm here to find out. Let's consider what we think we know about Monte, and why we think we know it.

"First, he's a huge globe in form, perhaps a hundred meters in diameter, with a stonelike shell of sufficient thickness and strength to support that tremendous weight on a planet of approximately Earth-gravity. Second, he's a one-member species that does not produce offspring, and presumably had his genesis in the earliest stages of the life-formation processes on his planet, perhaps a billion years ago. Third, a Lontastan exploration team entered his star's planetary system and discovered him, and he volunteered his services in the econo-war very soon thereafter.

"Now, we aren't dealing with impossibilities in any of those three areas—that is, Monte's present form, his history, or his discovery by man. But I suggest each of the three holds substantial improbabilities, and when all of them are combined the likelihood of truth is statistically slight.

"For example, such giant size and mass would create problems of inadequate muscular strength for mobility, of finding sufficient nourishment, and of dissipating body heat. A Monte creature ought to be immobile, and stewing in its own weak juices.

"And yet, this creature reportedly has survived and grown through most of the geologic ages of his planet. Earthquakes, floodings, volcanic eruptions, ice incrustations . . . he got through them all.

"And then this creature, after a billion years of total intellectual solitude, becomes a 'joiner' as soon as he encounters humanity!"

Tosen paused, then added, "I don't say all this is impossible. Merely improbable."

Frowning, Mergly countered, "Perhaps; perhaps not. Every difficulty you cite can be explained. The matter of nourishment, for instance, seems to be handled in large part by a process similar to photosynthesis, called radiosynthesis. Radioactive ores would have been plentiful and rich in Monte's youth—and incidentally there may have been many small Montes back then, making the survival of one far more probable. The nourishment problem would have built up with the passage of time, I agree. And according to some reports I've seen, that could explain Monte's eagerness for human associates. People can mine and refine radioactives for him to bed down in.

"I won't bother to cover all your 'improbables,'" Mergly concluded with a shrug. "Presumably you've studied the matter sufficiently to know the explanations yourself. My question is why do you even bother to bring the subject up?"

"Because despite the explanations, the improbables are still just that," retorted Tosen. "And if there is any reason to believe the account of Monte we have is based on misinformation, we might be well-advised to assume a more believable account of what he is, and how he got that way."

Mergly's eyebrows raised and he flickered annoyance. "Misinformation?" he said.

"That's what I want you to tell me," said Tosen quickly. "What are the sources of our data concerning Monte? How close has one of our own agents ever got to him? Have we ever captured and questioned a Lontastan who had *direct* knowledge of Monte's physical nature?"

There was a moment of silence. "You're suggesting the Lontastans have sold us a comet tail," Mergly said slowly.

"Could be. I want to know if any of our data on Monte is unimpeachable enough to prove me wrong."

"Well . . . as you know, Lontastan security around Orrbaune is extremely tight," said Mergly. "As soon as one of our agents breaks warp anywhere in the planetary system he's detected telepathically. And he can't stay long . . . everybody's jumpy about intruders these days, partly because of the crisis condition of the econo-war, and partly because Radge Morimet brought unsane motivation into play. The Lontastan Guardsmen blast away at an agent immediately, on the chance that he might be some kind of nut with a superweapon in his pocket.

"As for picking up direct data on Monte from a captured Lontastan, I'd have to check on that, but I believe all information from such sources is third-hand at best. For the moment, I'll go along with your notion that the Monte story has been falsified. The question remains, what good would this falsification do the Lontastans? And what can we gain by penetrating it?"

"Easy," smiled Tosen. "If Monte's not a living being, the most probable alternative is that he's a machine built by the Lontastans. If we are led to *think* the Monte machine is a being, we won't try to build one of our own. After all, anything the Lontastans can build, so can we. But a telepathic life form isn't one of those things . . . biotechnics just isn't up to it. Thus, the Lontastans develop a telepathic device, make us believe it's a natural life form, and keep a monopoly on their gadget."

"But why on such an out-of-the-way planet as Orrbaune?" protested Mergly. "Would they actually go to the trouble of shifting their capital way out there, if Monte were indeed a machine that could be built presumably anywhere?"

"Sure, for verisimilitude!" exclaimed Tosen. "And for security reasons, too. Keep in mind that, back before they had Monte, we had the upper hand in the war. They hadn't broken our monopoly on implanted emo-monitors then, and our undercover agents and saboteurs were having a field day on their central worlds. When they hit on the telepathy gimmick, they had to spirit their development team off somewhere, to such an undeveloped world as Orrbaune, to keep the project secret from us.

"But if they had started building Monte machines on all their major planets, we would have caught on quickly. So they built just the one . . . and on a planet where a startling life form might *possibly* have been discovered, and started spreading their tall story."

Mergly nodded slowly, and Tosen felt a calm elation.

"Of course," Mergly said, not quite willing to be convinced, "what you have here is a purely suppositional structure."

"Yes, but one that, if I'm right, could straighten out the entire econo-war mess and get everybody back in competition. But I agree it would help if we had more dependable data to go on."

"Such as what?"

"Such as an agent might get during a very close—though necessarily quite brief—approach to Orrbaune. For a moment our man would be in the thick of the telepathic communications network that Monte provides the personnel on the planet, not merely within range of telepathic detection. He might get a surprise reaction from Monte, especially if it is a living creature. And he might pick up thoughts from the local humans who have first-hand knowledge of the telepath."

Mergly was radiating impatience. "Who's dealing with extreme improbabilities now?" he snorted. "But never mind that for a moment, since I can see from your emo that you think you know how such a close approach could be made. If you're asking me to assign a Bureau agent to that mission, the answer is NO. For the very good reason that we no longer have an agent fit for that type of job."

"No agent?" murmured Tosen.

"They've all turned noncompetitive," grunted Mergly. "Which makes sense from their viewpoint. Agents are among the few people who actually risk their lives in the conduct of the econo-war. That takes strong motivation, which present conditions don't provide."

"But if it was explained to one that this mission might revitalize the econo-war . . ." Tosen began.

"He would laugh at you," Mergly responded. "Have you tried to explain your scheme to a noncompetitor?"

"Well, yes. To my wife."

"What did she think of it?"

"She laughed," Tosen admitted lamely.

Mergly's smile was sour. "So there you are. You have a suppositional structure, which you need more data to substantiate sufficiently to impress someone who has turned noncompetitive. But to get that data, you have to impress a noncompetitive agent with your suppositions. Quite a dilemma."

After a silence, Tosen said, "There's one answer to it: I can make the jaunt to Orrbaune myself if you'll agree."

"That's a deadly game for an amateur," replied Mergly.

"I know," said Tosen.

Four light-days away from Orrbaune's sun Tosen came out of warp, well outside telepathic detection range.

For an instant he felt a purely subjective chill, so distant from a sun's warmth and clad only in the shorts, sleeveless shirt and low boots normally worn by space travelers. However, the tiny implanted devices of his life-support system were keeping him warm while they protected him from the vacuum, and from the high-energy particles of interstellar space. And embedded in the tissues of his throat and nasal passages were gas-converting macromolecules to permit normal breathing.

He torqued his repulsor field to start himself spinning slowly, blinked tightly to turn on his amplisight, and peered about for the equipment pod which had been set to follow three seconds behind him through warp. This was an uncertainty-filled point in his mission —finding his equipment—because warping over a two-hundred-light-year jump was not totally precise. His pod might emerge on top of him or fifty thousand miles away. And it could not make any blatant announcement of its location so near the Lontastan capital system . . . it had a powerful red blinker for Tosen to look for, and that was all.

Without the equipment in the pod, he might as well warp for

home immediately. He had to have it, and it could not have made the trip through warp with him. A man-sized mass was about the maximum that could move at warp velocities without stirring up mind-wrecking turbulence in prime-field.

So Tosen spun slowly in space, straining for a glimpse of the red blinker.

He almost missed it. It was a dim flicker in his peripheral vision that vanished when he tried to look directly at it. But he had its direction spotted. He activated his propulsor field and zoomed toward it on semi-inert mode.

Within fifty yards of the pod he went full-inert and drifted in slowly. The pod was a slender torpedo of dull red, and the color went black when he reached and killed the blinker. After activating the automatic setup system, he drifted a few feet away while he watched the pod unfold, extend a framework of slender lattices, and fan out a thin pie-slice of silver into a six-meter telescope mirror. When the components clamped together and motion stopped, he drifted to the eyepiece and swung the instrument to point in the direction of Orrbaune.

Basically it was an ancient device that would have been readily recognized for what it was back in Earth-Only times—an astronomical reflector telescope. It was rendered more effective by an ampli-sight attachment and tight-line tracking, but its mirror optics differed little from those used by men to peer into space even before man himself could leave old Earth's atmosphere.

Tosen grinned at the sheer size of the instrument. Who would imagine a spy using such a big, cumbersome gadget?

And that was the whole point. Nobody had imagined it, and that was why it had never been tried. People were used to thinking of space equipment in pill-sized packages . . . devices small enough to place in the various available nooks and crannies of the human body without making noticeable bulges. Like ampli-sight, for example, for which a specialized field phenomenon was produced by specklike transmitters located within the eyeballs.

Being sane, Tosen mused as he busied himself with the telescope, only gave individuals access to such abilities as they inherently possessed. It was no guarantee of great wisdom, or of creative imagination. He felt himself fortunate to possess the latter of these.

He spent fifteen hours working with the telescope and its computer attachment, getting the data he needed. When his series of observations was complete, he knew his position and motion relative to Orrbaune with more exactitude than any earlier Commonality agent. He figured on a maximum margin of error of ten miles.

Satisfied at last, he activated the breakdown system and watched the telescope collapse back into the compact pod configuration. When the process was complete, he switched on the systems of the pod's record-and-home automatic sequence.

Then he drifted away from the pod, carefully set up his approach vector, and warped toward Orrbaune.

He exited into norm space almost sitting on the planet. His altitude was only two hundred miles, and his inert momentum in relation to the surface was near zero.

But he had no time to congratulate himself on this success. He was too busy observing with every implant-augmented sense he could bring to bear. He had a lot to try to learn in the two seconds he had allowed himself.

At that, he nearly overstayed. The Lontastans were skittish indeed about unheralded visitors—and especially one appearing almost on top of their heads. Tosen realized as he automatically went into warp and zipped away that he had felt the first few milliseconds of a zerburst flare that had blossomed within a few hundred meters of where he had been. He could feel the burn all across his back, and could detect his medicircuits going to work on the damage.

What had he learned?

He wasn't sure, but he hadn't expected to be at this stage. The important information, he hoped, was that which had been gathered by his special sensing devices and transmitted to the pod, to be recorded and transported home.

But at any rate, his memory of those two seconds held nothing to indicate Monte was not a device.

There *had* been telepathic contact. It had come so swiftly after his exit from warp that he had noticed no time lag.

But the . . . the *feel* of that contact was, at first, impersonal, without even mild emotion. Would a living telepath have such a feel? Tosen had never experienced telepathy before, but he doubted it.

Then, a split-second later, that impersonal feel was lost in a welter of obviously human thought-patterns as alerted Guardsmen came storming into the telepathic linkage with the expected reactions of alarm and anger, and harsh demands that the intruder identify himself instantly.

All in all, Tosen considered his mission to Orrbaune a complete success.

He left a confused flurry of exchanges behind him.

Who was that? demanded Frikason of the Lontastan High Board.

Monte replied: *His identity was not revealed, as his attention*

was so totally on receiving data that he transmitted very little. How-
ever, he was from the Commonality, and his purpose came through
clearly.

Oh? What was it?

To obtain information to verify his belief that I'm a machine, not
a living being. Monte's thought was obviously amused. *If I were a*
machine, it would be possible for the Commonality to build my
counterpart. That was his intention.

Frikason along with several others present shared Monte's
amusement.

Then from Frikason: *In a way it's too bad he's so completely off*
the track.

True, agreed Monte. *The deterioration of the econo-war game*
is regrettable, and my equivalent on the Primgranese team would be
the ideal way to restore the balance. But extensive studies by my-
self in collaboration with a number of your scientists has produced
the unavoidable conclusion: a telepathic device, or machine, lies
totally beyond all present skills and knowledge, and may, in fact, be
an impossibility. Whereas certain of the reasoning capabilities of the
mind can be duplicated by computing devices, telepathy lends itself
to no such mechanical production. It is too purely a life-function for
that.

After a moment of relative telepathic silence, a thought came
from Garsanne of the High Board: *Surely even the Primgranese*
should have figured that out. Why did this spy think otherwise? Did
he have an unsane motivator?

No, replied Monte. *My impression was that he bases his belief*
on a logical—if thoroughly wishful—interpretation of such data con-
cerning myself as the Commonality has obtained.

Wishful indeed, remarked Frikason. *By the way, did he warp*
out safely?

Yes, barely. He escaped with the equivalent of a bad case of
sunburn.

Sadder but wiser, huh?

No, not wiser, Monte informed them. *As you know, there is prac-*
tically nothing of what may be called personality in any one of my
billions of telepathic attention units. Each is simply a circuit. The
spy would not be able to distinguish the attention unit that de-
tached his presence and revealed him to the nearest Guardsmen as
the product of a living mind. As for the Guardsmen with whom he
was in mental contact, able though they are for their assignments
they are genetic barbarians of meager intellectual curiosity. Their
knowledge of me is only of the hearsay type the spy discountenances.

So he's going home, still thinking you're a machine he can dupli-

cate, observed Garsanne. *Look, Tedaboyd, you'd better dispatch a couple of agents to learn his identity and see what he comes up with, just in case.*

The Lontastan Intelligence chief's thought was annoyed: *What couple of agents? I told the High Board months ago that I haven't got a decent agent left! They've all become slackouts! And I can't say I blame them. Why should they stick their necks out for a war that is already won?*

Yes, I'm afraid we non-slack-outs are a vanishingly small minority, agreed Frikason. *Never mind trying to track down that spy. He can't possibly succeed, as Monte's told us. Let's get back to the task at hand of devising the least disastrous means of bringing the econo-war to an official close.*

Monte observed: *The Commonality of Primgran, though defeated, still has one strength we lack.*

Oh? What's that? Frikason asked.

One highly-motivated agent, still on the job.

Tosen soon found himself needing all his high motivation.

"Why," demanded Mergly, glowering across Tosen's desk, "didn't you tell me you didn't have even the backing of your own research man?"

Tosen glanced sideways at Clarn Rogers, who was emoting offended surprise, then replied, "Because I didn't know." He grinned wryly and added, "I didn't bother to check with him."

"Why not?"

"Because I suspected what his answer would be."

Mergly growled, "So you got me to go to bat for you before the Council to get you an R-and-D contract, with my neck way out—not that I give a damn about my neck, but wasting what competitive push we've got left is another matter!"

"I don't think it's a waste," Tosen returned. "I think Rogers is wrong."

"But, Rof," Rogers complained, "a telepathic machine just doesn't make sense. Every piece of substantial research on the subject indicates that telepathy is a function of the ego-field, or the spirit, or soul, or whatever you want to call it. Definitely, telepathy is *not* a function of the physiological nervous system. Or at any rate, not basically. A proper nervous system, such as that of the creature Monte, doubtless is essential machinery to facilitate an ego-field's telepathic abilities—otherwise all humans would have it. But you certainly can't produce telepathy with a mere machine!"

"Psionic devices have been around for several centuries," Tosen remarked softly.

"Certainly," Rogers said, showing impatience, "but they function as accessories of the users' nervous systems, as relatively simple additional nerve-ends, so to speak. Very useful as controls for our life-support implants and what not."

"But it's the ego-field that makes a psionic device work, isn't it?" said Tosen.

Rogers wriggled. "Well, of course. But as a *small* added part of the nervous system under the ego-field's control! What you're proposing wouldn't be small. It would be several orders of magnitude more complex than the human brain itself, according to my understanding of what Monte is. You couldn't merely focus your attention on such a thing and make it work. You don't have that much . . . that much *attention!* Certainly not that much to spare."

Mergly asked Rogers, "Then what would you expect to be the result of the project if we carried it out?"

Rogers shrugged. "We would have a very large, very expensive, and very inactive conglomerate of close-connected macromolecules."

"As large as Monte is reported to be?" demanded Mergly.

"No. We can crowd more functional capacity into artificially produced macromolecules than you find in living tissue, and use more concentrated energy sources. The construct would be less massive than Monte's living brain, but approximately as complex. I would estimate the diameter at two meters."

Tosen smiled inwardly at Rogers's insistence on thinking of Monte as a living creature, despite the flat, mechanical emo-quality of the telepathic contact made with him on his spying jaunt—that quality having been duly recorded and scrupulously analyzed since his return.

Now he kept silent as Mergly and Rogers continued the discussion. He was for the moment in the bad graces of both men for getting them involved in a project they considered half-baked at best. But they were both good constructive competitors who would, if they could, find a way to salvage something useful from the mess his "irresponsibility" had created.

In the meantime, his research man and the government's Information man were a team from which he was excluded. So the less he had to say, the better.

"Assuming that Monte is a natural life form," Mergly said, "with a brain as massive as that assumption would suggest, wouldn't our artificial construct be superior to him, provided it worked at all?"

"Interconnections would be much shorter," Rogers nodded, "which would permit faster responses. But, of course, it wouldn't work at all. It would be a sumptuous mock-up of a superior central nervous system, capable of producing billions of responses of the quality Rof picked up from Monte. But it would be an *uninhabited* mock-up. It would be dead."

After a pause, Mergly said, "Yes, but would it stay that way?"

"What do you mean?"

Mergly shifted in his seat and frowned. "There's much we don't know about the disembodied ego-field, even though that's a state we've all gone through. The experience just doesn't carry over to the normal embodied state; perhaps there are too few similarities to use as guides. My own impressions of disembodiment are completely vague. I'm wondering . . . would our artificial construct be attractive to a disembodied ego-field? Could it be *made* attractive?"

Rogers blinked. "That's a possibility, I suppose. We don't know what attracts an ego-field into a newly-created life form, such as a human baby, although there's no shortage of conflicting theories. There are, certainly, the physical pleasures, such as sex. Perhaps a structure that facilitated telepathic communication would have its attractions."

"O.K., and if that didn't do the trick," Mergly persisted, "couldn't pleasure-producing circuits, or physical structures, be added on?"

"Well, yes, in an artificial way. But let me put it like this: Would you want to live in a body composed completely of prosthetics?"

Mergly frowned. "No."

"Well, that's what we would be offering any interested ego-field. Strictly ersatz, second-rate physical pleasures. I think telepathy would be the real—perhaps the only—attraction we could offer."

Mergly considered this in silence, displaying a varying emo-pattern as he did so. Then suddenly his pattern went clean and he rose from his seat. Obviously, he had decided.

"O.K., Clarn," he said to Rogers. "Get on with the project. Build that structure, and we'll see if anyone moves in. We're taking a shot in the dark, but," he shrugged, "these are rather frantic times." His eyes moved to Tosen and he added, "Frantic enough to justify frantic schemes I'm sure."

Tosen was radiating triumph, and the contrite tone of his "Thank you, Dave" fooled nobody.

He stayed on the side lines of Project Bauble as the research and development work moved ahead. He assisted Rogers mostly by seeking out people in the company who hadn't gone completely noncompetitive, giving them exciting sales pitches about "something big and revolutionary" going on in the lab, and sending on to Rogers the recruits who responded with genuine interest.

Within a month, there was a notable difference in atmosphere at

Arbemel Systems Corporation. It wasn't back to the status of Hot Econo-war times, but had shifted in that direction. Even Tosen's secretaries were showing alert interest in their work, whereas before the project started their attention had been dispersed over such areas as the care and feeding of each other's children, beauty regimens, and in a few cases astrology. Now they were trying to outdo each other once more in demonstrating their efficiency.

Tosen was pleased. Whatever the outcome of the project, he had restored for a while, and within the limited confines of his company, the old spirit that had brought humanity so far and so fast.

But he knew the spirit would die quickly if the Bauble did not come alive.

Mergly was spending at least as much time on Haverly, at the Arbemel lab, as he was on the capital planet. Project Bauble was, after all, about the only real action going, so far as econo-war effort was concerned. Mergly wanted to keep an eye on it . . . and make sure there were no Lontastans doing the same.

"I've taken the liberty," he told Tosen after the project had been underway for several months, "of having the Arbemel floating stock purchased quietly for a Commonality trust."

Tosen nodded. "A good move," he said. "Since the bottom dropped out of the market three years ago, I've been uncomfortably aware of the possibility of being descended upon by a team of referees from Exchange World, with the news that Lontastans had bought a majority interest in the company for peanuts and had voted to liquidate."

"That wouldn't have been likely," said Mergly. "Why would they want this company, even for peanuts, the way things were? But now, because of the project, which they might find out about, we can't have a majority of the stock loosely held."

"How much did you buy for the trust?" Tosen asked.

"Forty-one percent."

"With my fourteen, that makes us safe." Tosen fiddled with the antique ballpoint pen he kept on his desk. "Been in the lab lately?" he asked.

"I just came from there."

"How are Rogers and his people doing?"

"They're coming along." Mergly paused, then added, "The Bauble will be complete next week, he says. This has been an expensive undertaking, Rof. The Council wouldn't have stood still for it if they had known what a gamble it is, or if other projects had been competing for R-and-D funds."

Tosen made a face. "O.K., you can consider me chastised. But despite all informed opinion to the contrary, I still believe the evidence favors Monte being an artificial, Lontastan-built structure, concerning which everyone but a few top Lontastans has been fed a load of misinformation."

"Maybe so," Mergly answered coolly. "We can hope so. If *they* haven't sold us misinformation, then *you* certainly have."

The Bauble had a pearllike luster, and Tosen decided as soon as he walked in the lab and saw it that it was well though deceptively named. A big bauble in appearance, but no bauble at all in price.

Rogers and Mergly were both there, gazing expressionlessly at the two-meter globe of glittery gray.

"That's it, huh?" Tosen said to announce his presence. "When are you going to turn it on?"

Rogers gave him a blank look. "It's turned on. It was built with its energy sources activated. It stays turned on."

"Well?"

Rogers said, "It's not doing anything. No life in it."

"O.K. So we wait for an interested ego-field to come along and discover it," said Tosen.

"We've already waited three hours," Mergly complained. "What's more, we've paraded every pregnant woman on the company payroll through here . . . two hundred and seven of them."

"What for?"

"Oh, one of the ego-field traditions that seems solider than most," shrugged Mergly. "Disembodied ego-fields are supposed to hang around pregnant women, waiting for the moment one of them can inhabit her child."

Tosen nodded. He had never thought highly of that idea. Ego-fields like a swarm of starving beggars, all of them after a tidbit only one could have! It carried the concept of competition to an unpleasantly ugly extreme.

"You may as well have a seat and a drink and be comfortable, if you're going to join the watch," said Rogers.

Tosen did so. The three of them sat with little conversation for over an hour.

At last Mergly said, "We ought to take this in shifts."

Rogers agreed. "This could keep up for days."

"I started last," said Tosen, "so I'll take the first shift if you like. Until midnight, say?"

"O.K."

The others left and Tosen got himself a fresh drink.

How long, he wondered, would it be reasonable to wait? With knowledge of ego-field characteristics so uncertain, a definite answer to the question was impossible. But his hunch was that, if an ego-field were ever going to inhabit the Bauble, it would have done so before now. From all accounts, ego-fields were numerous. And they moved around constantly. One should have discovered the Bauble before now. Probably one had—and had either considered it an undesirable habitation, or had not even regarded it as a *possible* habitation.

And unencumbered by a body and brain, an ego-field could presumably act with the swiftness of thought. Perhaps a hundredth of a second was all the time required for an ego-field to recognize a body's desirability and move in.

In which case the Bauble should have been inhabited within less than a full second after its completion. But that had not happened, not even in the first minute—nor the first hour—nor the first six hours.

Tosen sighed. So far as orders of magnitude were concerned, he realized uncomfortably, six hours resembled a century more closely than it did a hundredth of a second. So, if the Bauble were ever going to be occupied, chances were that it would have been so by now.

Another uncomfortable thought struck him for the first time, seriously undermining all his reasoning on the nature of Monte.

The Lontastans had, over the centuries, been less noted for innovation than the Primgranese. Usually, the Lontastans were content to copy, or improve upon, basic advances first made in the Commonality.

Would the Lontastans have gone to the extreme expense of a Project Bauble without foreknowledge that it would work?

It would have been most uncharacteristic of them, for sure. And Mergly could never have got Council support for *this* Project, except by arguing that this was something the Lontastans had already shown was possible.

Tosen chuckled, because in the final analysis none of that mattered in the least. The econo-war was lost, thanks to an obviously alive Monte on the Lontastan team. So what resources and effort had been spent on Project Bauble was merely decreasing the wealth that would be available for Lontastan claimancy, when the Lontastans got around to demanding settlement of the war.

So, as far as he was concerned, the project had been a good final try, even if a rather frantic and poorly thought-out one . . . at the enemy's eventual expense.

Tosen leaned back in his seat and relaxed, gazing at the Bauble.

A very handsome piece of workmanship, he mused, whether it did anything but look pretty or not. Actually it could be more accurately described as something grown rather than something built, being produced by chemical processes that had their genesis back in Earth-Only times when crystals were grown for solid-state electronic components. While the Bauble could theoretically be subdivided into millions of individual macromolecules, it was in fact one super-macromolecule, since the linkages between its theoretical units were themselves molecular in nature.

It would have been one hell of a gadget—if it had worked.

Why did the ego-fields turn up their ectoplasmic noses at it? he wondered with sudden irritation.

Maybe he could find out.

He put down his drink, let himself go limp, and left his body. This was something any psych-released adult could do easily enough, but was a rather useless trick except when the body was dying, at which time the ego-field usually went exterior to escape the death trauma.

Now Tosen drifted a few feet behind and above his head, still controlling his body from a distance and looking at the Bauble with normal sight and at the same time perceiving it with vague field senses. He drifted forward very slowly and entered the Bauble.

It was . . . like and unlike a body. Or more exactly, like and unlike a mind. It was difficult to pin down the flaw of the place as an abode. A poor analogy would be the interior of an empty house, with no furnishings, no fixtures, no doors. Just walls that were, strangely, both stark and indistinct at once.

He realized that he was exterior rather than fully disembodied, and that this might alter his view considerably from that of a totally detached ego-field. But his impression was strong that the Bauble was so totally lacking in *hominess* that no ego-field could possibly find it livable.

He pulled out of it and returned to his body. The mental exercise had, unaccountably, left him slightly exhausted and very hungry.

He walked over to an autospenser, dialed himself a tray of supper, and returned to his chair to eat. When he finished, he lay back and napped for a couple of hours.

Mergly came in promptly at midnight. "Nothing yet?" he asked.

"No, and I'm afraid not ever," said Tosen, He quickly explained why the time they had already waited should have been more than adequate for the Bauble to take on life, and why the Lontastans would not have tried to develop an artificial telepath.

"As a final check," he wound up, "I exteriorized and entered the thing to get the feel of the place. I wouldn't care to live there."

Mergly nodded slowly. "What was your feeling inside the . . ." he began, then hesitated. "Never mind describing it. I'll take a look for myself."

He sat down and relaxed. Tosen waited quietly for close to ten minutes before Mergly stirred and looked up.

"Well, what did you think of it?" Tosen asked.

"A vast empty place with hard echoes. That's about as close as I can describe it," Mergly replied thoughtfully. "Even with you along for company the emptiness felt overwhelming."

"I didn't go along," objected Tosen. "I stayed right here in my own comfortable noggin."

Mergly frowned. "Oh? Perhaps you didn't, at that. What I sensed, I believe, was that you had been there before me. Maybe some of you rubbed off inside."

Tosen laughed. "Could be. I felt half exhausted when I came out."

"So do I." Mergly yawned, and stared at the Bauble from beneath drooping eyelids.

"I'm going home," said Tosen heading for the door. "Tell Rogers I'll contact him around midday to see if he thinks it worthwhile for me to stand another watch."

"O.K.," replied Mergly. "I'll suggest that he take a feel inside the Bauble, too. He might have some ideas on how to make it more homey."

Walking down the hallway Tosen replied, "O.K., no harm in asking him. But I feel the Bauble's flaws are too basic to be remedied easily or cheaply." He paused outside the lab to gaze upward into the clear, starry night. Then he activated his transport implants and soared up and westward toward his home. "At the least," he added, "we would have to start again from scratch and build a completely different kind of Bauble. What would the Council say to that?"

Mergly emoted such a violent shudder that Tosen chuckled.

"I'm glad you can feel amused," complained Mergly with a flash of anger. "Unfortunately, I can't share that don't-give-a-damn attitude you've taken on. It smacks of noncompetitiveness to me."

Tosen flinched. "Sorry," he said. "I got us into this thing, and I'd have no business turning deserter now."

"I didn't say you were a deserter," Mergly denied.

"No, but you felt it . . . or thought it." Suddenly Tosen gasped and whirled his body, searching the upper atmosphere for sight of Mergly. "*Say, where the hell are you, anyway?*"

"Why . . . right here in the lab, in my body."

Tosen watched through Mergly's eyes as the Information man looked away from the Bauble to search the room for the man he had been talking to. "Where are *you?*" Mergly demanded, then added, "Oh . . . I . . . see."

The damned thing works! Tosen exulted.

But just for us? from Mergly, whose mind was tumbling confusedly.

Sure! The Bauble's not a living telepath like Monte. It's merely a gadget! It doesn't reach out. We have to reach in. Give it our individual punched cards, so to speak. And so far, only you and I have reached in! You felt I had been there before you, remember. That was because it had my pattern. It has yours, too. I'm going to flip on this antique toothmike of mine and call Rogers, while you warp for the capital to give the Council the news!

Very well, but . . . but this is difficult to take in, Rof. Not thirty minutes ago you had me convinced the Bauble couldn't possibly work, that the whole project was based solely on your wishful thinking and misinformation . . .

Tosen thought a big happy smile. *Dave, we'd all still be living in Earth caves if we hadn't wished for things we couldn't possibly have. And as for misinformation . . .*

Yes? Mergly prompted.

Well, when misinformation says the impossible can be done instead of the other way around, then it just might turn out to be the truest information you ever heard!

2

Social Organization and Culture

Social organization and culture are two of the most useful concepts for sociologists. In this chapter are readings relevant to both social organization and culture as well as to the related concepts of social and cultural change, collective behavior, and deviance.

(1) *Social Organization.* The sociologist studies patterned, recurrent human social behavior. These recurrent patterns form *social structures* that sociologists identify by using basic concepts of social structure, such as social relationship, role, status, group, association, and complex organization. Each structure can be analyzed as to its internal components and its relationship to larger structures of which it is a part. To study the interrelationship among components of a social structure is to investigate *social organization.*

Common to the perspectives of many sociologists throughout the development of sociology has been the concept of *social system.* Early sociologists often analyzed human groups or societies by drawing analogies between them and the physiological systems of organisms. The social system perspective survived its detachment from organicism and remains an analytical device for the sociologist. Viewing patterned social behavior as forming systems (relatively self-operating entities) comprised of interrelated components has increased understanding of both simple and complex patterns of social organization.

The basic social or group processes have been identified by sociologists as the dynamic forces keeping the social system operating. These patterned processes are identified by such terms as co-operation, competition, conflict, accommodation, assimilation, and so on. These processes describe the variable modes of patterned interaction between and among groups.

(2) *Culture.* Many definitions of culture have been developed by sociologists and anthropologists. Early anthropologists, studying small, self-contained, nonliterate societies, often conceptualized culture as the "total way of life" of the people in a given society. Their "way of life" included their shared beliefs, values, norms or rules guiding behavior, as well as their rituals, practices, and artifacts (material objects shaped and given meaning by the people—a tool, vessel, weapon, or religious totem, for example).

In conceptualizing culture, sociologists and anthropologists have emphasized the nonbiological products of man's behavior in society. These products range from abstract theory and ideology to the concrete objects and combinations of objects forming part of the technology of a people. Contemporary sociologists and anthropologists generally conceive of culture as the unique possession of the human species. Some nonhuman species live in societies with a division of tasks or labor (for example, bees and ants). Some species utilize objects as tools and some similar to man may even "make" tools (witness Jane Van Lawick-Goodall's discovery that chimpanzees strip bark from a twig so that it can be used as a tool). Insofar as we know at this time, however, only man creates a language that permits *symbolic* communication. Symbolic communication in association with others facilitates the *sharing, learning,* and *transmission* of culture that are essential features of the sociological concept of culture.

(3) *Social and Cultural Change.* The sociologists' study of social structures and of culture reveals that these phenomena are not static and unchanging but constantly in the process of change and that their change is patterned too. While some sociologists use the terms *social change* and *cultural change* interchangeably, it is useful to distinguish between them. The term social change is applied to changes in a society's structured interpersonal relationships as in the change from a familistic to a bureaucratic pattern of social organization. The term cultural change refers to change in the content or organization of culture, as, for example, in changes in the way of life of a people as they move from handicraft modes of production to machine technology.

The terms industrialization, urbanization, modernization, and secularization refer to patterns of long-term social change. Certain early sociologists identified contrasting models of social order in an attempt to describe and explain both structure and change. Toennies' *Gemeinschaft* and *Gesellschaft* or Spencer's military and industrial types of society are just two of many examples of this approach to portraying social change.

Culture changes in scope and content with the passage of time. As cultural patterns are transmitted from generation to generation, some cultural elements are lost, while others are added. The sum of culture at any given time is the *culture base* of a society, and since more elements are added than lost, the culture base expands, or culture "accumulates." The larger the culture base, the more possible recombinations of elements into new patterns through *innovation, invention* or *cultural diffusion*. Cultural change has seemed to accelerate with modernization and most assume it will continue to accelerate in the future.

Some 50 years ago the sociologist William Fielding Ogburn defined culture so as to include both the material productions of man's actions and the values, beliefs, norms, and ideologies that are also the product of man's social interaction. Ogburn called the former "material culture" and the latter "nonmaterial culture." Although a distinction rejected by many sociologists later, it was useful to Ogburn in developing his conception of *culture lag*. By this term he emphasized that material culture changes more rapidly than nonmaterial culture; that is, the latter lags behind the former as both change.

(4) *Collective Behavior.* Generally the behavior patterns studied by the sociologist take highly structured forms: for example, the formal structure of a complex organization such as a corporation, a governmental agency, or a church hierarchy. However, some social behavior takes much less structured forms. It is less bounded by cultural norms and regularized social roles and group structures. Sociologists call this relatively unstructured behavior *collective behavior.* They study several forms of collective behavior—among them are crowds, publics, and social movements. This study includes attention to such forms as riots, mob action, audiences, public opinion formation, and propaganda.

Social movements are of particular interest to sociologists because they evidence a greater degree of structure than more expressive forms of crowd action and because of their consequences for social stability and change. Social movements involve large numbers of people consciously participating in collective action that attempts to resist or bring about change in society. There are many types of social movements and they can be classified in a variety of ways. For example, there are youth movements, women's rights movements, minority group movements, peasants' movements, political or religious movements, and reactionary, reform, or revolutionary movements.

Social movements are collective responses to defined social circumstances, and therefore each movement has to be understood in the context of its society and the times. However, some movements widely separated in time are addressed to recurring ways in which societies are organized, and sociologists will trace the similarities of movements widely separated in time. For example, how is today's women's liberation movement like and unlike the woman's suffrage movement of half a century ago in the United States? Sociologists are also interested in the organization and types of leadership of social movements; how beliefs, values, and goals are organized into the ideology of a social movement; and the phases or stages through which a movement passes.

(5) *Deviance.* Social deviance is behavior in violation of normative expectations. All societies and all groups develop certain universal cultural forms. Among these are *norms,* that is, standards of expected behavior shared by members of the group or the society. Some of these rules are generally stated; others are very specific. Some apply to a wide variety of situations; others apply to a single situation. Sociologists identify three types of norms: *folkways, mores,* and *laws.* Folkways and mores are nonformalized norms. The difference between them is that mores carry a moral significance not attached to folkways, and sanctions for violating them are more severe than they are for violating folkways. Laws are officially enacted norms. They become more important and more pervasive as societies become more diverse and complex.

Behavior that meets normative expectations is referred to as *conformity.* Behavior violating standards of expected behavior is deviance. Violation of a folkway, such as a male not wearing a tie to a formal dinner party, is deviance. Violation of a criminal law, such as committing homicide, is deviance. These acts vary greatly in the seriousness with which they are viewed, but they are both deviant. It is important to view deviance as behavior vis-à-vis the encompassing norm, since in popular useage the term *deviant* can mean many things and is usually characterized by a negative evaluative tone.

To fully understand deviance, one must also ask several other questions: Whose norms are involved? Do the norms of one group conflict with those of another group? Is the deviance discovered? What response is made to it? What has caused the act to be committed? The study of deviant behavior is pursued in the *sociology of deviance,* and the same perspectives are common to *criminology,* the study of one type of deviance: violation of criminal law.

Social
Organization

Positive Feedback

Sociological study based on the social systems approach has revealed that man's social experiences are likely to involve him simultaneously in a number of different systems—"ecosystem," "technosystem," and so on. Concern has arisen about the possible conflict between the various systems and about the degree of control that man has over the systems he creates, which, once set in motion, seem to proceed with a momentum of their own.

"Positive Feedback" illustrates the problem of adjusting systems while they are in action so that they serve man's purpose. Systems theory recognizes the importance of information flows in systems. One type of information input—negative feedback—provides an error-correction capability. It helps to avoid repetition of mistakes and to allow the system to adapt to changing reality external to the system and to malfunction within the system itself. Another type of flow—positive feedback—generates action that impairs the system's ability to adapt itself to its environment, since it can create tendencies to adhere to the same ways of dealing with problems or can even add additional problems. In "Positive Feedback" auto repairs get "out of hand" because elements of the system are reinforced by positive feedback, not corrected by negative feedback.

The interaction that is the basis of every social system not only provides for necessary task completion, but also develops social expectations about what is necessary and proper. In "Positive Feedback," the plight of Joe Schramm derives from his having to fulfill expectations having to do with needed equipment. These generated needs dominate his business. The interaction among Schramm, Foresyte Insurance, and Superdee Equipment raises some major sociological questions: Do individuals participating in groups that form the basic structure of society develop their own expectations? Or is the process of interdependency in social organization itself a structural determinant that molds behavior in directions that "violate" the preferences and actual needs of individuals? Does social organization restrict and constrain or does it enhance the freedom of man to pursue a wider number of options?

Positive Feedback

CHRISTOPHER ANVIL

SCHRAMM'S GARAGE

To: Jack W. Bailey
413 Crescent Drive
City

Parts:	1 set 22-638 brushes	$ 1.18
Labor:	overhaul generator	
	set regulator	
	clean battery terminals	11.00
	total	$12.18

NOTE: Time for oil change and install new filter.
Noticed car seemed to pull to the left when we stepped on the brake. Can take care of it Wednesday if you want.

Joe Schramm

Dear Joe:
Check for $12.18 enclosed.
Will see about the oil change and filter later. The kids have been sick and we're going broke at this rate.
Maybe it pulls to the left, but I haven't noticed it.

Jack Bailey

SUPERDEE EQUIPMENT

Mr. Joseph Schramm
Schramm's Garage
1428 West Ave.
Crescent City
Dear Mr. Schramm:
Enclosed find literature on our new Automated Car Service Handling Machine.

With this great new machine, you can service anything from a little imported car to a big truck. The Handling Machine just picks the vehicle up, and the Glider on its Universal Arm enables your mechanic to get at any part, from above or below. By just turning a few knobs, he glides right to the spot on the end of the Arm. Power grapples, twisters, engine-lifters, transmission-holders, dozen-armed grippers and wrasslers—all these make the toughest job easy.

If you've got a dozen mechanics, buy this machine and you can get along with three or four.

This machine will be the best buy of your life.

Truly yours,
G. Wrattan
Sales Manager

SCHRAMM'S GARAGE

Dear Mr. Wrattan:

This machine of yours would take up my whole shop. It's all-electric, and looks to me as if it would take the Government to pay the electric bills. Your idea that I could buy this thing and then let most of my mechanics go is a little dull. When business gets bad, I can *always* let them go. But with this monster machine of yours, I couldn't let *anybody* go, except the few guys I still had, who would be my best mechanics.

Do you know how hard it is to find a good mechanic?

Let's have the prices and information on your line of hydraulic jacks. Spare me the million-dollar-Robot-Garage stuff.

Yours truly,
J. Schramm

SUPERDEE EQUIPMENT

Mr. Joseph Schramm
Schramm's Garage
1428 West Ave.
Crescent City

Dear Mr. Schramm:

Enclosed find prices and literature on our complete line of hydraulic jacks, jack-stands, and lifts.

Mr. Schramm, we feel that you do not fully appreciate the advantages of our great new Automated Car Service Handling Machine. This machine will more than pay for itself in speed, efficiency, and economical service. In bad times you could still cut down your repair staff. Mr. Schramm, *one man* can operate this machine.

We are enclosing a new brochure on this wonderful new labor- and expense-saving machine, which will turn your garage into an ultra-modern Servicatorium.

Cordially,
G. Wrattan
Sales Manager

Schramm's Garage

Dear Mr. Wrattan:

I'm enclosing an order sheet for jack and stands.

Your new brochure on your wonderful new labor- and expense-saving machine went straight into the furnace.

I think you are going to have plenty of trouble selling this machine. The reason is, all you're doing is to think how nice it will be for you if somebody buys it, not how lousy it will be for him to have the thing.

This machine will take cable as thick as my arm for the juice to run all those motors. It's bound to break down, and while I'm repairing it, I'm out of business.

You say I can let all my mechanics go but one. You must have a loose ground somewhere. If I fire all my mechanics but one, and he runs this machine, *who's the boss then?*

I could tell you what to do with this great new machine of yours, but I don't think you would do it.

Yours truly,
J. Schramm

Superdee Equipment
Interoffice Memo

To: W. W. Sanson, Pres.

Dear Mr. Sanson:

I am sending up a large envelope containing sample letters, from garages all over the country.

The response we've had on Handling Machines has been unusually large and emphatic, but unfortunately it has not been favorable.

G. Wrattan

Superdee Equipment
Interoffice Memo

To: G. Wrattan, Sales Mgr.

Dear Wrattan:

There are going to have to be some drastic changes around here.

Bring all the letters you have up to my office at once.

Sanson

Mr. Joseph Schramm
Schramm's Garage
1428 West Ave.
Crescent City
Dear Mr. Schramm:

There have been big changes at Superdee! Exciting changes!

Following a complete overhaul of top engineering management personnel, things are moving again!

Superdee is on the march!

Leading the van is our revamped ultramodern Supramatic Car Service Handling Machine, capable of repairing anything from a little foreign car to a huge truck! Fast! Economical! Efficient!

This new version embodies the most advanced methods, together with the actual suggestions of *practical automative repairmen like yourself!*

This machine is hydraulically operated, and even has a special High Efficiency Whirlamatic Hand Pump in case of emergency power failure!

There's practicality!

There's real manufacturer co-operation!

You asked for it! *Here it is!*

Superdee is on the march!

Are you?

> Cordially,
> G. Wrattan
> Sales Mgr.

SCHRAMM'S GARAGE

Dear Mr. Wrattan:

I am enclosing an order for one of your new Superdeeluxe jacks.

I have read the stuff about your new Supramatic Machine. This one doesn't take as much space, and seems to be pretty good.

But I can't afford it.

> Yours truly,
> J. Schramm

SUPERDEE EQUIPMENT
Interoffice Memo

To: W. W. Sanson, Pres.
Dear Mr. Sanson:

Well, we've sold three of them.

> G. Wrattan

Christopher Anvil   55

SUPERDEE EQUIPMENT
Interoffice Memo

To: G. Wrattan, Sales Mgr.

Dear Wrattan:

We've got to do better than this or we'll all be lined up at the employment office in just about six months.

How about a big advertising campaign?

Sanson

SUPERDEE EQUIPMENT
Interoffice Memo

To: W. W. Sanson, Pres.

Dear Mr. Sanson:

It won't work. This machine would theoretically improve just about any fair-sized repair shop's efficiency, but it's still too expensive.

To judge by the response, we now have an acceptable Handler here. In time, it's bound to take hold, despite the cost, and obtain wide acceptance.

But this won't happen in six months.

G. Wrattan

SUPERDEE EQUIPMENT
Interoffice Memo

To: W. Robert Schnitzer, Mgr.
Special Services Dept.

Dear Schnitzer:

Since you ran the computerized market simulation, on the basis of which we made this white elephant, I suggest you now find some way to unload it.

I would hate to be the man whose recommendations, presented in the guise of scientific certainty, were so disastrous that they destroyed the company that paid his salary.

A reputation such as that could make it quite difficult to find another job.

Sanson

SUPERDEE EQUIPMENT
Interoffice Memo

To: W. W. Sanson, Pres.

Dear Mr. Sanson:

I have been giving this matter a great deal of thought, and have analyzed it on the Supervac-666.

The trouble is, the average individual does not use the available automotive repair facilities to a sufficient extent to assure the garage owner of enough income to afford our machine.

This is roughly analogous to the situation in the health industries some years ago.

I believe we might find a similar solution to be useful in this case.

W. R. Schnitzer

Superdee Equipment
Interoffice Memo

To: W. Robert Schnitzer, Mgr.
Special Services Dept.
Dear Schnitzer:

I frankly don't follow what you're talking about, but I am prepared to listen.

Come on up, and let's have it.

Sanson

Superdee Equipment
Interoffice Memo

To: G. Wrattan, Sales Mgr.
Dear Wrattan:

Schnitzer has one of the damndest ideas I ever heard of, but it might just work.

I am getting everybody up here to meditate on this, and want to find out how it strikes you.

This *could* be a gold mine, provided we can get the insurance people interested.

Sanson

Superdee Equipment
Interoffice Memo

To: G. Wrattan, Sales Mgr.
Dear Wrattan:

You will be interested to know after that discussion we had about Schnitzer's idea, that the insurance people are closely studying it. I could see whirling dollar signs in their eyes as I gave them the exact pitch Schnitzer gave me.

If they *do* go ahead, the banks will take a much rosier view of our prospects. We may weather this thing yet.

Sanson

"In Unity, Strength"
Since 1906

Dear Car Owner:

How many times have you suffered inconvenience and delay, because of auto failures and breakdowns? Yet how often have you hesitated to have your car checked, and repairs carried out that might have prevented these delays and breakdowns—*because you were short of cash at the moment?*

You need no longer suffer this inconvenience. *Now you can prepay your car repair bills!*

Foresyte Insurance now offers an unique plan by which, for as little as two dollars a month, you can get *necessary repairs made on your car,* and *Foresyte will pay the bill!*

We call this our Blue Wheel car repair insurance plan. We are sure it will pay you to send in the coupon below, right away.

We can afford to make this offer because many cars will need no repairs, and the premiums for *those* cars will pay *your* repair bills! Send in the coupon today!

> Cordially,
> P. J. Devereaux
> President

Schramm's Garage
1428 West Ave.
City

Dear Joe:

About that oil change and new filter: I've got Blue Wheel insurance now, so take care of it.

While the car's in there, check that pull to the left you mentioned.

> Jack Bailey

SCHRAMM'S GARAGE

To: Jack W. Bailey
413 Crescent Drive
City

Parts:	6 qts oil	$ 3.90
	#14-66 oil filter	4.95
	#6612 brake shoes, 1 set	12.98
	total	$21.83
Labor:	change filter	
	drain oil	

put in fresh oil
install brake shoes
grind drums

	total	$24.00
	total	$45.83
	Blue Wheel	$45.83
	Paid—J. Schramm	

NOTE: Your transmission needs work. I can't work on it this week, because I'm swamped. How about next Wednesday morning?

Joe Schramm

Dear Joe:

Sure. I'll have the wife leave the car early.

Jack Bailey

Schramm's Garage

Dear Mr. Wrattan:

Please send me your latest information on your Automated Car Service Handling Machine.

I never saw so much business in my life. I am now running about a month behind.

Yours truly,
J. Schramm

Superdee Equipment
Interoffice Memo

To: W. Robert Schnitzer, Mgr.

Special Service Dept.

Dear Schnitzer:

We are now out of the woods, thanks to your stroke of genius on the prepayment plan.

Now see if you can find some way to step up production.

Sanson

Foresyte Insurance
Interoffice Memo

To: J. Beggs, Vice-Pres.

Blue Wheel Plan

Dear Beggs:

What on earth is going on here? After making money the first few months on Blue Wheel, we are now getting swamped.

What's happening?

Devereaux

FORESYTE INSURANCE
Interoffice Memo

To: P. J. Devereaux, Pres.

Dear Mr. Devereaux:

I don't exactly know what's going on, but it completely obsoletes these figures of Sanson's.

We are going to have to raise our premium.

Beggs

SCHRAMM'S SERVICATORIUM

Dear Mr. Wrattan:

Please put my name on the waiting list for another Handling Machine right away.

Yours truly,
J. Schramm

BLUE WHEEL
Prepaid Car Care

Dear Subscriber:

Owing to unexpectedly heavy use of the Blue Wheel insurance by you, the subscriber, we must raise the charge for Blue Wheel coverage to $3.75 per month, effective January 1st.

Cordially,
R. Beggs

SCHRAMM'S SUPER SERVICATORIUM

Dear Mr. Wrattan:

We're going to need another Handling Machine as soon as we get the new wing finished next month.

Yours truly,
J. Schramm

FORESYTE INSURANCE
Interoffice Memo

To: P. J. Devereaux, Pres.

Dear Mr. Devereaux:

I have to report that ordinary garages are now being replaced by "servicatoriums," "super servicatoriums," and "ultraservicatoriums."

These places charge more, which is justified by their heavier capital investment, and faster service.

Nevertheless, it now costs us more for the same job.

R. Beggs

BLUE WHEEL

Prepaid Car Care

Dear Subscriber:

Due to increasingly thorough car care offered by modern servicatoriums, and to continued heavy and wider use of such care, we find it necessary to increase the charge to $4.25 a month.

Cordially,
R. Beggs

SCHRAMM'S ULTRASERVICATORIUM

To: Jack W. Bailey
     413 Crescent Drive
     City

Parts:	1 set 22-638 brushes	$. 1.46
Labor:	clean battery terminals	
	set regulator	
	overhaul generator	21.00
	total	$22.46
	Blue Wheel	$22.46
		PAID

NOTE: There's a whine from the differential we ought to take care of on the Machine. How about Friday morning? I don't see why there was more trouble with the generator and regulator. I think we ought to check everything again. Your Blue Wheel will cover it.

Joe Schramm

SCHRAMM'S ULTRASERVICATORIUM

Dear Mr. Wrattan:

I want three of your All-Purpose Diagnostic Superanalyzers, that will test batteries, generators, starters, automatic transmissions, etc., etc. Rush the order. I can't get enough good mechanics to do this work.

Yours truly,
J. Schramm

FORESYTE INSURANCE
Interoffice Memo

To: P. J. Devereaux, Pres.

Dear Mr. Devereaux:

When I was a boy, I rode a bicycle with bad brakes down a steep hill one time, and got up to around 60 miles an hour as I came to a curve with a post-and-cable guardrail at the side, and about a 60-foot drop into a ravine beyond that.

This Blue Wheel plan gives me the same no-brakes sensation.

Incidentally, have you visited a garage lately?

R. Beggs

FORESYTE INSURANCE
Interoffice Memo

To: R. Beggs, Vice-Pres.
Blue Wheel

Dear Beggs:

What we seem to have here is some kind of weird mechanism that just naturally picks up speed by itself.

Without our insurance plan, the garages could never have gone up to these rates, because car owners wouldn't, or couldn't have paid them. Thanks to us, the car owners themselves now couldn't care less what the bill is. In fact, the higher it is, the more the car owner thinks he's getting out of his insurance.

The effect of this on the garage owner is to go overboard on every kind of expense.

Yes, I've visited a garage lately. I got a blowout over in Bayport, bought a new front tire, and on the way back noticed a vibration in the front end. Obviously, the wheel needed balancing.

However, when I tried to explain this to the Chief Automotive Repair Technician in Stull's Superrepairatorium, he wouldn't listen. Before I knew what was going on, the car was up in the air.

Parts:	4 22-612 balance weights	$ 1.60
Labor:	Complete diagnostic	$40.00
	Wheel removal	2.00
	Transport	1.50
	Superbalancomatic	6.50
	Transport	1.50
	Wheel attachment	2.00
	Car transport	3.25
	Total parts and labor	$58.35
	Blue Wheel	$58.35

PAID—L. Gnarth, C.A.R.T.

I think you can appreciate how I felt about Stull's Superrepair-atorium. I shoved past the Chief Automotive Repair Technician, and got hold of Stull himself. He listened, looked sympathetic, and said, "If you want, I will pay all of this but $2.75, which is about what it should have cost. But that won't change the fact that at least half of these bills are going to be higher than they should be, and it's going to get a lot worse, not better."

"Why?"

"Do you think anybody that learns how to tell what's wrong by using one of these diagnostic machines, and that learns how to repair a car with hydraulic pressers and handlers at his elbow, is ever going to be able to figure out what's wrong on his own, or do the work with ordinary tools? All he's learned to do is *work with the machine.* He *can't* do a simple job. He's *got* to make a big job out of it, *so he can use the machine.*

"Now," Stull went on, "a good, old-style mechanic narrows the trouble down with a few simple tests. For instance, if the car won't start, he tries the lights and horn, sees how the lights dim when he works the starter, watches the ammeter needle, notices how the starter sounds, checks the battery terminals and cables, checks the spark, bypasses the solenoid and sees if that's the trouble—in 15 minutes, a good mechanic with a few simple tools has a good idea where the trouble is, and then it's a question of putting in new points, pulling the starter to check for a short, or maybe working on the carburetor or fuel pump. To do this, *you've got to understand first-hand the things you're working with.* Then the know-how is in your brain and muscles, and you can use it anytime.

"But now, with these new machines, especially this damned Combination Handling Machine and Diagnostic Analyzer, the skill and know-how *is in the machine.*

"What kind of mechanics do you think we're going to turn out this way? How many of them will ever be able to do *anything* without using the machine? And since the machine costs so much, what is there to do but charge more?"

That was how it went at the garage. I thought that was bad enough, but this thing is snowballing, and there's more to it. After I left the garage, I happened to take another look at the bill and noticed that this Chief Automotive Repair Technician had written "C.A.R.T." after his name. This struck me as peculiar, so I stopped at a roadside phone, and called up Stull. He sounded embarrassed.

"It's his . . . well . . . degree. It used to be a mechanic would have laughed at that. He had his skill, and knew it, and that was enough. But now, with these machines, a lot of these new guys don't *have* the skill. Now they've got no way to prop up their feeling of being worth something. So, we've got this NARSTA, and—"

"You've got *what?*"

"N.A.R.S.T.A.—National Automotive Repair Specialists and Technicians Association. They award what amounts to *degrees.* They limit the number of people who can be mechanics, because anybody off the street could learn to run the machines in a few weeks."

"The mechanic who writes 'C.A.R.T.' after his name? Is he your *chief* mechanic?"

"Naturally."

"Why pick him for chief mechanic?"

"Because he has a 'C.A.R.T.' degree. If I use a guy with an A.A.R.T., or an A.R.T., I get in trouble with NARSTA. NARSTA says all its people are professional, and have to be treated according to their 'professional qualifications.' "

"That is, how good they are as mechanics?"

"Of course not. 'Professional qualifications' is whether the guy's got an A.R.T., an A.A.R.T., or a C.A.R.T. He may not be as good as another mechanic. What counts is that C.A.R.T. after his name. That changes his wage scale, changes his picture of himself, and makes an aristocrat out of him."

There was more to this phone conversation, but I think you get the picture.

This mess is compounding itself fast. I talked to Sanson over at Superdee about it, but Superdee is making so much money out of this that Sanson naturally won't listen to any objections. Instead, he went into a spiel about the Advance of Science. Sanson doesn't know it, but this trouble comes because there is one science, and the Master Science at that, that is being left out of this. But I think if we put it to use ourselves we can end this process before it wrecks the country.

I have hopes that you know what I am talking about, and will see how to put it to use.

Bear in mind, please, that when the rug is jerked out, we want *somebody else* to land on his head, not us.

I might mention that I have recently had cautious feelers from one Q. Snarden, who turns out to be the head of NARSTA. Snarden wants, I think, to take over Blue Wheel.

He would then, I suppose, run it as a "nonprofit" organization. Do you get the picture?

Devereaux

Interoffice Memo

To: P. J. Devereaux, Pres.

Dear Mr. Devereaux:

I don't know just what you mean by the "Master Science." But I have a good idea what we ought to do with this Blue Wheel insurance.

Suppose I come up this afternoon about 1:30 to talk it over?

R. Beggs

FORESYTE INSURANCE
Interoffice Memo

To: R. Beggs, Vice-Pres.
Blue Wheel

Dear Beggs:

I have now had a chance to analyze, and mentally review, your plan for dealing with Snarden and Blue Wheel. I think this is exactly what we should do.

We want to be sure to run out plenty of line on this.

Devereaux

BLUE WHEEL
A Nonprofit Organization
NARSTA-Approved

Dear Subscriber:

In these days of rising car-care costs, one of your most precious possessions is your Blue Wheel policy. To assure you the best possible service at the lowest cost, Blue Wheel is now operated under the supervision of the National Automotive Repair Specialists and Technicians Association, as a *nonprofit* organization.

Yes, Blue Wheel now gives you real peace-of-mind on the road. And your Blue Wheel card will continue to admit your car to the finest servicatoriums, whenever it needs care.

But as costs rise, the charges we pay rise.

As we spend only 4.21 percent on administrative expenses, you can see we are doing our best to hold prices down; but costs are, nevertheless, rising.

To meet the costs, we find it is necessary to raise our premium to $5.40 a month.

When you consider the cost of car care today, this is a real bargain.

Cordially,
Q. Snarden
Pres.

BLUE WHEEL
(Nonprofit)
NARSTA-Approved

Dear Subscriber:

For reasons mentioned in the enclosed brochure, we are forced to raise our premium to $6.25 a month.

> Cordially,
> Q. Snarden
> Pres.

BLUE WHEEL

Dear Subscriber:

Blue Wheel has fought hard to hold the line, but next year, rates must go up if Blue Wheel is to pay your car-care bills.

As we explain in the enclosed booklet, Blue Wheel will now cost $8.88 a month.

This is one of the greatest insurance bargains on earth, when you consider today's car-care costs.

> Cordially,
> Q. Snarden
> Pres.

BLUE WHEEL

Dear Subscriber:

Blue Wheel is going to have to raise its rates to meet its ever-increasing costs of paying *your* car-care bills.

Future rates will be only $10.25 a month.

> Cordially,
> Q. Snarden
> Pres.

BLUE WHEEL

Dear Subscriber:

Blue Wheel's new rates will be $13.40 a month.

> Cordially,
> Q. Snarden
> Pres.

BLUE WHEEL

Dear Subscriber:

Blue Wheel is going to $16.90 a month effective January 1st. See our enclosed explanation.

> Cordially,
> Q. Snarden
> Pres.

Dear Subscriber:

$22.42 a month is a small price to pay to be free of car-care expense worries nowadays.

This rate becomes effective next month.

Cordially,
Q. Snarden
Pres.

SCHRAMM'S SERVICATORIUM

To: Jack W. Bailey
413 Crescent Drive
City

Parts:	1 set 22-638 brushes		$ 2.36
Labor:	Super diagnostic		85.00
	Giant Lift		65.00
	Manipulatorium		55.00
	Extractulator		28.00
	Gen. transport		1.25
	Treatment		12.50
	Checkulator		4.50
	Gen. transport		1.25
	Ultramatatonic		5.00
	Installator		15.00
	Ch. transport		3.75
	Checkulator final		6.50
	Ch. transport		3.75
	Car transport		$5.25
		Total parts and labor	$291.75
		Blue Wheel	$291.75
			PAID

FORESYTE INSURANCE
Interoffice Memo

To: P. J. Devereaux, Pres.

Dear Mr. Devereaux:

The other day, the turn-signals on my car quit working, and before I got out of the garage, the bill ran up to $417.12.

In today's mail I got a notice that Blue Wheel, with Snarden at the helm, is going to raise its rates to $28.50 a month.

This notice, by the way, piously states that administrative costs now only come to 2.4 percent of Blue Wheel's total revenues. Naturally, if they keep raising their revenues by upping the premium, administrative costs will get progressively smaller, in proportion to the total. The percentage looks modest, but that's 2.4 percent of *what?*

I was talking to a physicist friend of mine the other day, and he says the trouble is, the car-repair setup now has "positive feedback," instead of "negative feedback." When the individual owner used to pay his own bills, his anger at high bills, and his reluctance or even inability to pay them, acted as negative feedback, reacting more strongly against the garage the higher the bills got. But now, not only is there none of this, but the garages are used *more* the higher the Blue Wheel premiums—because people feel that they should get *something* out of the policy. This is positive feedback, and my physicist friend says that if it continues long enough, it invariably ends by destroying the system.

Already there is talk of government regulation, and of plans to spread the burden further by taxation. This is just more of the same thing, on a wider scale. It will only delay the day of reckoning, and the trouble when the day of reckoning comes.

I think we'd better pull the plug on this pretty soon.

R. Beggs

FORESYTE INSURANCE
Interoffice Memo

To: R. Beggs, Vice-Pres.
   Special Project
Dear Beggs:

Snarden goes before the congressional investigating committee next week.

When he is about halfway through his testimony, and has them tied in knots with his pious airs and specious arguments, *then* we want to hit him.

Have everything ready for about the third day of the hearing.

Devereaux

FORESYTE INSURANCE
Interoffice Memo

To: R. Beggs, Vice-Pres.
   Special Project
Dear Beggs:

Now's the time. Snarden has pumped the hearing so full of red herrings that it looks like a fish hatchery.

Pull the plug.

Devereaux

To: P. J. Devereaux, Pres.
Dear Mr. Devereaux:
The first ten million circulars are in the mail.

Beggs

FORESYTE INSURANCE
"In Unity, Strength"
Since 1906

Dear Car Owner:
When car-care insurance cost two dollars a month, it was a bargain. Now it costs about 15 times as much.

This present-insurance plan is so badly set up that it *forces up car-care costs*. And when car-care costs go up, *that forces up insurance premiums*.

This is a vicious circle.

Before this bankrupts the whole country, Foresyte Insurance is determined to stop the endless climb of these premiums, by offering our *own* plan.

Possibly, after paying these present terrific bills, you will understand why we call our plan *Blue Driver*. But you won't feel blue when you learn that our monthly rates on this new insurance are as follows:

$90 deductible 90%	$18.50
$90 deductible 75%	$12.50
$90 deductible 50%	$5.25
$180 deductible 90%	$13.75
$180 deductible 75%	$7.95
$180 deductible 50%	$3.75

Compare this with what you are paying now.

We are convinced that the huge increase in car-care costs is due mainly to the fact that the system now used makes it *nobody's* business to keep costs down, and puts the ever-increasing burden just as heavily on the man who *doesn't* overuse the plan as on the man who does.

Our plan is different, and puts the burden where it belongs— *on the fellow who overuses the plan*. You don't have to pay for all *his* expenses. He can't get away *without* paying extra for them. This is how it should be. Moreover, this plan gives good protection, at a lower cost.

For instance, with our $90 deductible 90% plan, you pay the first

$90 of the bill yourself. True, $90 is a lot of money, *but in less than a year's time, you save that much or more in premiums.*

The 90% of the plan means that *we pay 90% of the rest of the bill.* You only have to pay 10%. On an $825 bill, for instance, you pay $90, which you have probably already saved because our premiums are so much lower. This leaves $735. We pay $661.50 of this, right away. *You pay only what's left.*

This lets you pay the small bills you can afford, while we take most of the big bills that everyone is afraid of these days.

Meanwhile, the less you use the plan, *the more you save.*

The larger the share of the risk you are willing to take, *the more you save.* Our $180 deductible 50% plan *costs only $3.75 a month.*

Because we may be able to lower premiums still further, these rates are not final. But at these rates, you can see that this plan rewards the person who doesn't overuse it.

We are already using this plan ourselves, and saving $10 to $24.75 a month on it.

How about you?

> Cordially,
> R. Beggs
> Vice-Pres.

413 Crescent Drive
Crescent City

Dear Mr. Beggs:

Here is my check for $7.95. I am signing up on your $180 deductible 75% plan, and saving $20.55 a month.

But you better not jack the rates way up, or I will go back to Blue Wheel. If we only burn one light in the house, heat one room, and eat cornmeal mush twice a day, we can still pay *their* premiums.

> Yours truly,
> Jack Bailey

Schramm's Superservicatorium

To: Jack W. Bailey
  413 Crescent Drive
  City

Note: Time for oil change, new filter. Our Automatic File Checker also says it is time your car had a Complete Super Diagnostic and Renewvational Overhaul on our special new Renewvator Machine. Your Blue Wheel will cover it.

> Joe Schramm

Dear Joe:

In a pig's eye my Blue Wheel will cover it. I'm a Blue Driver now, and I get socked 180 bucks plus 25 per cent of the rest of your bill, and it sounds to me like I will get hit for enough on this one to buy a new car.

Keep the Renewvational Overhaul. As for the Complete Super Diagnostic, I found an old guy out on a back road, and he can figure out more with a screw driver, a wrench, and a couple of meters than those stuck-up imitation mechanics of yours can find out with the whole Super Diagnostic Machine.

Don't worry about the oil change. I can unscrew the filter all by myself. I will pay myself $4.50 for the labor, and save anyway 100 bucks on the deal.

If the transmission falls out of this thing, or the rear axle climbs up into the back seat, I'll let you know about it. But don't bother me when it's time to oil the door handles and put grease on the trunk hinges.

Jack Bailey

SCHRAMM'S SUPER SERVICATORIUM

Dear Mr. Wrattan:

I just got your monthly booklet on "New Superdee Labor-Saving Giants."

Since the paper in this fancy booklet might clog up my new oil burner, I'm afraid I don't know what to do with it.

I am enclosing half-a-dozen letters from ex-customers, and maybe they will explain to you why business is off 20 per cent this month.

Yours truly,
J. Schramm

SUPERDEE EQUIPMENT
Interoffice Memo

To: W. W. Sanson, Pres.

Dear Mr. Sanson:

I am sending up a big envelope containing letters from garagemen and their customers. These letters are representative of a flood that's coming in.

What do we do now?

G. Wrattan

SUPERDEE EQUIPMENT
Interoffice Memo

To: G. Wrattan, Sales Mgr.

Dear Wrattan:

Christopher Anvil   71

I put this one to Schnitzer and his Supervac 666. It flattened them.

There's just one thing *to* do. We take a loss on this latest stuff, and get out while we're still ahead.

As for these questions as to how much we offer to repurchase Renewvators, Giant Lifts, etc., we don't want them at any price. Point out how well made they are, and how much good metal is in them. That's just a hint to the customer, and if he deduces from that that the best thing to do with them is scrap them, that's *his* business.

Do you realize it cost me $214.72 to get a windshield-wiper blade changed the other day? They ran the whole car through the Super Diagnostic first to be sure the wiper blade *needed* to be changed.

As far as I'm concerned, this whole bubble can burst anytime.

Sanson

SCHRAMM'S ECONOMY GARAGE

To: Jack W. Bailey
413 Crescent Drive
City

	Parts:	1 set 22-638 brushes	$1.48
	Labor:	overhaul generator	
		set regulator	8.50
		total	$9.98

NOTE: Time for oil change, new filter. We will take care of this for you next time you're in—no charge for labor on this job. Al Putz says there was a funny rumble from the transmission when he drove the car out to the lot. We better check this as soon as you can leave the car again. Once those gears in there start grinding up the oil slingers and melting down the bearings, it gets expensive fast.

Joe Schramm

Dear Joe:

Thanks for the offer, but I'll take care of the oil change myself. I want to keep in practice, just in case the country comes down with another epidemic of Super Giant Machinitis.

As for that rumble from the transmission, I jacked up a rear wheel, started the engine, and I heard it, too. It had me scared for a minute there, but I blocked the car up, crawled under, and it took about three minutes to track down the trouble. In this model, the emergency brake works off a drum back of the transmission. Since I brought the car down to your garage, one end of a spring had somehow come loose on the emergency brake, and this lets the brake chatter against the drum. It was easy to connect the spring up again. The transmission is now nice and quiet.

I am enclosing the check for $9.98.

Jack Bailey

To: P. J. Devereaux, Pres.

Dear Mr. Devereaux:

We were able to bring the rates on Blue Driver car-care down again last month. We are still making a mint from this plan, even with reduced premiums, and we are still getting enthusiastic letters.

I can see, in detail, how this works, by giving everyone involved an incentive to keep costs down. But I am still wondering about a comment you made earlier.

What is the "Master Science" you referred to, in first suggesting the idea of this plan?

R. Beggs

To: R. Beggs, Vice-Pres.
    Blue Driver

Dear Beggs:

I am delighted you were able to bring the premium down again. Maybe we will get this thing within reason yet.

What do you *suppose* the Master Science is? Isn't it true to say that Science first comes into existence when the mind intently studies actual physical phenomena? And the mind operates in this and other ways, doesn't it, when it is moved to do so by reasons arising out of *human nature?*

What is the result when the mind intently studies *human nature?*

Engineers, physical scientists, biological scientists, mathematicians, statisticians, and other highly-trained specialists do work that is useful and important. As a result, we have gradually built up what amounts to a tool kit, filled with a variety of skills and techniques.

They are all useful, but nearly every time we rely on them alone and ignore human nature, we pay for it.

All our tools are valuable.

But we can't forget the hand that holds them.

Devereaux

Deeper Than the Darkness

Sociologists are interested in the social bonds that bind people together in social units. Whether it is the bond of common likeness characteristic of less complex societies or the bond of mutual interdependence of more complex societies, patterns of social organization reflect linkages between and among human beings that develop from their mutual association.

Sociologists often explained the cohesion of small, nonliterate societies as the result of perceived common likenesses and mutual interest. When Ferdinand Toennies referred to a *Gemeinschaft* society, or Emile Durkheim referred to a society characterized by what he called *mechanical solidarity,* or when others used such concepts as *consciousness of kind* or *sense of community,* they were identifying this type of social bond.

Modern society is much more complex, heterogeneous, and interdependent. The social bond is more a reflection of the mutual interdependence of unlike and specialized social units linked together in larger systems. Toennies' *Gesellschaft* and Durkheim's *organic solidarity* refer to this different type of social bond. The modern assembly-line worker—a specialist performing a narrowly defined task that is part of a chain of such units, each unit dependent in a systematic way on each of the others—is perhaps our clearest example of this type of linkage in modern social order.

To many sociologists, the social bond characteristic of modern sociology is not as productive of social order and stability as was the social bond of premodern society. Durkheim reflects this view in his concern for the greater problems of *social control* in the society of organic solidarity. Lack of commonality of task experience and interest in a society comprised of interdependent specialists presents a potentially disruptive arrangement. The *cohesion* of such a society is much more tenuous, more fragile.

Sanjen, the central character in "Deeper Than the Darkness," is a member of a future society of heterogeneous people—a society with advanced technology but also vestiges of a tribal past. It is also a society with a social bond consciously based on a sense of common identity and purpose. As Sanjen believes, "sense of community was the glue that held a culture together." This story illustrates the fragility of the social bond and the consequences of emphasizing a sense of community where common background and identity do not exist, while ignoring the cohesion that can result from recognition of the positive consequences of mutual interdependence of diverse and unlike social units.

Many bemoan the "loss of community" characteristic of most of modern social organization, yet interdependency is a feature of modern reality—not so much because it is invaluable, but because it seems inevitable. Vast linkages of interdependent units in society make it possible to address vast undertakings in some rational way, and yet these organizational patterns make modern society so susceptible to disruption, because disturbances in one segment of society will affect other segments of the society. Hence, the density and social differentiation characteristics of modern social organization may breed conflict as well as cooperation, war as well as trade, the solution of problems as well as their creation.

Deeper Than the Darkness

GREG BENFORD

It was about an hour into morning shift. I was planning out my day. I had to arrange the routing work I could do using the screen so that it didn't conflict with the eating routine, the kids' use of the screen for school hours, and the best times to go for a walk in the tubes.

The kids were pouting for some reason, and I was having trouble concentrating on the alterations that had been made in the production schemes since yesterday. If you don't get the changes down pat in the morning, you'll be sending new goods to depots that don't handle that product any more and the losses can eat up your day's management commission before complaint feedback reaches you.

I'd just about gotten it down when it was time for the kids' first lecture, and I had to give up the screen. I settled down in the dining booth to review my notes, but it wasn't ten minutes before they started whining.

"*Dad*-dy, why do we have to watch this old stuff?" Romana said, jerking her chin up with a regal look. "None of the other cubes in this block even *carry* Schoolchannel any more."

"Uh," said Chark, "and it's *boring*. Everybody knows you can't learn fast without tapping. We're going to turn out to be rennies."

"Rennies?"

"Renegades," Angela said from the kitchen cloister. "It's new slang. You should watch the entertainment channel more." The words were normal but her tone had an edge on it. She'd tried the manual breakfast this morning, and it hadn't worked out, but indocing—or was that out-dated term still around?—was one of our flash points. She stood in the doorway and looked at me with her mouth tightened. "Don't you think it's about time you started to listen to what other people think, Sanjen? Finally?"

"No." I looked away and started underlining some parts of my notes. Chark dialed the 3D volume down and the room fell silent. I wasn't going to get away with a light dismissal.

"*Dad*-dy . . ."

"If you'd just read some of the articles we gave you," Chark began in a measured, reasonable tone, "and talked to a counselor at the Center, you'd understand why we need tapping now. You were out there yourself, Dad, so . . ."

"Yes," I said sharply. "I was out there. And none of you were. You believe anything the Assembly says is good for the common defense, but don't expect me . . ."

I stopped. It wasn't going to do any good. I wouldn't tell them the guts of what happened out there—that was buried away in a file somewhere with red Secret stickers all over it, and until the stickers came off I couldn't say anything.

Angela broke her rigid silence, and I could tell from the way she said it that it had been held back for a long time. "Why do you tell them such things? They'll respect you even less if you try to pretend there's some big mystery about what you did out there. You were just a shuttle captain, a pickup convoy to get the survivors off Regeln after the Quarm hit it. And you didn't even get many off, either."

"Something happened. Something really happened."

The children had gotten quiet, the way they do when they sense that the grownups have forgotten they're around, and maybe a fight was going to start. Angela and I both noticed it at the same time.

"All right. We'll talk about it later," I said. The kids went back to their lecture, grumbling to each other, and Angela walked into the bedroom, probably to pout. It was one more nick in a marriage that was already eroding.

We would talk later, and there would be accusations and complaints, and I couldn't solve them; I couldn't explain.

But it happened. It caught me in a wave of hard color, a menace, subtle and faceless, and the wave threw me up on this barren spiritual shore. To wait, and while waiting to die. It happened during that quick run to drop into the Regeln system and grab whatever was left before the Quarm returned.

The crew didn't take it well. Fleet took us off a routine run and outfitted the ships with enough extras to put the convoy on the lowest rung·of warship class. But men take time to adjust. Most of them were still nervous and edgy about the changes that had been made. They were suddenly *oraku,* warrior status. They didn't like it—neither did I—but there was nothing to be done. It was an emergency.

I had us roar out of port at full bore, giving the ships that hot gun-metal smell, and that kept them busy for a while. But maintenance is maintenance, and soon they found the time to tie themselves in knots, wringing out self-doubts with fidgeting fingers. In a few days the results began to come up through the confessional rings: anxieties, exclusion feelings, loss of phase.

"I told Fleet we'd have this," I said to Tonji, my Exec. "These men can't take a sudden change of status and role." I let go of the clipboard that held the daily report and watched it strike the table top with a slow-motion clatter in low gee.

Tonji blinked his simian eyes languidly. "I think they are overreacting to the danger involved. None of us signed for this. Give them time."

"Time? Where am I going to get it? We're only weeks out of Regeln now. This is a large group, spread over a convoy. We'll have to reach them quickly."

He unconsciously stiffened his lips, a gesture he probably associated with being tough-minded. "It will take effort, it's true. But I suppose you realize there isn't any choice."

Was that a hint of defiance in his voice, mingled with his habitual condescension? I paused, let it go. "More Sabal, then. Require senior officers to attend as well."

"You're sure that's enough, sir?"

"Of course I'm not sure! I haven't got all the answers in my pocket. This convoy hasn't had anything but shuttle jobs for years."

"But we've been reassigned . . ."

"Slapping a sticker on a ship doesn't change the men inside. The crews don't know what to do. There isn't any confidence in the group, because everyone can sense the uncertainty. Nobody knows what's waiting for us on Regeln. A crewman wouldn't be human if he didn't worry about it."

I looked across the small cabin at my kensdai altar. I knew I was losing control of myself too often and not directing the conversation the way I wanted. I focused on the solid, dark finish of the wood that framed the altar, feeling myself merge with the familiarity of it. Focus down, let the center flow outward.

Tonji flicked an appraising glance at me. "The Quarm were stopped on Regeln. That's why we're going."

"They'll be back. The colony there beat them off, but took a lot of losses. It's now been twenty-four days since the Quarm left. You've heard the signals from the surface—they're the only ones we got after their satellite link was destroyed. The correct code grouping is there, but the signal strength is down and transmission faded. Whoever sent them was working in bad conditions, or didn't understand the gear, or both."

"Fleet doesn't think it's a trap?" Tonji's features, Mongol-yellow in the diffused light of my cabin, took on a cool, sly look.

"They don't know. I don't either. But we need information on Quarm tactics and equipment. They're a race of hermits, individuals, but somehow they cooperate against us. We want to get an idea how."

"The earlier incidents . . ."

"They were just that—incidents. Raids. Fleet never got enough coherent information out of the surviving tapes, and what there was they can't unravel. There were no survivors."

"But this time the colonists stood off a concentrated attack."

"Yes. Perhaps there are good records on Regeln."

Tonji nodded, smiling, and left after proper ceremonies. I was sure he knew everything I'd told him, but he'd seemed to want to draw the details out of me, to savor them.

For the better the mission, the gaudier the reports, then all the faster would rise the fortunes of Mr. Tonji. A war—the first in over a century, and the first in deep space—has the effect of opening the staircases to the top. It relieves a young officer of the necessity for worming his way through the hierarchy.

I reached out, dialed a starchart of Regeln's neighbors, studied.

The Quarm had been an insect buzzing just beyond the range of hearing for decades now. Occasional glancing contacts, rumors, stories. Then war.

How? Security didn't bother to tell lowly convoy captains—probably only a few hundred men anywhere knew. But there had been a cautiously worded bulletin about negotiations in the Quarm home worlds, just before the War. The Council had tried to establish communal rapport with some segment of Quarm society. It had worked before, with the Phalanx and Angras.

Among the intellectual circles I knew—such as they were—it was holy dogma. Sense of community was the glue that held a culture together. Given time and correct phase it could bind even alien societies. In two cases it already had.

And it wove a universe for us. A world of soft dissonances muted into harmonies, tranquil hues of water prints fading together.

To it, the Quarm were a violent slash of strangeness. Hermit-like, they offered little and accepted less. Privacy extended to everything for them; we still had no clear idea of their physical appearances. Their meetings with us had been conducted with only a few individual negotiators.

Into this the Council had moved. Perhaps a taboo was ignored, a trifle overlooked. The mistake was too great for the Quarm to pass; they came punching and jabbing into the edge of the human community. Regeln was one of their first targets.

"First Sabal call," Tonji's voice came over the inboard. "You asked me to remind you, sir."

It was ironic that Tonji, with all his ancestors citizens of Old Nippon, should be calling a Sabal game to be led by me, a half-breed Caucasian—and I was sure it wasn't totally lost on him. My mother was a Polynesian and my father a truly rare specimen: one of the last pure Americans, born of the descendants of the few who had survived the Riot War. That placed me far down in the caste lots, even below Australians.

When I was a teenager it was still socially permissible to call us *ofkaipan*, a term roughly analogous to *nigger* in the early days of the American Republic. But since then had come the Edicts of Harmony. I imagine the Edicts are still ignored in the off-islands, but with my professional status it would be a grave breach of protocol if the word ever reached my ears. I'd *seen* it often enough, mouthed wordlessly by an orderlyman who'd just received punishment, or an officer who couldn't forget the color of my skin. But never aloud.

I sighed and got up, almost wishing there were another of us aboard, so I wouldn't have moments of complete loneliness like this. But we were rare in Fleet, and almost extinct on Earth itself.

I uncased my formal Sabal robes and admired their delicate sheen a moment before putting them on. The subtle reds and violets caught the eye and played tricks with vision. They were the usual lint-free polyester that shed no fine particles into the ship's air, but everything possible had been done to give them texture and depth beyond the ordinary uniform. They were part of the show, just like the bals and chants.

During the dressing, I made the ritual passes as my hands chanced to pass diagonally across my body, to induce emotions of wholeness, peace. The vague fears I had let slip into my thoughts would be in the minds of the crew as well.

The murmur in our assembly-room slackened as I appeared; I greeted them, took my place in the hexagon of men and began the abdominal exercises, sitting erect. I breathed deeply, slowly, and made hand passes. At the top of the last arc the power was with me and, breathing out, I came *down* into focus, outward-feeling, *kodakani*.

I slowed the juggling of the gamebals, sensing the mood of the hexagon. The bals and beads caught the light in their counter cadences, glancing tones of red and blue off the walls as they tumbled.

The familiar dance calmed us, and we moved our legs to counter-position, for meditation.

My sing-chant faded slowly in the softened acoustics of the room. I began the Game.

First draw was across the figure, a crewman fidgeting with his Sabal leafs. He chose a passage from the Quest and presented it as overture. It was a complex beginning—the Courier was endowed with subtleties of character and mission. Play moved on. The outline of our problem was inked in by the others as they read their own quotations from the leaves into the Game structure.

For the Royal Courier rode down the hills, and being he of thirst, hunger and weariness, he sought aid in the town. Such was his Mission that the opinion he gained here of the inhabitants of the village, their customs, honesty and justice (not only to the Courier, but to themselves) would be relayed to the Royal Presence as well. And thence, it is said, to Heaven. Having such items to barter, he went from house to house . . .

After most entries were made, the problem maze established had dark undertones of fear and dread. As expected.

I repeated the ritual of beads. And rippling them slowly through my fingers, began the second portion of Sabal: proposing of solution. Again the draw danced among the players.

You are one of two players. There are only two choices for you to make, say red and black. The other player is hidden; only his decisions are reported to you.

If both of you pick red, you gain a point each. If both are black, a point is lost. But if you choose red and your opponent votes black, he wins *two* points, and you lose two.

He who cooperates in spirit, he who senses the Total wins.

Sabal is infinitely more complex, but contains the same elements. The problem set by the men ran dark with subtle streams of anguish, insecurity.

But now the play was returning to me. I watched the solution as it formed around the hexagon. Rejoiced in harmony of spirit. Indicated slight displeasure when divergent modes were attempted. Rebuked personal gain. And drew closer to my men.

"Free yourself from all bonds," I chanted, "and bring to rest the ten thousand things. The way is near, but we seek it afar."

The mood caught slowly at first and uncertainty was dominant, but with the rhythm of repetition a compromise was struck. Anxiety began to submerge. Conflicting images in the Game weakened.

I caught the uprush of spirit at its peak, chanting joyfully of completion as I brought the play to rest. Imposed the dreamlike flicker of gamebal and bead, gradually toning the opticals until we were clothed in darkness. Then stillness.

The fire burning, the iron kettle singing on the hearth, a pine bough brushing the roof, water dripping.

The hexagon broke and we left, moving in concert.

The Game on our flagship was among the best, but it was not enough for the entire mission. I ordered Sabal as often as possible on all ships, and hoped it would keep us in correct phase. I didn't have time to attend all Games, because we were getting closer to drop and all details weren't worked out.

In the hour preceding the jump, I made certain that I was seen in every portion of the ship, moving confidently among the men. The number of ships lost in the jump is small, but rising dangerously and everyone knew it.

I ended up on the center bridge to watch the process, even though it was virtually automatic. The specialists and crewmen moved quickly in the dull red light that simulated nightfall—jump came at 2200—and fifteen minutes before the computers were set to drop us through, I gave the traditional order to proceed. It was purely a formalism, but in theory the synchronization could be halted even at the last instant. But if it was, the requirements of calculating time alone would delay the jump for weeks. The machines were the key.

And justly so. Converting a ship into tachyons in a nanosecond of real-space time is an inconceivably complex process. Men invented it, but they could never control it without the faultless coordination of micro-electronics.

I looked at the fixed, competent faces around me in the bridge. It was a little more than one minute to jump. The strain showed, even though some tried to hide it. The process wasn't perfect and they knew it.

Nothing was said about it at the Fleet level, but micro-electronic equipment had been deteriorating slowly for years. The techniques were gradually being lost, craftsmanship grew rare and half-measures were used. It was part of the slow nibbling decline our society had suffered for the last half century. It was almost expected.

But these men bet their lives on the jump rig, and they knew it might fail.

The silvery chimes rang down thin, padded corridors, sounding the approach of jump. I could feel the men in the decks around me, lying in near darkness on tatami mats, waiting.

There was a slightly audible count, a tense moment, and I closed my eyes at the last instant.

A bright arc flashed beyond my eyelids, showing the blood

vessels, and I heard the dark, whispering sound of the void. A pit opened beneath me, the falling sensation began.

Then the fluorescents hummed again and everything was normal, tension relieved, men smiling.

I looked out the foreward screen and saw the shimmering halo of gas that shrouded the star of Regeln. At our present velocity, we would be through it in a day and falling down the potential well directly toward the sun. There wasn't much time.

We had to come in fast, cutting the rim of plasma around Regeln's star to mask our approach. If we dropped in with that white-hot disk at our backs, we would have a good margin over any detection system that was looking for us.

Regeln is like any life-supporting world: endlessly varied, monotonously dull, spaced with contrast wherever you look, indescribable. It harbors belts of jungle, crinkling grey swaths of mountains, convoluted snake-rivers and frigid blue wastes. The hazy air carries the hum of insects, the pad of ambling vegetarians, the smooth click of teeth meeting. And winds that deafen, oceans that laugh, tranquillity beside violence. It is like any world that is worth the time of man.

But its crust contains fewer heavy elements than are necessary for the easy construction of a jump station or docking base. So it fell under the control of the colonization-only faction of Fleet. They had moved in quickly with xenobiologists to perform the routine miracles that made the atmosphere breathable.

Wildlife was some problem, but during the twenty-odd years the atmosphere was being treated, a continent was cleared of the more malignant varieties. There was a four-meter scorpion which could run like a deer, among other things. I saw it in an Earthside zoo, and shuddered.

Drop time caught us with only the rudiments of a defense network. There simply wasn't time to train the men, and we were constantly missing relevant equipment. I wished for better point-surveillance gear a hundred separate times as we slipped into the Regeln System.

But no Quarm ships were visible, no missiles rose to meet us. Tonji wanted to get out of the sky as soon as physically possible, even though it would've been expensive in reaction mass. I vetoed it and threw us into a monocycle "orange slice" orbit for a look before we went down, but there turned out to be nothing to see after all.

Our base was buttoned up. No vehicles moved on the roads, not even expendable drones for surveillance. I had prints of the base defenses, even the periscope holes, but when we checked there was no sign that they were open. Scattered bluish clouds slid over the farmhouses and fields of grain, but nothing moved on the surface.

There wasn't time to think, send down probes, play a game of cat and mouse. I had a drone mass info out to the system perimeter, where random radiation from the star wouldn't mask the torch of an incoming Quarm ship, but I couldn't rely on it completely.

"Skimmers ready, sir," Tonji said.

"Good. Order all three down immediately." The skimmers were fast and can usually maneuver around manual surface-air defenses.

They landed easily, formed a regulation triangle defense in the valley where the colony's HQ was buried under a low, crusty hill, and reported back. When their skins had cooled to the minimum safety point, they popped out their hovercraft and moved off, checking the covered entrances. No signals were coming out of the hill. There were no flash marks, no sign of the use of any weapons.

A pilot landed near the main entrance, shucked his radiation gear for speed and tried the manual alarms mounted for emergency purposes near the vault door. Nothing.

I got all this over TV, along with a running account of additional data from the other ships spread out in orbit around Regeln. The pilot on the ground asked for further instructions. From the sound of his voice I could tell the order he wanted was to pull out, and fast, but he didn't expect to get it.

And I couldn't give it. You don't walk away from a colony that's in trouble, even if it does look like an obvious trap.

"Tell him to use his sappers," I said. "Get the others over there, too, but keep watching the other entrances from orbit. It's going to take a while to kick in the door, but we've got to look inside."

Tonji nodded and started to code. "Tell him I'm coming down, too."

He looked at me, surprised for the first time since I'd known him.

I rang Matsuda over inboard and placed him in temporary command of the convoy in orbit. "Tonji is coming with me. If the Quarm show, give us an hour to get up here. If we don't make it, mass out. Don't hang around. These ships are worth more than we are."

I looked at Tonji and he smiled.

The shuttle down was slow but gentle, since it was designed for pushing soft flatlanders back and forth from orbit. I didn't have time to enjoy the ride because I was listening to the efforts of the ground crew to blow the hatch off the entrance. Regeln's sky flitted past, a creamy blend of reds and blues like a lunatic tropical drink, and then we were down.

The pilot of the hovercraft that took me out to the site was jumpy, but we made it faster than I would've thought possible. I was out the hatch before they got chocks under the wheels, and the lieutenant in charge came toward me at double time.

"Had to drill and tap, sir," he said quickly, saluting. "We're ready to blow it."

I gave the nod and we ducked behind a gentle rise at the base of the hill, a hundred meters away from the portal. Everything was dead still for a moment, and I thought for the first time that the ground beneath me was alien, a new planet. In the rush I'd accepted it as though it were Earth.

The concussion was as sharp as a bone snapping and debris showered everywhere. In a moment I was moving up with the main body of men, before the dirt had cleared. The portal was only partially opened, a testament to the shelter's designer, but we could get through.

Three runners went in with lights and were back in minutes.

"Deserted for the first few corridor levels," one of them said. "We need more men inside to keep a communications link."

Tonji led the next party. Most of the crewmen were inside before word came back that they'd found somebody. I went in then with three guards and some large arc lamps. None of the lighting in the corridors of the shelter was working—the bulbs were smashed.

Men were clustered at one end of the corridor on the second level, their voices echoing nervously off the glazed concrete.

"You've got something, Mr. Tonji?" I said. He turned away from the open door, where he had been talking to a man whose uniform was covered with dirt. He looked uncertain.

"I think so, sir. According to the maps we have of the base, this door leads to a large auditorium. But a few meters inside—well, look."

I stepped through the door and halted. A number of steps beyond, the cushioned walkway ended and a block of *something*—dirt, mostly partitions, unidentifiable rubble—rose to the ceiling.

I looked at Tonji, questioning.

"A ramp downward starts about there. The whole auditorium is filled with this—we checked the lower floors, but the doors off adjacent corridors won't open."

"How did it get here?"

"The levels around the auditorium have been stripped bare and most of the wall structure torn out, straight down to the bedrock and clay the base was built on. Somebody carted a lot of dirt away and dumped it in here." He glanced at me out of the corner of his eyes.

"What's that?" I pointed at a black oval depression sunk back into the grey mass of dirt, about two meters off the floor.

"A hole. Evidently a tunnel. It was covered with an office rug until Nahran noticed it." He gestured back at the man in the dirty uniform.

"So he went inside. What's there?"

Tonji pinched his lip with a well-manicured thumb and forefinger. "A man. He's pretty far back, Nahran says. That's all I can get out of Nahran, though—he's dazed. The man inside is hysterical. I don't think we can drag him out through that hole, it's too narrow."

"That's all? One man?"

"There might be a lot of people inside there. We've heard noises out of several of these holes. I think this thing that fills the auditorium is honeycombed with tunnels. We've seen the entrance of several more from the balcony."

I checked the time. "Let's go."

Tonji turned and started back through the door.

"No, Mr. Tonji. This way."

For a second he didn't believe it, and then the glassy impersonal look fell over his face. "We're both going to crawl in there, sir?"

"That's right. It's the only way I can find out enough to make a decision."

He nodded and we spent a few minutes arranging details, setting timetables. I tried to talk with Nahran while I changed into a tight pullover worksuit. He couldn't tell me very much. He seemed reticent and slightly dazed. Something had shocked him.

"Follow immediately after me, Mr. Tonji." We both carefully emptied out pockets, because the passage was obviously too narrow to admit anything jutting out. Tonji carried the light. I climbed up onto the slight ledge in front of the dark oval and looked across the slate grey face of the thing. It was huge.

Men were crowding in the doorway of the thing. I waved with false heartiness and began working my legs into the hole. I went straight down into a nightmare.

My thighs and shoulders braked me as the force of gravity slowly pulled me down the shaft. I held my arms above my head and close together, because there wasn't much room to keep them at my sides.

After a moment my feet touched, scraped, and then settled on something solid. I felt around with my boots and for a moment thought it was a dead end. But there was another hole in the side, off at an angle. I slowly twisted until I could sink into it up to my knees.

I looked up. It wasn't more than three meters over my standing height to the top of the shaft, but it seemed to have taken a long time to get this far. I could see Tonji slowly settling down behind me, towing a light above his head.

I wriggled into the narrow side channel, grunting and already beginning to hate the smell of packed dirt and garbage. In a moment I was stretched flat on my back, working my way forward by digging in my heels and pushing with my palms against the walls.

The ceiling of the tunnel brushed against my face in the utter blackness. I felt the oppressive weight of the packed dirt crushing down on me. My own breath was trapped in front of my face, and I could hear only my own gasps, amplified.

"Tonji?" I heard a muffled shout in reply. A trace of light illuminated the tunnel in front of me, and I noticed a large rock was embedded in the side. The auditorium was probably filled with a skeleton of stone that supported the packed soil.

I came to a larger space and was able to turn around and enter the next hole head first. The entrance way was wide, but it quickly narrowed, and I felt mud squeeze between my fingers. The walls pressed down. Some of the clay had turned to mud.

A chill seeped up my legs and arms as I inched forward. I twisted my shoulder blades and pulled with my fingers. The going was easier because the passage tilted slightly downward, but the ooze sucked at me.

I wondered how a man could have gotten in here, or out. With every lunge forward my chest scraped against the sides, rubbing the skin raw and squeezing my breath out. It seemed just possible that I could get through.

Tonji shouted and I answered. The reply was muffled against the wall and I wondered if he had heard. I could feel the irregular bumps in the wall with my hands, and I used them to measure how far I had come.

Progress was measured in centimeters, then even less. My forearms were beginning to stiffen with the effort.

A finger touched the wall, found nothing. I felt cautiously and discovered a sudden widening in the tunnel. At the same instant there was a scraping sound in the night ahead of me, the sound of something being dragged across a floor. It was moving away.

I got a good grip on the opening, pushed and was through it. I rolled to the side and kept close to the wall. Flickers of light from Tonji showed a small, rectangular room, but there was no one in it. A row of darkened holes were sunk into the opposite wall.

Tonji wriggled through the passage, breathing heavily in the cold air. The light he carried was almost blinding, even though it was on low beam.

I found I could get to my knees without bumping my head. I

stretched out my cramped legs and rubbed them to start circulation.

"Nothing here," he said in a whisper.

"Maybe. Throw the beam on those holes."

He played it across the opposite wall.

"Aeeeeeee!"

The shrill scream filled the surrounding area, and I caught sight of a head of filthy hair that wrenched further back into the upper-most hole.

I started toward him on hands and knees and stopped almost immediately. The floor below the holes was strewn with excrement and trash. Tonji swallowed and looked sick.

After a moment I moved forward and my foot rattled an empty food tin. I could barely see the man far back in his hole.

"Come out. What's wrong?" The man pressed himself further back as I picked my way toward him. He whispered, cried, hid his face from the light.

"He won't answer," Tonji said.

"I suppose not." I stopped and looked at some of the other holes. The rock on this side of the room was intolerable. I hadn't noticed it in the tunnel because there was a cool draft blowing out of one of the holes in the wall. It kept the air in the room circulating away from the tunnel we'd used.

"Flash the light up there," I said. A human hand hung out of one of the holes. Cloth and sticks had been stuffed into the opening to try to keep in the smell.

There were other holes like it. Some others were packed with food, most of it partially eaten.

"Can we go back?" Tonji asked.

I ignored him and moved closer to one of the openings with a larger mouth. It sucked the dank air around me down into a black hole. In the empty silence I could hear the faint echoes of wailing and sobbing from further inside. They mingled together in a dull hum of despair.

"Bring the light," I said.

"I think it's getting colder in here, sir." He hesitated a moment and then duck-walked closer.

The man was still moaning to himself in his hole. I clenched my jaw muscles in involuntary revulsion and with an effort of will reached out and touched him. He cringed away, burrowing down, sobbing with fear.

There was part of a sleeve left on his arm—the light blue cloth of the Fleet. I looked back at the tunnel we'd just used and estimated the difficulty of pulling a struggling man through it.

"We're not going to get any more out of this," I said.

The cold was clinging to my limbs again, but Tonji was sweating. He looked about the hole nervously, as if expecting attack. The silence was oppressive, but I seemed to hear more clearly now the convulsive sobbing from further inside the mound.

I motioned quickly to Tonji and we pressed ourselves into the tunnel. I made as rapid progress as I could, with him scrambling close at my heels.

The dead weight squeezed us with rigid jaws. I tried to notice markings on the sides that would measure how far we had come, but I began to get confused.

It took me a moment to realize the air was definitely getting worse. It clung to my throat and I couldn't get enough. My chest was caught in the tunnel's vice and my lungs would never fill.

Between wriggling to squirm up the slight grade, I stopped to listen for sounds from the men at the entrance. Nothing. The long tunnel pressed at me, and I gave myself over to an endless series of pushing and turning, rhythmically moving forward against the steady hand of gravity and the scraping of the walls.

Tonji's light sent dim traces of light along the walls. I noticed how smooth they were. How many people had worn them down? How many were in here? And, God, *why?*

The tunnel began to narrow, I got through one opening by expelling all my breath and pushing hard with my heels. Coming in hadn't seemed this hard.

There was an open space that temporarily eased the pressure, and then ahead I saw walls narrowing again. I pushed and turned, scrabbling on the slick dirt with all my strength. A flicker of light reflected over my shoulder, and I could see the passage closing even further.

Impossible. A massive hand was squeezing the life out of me and my mind clutched frantically at an escape. The air was positively foul. I felt ahead and grunted with the effort. The walls closed even more. I knew I couldn't get through.

My hand touched something, but I was too numbed with the cold to tell what it was.

"Light," I managed to whisper. I heard Tonji turning, breathing rapidly, and in a moment the beam got brighter.

It was a man's foot.

I recoiled; for a moment I couldn't think and my mind was a flood of horror.

"Back," I gasped. "We can't go this way."

"This . . . way . . . we came in."

"No." Suddenly the air was too thick to take it any longer. I started to slide backwards.

"Go on!" He hit my boots.

"Back up, Mr. Tonji."

I waited and the dirt pressed at me, closing in everywhere. It was only mud. What if it collapsed?

Tonji was silent and after a moment I felt him move back. I had been holding my breath ever since my hand felt something, and I let it out as I scrambled back down the tunnel. The man hadn't been there long, but it was enough. The air was heavy with it.

I noticed I was sweating now, despite the chill. Had we taken the right hole when we left the man back there? We could be working our way further into the mound, not out of it.

How long could I take the air? I could tell Tonji was on the edge already. Did we miss a turn coming out and go down the wrong way? It was hard to imagine, in the closeness of the tunnel.

My ribs were rubbed raw and they stung whenever I moved. The weight closed on me from every direction. I pulled backward slowly, trying to collect my thoughts. I moved automatically.

After a few moments my left hand reached out and touched nothing. I stopped, but Tonji went on, as if in a stupor. I listened to his moving away, blinking uncomprehendingly at the hole to my left and tried to think.

"Wait? This is it!"

We had both missed the turn, somehow. The air had dulled our minds until we noticed nothing without conscious effort.

I worked myself into the opening. Tonji was returning and the direct glare of the beam was almost painful. He moaned something but I couldn't understand.

The passage gradually widened and I caught glimmerings of light ahead. In a moment I was standing in the vertical shaft and a man was dropping a line down to me. My hands slipped on it several times as they pulled me up.

For a few minutes I sat by the entrance, numb with fatigue. The men crowded around us and I looked at them as if they were strangers. After a while I picked out a lieutenant.

"Get . . . Jobstranikan down here." Jobstranikan had psychotherapy training, and this was clearly his job.

Orders were given and men scattered. After a moment I got up and changed back into full uniform. A runner was waiting outside the door, his nose wrinkling at the stench which I had ceased to notice.

"Sir, reports from lower levels say there are more like this. There appear to be people in them, too. The coordination center was untouched, and it's five levels down. I think they've got some of the tapes ready to run."

I turned to Tonji. "Try to get that man out of there. Do it any way you can, but don't waste time. I'll be in the center."

The walk through the next two levels was like a trip through hell. The stink of human waste was overpowering, even though the ventilation system was working at full capacity. Arc lights we had brought down threw distorted crescents of faint blue and white along walls smeared with blood, food, excrement.

Echoes of a high, gibbering wail haunted the lower floors, coming from their hiding places. They had burrowed far back into the walls in spots, but most of the tunnel mouths were in monstrous, huge mounds like the one above. They weren't hiding from us alone; their warrens were surrounded by piles of refuse. They had been in there for weeks.

Jobstranikan caught up with us just before we worked our way to the center.

"It is difficult, sir," he said. "It is like the legends—the country of madness, possessed by devils and monsters."

"What's happened to them?"

"Everything. At first I thought they had a complete fear of anything that they could sense—light, movement, noise. But that is misleading. They screech at each other incoherently. They won't let us touch them and they cry, scream, and fight if we try."

"Has Tonji been able to get any of them out?"

"Only by knocking them unconscious. One of his men was bitten badly when they tried to drag that man out. Getting anyone out of this mess is going to be a major job."

There was a guard outside the center. Broken bits of furniture and electronic gear were strewn down the corridor, but inside the center itself everything was in order.

"The hatch was sealed electronically and coded, sir," the officer inside explained. "We brought down the tracers and opened it. Somebody must have seen what was happening and made certain no one could get in here before we arrived."

I walked over to the main display board. Technicians were taping the readouts we would need from the center's computer bank, working with feverish haste. I motioned Jobstranikan back to duty and turned to the officer.

"Have you got any preliminary results? Is there an oral log that covers the Quarm attack?"

"No oral yet. We do have a radar scan." He fitted a roll into the projector attachment of the display board. "I've cut it to begin with the first incursion into this system."

He dimmed the lights in this section of the center, and the green background grid of a radar scan leaped into focus. The relative locations of the other planets in the Regeln system were shown—here lumps of cold rock, for the most part—and a small Quarm dot was visible on the perimeter of the screen, glowing a soft red.

"They took their time getting here, apparently." The projection rate increased. More dots joined the first to form a wedge-shaped pattern. A blue line detached itself from the center of the screen and moved outward, shrinking to a point—a defensive move from Regeln.

"All available missiles seem to have been fired. The Quarm took a few hits, but they could outmaneuver most of them. I'm afraid we launched too soon, and by the time our seekers were within range, their fuel reserves weren't up to a long string of dodges."

The red dots moved quickly, erratically, in a pantomime dance with the blue defenders. The distance between them was never short enough to permit a probable kill with a nuclear charge, and eventually the blue dots fell behind and were lost. They winked out when their reaction mass was exhausted.

"Except for the atmospheric ships, that finished their defenses. This colony wasn't built to carry on a war. But something strange happened."

The Quarm ships drifted toward center screen at an almost leisurely pace. A small missile flared out, went into orbit around Regeln and disappeared.

"That was the satellite link. They got that and then . . ."

"And then left," I finished. The red dots were backing off. They gradually picked up velocity, regrouped and in a few minutes slipped off the grid. The screen went black.

"That is all we have. This clipping covered about eight days, but we can't be sure anybody was watching the last part of it because the recording mechanism was automatic. It stopped when it ran out of film. This room may have been sealed anytime after they launched their missiles."

"None of this explains what happened here. The Quarm didn't touch Regeln, but this shelter is full of lunatics. Something made the Quarm stop their attack and leave." I looked around at the banks and consoles. I could feel a tightness forming somewhere. That old feeling of rightness, certainty of position, was slipping away.

"Get every record you can, in duplicate tapes if possible," I ordered, trying to shrug off the mood. The officer saluted and I went back into the corridors with a guard detail. I made a note to get respiration packs down here as soon as possible and meanwhile held my breath as long as I could between gasps.

The route we took back was different, but no less horrible. Here there were bodies lying among the wreckage, most of them in advanced stages of decay. Two of my guards gagged in the close, putrid atmosphere of the corridors. We kept moving as quickly as we could, avoiding the half-open doors from which came the faint shrill gibbering of madmen. Most of the bodies we saw had been stabbed or clubbed and left to die. A large proportion were women. In any contest of strength they wouldn't last long, and they hadn't received any special consideration.

When we reached the perimeter Tonji had established, the air improved. Men were moving along the corridors in teams, spraying the walls with a soapy solution.

"The water and drainage systems are still working, so I decided to use them," Tonji said. He seemed to have recovered from the tunnel. "Wherever we can we're sealing off the places where they lived, and merely hope we can keep the halls clean."

Jobstranikan came around a nearby corner portal we'd blasted through only a short while before. "Any new ideas?"

"Not as yet, I fear." He shook his head and the long Mongolian locks tangled together on the back of his neck. He wore it in traditional semi-tribal fashion, like most of my officers. It was dull black, in the manner of the soldiers of the Khan and the Patriarch, and braided at the tail with bright leather thongs. The style was as old as the great central plains of Asia.

"I can make no sense of it. They fought among themselves at first, I think, for the bodies we've found are at least weeks old. Since then they've stayed back in those holes they made for themselves, eating the food supplies they'd gotten earlier. But they don't want to leave. Every one I've seen wants to burrow into the smallest volume possible and stay there. We've found them in cupboards, jammed into ventilation shafts, even. . . ."

"Signal for me?" I asked the crewman in charge. We'd reached a temporary communication link. He handed me a receiver and I pulled the hushpiece over my head. If this was what I thought it was, I didn't want anyone to know before I told them.

It was Matsuda. "Our drone is registering approaching extrasolar ships. Preliminary trajectory puts them into the Regeln orbit."

I let out a long breath. In a way I'd almost been expecting it. "What's their Doppler shift?"

There was a pause, then: "It is not enough for them to be braking from a star jump. The pectroscope says they're on full torch, however. They couldn't have been accelerating very long."

"In other words, this is the same group that hit—or didn't hit— Regeln the first time. How long can we have on the surface?"

"Sir, readout says you can stay down there about five hours and not incur more than five percent risk to the convoy. Can you get them out if I give you that much?"

"We'll see," I said, and went back to Tonji.

It was impossible. With all shuttles and skimmers we saved a little over three thousand, only a fraction of the colony's population. Most of the interior of the shelter was never reached.

As it was, we boosted late and a Quarm interceptor almost caught us. A yellow fusion burst licked at us as we pulled away, so we never saw what the rest of the Quarm did to Regeln, and I don't suppose anyone else will either because it's in the middle of their territory now.

After a few unsuccessful attempts, I decided to stop trying to communicate with the lunatics we had scattered among the ships. Jobstranikan wanted to try treatment on some of them, but the medics were having a hell of a time just patching up their injuries and infections, and treating malnutrition.

The Quarm didn't try to follow us out of the system. I thought this strange, and so did Tonji.

"It does not make sense," he said. "We don't know a lot about their drive systems, but they might have a good chance of catching us. It would certainly be worth a try. If you've set a trap, why spring it half-heartedly?"

"Maybe it's not that kind of trap," I said.

Tonji frowned. "Do you mean they might be waiting for us further along trajectory? We're already out of detection range of any Quarm ships, and the jump is coming up. They'll never trace us through that."

"No, nothing. It was just a thought." Not a well-defined one, at that. Still, something was bothering me. It wasn't lessened any when Tonji reported the results from Intelligence.

"The computer analysis of the colony's radar scan is finished," he began. "Regardless of what happened to the colony itself, the machines have a low opinion of Quarm tactics. Regard."

He flicked on a screen above my desk, and the pattern of red and blue points on a green grid began to repeat itself. "Notice this shortly after initial contact."

The blue dots danced and played as they moved in, performing an intricate pattern of opposing and coalescing steps. The red Quarm ships back-pedaled and moved uncertainly.

"The Quarm had ballistic superiority and more maneuverability. But notice how they avoided the Regeln missiles."

The red points dodged back, moving in crescents that narrowly avoided the feints and slashes of blue. The crescent formed, fell back. Again. And again. The Quarm were using the same tactic, relying on their superior power to carry them beyond Regeln attack at the cusp-point. I'm not a tactician, but I could see it was wasteful of energy and time.

"They continued this until the interceptors ran out of reaction mass. If they'd been pitted against equals, the engagement wouldn't have lasted two minutes."

I clicked off the screen. "What does it mean?"

Tonji poked the air with a finger. "It means we have got them. Over the last year they've had the luck to hit border planets that weren't first-line military emplacements. We haven't had a look at their techniques because they didn't let anyone get away. But these tactics are schoolbook examples! If this is the best they can do, we'll wipe them out when our fleets move in."

He was over-enthusiastic, but he was right. Our defenses were solidly based on the fleet-principle, with interlocking layers of tactical directorates, hundred-ship armadas and echelons of command. It was very much like the surface aquatic navies of Earth history. On these terms, the Quarm were disastrously inferior.

The news should have quieted the unease I felt, but instead it grew. I began to notice outbreaks of rudeness among the crew, signs of worry on the faces of the officers, disruption of spirit. The tedium of caring for the colonists could certainly account for some of it—they refused to be calmed and had to be restrained from destroying their room furniture. They were using it to construct the same sort of ratholes we'd found them in.

But that wasn't all. Crewmen began missing meals, staying in their cabins and not talking to anyone else. The ship took on a quiet, tense mood. I ordered resumption of the Games at once.

We almost got through it.

There was divisive talking and nervousness instead of the steady calm of self-contemplation, before the Sabal began, but the opening rituals damped and smoothed it. I thought I detected a relaxation running like a wave through the hexagon. Muscles unstiffened, consciousness cleared and we drew together.

It is usual in the Game to choose a theme which begins with a statement of the virtue of community, test it, and then return to initial configuration, the position of rest. I anticipated trouble, but not enough to make a change of game plot necessary. The plot ran smoothly at first, until we came to first resolution point.

One of the lower deckmen, who had been in the shelter caverns from the first entry, was called by the chance of the game to make the decision. He hesitated, looked guiltily at his card and beads, and made a choice that profited himself at the expense of the other players.

Everything came to a stop.

I could feel the group teetering on edge. The men were straining for sense of harmony and trying to decide how to play when their turn came. A bad play isn't unknown to Sabal, but now it could be dangerous.

I repeated the confirmation rituals hoping it would calm them —and myself—but the next play was a choice of withdrawal. No gain for the individual, but the group did not profit, and the net effect was bad. Fear began to slip from member to member down the hexagon.

The plays came rapidly now. Some men tried to reinforce the message and cast configurations that benefited the group. They were swamped, one by one, and the Game began to fall apart.

I used the chant. Tranquillity, detachment, the words rose and fell. Interpenetrating. Interconverting. The mosquito bit the bar of iron.

My own cast held them for a while out of respect for my position, but in a quick string of plays its advantage was nibbled away.

Then the flood came. A dozen casts went by, all having loss of phase. The theme was not gain, but a pulling away from the group, and that was what made the failure so serious. Withdrawal strikes at the social structure itself.

I seized control of the Game, breaking off a subplot that was dragging us deeper. I drew a moral, one I'd learned years before and hoped to never use. It slurred over the resolution of the Game and emphasized the quality of the testing, without questioning whether the test had been met. It was an obvious loss, but it was all I could do.

The hexagon broke and the men burst into conversation, nearly panic-stricken. They moved out of the room, jostling and shoving, and broke up as they reached the halls. A few glanced quickly at me and then looked away. In a moment the only sound was the hissing of the air system and the distant quick tapping of boots on deck.

Tonji remained. He looked puzzled.

"What do you think it means?" I said.

"Probably just that the mission was too much for us. We'll be all right after landfall."

"I don't think so. Our Games before worked well, but this one shattered before it was half finished. That's too much of a change."

"What, then?"

"It's something to do with this mission. Something . . . What percentage of the crew have regular contact with the Regeln survivors?"

"With the way the nursemaid shifts are set up now, about sixty percent. Every man who's replaceable for more than an hour on his job has to help feed and clean them, or assist the psych teams who are working on the problem."

"So even though we're off Regeln, most of the men continue to see them."

"Yes, but it's unavoidable. Our orders were to bring back as many as we could, and we are."

"Of course." I waved my hand irritably. "But the Game failed tonight because of those survivors, I'm sure of that. I can't prove it, but it's the only reasonable answer. The strain of putting this set of crews into war-status duty isn't small, but we've allowed for it in our planning. It doesn't explain this."

Tonji gave me a stiff look. "Then what does?"

"I don't know." I was irritated at the question, because I *did* know—in a vague, foreboding sense—and his question uncovered my own fear.

"The Sabal Game has something to do with it. That and the way our ships—hell, our whole society—has to be run. We emphasize cooperation and phase. We teach that a man's happiness depends on the well-being of the group, and the two are inseparable. Even in our contacts with alien races, until the Quarm, we spread that philosophy. We try to draw closer to beings who are fundamentally different from us."

"That is the way any advanced society must be structured. Anything else is suicide on the racial scale."

"Sure, sure. But the Quarm apparently don't fit that mold. They've got something different. They work almost completely alone and live in cities only, I suppose, because of economic reasons. Most of what we know about them is guesswork because they don't like contact with others, even members of their own race. We've had to dig out our own data bit by bit."

Tonji spread his hands. "That is the reason for this mission. The Regeln survivors may be able to tell us something about the Quarm. We need an idea of how they think."

"From what we've seen of them, I don't think they'll be any help. The survivors have gone too far over the edge, and already they're threatening the convoy."

"Threatening? With what?"

"Disruption, mutiny—something. All I can say is that when this Sabal started, the crew was in bad condition, but they could be reached. They still communicated.

"During the Game, though, the tension *increased*. We didn't witness here the exposure of what the men were thinking. Their fears were augmented, piled on top of each other. I could feel it running through the subplots they made a part of the Game. There's something we do—and the Game is just a way of concentrating it—that increases the imbalance we picked up from the Regeln survivors."

"But in the Game we duplicate our society, our way of living, if *that* amplifies the imbalance . . ."

"Exactly," I said despairingly. "Exactly."

I slept on it that night, hoping something would unravel the knot of worry while I slept. Over a lonely breakfast in my cabin I reviewed the conversation and tried to see where my logic was leading.

A sense of dread caught my stomach and twisted it, turning to lead the meal of rice and sea-culture broth.

How can a man step outside himself and guess the reactions of aliens utterly unlike him? I was trying to find the key to the riddle of Regeln with all the elements in full view.

Something formed. I let my senses out through the ship, feeling the usual rhythms of life, reaching for the . . . other. An alien element was there. I knew, with a new certainty, what it was.

I picked up my tea cup and focused on my kensdai altar. The deep mahogany gave me confidence. Power and resolution flowed outward from my body center. I balanced the cup lightly in my hand.

And slammed it down. Jump was coming. I had to stop it.

I had forgotten that Tonji was to be bridge officer during the jump. He was making routine checks in the somber green light of morning watch. Men moved expertly around him, with a quiet murmur.

"Great greetings of morn, sir," he said. "We have come to the point for your permission to jump."

Then it was already late, far later than I'd thought. I looked at him steadily.

"Permission denied, Mr. Tonji. Ready a fourspace transmission."

I could feel a hush fall on the bridge.

"May I ask what the transmission will say, sir?"

"It's a request to divert this convoy. I want the expedition put into decontamination status until this is understood."

Tonji didn't move. "There are only a few moments until jump, sir."

"It's an order, Mr. Tonji."

"Perhaps if you would explain the reasoning, sir?"

I glanced at the morning board. It showed a huge sick report, most of them accompanied by requests to remain in quarters. All divisions were undermanned.

It fitted. In a few days we wouldn't be able to operate at all.

"Look," I said impatiently, "the Quarm did something to our people. Probably a psychtape—except orders of magnitude more effective—smuggled into their communications system by an agent. I don't know exactly how, but those colonists have been given the worst trauma anybody's ever seen."

"An agent? One of our own people?"

"It's been done before, by idealists and thugs alike. But the important point is that when we picked up Quarm ships on our screens they weren't trying any maneuvers to throw off detectors or give false images. It was a classic ballistic problem they presented to us, and all we had to do was leave Regeln early enough to out-mass them. They *wanted* us to escape."

"But look at their maneuvers on that first run against Regeln, the one that ran our people underground. That's all the evidence we need. They're children when it comes to military tactics. The second approach was simple, yes, but it was probably all they could do."

"I don't think so, not if the Quarm are half as intelligent as the rest of our data tells us. So their first attack *did* drive the colonists under—fine. It got all the Regeln population in one place, inside the shelter where whatever techniques the Quarm knew could go to work. What looked like an error was a feint.

"Think. A knowledge of sophisticated tactics is a rather specialized cultural adaptation. For all we know, it may not be very useful in the kind of interstellar war we've just gotten into. The fact that the Quarm don't have it doesn't mean they're inferior. Quite the opposite, probably. Regeln was a trap."

"If it was, we escaped," Tonji said sharply.

"No, Mr. Tonji, we didn't. We're just serving as a convenient transport for what the Quarm want to get into the home worlds— the Regeln survivors."

"But *why?*"

"You know the analogy we use in the Game. Mankind is now, at last, an organism. Interdependent. We're forced to rely on each other because of the complexities of civilization." My own voice sounded strange to me. It was tired and a note of despair had crept in.

"Of course," Tonji said impatiently. "Go on."

"Has it ever occurred to you that once you admit society is like an organism, you admit the possibility of contagious diseases?"

"Quite frankly, I don't understand what you're talking about."

"The survivors. They're enough of a test sample to set it off, apparently. An average crew member spends several hours a day with them, and the continued exposure is enough."

"Why aren't you affected, then? And the men who aren't on the sick list—why don't they have it?"

"Minor variations in personality. And there's something else. I checked. Some of them are from the off-islands, like me. We're different. We didn't grow up with the Game. We learned it later on the mainlands. Maybe that weakens its effect."

He shook his head. "Yes, this thing the colonists have is different, but . . ."

"It claws at the mind. It's irrational. We're the product of our ancestors, Mr. Tonji, and these ancestors knew terrors we cannot comprehend. Remember, this is a new psychosis we've found on Regeln, a combination. Fear of light, heat, heights, open spaces. That last one, agoraphobia, seems strongest. The Quarm have worked up a first-class horror for us, and this convoy is the carrier."

"A carrier for a mental disease?" Tonji said contemptuously.

"Yes. But a disorder we've never seen before. An amalgam of the fundamental terrors of man. A collective society has the strength of a rope, because each strand pulls the same way. But it has weaknesses, too, *for the same reason.*"

The men were watching us, keeping very still. I could hear the thin beeping of monitoring units. Tonji's skin had a slight greenish cast; his eyes looked back at me impersonally.

"We're carrying it with us, Mr. Tonji. The survivors are striking the same resonant mode with us that the Quarm found in them. The Quarm hit at us through our weaknesses. They're hermits, and they see us more clearly than we see ourselves. Our interdependence, the Game and all of it, communicates the disease."

I noticed that my hand was tightening convulsively on the console at my side. Tonji stood motionless.

"Stop the jump, Mr. Tonji, and send the transmission."

He motioned to an assistant, and the jump was canceled. He stood motionless for a moment, looking at me. Then he took a quick backward step, came to attention and saluted. When he spoke, the words were measured carefully and he wore that same blank stare.

"Sir, it is my duty to inform you that I must file a Duty Officer's Report when your dispatch is transmitted. I invoke Article Twenty-seven."

I froze.

Article Twenty-seven provides that the duty officer may send a counterargument to the Commander's dispatch when it is transmitted. When he feels the Commander is no longer competent to conduct his duties.

"You're wrong, Mr. Tonji," I said slowly. "Taking these survivors —and by now, most of the crew—into a major port will cause more damage than you or I can imagine."

"I have been observing you, sir. I don't think you're capable of making a rational decision about this thing."

"Man, think! What other explanation can there be for what's happening to this ship? You've seen those tapes. Do you think the scraps of information on them are worth the risk of delivery? Do you think *anyone* can get even a coherent sentence out of those lunatics we're carrying?"

He shook his head mutely.

I looked across the dark void betwen us. He was a man of the East, and I represented the dead and dying. In the histories they wrote, the ideals my ancestors held were called a temporary abnormality, a passing alternative to the communal, the group-centered culture.

Perhaps they were right. But we had met something new out here, and I knew they wouldn't understand it. Perhaps the Americans would have, or the Europeans. But they were gone.

I should have anticipated that the lost phase we all felt would take different forms. Tonji chose ambition above duty, above the ship.

If Fleet upheld him there would be promotions, even though he had used Article Twenty-seven. And I stood here, bound by rules and precedents. If I made a move to silence Tonji, it would count against my case with Fleet. We were on a rigid schedule now that the Article was used, and nothing I could do would stop it.

"Mr. Tonji! You realize, don't you, that one of us will be finished when this is over?"

He turned and looked at me, and for a moment a flash of anticipation crossed his face. He must have hated me for a long time.

"Yes, I have thought of that. And I think I know which one of us it will be."

He didn't finish the sentence aloud. He mouthed it, so only I could see his lips move.

". . . ofkaipan."

He was right. Fleet wanted to talk to anyone who'd had battle contact with the Quarm, and they weren't ready to wait for a convoy commander with suspicions and a theory.

We lingered in real space for a week, waiting for the decision, and then jumped. The trial was short.

"Haven't you gone out for your walk yet?" Angela said.

The sound startled me, even though I'd been blocking out the noise of the kids and their view-screen. She stood in the door of our bedroom a few feet away, the lines of tension still set in the pale yellow cast of her face. I was beginning to think they would never smooth out again. She had been pretty, once.

"I guess I forgot it. Want to go with me?"

She nodded and I got up from the cramped breakfast nook, stacking the papers I still hadn't reviewed.

I cut the corridor lights before we stepped outside our apartment door, and we linked hands automatically. I put my right palm on the wall and we inched forward. The terror caught at me, but I fought it down.

"Honestly, I don't see why you're so set against tapping for the children." Her voice was hollow in the darkness. It reflected off the glazed concrete that was close and sheltering. "With all of us at war, any aid to increase education is a godsend. Without it they just fall further and further behind their playmates."

"What playmates? Children don't play any more. Games take space." We rounded a corner and stumbled on someone who was doubled up on the floor clutching at himself in spasms. From the sound of his breathing, I guessed he'd had an attack and couldn't go any further. We edged by him.

"Well, not the same way we did. But they have their games, new ones. You've got to accept the world as it is."

"Accept this crowding? Accept the fear that crushes you whenever you step outside? Accept the fact that a third of the population can't work and we who can—even with our guts twisted up inside—must support them?"

Her hand tightened convulsively on mine. "You know that can't be helped! We're in a . . . stage of evolution of society. Withdrawal is necessary to achieve a greater phase, later."

"And meanwhile the Quarm take one system after another. They've cut us off from most of our raw materials already, and we can't muster the men to stop them. Maybe if we're lucky they'll cut us off from our own lies before all this is over."

"Now *that* is completely unreasonable," she said icily. "It ties in with all your other ideas, like not letting Romana and Chark have tapping."

"Not letting the government tinker around in their minds, you mean, with one of their schemes for increasing the war effort. Let Chark have a brain tap so all he cares about is torch chamber design, say, and will never be happy when he's not doing it. That's right, I won't. Our kids will need every bit of mental balance they have to stay alive as a defeated race, and I don't intend to rob them of it."

We passed by some of the lower-level apartments hastily thrown up by the government for the more severe cases. Whimpering came from the little holes where things that had been human beings were curled up into tight balls, desperately trying to shut out the light, the sounds, all of the awful enormity of sheer open space.

Angela descended into her glacial silence, maintaining only a fingertip touch with me to retain her orientation. The walks don't seem to do either of us any good any longer, so I suppose there is a limit to their therapeutic value. I've gone about as far as I can go, as one of the original cases, and our small apartment is the largest volume my senses can stand.

Even then, the world isn't real to me. It's filled with a thousand devious terrors—the accidentally thrown light switch, an unsuspected window in an unfamiliar wall.

Out on the edge of our pitifully shrinking empire, the Fleet plays at war with the only toys it knows—guns, ships, beams—while their enemy (and what is he like, to be so wise?) fights with the only ultimate weapons between races: their weaknesses.

The men who climbed to the stars now cower in caves, driven by the horrors they inherited from the first amphibians. I do not feel at home on the earth any longer. My life lies in dark halls, jammed with people I can understand but whose fears I hate, because they are mine as well.

I will welcome the Quarm, when they come. I have been alone a long time.

Culture

Of Courſe

Although all peoples have a culture, the content of any given culture varies from one society to another. Cultures differ from one another. Where there is difference, there is a tendency toward comparison, and where there is comparison there is also a tendency to make judgments about the superiority or inferiority of differing ways of life. Sociologists use the term *ethnocentrism* to refer to a special evaluation people commonly make of their own and other cultures. Literally meaning "placing one's nation at the center of the universe," ethnocentrism is the belief that one's own culture is the superior arrangement of human activity. Taking one's own way of life for granted and valuing it strongly, the ethnocentric person assumes his culture to have "progressed" to the most "civilized" of states and that other cultural patterns are not just dissimilar, but inferior.

Each national leader in "Of Course" is convinced of the superiority of his own culture and views no other culture as its equal. We can find many examples of ethnocentric persons in contemporary society, from ordinary citizen to leader. Real life has its Archie Bunkers, and some critics of our foreign policy believe that this policy is arrogantly paternalistic in its unrecognized assumptions that America's ways are best for all people. Certainly, ethnocentrism is not uniquely American; for example, the literal translation into English of the Chinese name for the Chinese foreign ministry is "The Ministry for Barbarian Affairs."

Individuals learn their culture through a process sociologists call *socialization*. Through association with others the individual is presented with and incorporates certain core values of the cultural ethos of his or her society. Experience often reinforces these values. The consequent attachment to one's own way of life provides a cohesiveness or solidarity among the people of that society and therefore makes more binding the social bond holding them together. Yet, ethnocentrism can foster blind acquiescence to one's own culture, coupled with the devaluation of the culture of other peoples, and can distort recognition of cultural difference into a biased stance of derogation of those not pursuing ways and holding values like one's own.

Objectively, how does one "rate" or "rank" cultures? How does one judge the level of advancement? What criteria should be used for determining who is to make the decision? Understanding the cultures of other societies and recognizing that cultural difference does not indicate cultural inferiority are clearly important components of world peace and cooperation. And this recognition may just be the "progress" the aliens from Procyon in "Of Course" expect Earthlings to develop in a century or so. In their minds, cultures of earth are not yet "civilized."

Of Course

CHAD OLIVER

In Bern, Switzerland, quite early in the morning, the President
woke up with a splitting headache. He hadn't been sleeping well
for the past three weeks, and last night had been worse than usual.
He stayed in bed for a few minutes, frowning at the ceiling. It was
an unpleasant situation to be in; there was no denying that. The
President, however, had confidence. Surely, with its record since the
Congress of Vienna in 1815, the outlook was good for his country.
The President managed a smile. Switzerland would be the one, of
course.

In Moscow, Russia, seated at the end of a long table, the Premier
listened intently to his chief military advisors. He didn't like what
he heard, but he kept his face expressionless. He didn't like the
position in which he found himself, but he wasn't really worried.
There could be no doubt whatever that the Supreme Soviet would
be the one chosen. Of course!

In London, England, the Prime Minister stepped out of 10
Downing Street, his pipe smoking determinedly. He climbed into his
car for a drive to the Palace, and folded his strong hands. Things
might be a bit touch-and-go for a short time, but the Prime Minister
was undismayed. England, with its glorious history, was the only
possible choice. Of course, it would be England!

To the east of Lake Victoria in Africa, the tall, slender priest-
chief of the Masai, the Laibon, looked out upon the humped cattle
grazing on the grassland and smiled. There was but one true God,
Em-Gai, and the pastoral Masai were proud. At long last, ancient
wrongs would be corrected! The Masai would rise again. They were
the only logical choice. Of course . . .

And so it went, around the world.

The somewhat dumpy gentleman in the rimless spectacles and

the double-breasted suit had a name: Morton Hillford. He had a title to go with the name: presidential advisor.

Right now, he was pacing the floor.

"You say you've investigated *all* the possibilities, general?" he demanded. "All the . . . um-m-m . . . angles?"

The general, whose name was Larsen, had an erect bearing and iron-gray hair, both of which were very useful when senators had to be impressed. He was a general who knew his business. Naturally, he was upset.

He said: "Every possible line of action has been explored, Mr. Hillford. Every angle has been studied thoroughly."

Morton Hillford stopped pacing. He aimed a forefinger at the general as though it were a .45. His expression indicated strongly that if there had been a trigger he might have pulled it. "Do you mean to tell me, sir, that the United States Army is impotent?"

The general frowned. He coughed briefly. "Well," he said, "let's say that the United States Army is *helpless* in this matter."

"I don't care what words you use! Can you *do* anything?"

"No," said the general, "we can't. And neither, may I point out, can the Navy, the Air Force, or the Marines."

"Or the Coast Guard," mimicked Morton Hillford. He resumed his pacing. "Why *can't* you do anything? That's your job, isn't it?"

General Larsen flushed. "I'm sorry, Mr. Hillford. Our job, as you point out, is to defend this country. We are prepared to do that to the best of our ability, no matter what the odds—"

"Oh, forget it, Larsen. I didn't mean to get under your hide. I guess my breakfast just didn't agree with me this morning. I understand your position in this matter. It's . . . embarrassing, that's all."

"To say the least," agreed General Larsen. "But I venture to say that we've thought of everything from hydrogen bombs to psychological warfare. We have absolutely nothing that stands the ghost of a chance of working. A hostile move on our part would be suicide for all of us, Mr. Hillford. I deplore melodrama, but facts are facts. It wouldn't do to let the people know just how much in their power we *are*, but nevertheless we *are* on the hook and there isn't any way that I know of to get off again. We'll keep trying, naturally, but the President must have the correct facts at his disposal. There isn't a thing we can do at the present time."

"Well, general, I appreciate your candor, even if you have little else to offer. It looks as though we will have to keep our fingers crossed and a great big smile on our collective face. The President isn't going to like it though, Larsen."

"I don't like it either," Larsen said.

Morton Hillford paused long enough to look out the window at the streets of Washington. It was summer, and the sun had driven most people indoors, although there were a few helicopters and cars visible. The old familiar buildings and monuments were there, however, and they imparted to him a certain sense of stability, if not of security.

It's not the heat, his mind punned silently, *it's the humility.*

"We'll just have to trust to their good judgment, I suppose," Morton Hillford said aloud. "It could be worse."

"Much worse," the general agreed. "The position of the United States in the world today—"

Hillford brushed the words aside impatiently. "There isn't the slightest doubt of it! That isn't our problem. Of *course,* the United States will be chosen."

"Of course," echoed the general.

"And then everything will be all right, won't it, Larsen?"

"Of course!"

"Just the same," said Morton Hillford pointedly, "you find us a weapon that will work, and do it in a hurry."

"We'll try, Mr. Hillford."

"You *do* it, general. That's all for today."

The general left, keeping his thoughts to himself.

Morton Hillford, presidential advisor, resumed his pacing. Fourteen steps to the window, fourteen steps back. Pause. Light a cigarette. Fourteen steps to the window—

"Of course," he said aloud, "it will be the United States."

And his mind added a postscript: *It had BETTER be the United States.*

Three weeks ago, the ship had come out of space.

It was a big ship, at least as far as Earth was concerned. It was a good half-mile long, fat and sleek and polished, like a well-fed silver fish in the shallows of a deep and lonely sea. It didn't do much of anything. It just hung high in the air directly above the United Nations building in New York.

Waiting.

Like a huge trick cigar about to blow up in your face.

Simultaneously with its appearance, every government on Earth got a message. Every government got the same message. The ship wasn't fussy about defining "government," either. It contacted every sort of political division. In certain instances where the recipients were illiterate, or non-literate, the message was delivered vocally.

Every message was sent in the native language. In itself, that was enough to give a man food for thought. There were a lot of languages on Earth, and many of them had never been written down.

The people who came in the ship, what was seen of them, looked quite human.

There was a great deal of talk and frenzied activity when the spaceship and the messages appeared. For one thing, no one had ever seen a spaceship before. However, the novelty of that soon wore off. People had been more or less expecting a spaceship, and they tended to accept it philosophically, as they had accepted electricity and airplanes and telephones and atom bombs. Fine stuff, naturally. What's next?

The message was something else again.

The United Nations and the United States greeted the ship from space with about one and a half cheers. Contact with other worlds was very dramatic and important and all that, but it *did* pose a number of unpleasant questions.

It is difficult to negotiate unless you have something to offer, or else are strong enough so that you don't have to dicker.

Suppose the ship wasn't friendly?

The United States dug into its bag of military tricks and investigated. They weren't fools about it, either. No one went off half-cocked and tried to drop a hydrogen bomb on an unknown quantity. It was recognized at once that dropping a bomb on the ship might be like hunting a tiger with a cap pistol.

The military looked into the matter, subtly.

They probed, gently, and checked instruments.

The results were not encouraging.

The ship had some sort of a field around it. For want of a better name, it was called a force field. Definitely, it was an energy screen of some sort—and nothing could get through it. It was absolutely impregnable. It was the ultimate in armor.

If a man has really foolproof armor and you don't, then you're out of luck.

The military couldn't fight.

After digesting the message, there didn't seem to be much for the diplomats to do either.

The message contained no explicit threat; it was simply a statement of intentions. If anything, it suffered from a certain annoying vagueness that made it difficult to figure out exactly *what* the ship was going to do.

The message read:

"PLEASE DO NOT BE ALARMED. WE HAVE COME IN PEACE ON A MISSION OF GOOD WILL. OUR TASK HERE IS TO DETERMINE TO OUR SATISFACTION WHICH ONE AMONG YOU HAS THE MOST ADVANCED CULTURE ON YOUR PLANET. IT WILL BE NECESSARY TO TAKE ONE REPRESENTATIVE

FROM YOUR MOST ADVANCED CULTURE BACK WITH US FOR STUDY. HE WILL NOT BE HARMED IN ANY WAY. IN RETURN FOR HIM, WE WILL UNDERTAKE TO SUPPLY HIS CULTURE WITH WHATEVER IT MOST DESIRES, TO THE BEST OF OUR ABILITIES. WE SINCERELY HOPE THAT WE WILL CAUSE YOU NO INCONVENIENCE AS WE WORK. IT IS SUGGESTED THAT YOU DO NOT ATTEMPT TO COMMUNICATE WITH THIS SHIP UNTIL OUR CHOICE HAS BEEN ANNOUNCED. IT IS ALSO SUGGESTED THAT HOSTILE ACTION ON YOUR PART SHOULD BE CAREFULLY AVOIDED. WE HAVE COME IN PEACE AND WISH TO LEAVE THE SAME WAY WHEN OUR JOB IS DONE. THANK YOU FOR YOUR COURTESY. WE ARE ENJOYING YOUR PLANET."

That was all.

On the face of it, the message was not too alarming, however unprecedented it may have been. However, second thoughts came fast.

Suppose, thought the United States, that Russia is chosen. Suppose, further, that what Russia most desired was an unbeatable weapon to use against the United States—what then? And suppose, thought Russia, that the United States is chosen—

The situation was somewhat uncomfortable.

It was made decidedly worse by the complete helplessness of the contestants.

There wasn't a thing they could do except to wait and see.

Of course, every single government involved was quite sure that it would be the one chosen. That being the case, the more discerning among them realized that no matter *who* was selected it would come as a shocking surprise to all the rest.

It did.

Morton Hillford, advisor to the President, got the news from the chief American delegate to the United Nations. The delegate hadn't trusted anyone with *this* hot potato; he had come in person, and at full speed.

When he got the news, Morton Hillford sat down, hard.

"That's ridiculous," he said.

"I know it," said the delegate. The shock had partially worn off for him, and he kept on his feet.

"I don't believe it," said Morton Hillford. "I'm sorry, Charlie, but I just don't believe it."

"Here," said the delegate, handing him the message, "you read it."

Hillford read it. His first impulse was to laugh. "Why, they're crazy!"

"Hardly."

Hillford managed to get to his feet and resume his pacing. His rimless spectacles were getting fogged from the heat, so he wiped them off with his handkerchief.

"I feel like a fool," he said finally. He shook the message, almost angrily. "It's such a terrific anticlimax, Charlie! Are you sure they're not joking?"

"They're dead serious. They're going to exhibit the man in New York tomorrow. After that, they're going to show him off in every other capital on Earth. After *that*—"

He shrugged.

Morton Hillford felt a sick sinking in the pit of his stomach. "Do you want to tell the Boss, Charlie?"

"No," said the delegate. "A thousand times no. I've got to get back to the U.N., Mort. *You* tell him."

"Me?"

"Who else?"

Morton Hillford accepted his burden with what stoicism he could muster. His not to reason why—

"Let's have a drink first, Charlie," he said wearily. "Just a small one."

As it turned out, they both told him.

The President eyed them intently, hands on his hips, and demanded to see the message. They showed it to him.

The President was not a handsome man, but he had strength in his features. His rather cold blue eyes were alert and intelligent, and they seldom followed his mouth's lead when he smiled.

He wasn't smiling now, anywhere.

"Well, Boss," asked Morton Hillford, "what do we do now?"

The President frowned. "We'll have to go on with a telecast as soon as possible," he said, speaking with authority. "We'll have to tell the people *something*. Get Doyle and Blatski on that right away, Mort—and tell them to write it up with some sort of a positive slant if they can. Soothe their pride, indicate we're not unwilling to learn, throw in something about unknown science and mysterious factors . . . you know. After that, we'll have a project set up to study this whole affair." He consulted the message again. "Hm-m-m. I see they're coming back again in one hundred of our years to check up on us. Fine! By then we may have something to argue with in case they mean trouble, although I doubt it. I pity the man in office when they come back—I hope he's a member of the Loyal Opposition. Now! We've got to find out what this is all about."

The United Nations delegate ventured one word: "How?"

The President sat down at his desk and lit a cigarette. He blew smoke out through his compressed lips, slowly. It was a good pose, and he liked it. As a matter of fact, he was a man who relished difficult problems—even this one. He liked action, and routine bored him.

"We need a scientist," he announced. "And not a nuclear physicist this time. We need someone in here who can tell us something about these people. The fact is, we need a *social* scientist."

Morton Hillford warned: "Don't let the *Tribune* find out. They'll crucify you."

The President shrugged. "We'll keep it quiet," he said. "Now! As I said, we need a social scientist. The question is, which kind?"

"Not a psychologist," mused Morton Hillford. "Not yet, anyway. I'm afraid we need a sociologist. If the *Tribune* ever finds out—"

"Forget the papers, man! This is important."

The President got to work on his private phone. "Hello . . . Henry? Something has come up. I want you to get over here right away, and I want you to bring a sociologist with you. That's right, a *sociologist*. What's that? Yes, I KNOW about the *Tribune*! Bring him in the back door."

In due course of time, Henry—who was Secretary of State—arrived. He brought a sociologist with him. The sociologist was unexpectedly normal looking, and he listened respectfully to what the President had to say. He was naturally surprised when he heard about the ship's choice, but he recovered himself quickly.

The sociologist was an honest man. "I'm terribly sorry, Mr. President," he said. "I could take a stab at it if you like, but what you really need is an anthropologist."

The President drummed his fingers on his desk. "Henry," he said, "get me an anthropologist over here, and hurry."

Henry hurried.

Four hours later, the anthropologist was shown into the President's office. His name was Edgar Vincent, he had a beard, and he smoked a foreign-looking pipe. Well, that couldn't be helped.

Introductions were hastily made.

"You are an anthropologist?" asked the President.

"That's right, sir," said Dr. Vincent.

"Fine!" said the President. He leaned back in his chair and folded his hands. "Now we're getting somewhere."

Dr. Vincent looked blank.

"Tell me, doctor," said the President, "what do you know about the Eskimos?"

The anthropologist stared.

"You don't mean—"

To save time, the President handed him the message that had been sent by the ship to the United Nations. "You might as well read this, doctor," he said. "It will be released to the papers within an hour anyway, and then everybody will know."

Edgar Vincent puffed on his pipe and read the message:

"WE BRING YOU GREETINGS AND FAREWELL. OUR WORK AMONG YOU HAS NOW BEEN COMPLETED. WE HAVE FOUND THE MOST ADVANCED CULTURE AMONG YOU TO BE THAT OF THE CENTRAL ESKIMO OF BAFFIN LAND. WE HAVE SELECTED ONE MEMBER OF THAT CULTURE TO GO BACK WITH US FOR STUDY. AS INDICATED EARLIER, WE WILL UNDERTAKE TO PROVIDE HIS CULTURE WITH WHATEVER IT MOST DESIRES, BY WAY OF PAYMENT. THE REPRESENTATIVE OF THE HIGHEST CULTURE ON YOUR PLANET WILL BE EXHIBITED IN ALL YOUR POLITICAL CENTERS, AT TIMES WHICH WILL BE INDICATED IN A SEPARATE COMMUNICATION, TO PROVE TO YOU THAT HE HAS NOT BEEN HARMED. WE WILL RETURN TO YOUR WORLD IN ONE HUNDRED EARTH-YEARS, AT WHICH TIME WE HOPE TO DISCUSS MUTUAL PROBLEMS WITH YOU AT GREATER LENGTH. THANK YOU AGAIN FOR YOUR COURTESY. WE HAVE ENJOYED YOUR PLANET."

"Well?" asked the President.

"I hardly know what to say," said the anthropologist. "It's fantastic."

"We already know that, doctor. Say *something*."

Edgar Vincent found a chair and sat down. He stroked his beard thoughtfully. "In the first place," he said, "I'm not really the man you want."

Henry groaned. "You're an anthropologist, aren't you?"

"Yes, yes, of course. But I'm a *physical* anthropologist. You know —bones and evolution and blood types and all that. I'm afraid that isn't quite what you're after here." He held up his hand, holding off a wave of protest. "What you need is an ethnologist or social anthropologist, and the man you ought to get is Irvington; he's the Central Eskimo man." He held up his hand again. "Just a moment, please gentlemen! As I say, you need Irvington. You won't be able to get him for some time, however. I suggest you put in a call for him— he's in Boston now—and in the meantime I'll fill you in as best I can. I do know a *little* cultural anthropology; we're not as specialized as all that."

Henry left to put in the call, and then hurried back. Vincent permitted himself a faint smile. It had been a long time since he had an audience *this* attentive!

"Can you think of any possible reason why an Eskimo might have been chosen?" asked Morton Hillford.

"Frankly, no."

"A secret civilization?" suggested the United Nations delegate. "A lost tribe? Something like that?"

Vincent snorted. "Nonsense," he said. "Sir," he added.

"Look," said the President. "We know they live in igloos. Go on from there."

Vincent smiled. "Even that isn't quite correct, I'm afraid," he said. "Begging your pardon, sir, but the Eskimos don't *live* in igloos, at least not most of the time. They live in skin tents in the summer, stone and earth houses in early winter—"

"Never mind that," the President said. "That's not important."

Vincent puffed on his pipe. "How do you know it isn't?"

"What? Oh . . . yes. Yes, I see what you mean." The President was nobody's fool. It was hardly his fault that he knew nothing about Eskimos. Who did?

"That's the catch, as you are beginning to understand, sir," Vincent said.

"But look here," put in Morton Hillford. "I don't mean to belittle your field of learning, doctor, but the Eskimos simply aren't the most advanced civilization on this planet! Why, we've got a technology hundreds of years ahead of theirs, science they can't even guess at, a Bill of Rights, a political system centuries in the making—thousands of things! The Eskimos just don't rate."

Vincent shrugged. "To you they don't," he corrected. "But you're not doing the evaluation."

Morton Hillford persisted. "Suppose you were making the choice, doctor. Would *you* choose an Eskimo?"

"No," admitted the anthropologist. "Probably not. But then, I'm looking at it from roughly the same values that you are. I'm an American too, you know."

"I think I see the problem," the President said slowly. "The people on that ship are far ahead of us—they must be, or they wouldn't *have* that ship. Therefore, their standards aren't the same as our standards. They're not adding up the points the same way we are. Is that right, doctor?"

Vincent nodded. "That's what I would say, at a guess. It stands to reason. Maybe our culture has overlooked something important—something that outweighs all the big buildings and mass production and voting and all the rest of it. How do we know?"

The President drummed his fingers on his desk. "Let's look at it this way," he suggested. "Could it be that spiritual values are more important than technological progress—something like that?"

Vincent considered. "I don't think so," he said finally. "It might be *something* like that, but then why choose the Eskimos? There are plenty of people worse off in a technological sense than they are—the Eskimos are quite skilled mechanically. They've invented a number of things, such as snow goggles and hunting techniques and intricate harpoon heads. They're quite good at gadgetry, as a matter of fact. I don't think we can throw technology out the window; it isn't that simple. And as for 'spiritual values,' they're apt to be tricky to handle. Offhand, I wouldn't say that Eskimos had any more than other people, and it's even possible that they have less. Look at India, say— they have *really* put the emphasis on religion. I think you're headed in the right direction, maybe, but you're not on the right track yet."

The delegate from the United Nations wiped his brow. "Well then, what *have* the Eskimos got?"

"I can only give you one answer to that," Vincent said. "At any rate, only one *honest* answer: I don't know. You'll have to wait for Irvington, and my guess is that he'll be just as surprised as anyone else. I haven't the faintest idea why the Eskimos should be picked out of all the peoples on Earth. We'll just have to find out, that's all—and that means we'll have to know a lot more about *every* group of people on this planet than we know now, to find out what the Eskimos have got that the others *haven't* got."

"More money," sighed the President, a trifle grimly. "Doctor, can't you give us something to go on, just provisionally? I've got a cabinet meeting in an hour, and I have to go in there and say something. And after that, there'll be a television address, and the newspapers, and the foreign diplomats, and Congress, and God knows what all. This won't be so funny a few years from now. Any ideas, doctor?"

Vincent did his best. "The Eskimos have made a remarkable adjustment to their environment at their technological level," he said slowly. "They're often used as examples of that. I recall one anthropologist who mentioned that they have no word for war, and no conception of it. That might be a good angle to work on. For the rest, you'll have to talk to Irvington. I'm out of my element."

"Well, thanks very much, Dr. Vincent," the President said. "I appreciate your help. And now, let's *all* have a small drink."

They adjourned to another room, all talking furiously, to get ready for the cabinet meeting to come.

Morton Hillford was the last to leave the President's office.

"Eskimos," he said sadly, shaking his head. "*Eskimos.*"

Next morning, strictly according to schedule, a smaller ship detached itself from the huge spaceship that hovered high in the sky above the United Nations building in New York.

For the onlooking millions, in person and via television, it was difficult to avoid the impression of a cigarette emerging from a large silver cigar.

The little ship landed, as gently as a falling leaf, in the area that had been cleared for it. A small bubble of force, glinting slightly in the morning sun, surrounded the ship. A circular portal slid open and the exhibition began.

It was simplicity itself.

Two tall, pleasant-looking men stepped out of the ship, staying within the energy shield. Their dress was unique, but rather on the conservative side. They leaned back into the portal and appeared to be speaking to someone.

A bit reluctantly, the Eskimo stepped outside and stood with them. He was dressed in new clothes and looked uncomfortable. He was short, a little on the plump side, and his hair was uncombed.

He gaped at New York City in frank astonishment.

He smiled with shy pleasure.

With only a trace of prompting from the two men, he waved cheerfully to the crowd that had gathered to see him. He stood there, smiling, for two minutes, and then he was escorted back into the ship.

The ship floated soundlessly into the air, and curved up to rejoin the larger ship above.

That was all there was.

The exhibition was over.

Right on schedule, it was repeated elsewhere.

In Bern, Switzerland.

In Moscow, Russia.

In London, England.

In the land of the Masai, in East Africa.

In China, Sweden, Australia, Mexico, Finland, Brazil, Samoa, Turkey, Greece, Japan, Tibet—

All around the world.

And, of course, everywhere the ship went it raised some highly annoying questions. Of course, every government *knew* that a mistake had somehow been made.

But just the same—

As suddenly as it had come, the great spaceship was gone. Its jets flickered with atomic flame, its outlines blurred, and it flashed back into the dark sea from which it had come.

It was headed for Procyon, eleven light-years distant, to check up on the results of a previous experiment that had taken place roughly a century ago.

The Eskimo wandered about the ship, munching on a fish, and tried to figure out what was going on.

Two men watched him, amused but not impressed.

"Well, anyhow," observed the first man, "his people will have plenty of seals from now on."

"Right enough," agreed the second man. "And we can put *him* down on Armique—he should be right at home there, and no harm done."

"It's high time we got around to Earth, if you ask me," said the first. "That planet is getting to be the eyesore of our sector."

"Oh, Earth will come along," said the second. "They really *are* making some progress down there, finally."

The Eskimo selected another fish out of his private bucket and watched the two men without interest.

"It must have been something of a shock when we selected *him*. An awfully nice chap, but he *is* a bit on the primitive side."

"A slight stimulus never hurt anyone, my friend. By the time they get through worrying about that Eskimo, they ought to have a *real* science down there."

The first man yawned and stretched. "And when we come back in a hundred years," he said, "you know which one of them we'll find with a culture *really* advanced enough so that we can offer them a place in Civilization."

The second man nodded. "Of course," he said, and smiled.

The Eskimo helped himself to another fish out of the bucket and wandered over to the window.

Social and Cultural Change

Slow Tuesday Night

How do individuals perceive cultural change? In earlier societies culture accumulated slowly, and change was minimal. The individual experienced a consistency and stability in social setting. Change was sufficiently slow and what was transmitted from elders to new generations fitted social reality during the lifetimes of subsequent generations. With rapid change, however, "new social realities" might occur several times within a lifetime, and old ways might become rapidly outdated. Successive generations live in different social worlds. For example, can the generation coming to maturity now understand what life was like without television, or what it meant to live through the Great Depression? Can their fathers and mothers understand a world without radio, motion pictures, or the automobile? These changes are not just in technological devices, but in such areas as information. Witness the "knowledge explosion." New knowledge accumulates so quickly that one trained to "know" a body of knowledge to accomplish his occupational tasks will find within his lifetime—in fact, within his early productive years—that his knowledge is "obsolete," and perhaps with it his ability to hold that job. Today educators often speak of educating not as a task of imparting *what* is to be learned, but as teaching one *how* to learn.

Ever-increasing rates of change demand a flexibility and adaptability among human beings that few possess or even recognize. It is out of this situation that the individual can become vaguely uneasy about the future or alienated to the present. Alvin Toffler made these points well in *Future Shock*, and R. A. Lafferty in "Slow Tuesday Night" describes a world in which change appears to us to be absurd in its rapidity. This story is an example of one of the things that science fiction does best: it reduces abstract concepts to a microcosmic level, where their content and implication can be concretely understood. In this story rapid change is reflected in the lives of the individuals concerned, and as one follows the characters in the story through the events of one Tuesday night one can grasp the future consequences of a rate of change that continues to accelerate.

Slow Tuesday Night

R. A. LAFFERTY

A panhandler intercepted the young couple as they strolled down the night street.

"Preserve us this night," he said as he touched his hat to them, "and could you good people advance me a thousand dollars to be about the recouping of my fortunes?"

"I gave you a thousand last Friday," said the young man.

"Indeed you did," the panhandler replied, "and I paid you back tenfold by messenger before midnight."

"That's right, George, he did," said the young woman. "Give it to him dear. I believe he's a good sort."

So the young man gave the panhandler a thousand dollars; and the panhandler touched his hat to them in thanks, and went on to the recouping of his fortunes.

As he went into Money Market, the panhandler passed Ildefonsa Impala the most beautiful woman in the city.

"Will you marry me this night, Ildy?" he asked cheerfully.

"Oh, I don't believe so, Basil," she said. "I marry you pretty often, but tonight I don't seem to have any plans at all. You may make me a gift on your first or second, however. I always like that.

But when they had parted she asked herself: "But whom will I marry tonight?"

The panhandler was Basil Bagelbaker who would be the richest man in the world within an hour and a half. He would make and lose four fortunes within eight hours; and these not the little fortunes that ordinary men acquire, but titanic things.

When the Abebaios block had been removed from human minds, people began to make decisions faster, and often better. It had been the mental stutter. When it was understood what it was, and that it had no useful function, it was removed by simple childhood meta-surgery.

Transportation and manufacturing had then become practically instantaneous. Things that had once taken months and years now took only minutes and hours. A person could have one or several pretty intricate careers within an eight hour period.

Freddy Fixico had just invented a manus module. Freddy was a Nyctalops, and the modules were characteristic of these people. The people had then divided themselves—according to their natures and inclinations—into the Auroreans, the Hemerobians, and the Nyctalops; or the Dawners who had their most active hours from 4 A.M. till Noon, the Day-Flies who obtained from Noon to 8 P.M., and the Night-Seers whose civilization thrived from 8 P.M. to 4 A.M. The cultures, inventions, markets and activities of these three folk were a little different. As a Nyctalops, Freddy had just begun his working day at 8 P.M. on a slow Tuesday night.

Freddy rented an office and had it furnished. This took one minute, negotiation, selection and installation being almost instantaneous. Then he invented the manus module; that took another minute. He then had it manufactured and marketed; in three minutes it was in the hands of key buyers.

It caught on. It was an attractive module. The flow of orders began within 30 seconds. By 8:10 every important person had one of the new manus modules, and the trend had been set. The module began to sell in the millions. It was one of the most interesting fads of the night, or at least the early part of the night.

Manus modules had no practical function, no more than had Sameki verses. They were attractive, of a psychologically satisfying size and shape, and could be held in the hands, set on a table, or installed in a module niche of any wall.

Naturally Freddy became very rich. Ildefonsa Impala the most beautiful woman in the city was always interested in newly rich men. She came to see Freddy about 8:30. People made up their minds fast, and Idlefonsa had hers made up when she came. Freddy made his own up quickly and divorced Judy Fixico in Small Claims Court. Freddy and Ildefonsa went honeymooning to Paraiso Dorado, a resort.

It was wonderful. All of Ildy's marriages were. There was the wonderful floodlighted scenery. The recirculated water of the famous falls was tinted gold; the immediate rocks had been done by Rambles; and the hills had been contoured by Spall. The beach was a perfect copy of that at Merevale, and the popular drink that first part of the night was blue absinthe.

But scenery—whether seen for the first time or revisited after an interval—is striking for the sudden intense view of it. It is not meant to be lingered over. Food, selected and prepared instantly, is eaten with swift enjoyment: and blue absinthe lasts no longer than its own novelty. Loving, for Ildefonsa and her paramours, was quick and consuming; and repetition would have been pointless to her. Besides Ildefonsa and Freddy had taken only the one hour luxury honeymoon.

Freddy wished to continue the relationship, but Ildefonsa glanced at a trend indicator. The manus module would hold its popularity for only the first third of the night. Already it had been discarded by people who mattered. And Freddy Fixico was not one of the regular successes. He enjoyed a full career only about one night a week.

They were back in the city and divorced in Small Claims Court by 9:35. The stock of manus modules was remaindered, and the last of it would be disposed to bargain hunters among the Dawners who will buy anything.

"Whom shall I marry next?" Ildefonsa asked herself. "It looks like a slow night."

"Bagelbaker is buying," ran the word through Money Market, but Bagelbaker was selling again before the word had made its rounds. Basil Bagelbaker enjoyed making money, and it was a pleasure to watch him work as he dominated the floor of the Market and assembled runners and a competent staff out of the corner of his mouth. Helpers stripped the panhandler rags off him and wrapped him in a tycoon toga. He sent one runner to pay back twentyfold the young couple who had advanced him a thousand dollars. He sent another with a more substantial gift to Ildefonsa Impala, for Basil cherished their relationship. Basil acquired title to the Trend Indication Complex and had certain falsifications set into it. He caused to collapse certain industrial empires that had grown up within the last two hours, and made a good thing of recombining their wreckage. He had been the richest man in the world for some minutes now. He became so money-heavy that he could not maneuver with the agility he had shown an hour before. He became a great fat buck, and the pack of expert wolves circled him to bring him down.

Very soon he would lose that first fortune of the evening. The secret of Basil Bagelbaker is that he enjoyed losing money spectacularly after he was full of it to the bursting point.

A thoughtful man named Maxwell Mouser had just produced a work of actinic philosophy. It took him seven minutes to write it. To write works of philosophy one used the flexible outlines and the idea indexes; one set the activator for such a wordage in each subsection; an adept would use the paradox feed-in, and the striking analogy blender; one calibrated the particular-slant and the personality-signature. It had to come out a good work, for excellence had become the automatic minimum for such productions.

"I will scatter a few nuts on the frosting," said Maxwell, and he pushed the lever for that. This sifted handfuls of words like chthonic and heuristic and prozymeides through the thing so that nobody could doubt it was a work of philosophy.

Maxwell Mouser sent the work out to publishers, and received it back each time in about three minutes. An analysis of it and reason for rejection was always given—mostly that the thing had been done before and better. Maxwell received it back ten times in 30 minutes, and was discouraged. Then there was a break.

Ladion's work had become a hit within the last ten minutes, and it was now recognized that Mouser's monograph was both an answer and a supplement to it. It was accepted and published in less than a minute after this break. The reviews of the first five minutes were cautious ones; then real enthusiasm was shown. This was truly one of the greatest works of philosophy to appear during the early and medium hours of the night. There were those who said it might be one of the enduring works and even have a hold-over appeal to the Dawners the next morning.

Naturally Maxwell became very rich, and naturally Ildefonsa came to see him about midnight. Being a revolutionary philosopher, Maxwell thought that they might make some free arrangement, but Ildefonsa insisted it must be marriage. So Maxwell divorced Judy Mouser in Small Claims Court and went off with Ildefonsa.

This Judy herself, though not so beautiful as Ildefonsa, was the fastest taker in the City. She only wanted the men of the moment for a moment, and she was always there before even Ildefonsa. Ildefonsa believed that she took the men away from Judy; Judy said that Ildy had her leavings and nothing else.

"I had him first," Judy would always mock as she raced through Small Claims Court.

"Oh that damned Urchin!" Ildefonsa would moan. "She wears my very hair before I do."

Maxwell Mouser and Ildefonsa Impala went honeymooning to Musicbox Mountain, a resort. It was wonderful. The peaks were done with green snow by Dunbar and Fittle. (Back at Money Market Basil Bagelbaker was putting together his third and greatest fortune of the night which might surpass in magnitude even his fourth fortune of the Thursday before.) The chalets were Switzier than the real Swiss and had live goats in every room. (And Stanley Skuldugger was emerging as the top actor-imago of the middle hours of the night.) The popular drink for that middle part of the night was Glotzengubber, Eve Cheese and Rhine wine over pink ice. (And back in the city the leading Nyctalops were taking their midnight break at the Toppers' Club.)

Of course it was wonderful, as were all of Ildefonsa's—but she had never been really up on philosophy so she had scheduled only the special 35 minute honeymoon. She looked at the trend indicator to be sure. She found that her current husband had been obsoleted, and his opus was now referred to sneeringly as Mouser's Mouse. They went back to the city and were divorced in Small Claims Court.

The membership of the Toppers' Club varied. Success was the requisite of membership. Basil Bagelbaker might be accepted as a member, elevated to the presidency and expelled from it as a dirty pauper from three to six times a night. But only important persons could belong to it, or those enjoying brief moments of importance.

"I believe I will sleep during the Dawner period in the morning," Overcall said. "I may go up to this new place Koimopolis for an hour of it. They're said to be good. Where will you sleep, Basil?"

"Flop-house."

"I believe I will sleep an hour by the Midian Method," said Burnbanner. "They have a fine new clinic. And perhaps I'll sleep an hour by the Prasenka Process, and an hour by the Dormidio."

"Crackle has been sleeping an hour every period by the natural method," said Overcall.

"I did that for a half hour not long since," said Burnbanner. "I believe an hour is too long to give it. Have you tried the natural method, Basil?"

"Always. Natural method and a bottle of red-eye."

Stanley Skuldugger had become the most meteoric actor-imago for a week. Naturally he became very rich, and Ildefonsa Impala went to see him about 3 A.M.

"I had him first!" rang the mocking voice of Judy Skuldugger as she skipped through her divorce in Small Claims Court. And Ildefonsa and Stanley-boy went off honeymooning. It is always fun to finish up a period with an actor-imago who is the hottest property in the business. There is something so adolescent and boorish about them.

Besides, there was the publicity, and Ildefonsa liked that. The rumor-mills ground. Would it last ten minutes? Thirty? An hour? Would it be one of those rare Nyctalops marriages that lasted through the rest of the night and into the daylight off hours? Would it even last into the next night as some had been known to do?

Actually it lasted nearly 40 minutes, which was almost to the end of the period.

It had been a slow Tuesday night. A few hundred new products had run their course on the markets. There had been a score of dramatic hits, three minute and five minute capsule dramas, and several of the six minute long-play affairs. *Night Street Nine*—a solidly sordid offering—seemed to be in as the drama of the night unless there should be a late hit.

Hundred-storied buildings had been erected, occupied, obsoleted, and demolished again to make room for more contemporary structures. Only the mediocre would use a building that had been left over from the Day-Flies or the Dawners, or even the Nyctalops of the night before. The city was rebuilt pretty completely at least three times during an eight-hour period.

The Period drew near its end. Basil Bagelbaker, the richest man in the world, the reigning president of the Toppers' Club, was enjoying himself with his cronies. His fourth fortune of the night was a paper pyramid that had risen to incredible heights; but Basil laughed to himself as he savored the manipulation it was founded on.

Three ushers of the Toppers' Club came in with firm step.

"Get out of here, you dirty bum!" they told Basil savagely. They tore the tycoon's toga off him and then tossed him his seedy panhandler's rags with a three-man sneer.

"All gone?" Basil asked. "I gave it another five minutes."

"All gone," said a messenger from Money Market. "Nine billion gone in five minutes, and it really pulled some others down with it."

"Pitch the busted bum out!" howled Overcall and Burnbanner and the other cronies. "Wait, Basil," said Overcall. "Turn in the President's Crosier before we kick you downstairs. After all, you'll have it several times again tomorrow night."

The Period was over. The Nyctalops drifted off to sleep clinics or leisure-hour hide-outs to pass their ebb time. The Auroreans, the Dawners, took over the vital stuff.

Now you would see some action! Those Dawners really made fast decisions. You wouldn't catch them wasting a full minute setting up a business.

A sleepy panhandler met Ildefonsa Impala on the way.

"Preserve us this morning, Ildy," he said, "and will you marry me the coming night?"

"Likely I will, Basil," she told him. "Did you marry Judy during the night past?"

"I'm not sure. Could you let me have two dollars, Ildy?"

"Out of the question. I believe a Judy Bagelbaker was named one of the ten best-dressed women during the frou-frou fashion period about two o'clock. Why do you need two dollars?"

"A dollar for a bed and a dollar for red-eye. After all, I sent you two million out of my second."

"I keep my two sorts of accounts separate. Here's a dollar, Basil. Now be off! I can't be seen talking to a dirty panhandler."

"Thank you, Ildy. I'll get the red-eye and sleep in an alley. Preserve us this morning."

Bagelbaker shuffled off whistling Slow Tuesday Night.

And already the Dawners had set Wednesday morning to jumping.

Gadget Vs. Trend

The application of science to human problems and the accompanying invention of devices were at the heart of the vast changes in production that social scientists call industrialization. Burgeoning technology brought vast changes to the social contexts in which new devices were used. Sociologists tend to use the term technology to refer to material products of industrial enterprise and to the attitudes, values, and norms of use that grow up around the devices themselves. Although the functional purpose of the device itself is a major and conscious part of the inventor's effort, the uses to which the device is put and the values and norms surrounding its use are rarely totally understood when the device is initially completed. Many of the consequences following invention are unanticipated. Perhaps it is not the responsibility of the scientist (that is, *physical* scientist) who invents to be concerned with the uses to which a device is put, but sociologists (as *social* scientists) are concerned with what have been called "the unanticipated consequences of purposive social action," whether the action in question is the invention of a device or some nonmaterial policy or act. In "Gadget Vs. Trend," the "QuietWall" produced far-sweeping consequences vaguely anticipated by its inventor, but unanticipated by those who chose to introduce the device. In fact, Anvil's sociologist, Dr. R. Milton Schummer, is more concerned with condemning what he sees to be the contemporary human condition than with asking the sociological question: What are the consequences of this change and how might they be responded to?

The "quiet wall" device in Gadget Vs. Trend" was a development of material culture. The nonmaterial elements pertinent to the norms and values of its use were undeveloped, and in consequence the disruptions of the social order following its introduction were severe. This is a consequence of what William Ogburn called *culture lag*. Much of technological change is of this nature. The consequences of the development and widespread acceptance of the automobile were slow to be recognized and the effects of television and computer technology on the social order are still imperfectly understood. Medical science is developing mechanical substitutes for human organs and can keep a person "alive" after consciousness and many physiological functions have stopped. The medical ethics, moral values, and legal issues pertaining to the use of this technology reflect the lack of any developed consensus. Certainly, in each of these cases, the values and norms ordering their use developed more slowly than the perfection of the devices themselves. Whether sociologists choose to use Ogburn's terms or not, the social context within which technological change develops and the consequences of technology for social patterns are important interests within the "sociological perspective."

Gadget Vs. Trend

CHRISTOPHER ANVIL

Boston, Sept. 2, 1976. Dr. R. Milton Schummer, Professor of Sociology at Wellsford College, spoke out against "creeping conformism" to an audience of twelve hundred in Swarton Hall last night.

Professor Schummer charged that America, once the land of the free, is now "the abode of the stereotyped mass-man, shaped from infancy by the moron-molding influences of television, mass-circulation newspapers and magazines, and the pervasive influence of advertising manifest in all these media. The result is the mass-production American with interchangeable parts and built-in taped programme."

What this country needs, said Dr. Schummer, is "freedom to differ, freedom to be eccentric." But, he concluded, "the momentum is too great. The trend, like the tide, cannot be reversed by human efforts. In two hundred years, this nation has gone from individualism to conformism, from independence to interdependence, from federalism to fusionism, and the end is not yet. One shrinks at the thought of what the next one hundred years may bring."

Rutland, Vt., March 16, 1977. Dr. J. Paul Hughes, grandson of the late inventor, Everett Hughes, revealed today a device which his grandfather kept under wraps because of its "supposedly dangerous side-effects." Dubbed by Dr. Hughes a "privacy shield," the device works by the "exclusion of quasi-electrons." In the words of Dr. Hughes:

"My grandfather was an eccentric experimenter. Surprisingly often, though, his wild stabs would strike some form of pay dirt, in a commercial sense. In this present instance, we have a device unexplainable by any sound scientific theory, but which may be commercially quite useful. When properly set up, and connected to a suitable electrical outlet, the device effectively soundproofs material surfaces, such as walls, doors, floors, and the like, and thus may be quite helpful in present-day crowded living conditions."

Dr. Hughes explained that the device was supposed to operate by "the exclusion of 'quasi-electrons,' which my grandfather thought governed the transmission of sound through solid bodies, and performed various other esoteric functions. But we needn't take this too seriously."

New York, May 12, 1977. Formation of Hughes QuietWall Corporation was announced here today.

President of the new firm is J. Paul Hughes, grandson of the late inventor, Everett Hughes.

New York, Sept. 18, 1977. One of the hottest stocks on the market today is Hughes QuietWall. With demand booming, and the original president of the firm kicked upstairs to make room for the crack management expert, Myron L. Sams, the corporation has tapped a gold mine.

Said a company spokesman: "The biggest need in this country today is privacy. We live practically in each other's pockets, and if we can't do anything else, at least QuietWall can soundproof the pockets."

The QuietWall units, which retail for $289.95 for the basic room unit, are said to offer dealer, distributor, and manufacturer a generous profit. And no one can say that $289.95 is not a reasonable price to pay to keep out the noise of other people's TV, record players, quarrels and squalling babies.

Detroit, December 23, 1977. Santa left an early present for the auto industry here today.

A test driver trying out a car equipped with a Hughes Quiet-Wall unit went into a skid on the icy test track, rolled over three times, and got out shaken but unhurt. The car itself, a light supercompact, was found to be almost totally undamaged.

Tests with sledgehammers revealed the astonishing fact that with the unit turned on, the car would not dent, and the glass could not be broken. The charge filler cap could not be unscrewed. The hood could not be raised. And neither windows nor doors could be opened till the unit was snapped off. With the unit off, the car was perfectly ordinary.

This is the first known trial of a QuietWall unit in a motor vehicle.

Standard house and apartment installations use a specially designed basic unit to soundproof floor and walls, and small additional units to soundproof doors and windows. This installation tested today apparently lacked such refinements.

December 26, 1977. J. Paul Hughes, chairman of the board of directors of the QuietWall Corp., stated to reporters today that his firm has no intention to market the Hughes QuietWall unit for use in motor cars.

Hughes denied the Detroit report of a QuietWall-equipped test car that rolled without damage, calling it "impossible."

Hartford, January 8, 1978. Regardless of denials from the Quiet-Wall Corporation, nationwide experiments are being conducted into the use of the corporation's sound-deadening units as a safety device in cars. Numerous letters, telegrams, and phone calls are being received at the head offices of some of the nation's leading insurance companies here.

Hartford, January 9, 1978. Tests carried out by executives of the New Standard Insurance Group indicate that the original Detroit reports were perfectly accurate.

Cars equipped with the Quiet Wall units cannot be dented, shattered, scratched, or injured in any way by ordinary tools.

Austin J. Ramm, Executive Secretary of New Standard Group, stated to reporters:

"It's the damndest thing I ever saw.

"We've had so many communications, from people all over the country who claim to have connected QuietWall units to their cars, that we decided to try it out ourselves.

"We tried rocks, hammers, and so forth, on the test vehicle. When these didn't have any effect, I tried a quarter-inch electric drill and Steve Willoughby—he's our president—took a crack at the center of the windshield with a railroad pickaxe. The pickaxe bounced. My drill just slid around over the surface and wouldn't bite in.

"We have quite a few other things we want to try.

"But we've seen enough to know there definitely is truth in these reports."

New York, January 10, 1978. Myron L. Sams, president of the Hughes QuietWall Corporation, announced today that a special automotive attachment is being put on sale throughout the country. Mr. Sams warns that improper installation may, among other things, seize up all or part of the operating machinery of the car. He urges that company representatives be allowed to carry out the installation.

❋   ❋   ❋

Dallas, January 12, 1978. In a chase lasting an hour, a gang of bank robbers got away this afternoon with $869,000 in cash and negotiable securities.

Despite a hail of bullets, the escape car was not damaged. An attempt to halt it at a roadblock failed, as the car crashed through without injury.

There is speculation here that the car was equipped with one of the Hughes QuietWall units that went on sale a few days ago.

Las Vegas, January 19, 1978. A gang of eight to ten criminals held up the Silver Dollar Club tonight, escaping with over a quarter of a million dollars.

It was one of the most bizarre robberies in the city's history.

The criminals entered the club in golf carts fitted with light aluminum- and transparent-plastic covers, and opened a gun battle with club employees. A short fight disclosed that it was impossible to even dent the light shielding on the golf carts. Using the club's patrons and employees as hostages, the gunmen received the cash they demanded, rolled across the sidewalk and up a ramp into the rear of a waiting truck, which drove out of town, smashing through a hastily erected roadblock.

As police gave chase, the truck proved impossible to damage. In a violent exchange of gunfire, no one was injured, as the police cars were equipped with newly installed QuietWall units, and it was evident that the truck was also so equipped.

Well outside of town, the truck reached a second roadblock. The robbers attempted to smash through the seemingly flimsy barrier, but were brought to a sudden stop when the roadblock, fitted with a QuietWall unit, failed to give way.

The truck, and the golf carts within, were found to be undamaged. The bandits are now undergoing treatment for concussion and severe whiplash injuries.

The $250,000.00 has been returned to the Silver Dollar Club, and Las Vegas is comparatively quiet once more.

New York, January 23, 1978. In a hastily called news conference, J. Paul Hughes, chairman of the board of Hughes QuietWall Corporation, announced that he is calling upon the Federal Government to step in and suspend the activities of the corporation.

Pointing out that he has tried without success to suspend the company's operations on his own authority, Dr. Hughes stated that as a scientist he must warn the public against a dangerous technological development, "the menacing potentialities of which I have only recently come to appreciate."

No response has as yet been received from Washington.

New York, January 24, 1978. President Myron L. Sams today acknowledged the truth of reports that a bitter internal struggle is being waged for control of the Hughes QuietWall Corporation.

Spring Corners, Iowa, January 26, 1978. Oscar B. Nelde, a farmer on the outskirts of town, has erected a barricade that has backed up traffic on the new Cross-State Highway for twenty miles in both directions.

Mr. Nelde recently lost a suit for additional damages when the highway cut his farm into two unequal parts, the smaller one containing his house and farm buildings, the larger part containing his fields.

The barricade is made of oil drums, saw horses, and barbed wire. The oil drums and saw horses cannot be moved, and act as if welded to the frozen earth. The barbed wire is weirdly stiff and immovable. The barricade is set up in a double row of these immovable obstacles, spaced to form a twenty-foot-wide lane connecting the two separated parts of Mr. Nelde's farm.

Mr. Nelde's manure spreader was seen crossing the road early today.

Heavy road machinery has failed to budge the obstacles. The experts are stumped. However, the local QuietWall dealer recalls selling Mr. Nelde a quantity of small units recently and adds, "but no more than a lot of other farmers have been buying lately."

It may be worth mentioning that Mr. Nelde's claim is one of many that have been advanced locally.

New York, January 27, 1978. The Hughes QuietWall Corporation was today reorganized as QuietWall, Incorporated, with Myron L. Sams holding the positions of president and chairman of the board of directors. J. Paul Hughes, grandson of Everett Hughes, continues as a director.

Spring Corners, Iowa, January 28, 1978. Traffic is flowing once again on the Cross-State Highway.

This morning a U.S. Army truck-mounted earth auger moved up the highway and drilled a number of holes six feet in diameter, enabling large chunks of earth to be carefully loosened and both sections of the barricade to be lifted out as units. The wire, oil drums, saw horses, and big chunks of earth, which remained rigid when lifted out, are being removed to the U.S. Army Research and Development Laboratories for study. No QuietWall units have been found, and it is assumed that they are imbedded, along with their power source, inside the masses of earth.

The sheriff, the police chief of Spring Corners, and state and federal law enforcement agents are attempting to arrest Oscar B. Nelde, owner of the farm adjacent to the highway.

This has proved impossible, as Mr. Nelde's house and buildings are equipped with a number of QuietWall units controlled from within.

Boston, February 1, 1978. Dr. R. Milton Schummer, Professor of Sociology at Wellsford College, and a severe critic of "creeping conformism," said tonight, when questioned by reporters, that some of the effects of the QuietWall units constitute a hopeful sign in the long struggle of the individual against the State and against the forces of conformity. However, Dr. Schummer does not believe that "a mere technological gadget can affect these great movements of sociological trends."

Spring Corners, Iowa, February 2, 1978. A barbed-wire fence four feet high, fastened to crisscrossed railroad rails, now blocks the Cross-State Highway near the farm home of Leroy Weaver, a farmer whose property was cut in half by the highway, and who has often stated that he has received inadequate compensation.

It has proved impossible for highway equipment on the scene to budge either wire or rails.

Mr. Weaver cannot be reached for comment, as his house and buildings are equipped with QuietWall units, and neither the sheriff nor federal officials have been able to effect entry on to the premises.

Washington, D.C., February 3, 1978. The Bureau of Standards reports that tests on QuietWall units show them to be essentially "stasis devices." That is to say, they prevent change in whatever material surface they are applied to. Thus, sound does not pass, because the protected material is practically noncompressible, and is not affected by the alternate waves of compression and rarefaction in the adjacent medium.

Many potential applications are suggested by Bureau of Standards spokesmen who report, for instance, that thin slices of apples and pears placed directly inside the surface field of the QuietWall device were found totally unchanged when the field was switched off, after test periods of more than three weeks.

New York, February 3, 1978. Myron L. Sams, president of Quiet-Wall, Incorporated, reports record sales, rising day by day to new peaks. QuietWall, Inc., is now operating factories in seven states, Great Britain, the Netherlands, and West Germany.

Spring Corners, Iowa, February 4, 1978. A U.S. Army truck-mounted earth auger has again removed a fence across the Cross-State Highway here. But the giant auger itself has now been immobilized, apparently by one or more concealed stasis (Quiet-Wall) devices.

As the earth auger weighs upwards of thirty tons, and all the wheels of truck and trailer appear to be locked, moving it presents no small problem.

Los Angeles, February 5, 1978. Police here report the capture of a den of dope fiends and unsavory characters of all descriptions, after a forty-hour struggle.

The hideout, known as the "Smoky Needle Club," was equipped with sixteen stasis devices manufactured by QuietWall, Inc., and had an auxiliary electrical supply line run in through a drain pipe from the building next door. Only when the electrical current to the entire neighborhood was cut off were the police able to force their way in.

New York, February 5, 1978. Myron L. Sams, president of Quiet-Wall, Inc., announced today a general price cut, due to improved design and volume production economies, on all QuietWall products.

In future, basic QuietWall room units will sell for $229.95 instead of $289.95. Special small stasis units, suitable for firming fence posts, reinforcing walls, and providing barred-door household security, will retail for as low as $19.95. It is rumored that this price, with improved production methods, still provides an ample profit for all concerned, so that prices may be cut in some areas during special sales events.

Spring Corners, Iowa, February 6, 1978. A flying crane today lifted the immobilized earth auger from the eastbound lanes of Cross-State Highway.

A total of fourteen small stasis units have thus far been removed from the auger, its truck and trailer, following its removal from the highway by air. Difficulties were compounded by the fact that each stasis unit apparently "freezes" the preceding units applied within its range. The de-stasis experts must not only locate the units. They must remove them in the right order, and some are very cleverly hidden.

Seaton Bridge, Iowa, February 9, 1978. The Cross-State Highway has again been blocked, this time by a wall of cow manure eighty-three feet long, four feet wide at the base, and two and a half feet high, apparently stabilized by imbedded stasis units and as hard as cement. National Guard units are now patrolling the Seaton Bridge section of road on either side of the block.

New York, February 10, 1978. Representatives of QuietWall, Inc., report that study of stasis devices removed from the auger at Spring Center, Iowa, reveals that they are "not devices of QW manufacture, but crude, cheap bootleg imitations. Nevertheless, they work."

Spring Center, Iowa, February 12, 1978. The Cross-State Highway, already cut at Seaton Bridge, is now blocked in three places by walls of snow piled up during last night's storm by farmers' bulldozers, and stabilized by stasis devices. Newsmen who visited the scene report that the huge mounds look like snow, but feel like concrete. Picks and shovels do not dent them, and flame throwers fail to melt them.

New York, February 15, 1978. Dr. J. Paul Hughes, a director of QuietWall, Inc., tonight reiterated his plea for a government ban on stasis devices. He recalled the warning of his inventor grandfather Everett Hughes, and stated that he intends to spend the rest of his life "trying to undo the damage the device has caused."

New York, February 16, 1978. Myron L. Sams, president of QuietWall, Inc., announced today that a fruit fly had been kept in stasis for twenty-one days without suffering visible harm. QW's research scientists, he said, are now working with the problem of keeping small animals in stasis. If successful, Sams said, the experiment may open the door to "one-way timetravel," and enable persons suffering from serious diseases to wait, free from pain, until such time as a satisfactory cure has been found.

Bonn, February 17, 1978. Savage East German accusations against the West today buttressed the rumors that "stasis-unit enclaves" are springing up like toadstools throughout East Germany.

Similar reports are coming in from Hungary, while Poland reports a number of "stasis-frozen" Soviet tanks.

Havana, February 18, 1978. In a frenzied harangue tonight, "Che" Garcia, First Secretary of the Cuban Communist Party, announced that the government is erecting "stasis walls" all around the island, and that "stasis blockhouses" now being built will resist "even the Yankees' worst hydrogen weapons." In a torrent of vitriolic abuse, however, Mr. Garcia threatened that "any further roadblocks and centers of degenerate individualism that spring up will be eradicated from the face of the soil of the motherland by blood, iron, sweat, and the forces of monolithic socialism."

There have been rumors for some time of dissatisfaction with the present regime.

Mr. Garcia charged that the C.I.A. had flagrantly invaded Cuban air space by dropping "millions of little vicious stasis units, complete with battery packs of fantastic power," all over the island, from planes which could not be shot down because they were protected by "still more of these filthy sabotage devices."

Des Moines, February 21, 1978. The Iowa state government following the unsuccessful siege of four farm homes near the Cross-State Highway today announced that it is opening new hearings on landowners' compensation for land taken for highway-construction purposes.

The governor appealed to owners of property adjoining the highway to be patient, bring their complaints to the capital, and meanwhile open the highway to traffic.

Staunton, Vt., February 23, 1978. Hiram Smith, a retired high school science teacher whose family has lived on the same farm since before the time of the Revolution, was ordered last fall to leave his family home.

A dam is to be built nearby, and Mr. Smith's home will be among those inundated.

At the time of the order, Mr. Smith, who lives on the farm with his fourteen-year-old grandson, stated that he would not leave "until carried out dead or helpless."

This morning, the sheriff tried to carry out the eviction order, and was stopped by a warning shot fired from the Smith house. The warning shot was followed by the flight of a small, battery-powered model plane, apparently radio-controlled, which alighted about two thousand yards from the Smith home, near an old apple orchard.

Mr. Smith called to the sheriff to get out of his car and lie down, if the car was not stasis-equipped, and in any case to look away from the apple orchard.

There was a brilliant flash, a shock, and a roar which the sheriff likened to the explosion of "a hundred tons of TNT." When he looked at the orchard, it was obscured by a pink glow and boiling clouds, apparently of steam from vaporized snow.

Mr. Smith called out to the sheriff to get off the property, or the next "wink bomb" would be aimed at him.

No one has been out to the Smith property since the sheriff's departure.

New York, February 25, 1978. Mr. Myron L. Sams, president of QuietWall, Inc., announced today that "there is definitely no connection between the Staunton explosion and the QW Corp. stasis unit. The stasis unit is a strictly defensive device and cannot be used for offensive purposes."

New York, February 25, 1978. Dr. J. Paul Hughes tonight asserted that the "wink bomb" exploded at Staunton yesterday, and now known to have left a radioactive crater, "probably incorporated a stasis unit." The unit was probably "connected to a light metallic container holding a small quantity of radioactive material. It need not necessarily be the radioactive material we are accustomed to think of as suitable for fission bombs. It need not be the usual amount of such material. When the stasis unit was activated by a radio signal or timing device, high-energy particles thrown off by the radioactive material would be unable to pass out through the container, now in stasis, and equivalent to a very hard, dense, impenetrable, nearly ideal boundary surface. The high-energy particles would bounce back into the interior, bombarding the radioactive material. As the population of high-energy particles within the enclosing stasis field builds up, the radioactive material, regardless of its quantity, reaches the critical point. Precisely what will happen depends on the radioactive material used, the size of the sample, and the length of the 'wink'—that is, the length of time the stasis field is left on."

Dr. Hughes added that "this is a definite, new, destructive use of the stasis field, which Mr. Myron Sams assures us is perfectly harmless."

Montpelier, Vt., February 26, 1978. The governor today announced temporary suspension of the Staunton Dam Project, while an investigation is carried out into numerous landowners' complaints.

Moscow, February 28, 1978. A "certain number" of "isolated cells" of "stasis-controlled character" are admitted to have sprung up within the Soviet Union. Those that are out of the way are said to be left alone, on the theory that the people have to come out sometime. Those in important localities are being reduced by the Red Army, using tear gas, sick gas, toothache gas, flashing searchlights, "war of nerves" tactics, and, in some cases, digging out the "cell" and carrying it off wholesale. It is widely accepted that there is nowhere near the amount of trouble here as in the satellite countries, where the problem is mounting to huge proportions.

Spring Corners, Iowa, May 16, 1978. The extensive Cross-State Highway claims having been settled all around, traffic is once again flowing along the highway. A new and surprising feature is the sight of farm machinery disappearing into tunnels constructed under the road to allow the farmers to pass from one side to the other.

Staunton, Vt., July 4, 1978. There was a big celebration here today as the governor and a committee of legislators announced that the big Staunton Dam Project has been abandoned, and a number of smaller dams will be built according to an alternative plan put forth earlier.

Bonn, August 16, 1978. Reports reaching officials here indicate that the East German government, the Hungarian government, and also to a considerable extent the Polish government, are having increasing difficulties as more and more of the "stasis-unit enclaves" join up, leaving the governments on the outside looking in. Where this will end is hard to guess.

Washington, September 30, 1978. The Treasury Department sent out a special "task force" of about one hundred and eighty men this morning. Their job is to crack open the mushrooming Anti-Tax League, whose membership is now said to number about one million enthusiastic businessmen. League members often give Treasury agents an exceedingly rough time, using record books and files frozen shut with stasis units, office buildings stasis-locked against summons-servers, stasis-equipped cars which come out of stasis-equipped garages connected with stasis-locked office buildings, to drive to stasis-equipped homes where it is physically impossible for summons-servers to enter the grounds.

Princeton, N.J., October 5, 1978. A conference of leading scientists, which gathered here today to exchange views on the nature of the stasis unit, is reported in violent disagreement. One cause of the disagreement is the reported "selective action" of the stasis unit, which permits ordinary light to pass through transparent bodies, but blocks the passage of certain other electromagnetic radiations.
Wild disorders broke out this afternoon during a lecture by Dr. J. Paul Hughes, on the "Quasi-Electron Theory of Wave Propa-

gation." The lecture was accompanied by demonstration of the original Everett Hughes device, powered by an old-fashioned generator driven by the inventor's original steam engine. As the engine gathered speed, Dr. Hughes was able to demonstrate the presence of a nine-inch sphere of completely reflective material in the supposedly empty focus of the apparatus. This sphere, Dr. Hughes asserted, was the surface of a space totally evacuated of quasi-electrons, which he identified as "units of time."

It was at this point that the disturbance broke out.

Despite the disorder, Dr. Hughes went on to explain the limiting value of the velocity of light in terms of the quasi-electron theory, but was interrupted when the vibration of the steam engine began to shake down the ceiling.

There is a rumor here that the conference may recess at once without issuing a report.

Washington, D.C., August 16, 1979. Usually reliable sources report that the United States has developed a "missile screen" capable of destroying enemy missiles in flight, and theoretically capable of creating a wall around the nation through which no enemy projectile of any type could pass. This device is said to be based on the original Everett Hughes stasis unit, which creates a perfectly rigid barrier of variable size and shape, which can be projected very rapidly by turning on an electric current.

Other military uses for stasis devices include protection of missile sites, storage of food and munitions, impenetrizing of armor plate, portable "turtle-shields" for infantry, and quick-conversion units designed to turn any ordinary house or shed into a bombardment-proof strongpoint.

Veteran observers of the military scene say that the stasis unit completely reverses the advantage until recently held by offensive, as opposed to defensive weapons. This traditionally alternating advantage, supposed to have passed permanently with the development of nuclear explosives, has now made one more pendulum swing. Now, in place of the "absolute weapon," we have the "absolute defence." Properly set up, hydrogen explosions do not dent it.

But if the nation is not to disintegrate within as it becomes impregnable without, officials say we must find some effective way to deal with stasis-protected cults, gangsters, anti-tax enthusiasts, seceding rural districts, space-grabbers, and proprietors of dens. Latest problem is the traveling roadblock, set up by chiselers who select a busy highway, collect "toll" from motorists who must pay or end up in a traffic jam, then move on quickly before police have time to react, and stop again in some new location to do the same thing all over. There must be an answer to all these things, but the answer has yet to be found.

Boston, September 2, 1979. Dr. R. Milton Schummer, Professor of Sociology at Wellsford College, spoke out against "galloping individualism" to an audience of six hundred in Swarton Hall last night.

Professor Schummer charged that America, once the land of cooperative endeavor, is now "a seething hotbed of rampant individualists, protesters, quick-rich artists, and minute-men of all kinds, each over-reacting violently from a former condition which may have seemed like excessive conformism at the time, but now in the perspective of events appears as a desirable cohesiveness and unity of direction. The result today is the fractionating American with synthetic rough edges and built-in bellicose sectionalism."

What this country needs, said Dr. Schummer, is "coordination of aims, unity of purpose, and restraint of difference." But, he concluded, "the reaction is too violent. The trend, like the tide, cannot be reversed by human efforts. In three years, this nation has gone from cohesion to fractionation, from interdependence to chaos, from federalism to splinterism, and the end is not yet. One shrinks at the thought of what the next hundred years may bring."

Collective
Behavior

Nobody Lives on Burton Street

Riotous mob behavior, although found in many societies and in most times, has been vividly brought to the attention of Americans in the late 1960s as dissent and protest broke the boundaries of nonviolence and produced destruction of lives and property by both rioters and those who sought to control violent disturbances.

There are sociological and psychological approaches to explaining contemporary riots. Sociologists, interested in the conditions of social structure that produced violent dissent, have focused their attention on the poverty of the lower class and the life-chances of discriminated against minorities. They discovered that it is not the absolute conditions of material deprivation that are conducive to violent protest, since many living at minimal survival levels fatalistically accept their "lot in life." Instead, those in a society who define themselves as denied the "good things" in life while others possess these things are often participants in violent protest. This protest often comes not when there is no hope for things to get better, but when improvement is thought to be possible or has been achieved by some while unfairly denied to others. When rising expectations are thwarted, a particularly volatile situation results, and riots are often a consequence. Sociologists refer to this situation, which is common today here and abroad in the newly modernizing nations, as "the Revolution of Rising Expectations."

A psychologist looking at riotous dissent might see it as a classic example of the "frustration-aggression" hypothesis. The frustrated individual responds aggressively—in this case toward objects in the environment rather than turning that aggression destructively inward toward himself. In this view, mob behavior could be the acting out of collective aggressions, and one structural remedy for the problem generating the behavior would be to provide outlets for that aggression that are socially acceptable or not destructive to the social order. Of course, it would seem advisable to some to deal with the psychodynamics of the frustration through therapy or by coercive measures by the state in the interest of order and stability. The last option raises a vital question: How much can the right of individual dissent be denied in the interest of social order and stability? And at what price to both the citizen and society?

Greg Benford's "Nobody Lives on Burton Street" reflects the psychological view of violent dissent described here more than the sociological view. Burton Street permits a socially managed riot that controls without addressing itself to social injustice and inequity generating dissent. This story also raises the specter of "psychological thought control" by government. As the central character says, "the psychers are public health! . . . You don't have to go around to some expensive guy who'll have you lay on a couch and talk to him. You can get better stuff right from the government. It's free!"

Nobody Lives on Burton Street

GREG BENFORD

I was standing by one of our temporary command posts, picking my teeth after breakfast and talking to Joe Murphy when the first part of the Domestic Disturbance hit us.

Spring had lost its bloom a month back and it was summer now —hot, sticky, the kind of weather that leaves you with a half-moon of sweat around your armpits before you've had time to finish your morning coffee. A summer like that is always more trouble. This one looked like the worst I'd seen since I got on the Force.

We knew they were in the area, working toward us. Our communications link had been humming for the last half hour, getting fixes on their direction and asking the computers for advice on how to handle them when they got here.

I looked down. At the end of the street was a lot of semi-permanent shops and the mailbox. The mailbox bothers me—it shouldn't be there.

From the other end of Burton Street I could hear the random dull bass of the mob.

So while we were getting ready Joe was moaning about the payments on the Snocar he'd been suckered into. I was listening with one ear to him and the other to the crowd noises.

"And it's not just that," Joe said. "It's the neighborhood and the school and everybody around me."

"Everybody's wrong but Murphy, huh?" I said, and grinned.

"Hell no, you know me better than that. It's just that nobody's *going* anyplace. Sure, we've all got jobs, but they're most of them just make-work stuff the unions have gotten away with."

"To get a real job you gotta have training," I said, but I wasn't chuffing him up. I like my job, and it's better than most, but we weren't gonna kid each other that it was some big technical deal. Joe and I are just regular guys.

"What're you griping about this now for, anyway?" I said. "You didn't used to be bothered by anything."

Joe shrugged. "I dunno. Wife's been getting after me to move out of the place we're in and make more money. Gets into fights with the neighbors." He looked a little sheepish about it.

"More money? Hell, y'got everything you need, we all do. Lot of people worse off than you. Look at all those lousy Africans, living on nothing."

I was going to say more, maybe rib him about how he's married and I'm not, but then I stopped. Like I said, all this time I was half-listening to the crowd. I can always tell when a bunch has changed its direction like a pack of wolves off on a chase, and when that funny quiet came and lasted about five seconds I knew they were heading our way.

"Scott!" I yelled at our communications man. "Close it down. Get a final printout."

Murphy broke off telling me about his troubles and listened to the crowd for a minute, like he hadn't heard them before, and then took off on a trot to the AnCops we had stashed in the truck below. They were all warmed up and ready to go, but Joe likes to make a final check and maybe have a chance to read in any new instructions Scott gets at the last minute.

I threw away the toothpick and had a last look at my constant-volume joints, to be sure the bulletproof plastiform was matching properly and wouldn't let anything through. Scott came doubletiming over with the diagnostics from HQ. The computer compilation was neat and confusing, like it always is. I could make out the rough indices they'd picked up on the crowd heading our way. The best guess—and that's all you ever get, friends, is a guess—was a lot of Psych Disorders and Race Prejudice. There was a fairly high number of Unemployeds, too. We're getting more and more Unemployeds in the city now, and they're hard for the Force to deal with. Usually mad enough to spit. Smash up everything.

I penciled an ok in the margin and tossed it Scott's way. I'd taken too long reading it; I could hear individual shouts now and the tinkling of glass. I flipped the visor down from my helmet and turned on my external audio. It was going to get hot as hell in there, but I'm not chump enough to drag around an air conditioning unit on top of the rest of my stuff.

I took a look at the street just as a gang of about a hundred people came around the corner two blocks down, spreading out like a dirty gray wave. I ducked over to the edge of the building and waved to Murphy to start off with three AnCops. I had to hold up three fingers for him to see because the noise was already getting high. I looked at my watch. Hell, it wasn't nine A.M. yet.

Scott went down the stairs we'd tracted up the side of the building. I was right behind him. It wasn't a good location for observation now; you made too good a target up there. We picked up Murphy, who was carrying our control boards. All three of us angled down the alley and dropped down behind a short fence to have a look at the street.

Most of them were still screaming at the top of their lungs like they'd never run out of air, waving whatever they had handy and gradually breaking up into smaller units. The faster ones had made it to the first few buildings.

A tall Negro came trotting toward us, moving like he had all the time in the world. He stopped in front of a wooden barber shop, tossed something quickly through the front window and *whump!* Flames licked out at the upper edges of the window, spreading fast.

An older man picked up some rocks and began methodically pitching them through the smaller windows in the shops next door. A housewife clumped by awkwardly in high heels, looking like she was out on a shopping trip except for the hammer she swung like a pocket book. She dodged into the barbershop for a second, didn't find anything and came out. The Negro grinned and pointed at the barber pole on the sidewalk, still revolving, and she caught it in the side with a swipe that threw shattered glass for ten yards.

I turned and looked at Murphy. "All ready?"

He nodded. "Just give the word."

The travel agency next door to the barber shop was concrete-based, so they couldn't burn that. Five men were lunging at the door and on the third try they knocked it in. A moment later a big travel poster sailed out the front window, followed by a chair leg. They were probably doing as much as they could, but without tools they couldn't take much of the furniture apart.

"Okay," I said. "Let's have the first AnCops."

The thick acrid smell from the smoke was drifting down Burton Street to us, but my air filters would take care of most of it. They don't do much about human sweat, though, and I was going to be inside the rest of the day.

Our first prowl car rounded the next corner, going too fast. I looked over at Murphy, who was controlling the car, but he was too busy trying to miss the people who were standing around in the street. Must have gotten a little over-anxious on that one. Something was bothering his work.

I thought sure the car was going to take a tumble and mess us up, but the wheels caught and it righted itself long enough for the driver to stop a skid. The screech turned the heads of almost everybody in the crowd and they'd started to move in on it almost before the car stopped laying down rubber and came to a full stop. Murphy punched in another instruction and the AnCop next to the driver started firing at a guy on the sidewalk who was trying to light a Molotov cocktail. The AnCop was using something that sounded like a repeating shotgun. The guy looked at him a second before scurrying off into a hardware store.

By this time the car was getting everything—bricks, broken pieces of furniture, merchandise from the stores. Something heavy shattered the windshield and the driver ducked back too late to avoid getting his left hand smashed with a bottle. A figure appeared on the top of the hardware shop—it looked like the guy from the sidewalk—and took a long windup before throwing something into the street.

There was a tinkling of glass and a red circle of flame slid across the pavement where it hit just in front of the car, sending smoke curling up over the hood and obscuring the inside. Murphy was going to have to play it by feel now; you couldn't see a thing in the car.

A teenager with a stubby rifle stepped out of a doorway, crouched down low like in a Western. He fired twice, very accurately and very fast, at the window of the car. A patrolman was halfway out the door when it hit him full in the face, sprawling the body back over the roof and then pitching it forward into the street.

A red blotch formed around his head, grew rapidly and ran into the gutter. There was ragged cheering and the teenager ran over to the body, tore off its badge and backed away. "Souvenir!" he called out, and a few of the others laughed.

I looked at Murphy again and he looked at me and I gave him the nod for the firemen, switching control over to my board. Scott was busy talking into his recorder, taking notes for the writeup later. When Murphy nudged him he stopped and punched in the link for radio control to the firefighting units.

By this time most of Burton Street was on fire. Everything you saw had a kind of orange look to it. The crowd was moving toward us once they'd lost interest in the cops, but we'd planned it that way. The firemen came running out in that jerky way they have, just a little in front of us. They were carrying just a regular hose this time because it was a medium-sized group and we couldn't use up a fire engine and all the extras. But they were wearing the usual red uniforms. From a distance you can't tell them from the real thing.

Their subroutine tapes were fouled up again. Instead of heading for the barber shop or any of the other stuff that was burning, like I'd programmed, they turned the hose on a stationery store that nobody had touched yet. There were three of them, holding onto that hose and getting it set up. The crowd had backed off a minute to see what was going on.

When the water came through it knocked in the front window of the store, making the firemen look like real chumps. I could hear the water running around inside, pushing over things and flooding out the building. The crowd laughed, what there was of it—I noticed some of them had moved off in the other direction, over into somebody else's area.

In a minute or so the laughing stopped, though. One guy who looked like he had been born mad grabbed an ax from somewhere and took a swing at the hose. He didn't get it the first time but people were sticking around to see what would happen and I guess he felt some kind of obligation to go through with it. Even under pressure, a thick hose isn't easy to cut into. He kept at it and on the fourth try a seam split—looked like a bad repair job to me—and a stream of water gushed out and almost hit this guy in the face.

The crowd laughed at that too, because he backed off real quick then, scared for a little bit. A face full of high-velocity water is no joke, not at that pressure.

The fireman who was holding the hose just a little down from there hadn't paid any attention to this because he wasn't programmed to, so when this guy thought about it he just stepped over and chopped the fireman across the back with the ax.

It was getting hot. I didn't feel like overriding the stock program, so it wasn't long before all the firemen were out of commission, just about the same way. A little old lady—probably with a welfare gripe—borrowed the ax for a minute to separate all of a fireman's arms and legs from the trunk. Looking satisfied, she waddled away after the rest of the mob.

I stood up, lifted my faceplate and looked at them as they milled back down the street. I took out my grenade launcher and got off a tear gas cartridge on low charge, to hurry them along. The wind was going crosswise so the gas got carried off to the side and down the alleys. Good; wouldn't have complaints from somebody who got caught in it too long.

Scott was busy sending orders for the afternoon shift to get more replacement firemen and cops, but we wouldn't have any trouble getting them in time. There hadn't been much damage, when you think how much they could've done.

"Okay for the reclaim crew?" Murphy said.

"Sure. This bunch won't be back. They look tired out already."

They were moving toward Horton's area, three blocks over.

A truck pulled out of the alley and two guys in coveralls jumped out and began picking up the androids, dousing fires as they went. In an hour they'd have everything back in place, even the prefab barber shop.

"Hellava note," Murphy said.

"Huh?"

"All this stuff." He waved a hand down Burton Street. "Seems like a waste to build all this just so these jerks can tear it down again."

"Waste?" I said. "It's the best investment you ever saw. How many people were in the last bunch—two hundred? Every one of them is going to sit around for weeks bragging about how he got him a cop or burned a building."

"Okay, okay. If it does any good, I guess it's cheap at the price."

"If, hell! You know it is. If it wasn't they wouldn't be here. You got to be cleared by a psycher before you even get in. The computer works out just what you'll need, just the kind of action that'll work off the aggressions you've got. Then shoots it to us in the profile from HQ before we start. It's foolproof."

"I dunno. You know what the Consies say—the psychers and the probes and drugs are an in—"

"Invasion of privacy?"

"Yeah," Murphy said sullenly.

"Privacy? Man, the psychers are public health! It's part of the welfare! You don't have to go around to some expensive guy who'll have you lay on a couch and talk to him. You can get better stuff right from the government. It's free!"

Murphy looked at me kind of funny. "Sure. Have to go in for a checkup sometime soon. Maybe that's what I need."

I frowned just the right amount. "Well, I dunno, Joe. Man lets his troubles get him down every once in a while, doesn't mean he needs professional help. Don't let it bother you. Forget it."

Joe was okay, but even a guy like me who's never been married could tell he wasn't thinking up this stuff himself. His woman was pushing him. Not satisfied with what she had.

Now, *that* was wrong. Guy like Joe doesn't have anywhere to go. Doesn't know computers, automation. Can't get a career rating in the Army. So the pressure was backing up on him.

Supers like me are supposed to check out their people and leave it at that, and I go by the book like everybody else. But Joe wasn't the problem.

I made a mental note to have a pyscher look at his wife.

"Okay," he said, taking off his helmet. "I got to go set up the

AnCops for the next one."

I watched him walk off down the alley. He was a good man. Hate to lose him.

I started back toward our permanent operations center to check in. After a minute I decided maybe I'd better put Joe's name in too just in case. Didn't want anybody blowing up on me.

He'd be happier, work better. I've sure felt a lot better since I had it. It's a good job I got, working in public affairs like this, keeping people straight with themselves.

I went around the corner at the end of the street, thinking about getting something to drink, and noticed the mailbox. I check on it every time because it sure looks like a mistake.

Everything's supposed to be pretty realistic on Burton Street, but putting in a mailbox seems like a goofy idea.

Who's going to try to burn up a box like that, made out of cast iron and bolted down? A guy couldn't take out any aggressions on it.

And it sure can't be for real use. Not on Burton Street.

Nobody lives around there.

The Shaker Revival

There have been many religious social movements in human history. Some have been revolutionary in design or impact, such as Calvinism, which forms the basis of the Protestant Ethic. Others have involved the members' attempts to establish their own beliefs, values, and life-style without militant challenge to the values of the social order of the society in which the movement has developed. Many religious movements have tried to abide by ascetic values that deny the worldly pleasures of secular society. Finally, although reform or revolutionary movements are commonly thought to be the actions of poverty-stricken, lower-class persons, these and other types of social movement can be based in the middle class.

Over the last century sociologists and other social thinkers foresaw that developments in technology and the rise of the industrial nation-state would challenge and change traditional patterns. Modern society is in a state of diversity and change, and social movements are common. From gay liberation to women's liberation, from John Birchers and the fundamentalist right wing to the hippies, yippies, and radical left, contemporary society is characterized by social movements that reflect, among others, political, religious, age, sex, and social class divisions.

In modern society, many who feel alienated and estranged from "impersonal" social structures feel unable to cope with the conditions of their lives as individuals. Believing that social ills and inequities can be overcome through joint effort in a cause with those who share their values and beliefs, many join in collective action.

The Shakers in Gerald Jonas's story are an ascetic religious group, made up of white middle-class youths who have rejected what they feel to be the overabundance and overindulgence of late twentieth-century society. The Shakers attempt to segregate themselves socially in order to establish values and a way of life quite in opposition to those around them. This story reflects the social context within which a social movement develops and is vividly contemporary.

History is not simple cyclical repetition of patterns previously experienced, but neither is history an unrelated sequence of isolated and unique events. Looking at youth movements in the United States in the 1960s, few would deny that many young adults rejected the Puritan values of the Protestant Ethic common among generations preceding their own. And yet, few recognized that some of this generation of young adults and more of the generation becoming young adults in the 1970s would *reject* this *rejection* and its secular permissiveness and would reassert sexual and social puritanism. That many unorganized religious sects of today's young have made this attempt is recognized today. What of the future?

The Shaker Revival

GERALD JONAS

To: Arthur Stock, Executive Editor, *Ideas Illustrated*, New York City, 14632008447
FROM: Raymond Senter, c/o Hudson Junction Rotel, Hudson Junction, N.Y. 28997601910
ENCLOSED: Tentative Lead for "The Shaker Revival." Pix, tapes upcoming.
JERUSALEM WEST, N.Y., Thursday, June 28, 1995—The work of Salvation goes forward in this green and pleasant Hudson Valley hamlet to the high-pitched accompaniment of turbo-car exhausts and the amplified beat of the "world's loudest jag-rock band." Where worm-eaten apples fell untended in abandoned orchards less than a decade ago a new religious sect has burst into full bloom. In their fantastic four-year history the so-called New Shakers—or United Society of Believers (Revived), to give them their official title—have provoked the hottest controversy in Christendom since Martin Luther nailed his ninety-five theses to the door of All Saints Church in Wittenberg, Germany, on October Thirty-one, Fifteen-seventeen. Boasting a membership of more than a hundred thousand today, the New Shakers have been processing applications at the rate of nine hundred a week. Although a handful of these "recruits" are in their early and middle twenties—and last month a New Jersey man was accepted into the Shaker Family at Wildwood at the ripe old age of thirty-two—the average New Shaker has not yet reached his eighteenth birthday.

Richard F, one of the members of the "First Octave" who have been honored with "uncontaminated" Shaker surnames, explains it this way: "We've got nothing against feebies. They have a piece of the Gift inside just like anyone else. But it's hard for them to travel with the Family. Jag-rock hurts their ears, and they can't sync with the Four Noes, no matter how hard they try. So we say to them,

'Forget it, star. Your wheels are not our wheels. But we're all going somewhere, right? See you at the other end.' "

It is hardly surprising that so many "feebies"—people over thirty—have trouble with the basic Believers' Creed: "No hate, No war, No money, No sex." Evidently, in this final decade of the twentieth century, sainthood is only possible for the very young.

The "Roundhouse" at Jerusalem West is, in one sense, the Vatican of the nationwide movement. But in many ways it is typical of the New Shaker communities springing up from La Jolla, California, to Seal Harbor, Maine. At last count there were sixty-one separate "tribes," some containing as many as fifteen "families" of a hundred and twenty-eight members each. Each Shaker family is housed in an army-surplus pliodesic dome—covering some ten thousand square feet of bare but vinyl-hardened earth—which serves as bedroom, living room, workshop and holy tabernacle, all in one. There is a much smaller satellite dome forty feet from the main building which might be called the Outhouse, but isn't—the New Shakers themselves refer to it as Sin City. In keeping with their general attitude toward the bodily functions, Sin City is the only place in the Jerusalem West compound that is off-limits to visitors.

As difficult as it may be for most North Americans to accept, today's typical Shaker recruit comes from a background of unquestioned abundance and respectability. There is no taint of the Ghetto and no evidence of serious behavioral problems. In fact, Preliminary School records show that these young people often excelled in polymorphous play and responded quite normally to the usual spectrum of chemical and electrical euphorics. As underteens, their proficiency in programmed dating was consistently rated "superior" and they were often cited as leaders in organizing multiple-outlet experiences. Later, in Modular School, they scored in the fiftieth percentile or better on Brand-Differentiation tests. In short, according to all the available figures, they would have had no trouble gaining admission to the college of their choice or obtaining a commission in the Consumer Corps or qualifying for a Federal Travel Grant. Yet for some reason, on the very brink of maturity, they turned their backs on all the benefits their parents and grandparents fought so hard for in the Cultural Revolution—and plunged instead into a life of regimented sense-denial.

On a typical summer's afternoon at Jerusalem West, with the sun filtering through the translucent dome and bathing the entire area in a soft golden glow, the Roundhouse resembles nothing so much as a giant, queenless beehive. In the gleaming chrome-and-copper kitchen, blenders whirr and huge pots bubble as a squad of white-smocked Food Deacons prepares the copious vegetable stew that forms the staple of the Shaker diet. In the sound-proofed garage sector the Shop Deacons are busily transforming another hopeless-looking junkheap into one of the economical, turbine-powered "hot-rods" already known to connoisseurs in this country and abroad as Shakerbikes. The eight Administrative Deacons and their assistants are directing family business from a small fiber-walled cubicle known simply as The Office. And in a large, fully instrumented studio, the sixteen-piece band is cutting a new liturgical tape for the Evening Service—a tape that may possibly end up as number one on the federal pop charts like the recent Shaker hit, *This Freeway's Plenty Wide Enough*. No matter where one turns beneath the big dome one finds young people humming, tapping their feet, breaking into snatches of song and generally living up to the New Shaker motto: "Work is Play." One of their most popular songs—a characteristic coupling of Old Shaker words to a modern jag-rock background—concludes with this no-nonsense summation of the Shaker life-style:

> *It's the Gift to be simple,*
> *The Gift to be free,*
> *The Gift to come down*
> *Where the Gift ought to be.*

—MORE TO COME—

XEROGRAM: June 28 (11:15 P.M.)
TO: The Dean, Skinner Free Institute, Ronkonkoma, New Jersey 72441333965
FROM: Raymond Senter, c/o Hudson Junction Rotel, Hudson Junction, N.Y. 28997601910
Friend:

My son Bruce Senter, age 14, was enrolled in your institute for a six-week seminar in Applied Physiology beginning May 10. According to the transcript received by his Modular School (NYC118A), he successfully completed his course of studies on June 21. Mrs. Senter and I have had no word from him since. He had earlier talked with his Advisor about pursuing a Field-research project in Intensive Orgasm. I would appreciate any further information you can give me as to his post-seminar whereabouts. Thank you.

TO: Stock, Ex-Ed, *I.I.*
FROM: Senter
ENCLOSED: Background tape. Interview with Harry G (born "Guardino"), member of First Octave. Edited Transcript, June 29.
Q: Suppose we begin by talking a little about your position here as

one of the—well, what shall I say? Founding Fathers of the Shaker Revival?

A: First you better take a deep breath, star. That's all out of sync. There's no Founding Fathers here. Or Founding Mothers or any of that jag. There's only one Father and one Mother and they're everywhere and nowhere, understand?

Q: What I meant was—as a member of the First Octave you have certain duties and responsibilities—

A: Like I said, star, everyone's equal here.

Q: I was under the impression that your rules stress obedience to a hierarchy.

A: Oh, there has to be order, sure, but it's nothing personal. If you can punch a computer—you sync with The Office Deacons. If you make it with wheels—you're in the Shop crew. Me—I fold my bed in the morning, push a juice-horn in the band and talk to reporters when they ask for me. That doesn't make me Pope.

Q: What about the honorary nomenclature?

A: What's that?

Q: The initials. Instead of last names.

A: Oh, yeah. They were given to us as a sign. You want to know what of?

Q: Please.

A: As a sign that no one's stuck with his birth kit. Sure, you may start with a Chevvie Six chassis and I have to go with a Toyota. That's the luck of the DNA. But we all need a spark in the chamber to get it moving. That's the Gift. And if I burn clean and keep in tune I may leave you flat in my tracks. Right?

Q: What about the Ghetto?

A: Even the Blacks have a piece of the Gift. What they do with it is their trip.

Q: There's been a lot of controversy lately about whether your movement is really Christian—in a religious sense. Would you care to comment on that?

A: You mean like "Jesus Christ, the Son of God"? Sure, we believe that. And we believe in Harry G, the Son of God and Richard F, the Son of God and—what's your name, star?—Raymond Senter, the Son of God. That's the Gift. That's what it's all about. Jesus found the Gift inside. So did Buddha, Mother Ann, even Malcolm X—we don't worry too much about who said what first. First you find the Gift— then you live it. The Freeway's plenty wide enough.

Q: Then why all the emphasis on your Believers' Creed, and the Articles of Faith, and your clothes?

A: Look, star, every machine's got a set of specs. You travel with us, you learn our set. We keep the chrome shiny, the chambers clean. And we don't like accidents.

Q: Your prohibitions against money and sex—

A: "Prohibitions" is a feebie word. We're free from money and sex. The Four Noes are like a Declaration of Independence. See, everybody's really born free—but you have to know it. So we don't rob cradles. We say, let them grow up, learn what it's all about—the pill, the puffer, the feel-o-mat—all the perms and combos. Then, when they're fifteen or sixteen, if they still crave those chains, okay. If not, they know where to find us.

Q: What about the people who sign up and then change their minds?

A: We have no chains—if that's what you mean.

Q: You don't do anything to try to keep them?

A: Once you've really found the Gift inside there's no such thing as "changing your mind."

Q: What's your attitude toward the Old Shakers? They died out, didn't they, for lack of recruits?

A: Everything is born and dies and gets reborn again.

Q: Harry, what would happen if this time the whole world became Shakers?

A: Don't worry, star. You won't be around to see it.

—MORE TO COME—

XEROGRAM: June 29 (10:43 p.m.)
TO: Connie Fine, Director, Camp Encounter, Wentworth, Maine, 47119650023
FROM: Raymond Senter, Hudson Junction Rotel, Hudson Junction, N.Y., 28997601910
Connie:

Has Bruce arrived yet? Arlene and I have lost contact with him in the last week, and it occurred to me that he may have biked up to camp early and simply forgotten to buzz us—he was so charged up about being a full counselor-leader of his own T-group this season. Anyway, would you please buzz me soonest at the above zip? You know how mothers tend to overload the worry-circuits until they know for sure that their little wriggler is safely plugged in somewhere. Joy to you and yours, Ray.

TO: Stock, Ex-Ed. *I.I.*
FROM: Senter
ENCLOSED: Fact sheet on Old Shakers

Foundress—Mother Ann Lee, b. Feb. 29, 1736, Manchester, England.

Antecedents—Early Puritan "seekers" (Quakers), French "Prophets" (Camisards).

Origin—Following an unhappy marriage—four children, all dead in infancy—Mother Ann begins to preach that "concupiscence" is the root of all evil. Persecutions and imprisonment.

1774—Mother Ann and seven early disciples sail to America aboard the ship *Mariah*. Group settles near Albany. Public preaching against concupiscence. More persecutions. More converts. Ecstatic, convulsive worship. Mother Ann's "miracles."

1784—Mother Ann dies.

1787—Mother Ann's successors, Father Joseph and Mother Lucy, organize followers into monastic communities and "separate" themselves from sinful world.

1787–1794—Expansion of sect through New York State and New England.

1806–1826—Expansion of sect across Western frontier—Ohio, Kentucky, Indiana.

1837–1845—Mass outbreak of spiritualism. Blessings, songs, spirit-drawings and business advice transmitted by deceased leaders through living "instruments."

1850's—Highpoint of Society. Six thousand members, 18 communities, fifty-eight "Families."

*Total recorded membership—from late 18th century to late 20th century—approximately seventeen thousand.

*Old Shakers noted for—mail-order seed business, handicrafts (brooms, baskets and boxes), furniture-manufacture.

*Credited with invention of—common clothes pin, cut nails, circular saw, turbine water-wheel, steam-driven washing machine.

Worship—Emphasis on communal singing and dancing. Early "convulsive" phase gives way in nineteenth century to highly organized performances and processions—ring dances, square order shuffles.

Beliefs—Celibacy, Duality of Deity (Father and Mother God), Equality of the Sexes, Equality in Labor, Equality in Property. Society to be perpetuated by "admission of serious-minded persons and adoption of children."

Motto—"Hands to Work and Hearts to God."

—MORE TO COME—

XEROGRAM: June 30 (8:15 (A.M.))

TO: Mrs. Rosemary Collins, 133 Escorial Drive, Baywater, Florida, 92635776901

FROM: Raymond Senter, Hudson Junction Rotel, Hudson Junction, N.Y. 28997601910
Dear Rosie:

Has that little wriggler of ours been down your way lately? Bruce is off again on an unannounced sidetrip, and it struck me that he might have hopped down south to visit his favorite aunt. Not to mention his favorite cousin! How is that suntanned teaser of yours? Still taking after you in the S-L-N department? Give her a big kiss for me—you know where! And if Bruce does show up please buzz me right away at the above zip. Much Brotherly Love, Ray.

TO: Stock, Ex-Ed., *I.I.*
FROM: Senter
ENCLOSED. Caption tape for film segment on Worship Service.

JERUSALEM WEST, Saturday, June 30—I'm standing at the entrance to the inner sanctum of the huge Roundhouse here, the so-called Meeting Center, which is used only for important ceremonial functions—like the Saturday Night Dance scheduled to begin in exactly five minutes. In the Holy Corridor to my right the entire congregation has already assembled in two rows, one for boys and one for girls, side by side but not touching. During the week the Meeting Center is separated from the work and living areas by curved translucent partitions which fit together to make a little dome-within-a-dome. But when the sun begins to set on Saturday night the partitions are removed to reveal a circular dance floor, which is in fact the hub of the building. From this slightly raised platform of gleaming fibercast, I can look down each radical corridor—past the rows of neatly folded beds in the dormitories, past the shrouded machines in the repair shops, past the partly finished Shakerbikes in the garage, past the scrubbed formica tables in the kitchen—to the dim horizon line where the dome comes to rest on the sacred soil of Jerusalem West.

All artificial lights have been extinguished for the Sabbath celebration. The only illumination comes from the last rays of the sun, a dying torch that seems to have set the dome material itself ablaze. It's a little like standing inside the fiery furnace of Nebuchadnezzar with a hundred and twenty-eight unworried prophets of the Lord. The silence is virtually complete—not a cough, not the faintest rustle of fabric is heard. Even the air vents have been turned off—at least for the moment. I become aware of the harsh sound of my own respiration.

At precisely eight o'clock the two lines of worshippers begin to move forward out of the Holy Corridor. They circle the dance floor, the boys moving to the right, the girls to the left. Actually, it's difficult to tell them apart. The Shakers use no body ornaments at all—no paints, no wigs, no gems, no bugs, no dildoes, no flashers. All wear their hair cropped short, as if sheared with the aid of an overturned bowl. And all are dressed in some variation of Shaker gear—a loosely fitting, long-sleeved, buttonless and collarless shirt slit open at the neck for two inches and hanging free at the waist over a pair of baggy trousers pulled tight around each ankle by a hidden elastic band.

The garments look vaguely North African. They are made of soft dynaleen and they come in a variety of pastel shades. One girl may be wearing a pale pink top and a light blue bottom. The boy standing opposite her may have on the same colors, reversed. Others in the procession have chosen combinations of lilac and peach, ivory and lemon or turquoise and butternut. The range of hues seems endless but the intensity never varies, so that the entire spectacle presents a living demonstration of one of the basic Articles of Faith of the Shaker Revival—Diversity in Uniformity.

Now the procession has ended. The worshippers have formed two matching arcs, sixty-four boys on one side, sixty-four girls on the other, each standing precisely an arm's length from each neighbor. All are barefoot. All are wearing the same expression—a smile so modest as to be virtually undetectable if it were not mirrored and remirrored a hundred and twenty-eight times around the circumference of the ritual circle. The color of the dome has begun to change to a darker, angrier crimson. Whether the natural twilight is being artificially augmented—either from inside or outside the building—is impossible to tell. All eyes are turned upward to a focus about twenty-five feet above the center of the floor, where an eight-sided loudspeaker hangs by a chrome-plated cable from the midpoint of the dome. The air begins to fill with a pervasive vibration like the rumble of a distant monocar racing toward you in the night. And then the music explodes into the supercharged air. Instantly the floor is alive with jerking, writhing bodies—it's as if each chord were an electrical impulse applied directly to the nerve ends of the dancers—and the music is unbelievably loud.

The dome must act as an enormous soundbox. I can feel the vibrations in my feet and my teeth are chattering with the beat—but as wild as the dancing is, the circle is still intact. Each Shaker is "shaking" in his own place. Some are uttering incomprehensible cries, the holy gibberish that the Shakers call their Gift of Tongues—ecstatic prophecies symbolizing the Wordless Word of the Deity. One young girl with a gaunt but beautiful face is howling like a coyote. Another is grunting like a pig. A third is alternately spitting into the air and slapping her own cheeks viciously with both hands.

Across the floor a tall skinny boy has shaken loose from the rim of the circle. Pirouetting at high speed, his head thrown straight back so that his eyes are fixed on the crimson membrane of the dome, he seems to be propelling himself in an erratic path toward the center of the floor. And now the dome is changing color again, clotting to a deeper purple—like the color of a late evening sky but flecked with scarlet stars that seem to be darting about with a life of their own, colliding, coalescing, reforming.

A moment of relative calm has descended on the dancers. They are standing with their hands at their sides—only their heads are moving, lolling first to one side, then the other, in keeping with the new, subdued rhythm of the music. The tall boy in the center has begun to spin around and around in place, picking up speed with each rotation—now he's whirling like a top, his head still bent back, his eyes staring sightlessly. His right arm shoots out from the shoulder, the elbow locked, the fingers stiff, the palm flat—this is what the Shakers call the Arrow Sign, a manifestation of the Gift of Prophecy, directly inspired by the Dual Deity, Father Power and Mother Wisdom. The tall boy is the "instrument" and he is about to receive a message from on high.

His head tilts forward. His rotation slows. He comes to a halt with his right arm pointing at a short red-haired girl. The girl begins to shake all over as if struck by a high fever. The music rises to an ear-shattering crescendo and ends in mid-note.

"Everyone's a mirror," the tall boy shouts. "Clean, clean, clean—oh, let it shine! My dirt's not my own but it stains the earth. And the earth's not my own—the Mother and Father are light above light but the light can't shine alone. Only a mirror can shine, shine, shine. Let the mirror be mine, be mine, be mine!"

The red-haired girl is shaking so hard her limbs are flailing like whips. Her mouth has fallen open and she begins to moan, barely audibly at first. What she utters might be a single-syllable word like "clean" or "mine" or "shine" repeated so rapidly that the consonants break down and the vowels flow into one unending stream of sound. But it keeps getting louder and louder and still louder, like the wail of an air-raid siren, until all resemblance to speech disappears and it seems impossible that such a sound can come from a human throat. You can almost hear the blood vessels straining, bursting.

Then the loudspeaker cuts in again in mid-note with the loudest, wildest jag-rock riff I have ever heard, only it's no longer something you can hear—it's inside you or you're inside it. And the dome has burst into blooms of color! A stroboscopic fireworks display that obliterates all outlines and shatters perspective and you can't tell whether the dancers are moving very, very slowly or very, very fast. The movement is so perfectly synchronized with the sound and the sound with the color that there seems to be no fixed reference point anywhere.

All you can say is: "There is color, there is sound, there is movement—"

This is the Gift of Seizure, which the New Shakers prize so highly—and whether it is genuinely mystical, as they claim, or auto-hypnotic or drug-induced, as some critics maintain, or a combination of all of these or something else entirely, it is an undeniably real— and profoundly disturbing—experience.

—MORE TO COME—

XEROGRAM: July 1 (7:27 A.M.)
TO: Frederick Rickover, Eastern Supervisor, Feel-O-Mat Corp., Baltimore, Maryland, 6503477502
FROM: Raymond Senter, Hudson Junction Rotel, Hudson Junction, N.Y. 28997601910
(*WARNING: PERSONALIZED ENVELOPE: CONTENTS WILL POWDER IF OPENED IMPROPERLY*)
Fred:

I'm afraid it's back-scratching time again. I need a code-check on DNA No. 75/62/HR/tl/4-9-06^5. I'm interested in whether the codee has plugged into a feel-o-mat anywhere in the Federation during the past two weeks. This one's a family matter, not business, so buzz me only at the above zip. I won't forget it. Gratefully, Ray.

TO: Stock, Ex-Ed., *I.I.*
FROM: Senter
ENCLOSED: Three tapes. New Shaker "Testimonies." Edited transcripts, July 1.

TAPE I (Shaker name, "Farmer Brown"): What kind of mike is this? No kidding. I didn't know they made a reamper this small. Chinese? Oh. Right. Well, let's see—I was born April seventeenth, nineteen seventy-four, in Ellsworth, Saskatchewan. My breath-father's a foreman at a big refinery there. My breath-mother was a consumer-housewife. She's gone now. It's kind of hard to remember details. When I was real little, I think I saw the feds scratch a Bomb-thrower on the steps of City Hall. But maybe that was only something I saw on 2-D. School was—you know, the usual. Oh, once a bunch of us kids got hold of some fresh spores from the refinery—I guess we stole them somehow. Anyway, there was still a lot of open land around and we planted them and raised our own crop of puffers. I didn't come down for a week. That was my farming experience. (LAUGH-TER) I applied for a bummer-grant on my fifteenth birthday, got a two-year contract and took off the next day for the sun. Let's see—Minneapolis, Kansas City, Mexico—what a jolt! There weren't so many feel-o-mats in the small towns down there and I was into all the hard stuff you could get in those days—speed, yellow, rock-juice, little-annie—I guess the only thing I never tried for a jolt was the Process and there were times when I was just about ready.

When the grant ran out, I just kept bumming on my own. At first you think it's going to be real easy. Half the people you know are still on contract and they share it around. Then your old friends start running out faster than you make new ones and there's a whole new generation on the road. And you start feeling more and more like a feebie and acting like one. I was lucky because I met this sweet little dove in Nashville—she had a master's in Audio-Visual but she was psycho for bummers, especially flat ones.

Anyway, she comes back to her coop one day with a new tape and puts it on any says, "This'll go right through you. It's a wild new group called the Shakers."

She didn't know two bobby's worth about the Shakers and I didn't either—the first Shaker tapes were just hitting the market about then. Well, I can tell you, that jagged sound gave me a jolt. I mean, it was bigger than yellow, bigger than juice, only it let you down on your feet instead of your back. I had this feeling I had to hear more. I got all the tapes that were out but they weren't enough. So I took off one night for Wildwood and before I knew it I was in a Prep Meeting and I was home free—you know, I've always kind of hoped that little dove makes it on her own—Oh, yeah, the band . . .

Well, I'm one of the Band Deacons, which is what's called a Sacrificial Gift because it means handling the accounts—and that's too close to the jacks and bobbys for comfort. But someone has to do it. You can't stay alive in an impure world without getting a little stained and if outsiders want to lay the Kennedys on us for bikes and tapes, that's a necessary evil. But we don't like to spread the risk in the Family. So the Deacons sign the checks and deal with the agents and the stain's on us alone. And everyone prays a little harder to square it with the Father and Mother.

TAPE II (Shaker name, "Mariah Moses"): I was born in Darien, Connecticut. I'm an Aquarius with Leo rising. Do you want my breath-name? I don't mind—it's Cathy Ginsberg. My breath-parents are both full-time consumers. I didn't have a very interesting childhood, I guess. I went to Mid-Darian Modular School. I was a pretty good student—my best subject was World Culture. I consummated on my third date, which was about average, I've been told, for my class. Do you really want all this background stuff? I guess the biggest thing that happened to the old me was when I won a second prize in the Maxwell Puffer Civic Essay contest when I was fourteen. The subject was *The Joys of Spectatorism* and the prize was a Programmed Weekend in Hawaii for two. I don't remember who I went with. But Hawaii was really nice. All those brown-skinned boys—we went to a big luau on Saturday night. That's a native-style orgy. They taught me things we never even learned in school.

I remember thinking, *Oh, star, this is the living end!*

But when it was all over I had another thought. If this was the living end—what came next? I don't know if it was the roast pig or what but I didn't feel so good for a few days. The night we got back home—Herbie! That was the name of my date, Herbie Alcott—he had short curly hair all over his back—anyway, the night I got home my breath-parents picked me up at the airport and on the way back to Darien they started asking me what I wanted to do with my life. They were trying to be so helpful, you know. I mean, you could see they would have been disappointed if I got involved in production of some kind but they weren't about to say that in so many words. They just asked me if I had decided how I wanted to plug into the Big Board. It was up to me to choose between college or the Consumer Corps or a Travel Grant—they even asked me if Herbie and I were getting serious and if we wanted to have a baby—because the waiting-list at the Marriage Bureau was already six-months long and getting longer. The trouble was I was still thinking about the luau and the roast pig and I felt all—burned out. Like a piece of charcoal that still looks solid but is really just white ash—and if you touch it it crumbles and blows way. So I said I'd think about it but what I was really thinking was *I'm not signing up for any more orgies just yet.*

And a few days later the miracle happened. A girl in our class was reported missing and a friend of mine heard someone say that she'd become a Shaker.

I said, "What's that?"

My friend said, "It's a religion that believes in No hate, No War, No money, No sex."

And I felt this thrill go right through me. And even though I didn't know what it meant at the time, that was the moment I discovered my Gift. It was such a warm feeling, like something soft and quiet curled up inside you, waiting. And the day I turned fifteen I hiked up to Jerusalem and I never went home. That was eleven months ago . . . oh, you can't describe what happens at Preparative Meeting. It's what happens inside you that counts. Like now, when

I think of all my old friends from Darien, I say a little prayer.

Father Power, Mother Wisdom, touch their Gifts, set them free. . . .

TAPE III (Shaker name, "Earnest Truth"): I'm aware that I'm something of a rarity here. I assume that's why you asked me for a testimony. But I don't want you categorizing me as a Shaker intellectual or a Shaker theologian or anything like that. I serve as Legal Deacon because that's my Gift. But I'm also a member of the vacuum detail in Corridor Three and that's my Gift too. I'd be just as good a Shaker if I only cleaned the floor and nothing else. Is that clear? Good. Well then, as briefly as possible: (READS FROM PREPARED TEXT) I'm twenty-four years old, from Berkeley, California. Breath-parents were on the faculty at the University; killed in an air crash when I was ten. I was raised by the state. Pacific Highlands Modular School: First honors. Consumer Corps: Media-aide First-class. Entered the University at seventeen. Pre-law. Graduated *magna cum* in nineteen ninety. Completed four-year Law School in three years. In my final year I became interested in the literature of religion—or, to be more precise, the literature of mysticism—possibly as a counterpoise to the increasing intensity of my formal studies. Purely as an intellectual diversion I began to read St. John of the Cross, George Fox, the Vedas, Tao, Zen, the Kabbala, the Sufis. But when I came across the early Shakers I was struck at once with the daring and clarity of this purely American variant. All mystics seek spiritual union with the Void, the Nameless, the Formless, the Ineffable. But the little band of Shaker pilgrims, confronted with a vast and apparently unbounded wilderness, took a marvelous quantum leap of faith and decided that the union had already been accomplished. The wilderness was the Void. For those who had eyes to see—this was God's Kingdom. And by practicing a total communism, a total abnegation, a total dedication, they made the wilderness flower for two hundred years. Then, unable to adjust to the methodologies of the Industrial Revolution, they quietly faded away; it was as if their gentle spirit had found a final resting place in the design of their utterly simple and utterly beautiful wooden furniture—each piece of which has since become a collector's item. When I began reading about the Old Shakers I had of course heard about the New Shakers —but I assumed that they were just another crackpot fundamentalist sect like the Holy Rollers or the Snake Handlers, an attempt to keep alive the pieties of a simpler day in the present age of abundance. But eventually my curiosity—or so I called it at the time—led me to investigate a Preparative Meeting that had been established in the Big Sur near Jefferstown. And I found my Gift. The experience varies from individual to individual. For me it was the revelation that the complex machine we refer to as the Abundant Society is the real anachronism. All the euphorics we feed ourselves cannot change the fact that the machinery of abundance has long since reached its limit as a vital force and is now choking on its own waste products—Pollution, Overpopulation, Dehumanization. Far from being a break-through, the so-called Cultural Revolution was merely the last gasp of the old order to maintain itself by programming man's most private senses into the machine. And the childish Bomb-throwers were nothing but retarded romantics, an anachronism within an anachronism. At this juncture in history, only the Shaker Revival offers a true alternative—in the utterly simple, and therefore utterly profound, Four Noes. The secular world usually praises us for our rejection of Hate and War and mocks us for our rejection of Money and Sex. But the Four Noes constitute a beautifully balanced ethical equation, in which each term is a function of the other three. There are no easy Utopias. Non-Shakers often ask: What would happen if everyone became a Shaker? Wouldn't that be the end of the human race? My personal answer is this: Society is suffering from the sickness unto death—a plague called despair. Shakerism is the only cure. As long as the plague rages more and more people will find the strength to take the medicine required, no matter how bitter it may seem. Perhaps at some future date, the very spread of Shakerism will restore Society to health, so that the need for Shakerism will again slacken. Perhaps the cycle will be repeated. Perhaps not. It is impossible to know what the Father and Mother have planned for their children. Only one thing is certain. The last of the Old Shaker prophetesses wrote in nineteen fifty-six: "The flame may flicker but the spark can never be allowed to die out until the salvation of the world is accomplished."

I don't think you'll find the flame flickering here.

—MORE TO COME—

XEROGRAM: July 1 (11:30 P.M.)
TO: Stock, Ex-Ed., *I.I.*
FROM: Raymond Senter, c/o Hudson Junction Rotel (*WARNING: PERSONALIZED ENVELOPE: CONTENTS WILL POWDER IF OPENED IMPROPERLY*)
Art:

Cooperation unlimited here—until I mention "Preparative Meeting." Then they all get tongue-tied. Too holy for impure ears. No one will even say where or when. Working hypothesis: It's a compulsory withdrawal session. Recruits obviously must kick all worldly habits before taking final vows. Big question: how do they do it? Conscious or unconscious? Cold-turkey, hypno-suggestion, or re-conditioning? Legal or illegal? Even Control would like to know. I'm taping the Reception Deacon tomorrow. If you approve, I'll start putting the pressure on. The groundwork's done. We may get a story yet. Ray.

XEROGRAM: July 2 (2:15 A.M.)
TO: Joseph Harger, Coordinator, N.Y. State Consumer Control, Albany N.Y. 31118002311
FROM: Raymond Senter, c/o Hudson Junction Rotel, Hudson Junction, N.Y. 28997601910
(*WARNING: PERSONALIZED ENVELOPE: CONTENTS WILL POWDER IF OPENED IMPROPERLY*)
Joe:

I appreciate your taking a personal interest in this matter. My wife obviously gave the wrong impression to the controller she contacted. She tends to get hysterical. Despite what she may have said I assure you my son's attitude toward the Ghetto was a perfectly healthy blend of scorn and pity. Bruce went with me once to see the Harlem Wall—must have been six or seven—and Coordinator Bill Quaite let him sit in the Scanner's chair for a few minutes. He heard a muzzein call from the top of one of those rickety towers. He saw the wild rats prowling in the stench and garbage. He also watched naked children fighting with wooden knives over a piece of colored glass. I am told there are young people today stupid enough to think that sneaking over the Wall is an adventure and that the Process is reversible—but my son is definitely not one of them. And he is certainly not a Bomb-thrower. I know that you have always shared my publication's view that a selective exposure to the harsher realities makes for better consumers. (I'm thinking of that little snafu in data-traffic in the Albany Grid last summer.) I hope you'll see your way clear to trusting me again. I repeat: there's not the slightest indication that my son was going over to the Blacks. In fact, I have good reason to believe that he will turn up quite soon, with all discrepancies accounted for. But I need a little time. A Missing Persons Bulletin would only make things harder at the moment. I realize it was my wife who initiated the complaint. But I'd greatly appreciate it if she got misfiled for 48 hours. I'll handle any static on this side. Discreetly, Ray.

TO: Stock, Ex-Ed., *I.I.*
FROM: Senter
ENCLOSED: Background tape; interview with Antonia Cross, age 19, Reception Deacon, Jerusalem West. Edited Transcript, July 2.
Q: (I waited silently for her to take the lead.)

A: Before we begin, I think we better get a few things straight. It'll save time and grief in the long run. First of all, despite what your magazine and others may have said in the past, we never proselytize. Never. So please don't use that word. We just try to live our Gift—and if other people are drawn to us, that's the work of the Father and Mother, not us. We don't have to preach. When someone's sitting in filth up to his neck he doesn't need a preacher to tell him he smells. All he needs to hear is that there's a cleaner place somewhere. Second, we don't prevent anyone from leaving, despite all rumors to the contrary. We've had exactly three apostates in the last four years. They found out their wheels were not our wheels and they left.

Q: Give me their names.

A: There's no law that says we have to disclose the names of backsliders. Find them yourself. That shouldn't be too hard, now that they're plugged back in to the Big Board.

Q: You overestimate the power of the press.

A: False modesty is not considered a virtue among Shakers.

Q: You mentioned three backsliders. How many applicants are turned away before taking final vows?

A: The exact percentage is immaterial. Some applicants are more serious than others. There is no great mystery about our reception procedure. You've heard the expression "Weekend Shakers." Anybody can buy the gear and dance and sing and stay pure for a couple of days. It's even considered a "jolt," I'm told. We make sure that those who come to us know the difference between a weekend and a lifetime. We explain the Gift, the Creed, the Articles of Faith. Then we ask them why they've come to us. We press them pretty hard. In the end, if they're still serious, they are sent to Preparative Meeting for a while, until a Family is ready to accept them.

Q: How long is a while?

A: Preparative Meeting can take days or weeks. Or longer.

Q: Are they considered full-fledged Shakers during that time?

A. The moment of Induction is a spiritual, not a temporal phenomenon.

Q: But you notify the authorities only after a recruit is accepted in a Family?

A: We comply with all the requirements of the Full Disclosure Law.

Q: What if the recruit is underage and lies about it? Do you run a routine DNA check?

A: We obey the law.

Q: But a recruit at a Prep Meeting isn't a Shaker and so you don't have to report his presence. Is that right?

A: We've had exactly nine complaints filed against us in four years. Not one has stuck.

Q: Then you do delay acceptance until you can trace a recruit's identity?

A: I didn't say that. We believe in each person's right to redefine his set, no matter what the Big Board may say about him. But such administrative details tend to work themselves out.

Q: How? I don't understand.

A: The ways of the Father and Mother sometimes passeth understanding.

Q: You say you don't proselytize, but isn't that what your tapes are —a form of preaching? Don't most of your recruits come to you because of the tapes? And don't most of them have to be brought down from whatever they're hooked on before you'll even let them in?

A: The world—your world—is filth. From top to bottom. We try to stay as far away as we can. But we have to eat. So we sell you our tapes and our Shakerbikes. There's a calculated risk of contamination. But it works the other way too. Filth can be contaminated by purity. That's known as Salvation. It's like a tug of war. We'll see who takes the greatest risk.

Q: That's what I'm here for—to see at first hand. Where is the Jerusalem West Preparative Meeting held?

A: Preparative Meetings are private. For the protection of all concerned.

Q: Don't you mean secret? Isn't there something going on at these meetings that you don't want the public to know?

A: If the public is ignorant of the life of the spirit, that is hardly our fault.

Q: Some people believe that your recruits are "prepared" with drugs or electro-conditioning.

A: Some people think that Shaker stew is full of saltpeter. Are you going to print that, too?

Q: You have been accused of brain-tampering. That's a serious charge. And unless I get a hell of a lot more cooperation from you than I've been getting I will have to assume that you have something serious to hide.

A: No one ever said you'd be free to see everything. You'll just have to accept our—guidance—in matters concerning religious propriety.

Q: Let me give you a little guidance, Miss Cross. You people already have so many enemies in that filthy world you despise that one unfriendly story from I.I. might just tip the scales.

A: The power of the press? We'll take our chances.

Q: What will you do if the police crack down?

A: We're not afraid to die. And the Control authorities have found that it's more trouble than it's worth to put us in jail. We seem to upset the other inmates.

Q: Miss Cross—

A: We use no titles here. My name is Antonia.

Q: You're obviously an intelligent, dedicated young woman. I would rather work with you than against you. Why don't we try to find some middle ground? As a journalist my primary concern is human nature—what happens to a young recruit in the process of becoming a full-fledged Shaker. You won't let me into a Prep Meeting to see for myself. All right, you have your reasons, and I respect them. But I ask you to respect mine. If I can look through your Reception files—just the last two or three weeks will do—I should be able to get some idea of what kind of raw material you draw on. You can remove the names, of course.

A: Perhaps we can provide a statistical breakdown for you.

Q: I don't want statistics. I want to look at their pictures, listen to their voices—you say you press them pretty hard in the first interview. That's what I need: their responses under pressure, the difference between those who stick it through and those who don't.

A: How do we know you're not looking for something of a personal nature—to embarrass us?

Q: For God's sakes, I'm one of the best-known tapemen in the Federation. Why not just give me the benefit of the doubt?

A: You invoke a Deity that means nothing to you.

Q: I'm sorry.

A: The only thing I can do is transmit your request to the Octave itself. Any decision on such a matter would have to come from a Full Business Meeting.

Q: How long will it take?

A: The Octave is meeting tomorrow, before Evening Service.

Q: All right. I can wait till then. I suppose I should apologize again for losing my temper. I'm afraid it's an occupational hazard.

A: We all have our Gift.

—MORE TO COME—

TO: Stock, Ex-Ed., *I.I.*

FROM: Senter

ENCLOSED: First add on Shaker Revival; July 3.

It is unclear whether the eight teenagers—six boys and two girls—who banded together one fateful evening in the spring of 1991 to form a jag-rock combo called The Shakers had any idea of the religious implications of the name. According to one early account in

Riff magazine, the original eight were thinking only of a classic rock-and-roll number of the nineteen-fifties called *Shake, Rattle and Roll* (a title not without sexual as well as musicological overtones). On the other hand, there is evidence that Harry G was interested in astrology, palmistry, scientology and other forms of modern occultism even before he left home at the age of fifteen. (Harry G was born Harry Guardino, on December eighteen, nineteen seventy-four, in Schoodic, Maine, the son of a third-generation lobster fisherman.) Like many members of his generation he applied for a Federal Travel Grant on graduation from Modular School and received a standard two-year contract. But unlike most of his fellow-bummers, Harry did not immediately take off on an all-expenses-paid tour of the seamier side of life in the North American Federation. Instead, he hitched a ride to New York City, where he established a little basement coop on the lower west side that soon became a favorite way-station for other, more restless bummers passing through the city. No reliable account of this period is available. The rumors that he dabbled in a local Bomb-throwers cell appear to be unfounded. But it is know that sometime during the spring of nineteen ninety-one a group of bummers nearing the end of their grants gathered in Harry G's coop to discuss the future. By coincidence or design the eight young people who came together that night from the far corners of the Federation all played some instrument and shared a passion for jag-rock. And as they talked and argued among themselves about the best way possible to "plug into the Big Board," it slowly began to dawn on them that perhaps their destinies were linked— or, as Harry G himself has put it, "We felt we could make beautiful music together. Time has made us one."

Building a reputation in the jag-rock market has never been easy—not even with divine intervention. For the next two months, The Shakers scrambled for work, playing a succession of one-night stands in consumers' centers, schools, fraternal lodges—wherever someone wanted live entertainment and was willing to put the group on. The Shakers traveled in a second-hand Chevrolet van which was kept running only by the heroic efforts of the group's electricoud player, Richard Fitzgerald (who later—as Richard F—helped to design the improved version of the turbo-adapter which forms the basis of today's Shakerbike).

On the night of June the first the group arrived in Hancock, Massachusetts, where they were scheduled to play the next evening at the graduation dance of the Grady L. Parker Modular School. They had not worked for three days and their finances had reached a most precarious stage—they were now sharing only four bummer-grants between them, the other four contracts having expired in the previous weeks. From the very beginning of their relationship the eight had gone everywhere and done everything as a group—they even insisted on sleeping together in one room on the theory that the "bad vibrations" set up by an overnight absence from each other might adversely affect their music. As it turned out, there was no room large enough at the local Holiday Inn, so, after some lengthy negotiation, the Modular School principal arranged for them to camp out on the grounds of the local Shaker Museum, a painstaking restoration of an early New England Shaker community dating back to seventeen ninety. Amused but not unduly impressed by the coincidence in names, the eight Shakers bedded down for the night within sight of the Museum's most famous structure, the Round Stone Barn erected by the original Shakers in eighteen twenty-six. Exactly what happened between midnight and dawn on that fog-shrouded New England meadow may never be known—the validation of mystical experience being by its very nature a somewhat inexact science. According to Shaker testimony, however, the spirit of Mother Ann, sainted foundress of the original sect, touched the Gifts of the eight where they lay and in a vision of the future—which Amelia D later said was "as clear and bright as a holograph"—revealed why they had been chosen: The time had come for a mass revival of Shaker beliefs and practices. The eight teenagers awoke at the same instant, compared visions, found them to be identical and wept together for joy. They spent the rest of the day praying for guidance and making plans. Their first decision was to play as scheduled at the Grady L. Parker graduation dance.

"We decided to go on doing just what we had been doing—only more so," Amelia D later explained. "Also, I guess, we needed the jacks."

Whatever the reason, the group apparently played as never before. Their music opened up doors to whole new ways of hearing and feeling—or so it seemed to the excited crowd of seniors who thronged around the bandstand when the first set was over. Without any premeditation, or so he later claimed, Harry Guardino stood up and announced the new Shaker dispensation, including the Believers' Creed (the Four Noes) and a somewhat truncated version of the Articles of Faith of the United Society of Believers (Revived): "All things must be kept decent and in good order," "Diversity in Uniformity," and "Work is Play." According to the Hancock newspaper, seventeen members of the senior class left town that morning with the Shakers—in three cars "borrowed" from parents and later returned. Drawn by a Gift of Travel, the little band of pilgrims made their way to the quiet corner of New York State now known as Jerusalem West, bought some land—with funds obtained from anonymous benefactors—and settled down to their strange experiment in monastic and ascetic communism.

The actual historical connections between Old Shakers and New Shakers remains a matter of conjecture. It is not clear, for instance, whether Harry G and his associates had a chance to consult the documentary material on display at the Hancock Museum. There is no doubt that the First Article of Faith of the Shaker Revival is a word-for-word copy of the first part of an early Shaker motto. But it has been given a subtly different meaning in present-day usage. And while many of the New Shaker doctrines and practices can be traced to the general tenor of traditional Shakerism, the adaptations are often quite free and sometimes wildly capricious. All in all, the Shaker Revival seems to be very much a product of our own time. Some prominent evolutionists even see it as part of a natural process of weeding out those individuals incapable of becoming fully consuming members of the Abundant Society. They argue that Shakerism is a definite improvement, in this respect, over the youthful cult of Bomb-throwers which had to be suppressed in the early days of the Federation.

But there are other observers who see a more ominous trend at work. They point especially to the serious legal questions raised by the Shakers' efforts at large-scale proselytization. The Twenty-seventh Amendment to the Federal Constitution guarantees the right of each white citizen over the age of fifteen to the free and unrestricted enjoyment of his own senses, provided that such enjoyment does not interfere with the range or intensity of any other citizen's sensual enjoyment. Presumably this protection also extends to the right of any white citizen to deny himself the usual pleasures. But what is the status of corporate institutions that engage in such repression? How binding, for example, is the Shaker recruit's sworn allegiance to the Believers' Creed? How are the Four Noes enforced within the sect? Suppose two Shakers find themselves physically attracted to each other and decide to consummate—does the United Society of Believers have any right to place obstacles between them? These are vital questions that have yet to be answered by the Control authorities. But there are influential men in Washington who read the Twenty-seventh Amendment as an obligation on the government's part not merely to protect the individual's right to sensual pleasure but also to help them maximize it. And in the eyes of these broad constructionists the Shakers are on shaky ground.

—MORE TO COME—

TO: Stock, Ex-Ed., *I.I.*

FROM: Senter

(WARNING: CONFIDENTIAL UNEDITED TAPE: NOT FOR PUBLICATION: CONTENTS WILL POWDER IF OPENED IMPROPERLY)

FIRST VOICE: Bruce? Is that you?

SECOND VOICE: It's me.

FIRST: For God's sake, come in! Shut the door. My God, I thought you were locked up in that Prep Meeting. I thought—

SECOND: It's not a prison. When I heard you were prowling around town I knew I had to talk to you.

FIRST: You've changed your mind then?

SECOND: Don't believe it. I just wanted to make sure you didn't lie about everything.

FIRST: Do they know you're here?

SECOND: No one followed me, if that's what you mean. No one even knows who I am. I've redefined my set, as we say.

FIRST: But they check. They're not fools. They'll find out soon enough—if they haven't already.

SECOND: They don't check. That's another lie. And anyway, I'll tell them myself after Induction.

FIRST: Brucie—it's not too late. We want you to come home.

SECOND: You can tell Arlene that her little baby is safe and sound. How is she? Blubbering all over herself as usual?

FIRST: She's pretty broken up about your running away.

SECOND: Why? Is she worried they'll cut off her credit at the feel-o-mat? For letting another potential consumer get off the hook?

FIRST: You wouldn't have risked coming to me if you didn't have doubts. Don't make a terrible mistake.

SECOND: I came to see you because I know how you can twist other people's words. Are you recording this?

FIRST: Yes.

SECOND: Good. I'm asking you straight out—please leave us alone.

FIRST: Do you know they're tampering with your mind?

SECOND: Have you tasted your local drinking water lately?

FIRST: Come home with me.

SECOND: I am home.

FIRST: You haven't seen enough of the world to turn your back on it.

SECOND: I've seen you and Arlene.

FIRST: And is our life so awful?

SECOND: What you and Arlene have isn't life. It's the American Dream Come True. You're in despair and don't even know it. That's the worse kind.

176   The Shaker Revival

FIRST: You repeat the slogans as if you believed them.

SECOND: What makes you think I don't?

FIRST: You're my flesh and blood. I know you.

SECOND: You don't. All you know is that your little pride and joy ran away to become a monk and took the family genes. And Arlene is too old to go back to the Big Boards and beg for seconds.

FIRST: Look—I know a little something about rebellion, too. I've had a taste of it in my time. It's healthy, it's natural—I'm all for it. But not an overdose. When the jolt wears off, you'll be stuck here. And you're too smart to get trapped in a hole like this.

SECOND: It's my life, isn't it? In exactly one hour and ten minutes I'll be free, white and fifteen—Independence Day, right? What a beautiful day to be born—it's the nicest thing you and Arlene did for me.

FIRST: Brucie, we want you back. Whatever you want—just name it and if it's in my power I'll try to get it. I have friends who will help.

SECOND: I don't want anything from you. We're quits—can't you understand? The only thing we have in common now is this: (SOUND OF HEAVY BREATHING). That's it. And if you want that back you can take it. Just hold your hand over my mouth and pinch my nose for about five minutes. That should do it.

FIRST: How can you joke about it?

SECOND: Why not? Haven't you heard? There're only two ways to go for my generation—The Shakers or the Ghetto. How do you think I'd look in black-face with bushy hair and a gorilla nose? Or do you prefer my first choice?

FIRST: I'm warning you, the country's not going to put up with either much longer. There's going to be trouble—and I want you out of here when it comes.

SECOND: What are the feebies going to do? Finish our job for us?

FIRST: Is that what you want then? To commit suicide?

SECOND: Not exactly. That's what the Bomb-throwers did. We want to commit your suicide.

FIRST: (Words unintelligible.)

SECOND: That really jolts you, doesn't it? You talk about rebellion as if you knew something about it because you wore beads once and ran around holding signs.

FIRST: We changed history.

SECOND: You didn't change anything. You were swallowed up, just like the Bomb-throwers. The only difference is, you were eaten alive.

FIRST: Bruce—

SECOND: Can you stretch the gray-stuff a little, and try to imagine what real rebellion would be like? Not just another chorus of "gimme,

gimme, gimme—" but the absolute negation of what's come before?
The Four Noes all rolled up into One Big No!

FIRST: Brucie—I'll make a deal—

SECOND: No one's ever put it all together before. I don't expect
you to see it. Even around here, a lot of people don't know what's
happening. Expiation! That's what rebellion is all about. The young
living down the sins of the fathers and mothers! But the young are
always so hungry for life they get distracted before they can finish
the job. Look at all the poor, doomed rebels in history—whenever
they got too big to be crushed the feebies bought them off with a
piece of the action. The stick or the carrot and then—business as
usual. Your generation was the biggest sellout of all. But the big
laugh is, you really thought you won. So now you don't have any
carrot left to offer, because you've already shared it all with us—
before we got old. And we're strong enough to laugh at your sticks.
Which is why the world is going to find out for the first time what
total rebellion is.

FIRST: I thought you didn't believe in violence and hate?

SECOND: Oh, our strength is not of this world. You can forget all
the tapes and bikes and dances—that's the impure shell that must
be sloughed off. If you want to get the real picture, just imagine us—
all your precious little genemachines—standing around in a circle, our
heads bowed in prayer holding our breaths and clicking off one by
one. Don't you think that's a beautiful way for your world to end?
Not with a bang or a whimper—but with one long breathless Amen?

TO: Stock, Ex-Ed., *I.I.*

FROM: Senter

ENCLOSED: New first add on "Shaker Revival" (scratch earlier
transmission; new lead upcoming).

JERUSALEM WEST, N.Y., Wednesday, July 4—An early critic of
the Old Shakers, a robust pamphleteer who had actually been a
member of the sect for ten months, wrote this prophetic appraisal of
his former cohorts in the year seventeen eighty-two: "When we
consider the infant state of civil power in America since the Revolution began, every infringement on the natural rights of humanity,
every effort to undermine our original constitution, either in civil or
ecclesiastical order, saps the foundation of Independency."

That winter, the Shaker foundress, Mother Ann, was seized in
Petersham, Massachusetts, by a band of vigilantes who, according to
a contemporary account, wanted "to find out whether she was a
woman or not." Various other Shaker leaders were horsewhipped,
thrown in jail, tarred and feathered and driven out of one New
England town after another by an aroused citizenry. These severe

persecutions, which lasted through the turn of the century, were the almost inevitable outcome of a clash between the self-righteous, unnatural, uncompromising doctrines of the Shakers—and the pragmatic, democratic, forward-looking mentality of the struggling new nation, which would one day be summed up in that proud emblem: The American Way of Life.

This conflict is no less sharp today. So far the New Shakers have been given the benefit of the doubt as just another harmless fringe group. But there is evidence that the mood of the country is changing —and rapidly. Leading educators and political figures, respected clergymen and prominent consumer consultants have all become more outspoken in denouncing the disruptive effect of this new fanaticism on the country as a whole. Not since the heyday of the Bomb-throwers in the late Seventies has a single issue shown such potential for galvanizing informed public opinion. And a chorus of distraught parents has only just begun to make itself heard—like the lamentations of Rachel in the wilderness.

Faced with the continuing precariousness of the international situation, and the unresolved dilemma of the Ghettoes, some Control authorities have started talking about new restrictions on all monastic sects—not out of desire to curtail religious freedom but in an effort to preserve the constitutional guarantees of free expression and consumption. Some feel that if swift, firm governmental action is not forthcoming it will get harder and harder to prevent angry parents—and others with legitimate grievances—from taking the law into their own hands.

—MORE TO COME—

Deviance

Guilty A/ Charged

Within sociology, the *sociology of deviance* includes the study of the social definition, extent, causes, and responses to deviant behavior. Sociologists and criminologists have spent much effort measuring crime (violation of one type of norm—a criminal law) and trying to develop *a* theory of crime, or *a* broader theory of deviance (violation of any type of norm—folkway, more, or law). Lack of satisfaction with the results of these efforts has led many to ask new questions and to focus on a new aspect of deviance. Dissatisfied with studying the characteristics of deviant or criminal *persons*, these scholars have focused on the *process* of becoming deviant and have discovered that the *social response to deviance*, especially the act of formally and publicly *labeling* the deviant through arrest, trial, and imprisonment, often contributes to, rather than inhibits or prevents, deviance. Inroads to understanding the social response to deviance have been made.

Social norms define deviance, and societies respond to behavior that violates the norms in a variety of ways. Some of these ways include formal *agencies for processing deviants*, such as the police, courts, prisons, mental hospitals, and so on. As attention turns to this processing, renewed study of *law enforcement, criminal justice, and corrections* results.

Following the lead of Emile Durkheim, who argued some 75 years ago that crime is "normal" in a society (it provides some social benefits), some sociologists are arguing that deviance fulfills some *positive functions* for a society. Responding to the deviant by labeling and stigmatizing the norm violator helps clarify the norms and enhances in-group cohesion as the criminal out-group is stigmatized. If this view is correct, then deviance will be found in all societies— past, present, and future. As culture changes, the types of things prohibited by norms will change, but in the long run there will be stability in the *amount* of deviance and similarity in the *kinds* of deviance.

"Guilty As Charged" tells of a time machine that permits two men to see but not hear or be present in the future. They find themselves viewing a criminal trial in the late twenty-second century. Criminal justice in 2183 does not fit their expectations of what they think two centuries of "advance" in criminal justice should have produced. What would one expect to witness in a criminal trial 200 years in the future? Would court procedures be the same? Would punishments be less severe than they are today? Would there still be deviance? Would the same types of crime be found?

Guilty As Charged

ARTHUR PORGES

His hand on a dial, Manton turned to Kramer, ready with the video-audio tape-recorder.

"All set, Dave?" he asked, a slight hum in his voice.

"Okay," Kramer replied, ostentatiously cool. The tape began to unwind with whispery precision, and Manton faced the screen, now beginning to glow. Shadowy images flitted across it, gradually sharpening to familiar shapes.

It was too bad, Manton felt, that he had been forced to choose a single small region of space-time on which to focus; the restriction was very annoying. But the field equations did indicate an additional range of about forty feet straight ahead, obtainable by varying a particular input factor. And even with all these limitations, the basic calculations had required months of expensive time on one of the fastest electronic brains available.

It had been something of a problem, too, deciding what unique setting should be computed. Manton believed that his conclusion was a logical one. Obviously, there was no point in going too far ahead; the limited view on the screen might seem chaotic—everything new and different, with few ties to his own day. Nor would it be reasonable to look forward a mere fifty years. One couldn't expect really significant changes in so brief a period. About 225 years, he decided, was probably best—not that the machine would hit it on the nose, anyway. And on that basis the months of brain-twisting mathematics, the design of thousands of electronic units, and the hair-splitting calibration of a dozen complex servomechanisms, had all been undertaken and successfully completed.

Gratified as he was, Manton couldn't help feeling a little disappointment. He had focused on the heart of this city in Massachusetts, hoping to capture the image of some busy public place: a scene sure to convey the maximum information about the mores of 2181. It was rather a let-down, then, to find himself viewing what was obviously a mere courtroom. True it was a magnificent, soaring chamber, with countless fascinating innovations of a minor sort, which he planned to study later; but Manton feared that two centuries and a quarter could not have seen any vast changes in English common law, already hallowed by time.

There would be new crimes, no doubt, either political or related to novel, intricate technologies; and a humane, streamlined, efficient courtroom procedure. Certainly, one would look in vain for either a Jeffreys or a Darrow in this enlightened age. The former would not be tolerated; and the latter would not be needed. Yet a court of law would not have changed to the extent, for example, of transportation, communication, or recreation, just to mention a few categories of human activity.

It was with mixed feelings, therefore, that he watched the two-foot-square, glowing screen, less interested at first in the trial itself than in the triumph of his genius, and the people, with their odd clothing, so loose and light, and their vigorous, almost beefy, bodies that radiated health.

There was a huge, illuminated clock calendar just at the border of his field of view; it gave him a glad thrill to see the date: April 14, 2183. He wrenched his eyes away for a brief glance at Kramer. Dave pointed to the calendar and grinned.

"Missed it by only a couple years," he said. "Nice work."

"Lucky," Manton grunted. "Plain lucky." He turned back to the screen.

Just beyond the calendar, against the same wall, was a sort of bulletin board, giving data about the case being tried. Manton could read "State vs. Frances Wills," but the next line, which presumably named the charge, was out of focus. And the machine had no leeway laterally. Too bad, but the proceedings themselves ought to clear up that point soon enough. He should be able to tell a murder case from a trial for bigamy, even in pantomime.

Now, as he watched, the accused was seating herself with obvious reluctance in the flowing contours of a witness chair. She had something about her, Manton thought, an air of strange vitality, perhaps. She was not young, about fifty, he guessed, although it occurred to him that anybody who looked only fifty in 2183 was more likely pushing ninety. Even in his day, the visible signs of senescence had been thrust ahead a decade or more within a few years.

The jurors filed in; apparently the court had been in recess. He noted that there were fifteen, and snorted. Fifteen-twelfths more chance (he couldn't help thinking mathematically) for illogical verdicts, if this bunch retained anything in common with 1956 juries. Still, they were not a bad looking group, really. Nine men and six women, of middle age mostly, but with three boys and two elderly ladies for balance.

There was the judge. Not much difference in his case. Portly, grave, and seemingly a bear for dignity. No robe. Thank God they'd given up that absurd hangover. Odd; no spectators either. A change for the better; they often put improper pressure on jurymen, just as the papers did. The judge's eyes, Manton noted, redeemed him. They were caverns of melancholy compassion. A jurist who found no perverted pleasure in sentencing social misfits had much to recommend him in Manton's opinion. But then, the cynical thought came, for whom was the compassion? Maybe the judge had ulcers—or were they finally licked after more than two centuries? He doubted it.

It was most unfortunate that he couldn't read lips; understanding this trial was not going to be so easy after all. The prosecuting attorney, a youngish man, with a surprisingly round, good-humored face, was addressing the jury, pointing now and then at the defendant. Although he seemed not unsympathetic to her, she glared at him with alarming malice. She must be, Manton concluded, a vindictive old harridan indeed. You'd think that after so many years the principles of psychiatry would have made such social unfortunates very rare. This one probably owned a fire-trap tenement; she looked the type. No, there wouldn't be tenements in 2183; it must be a more enlightened age than that. A clean courtroom proved something. Public buildings are always cleaned and modernized last. Those even in the biggest cities in his own day: Chicago, New York— why, prison was hardly more depressing than the courtrooms.

Although he knew little enough about law, Manton felt sure that procedures had changed greatly. Witnesses were seated facing the accused, for example. Most of them were restrained, but one woman, with a ravaged, unhappy face, got quite emotional, even waving before the jury a photograph, a wonderful, three-dimensional one, he noted with interest, apparently of a young girl. Later, she tried to attack the prisoner, but guards smoothly intervened. The prosecutor, looking like a chubby, brooding child, helped calm her, but she spat like an angry cat towards the accused, who merely gave her repeated, sidelong glances, half malicious, half contemptuous.

"Whistler's mother," Dave said, pointing at the defendant. "Poisonous old biddy."

Manton pulled his gaze from the bright square, a little annoyed at the comment. He liked to be judicial.

"Lucky you're not on the jury," he said evenly.

The defense attorney, tall and casual, seemed to have very little part in the trial, except for an occasional unemphatic objection. Manton guessed his case had been presented earlier, and that this was the prosecutor's second and last summation. There was an air of fait accompli about the case; it seemed that the defense was merely a routine gesture.

But it was by no means clear just what crime the old woman had committed. Apparently she had offended a number of people, for several of the witnesses showed dislike of a personal nature. There was even a touch of comedy—or so Manton accounted it, although nobody present seemed amused—when one old man, a very shaky and garrulous individual, displayed a photograph of a magnificient prime steer. As a former farm boy, Manton gasped at the meaty perfection of the animal. The old man pointed to the likeness, and shed senile tears; once he shook a trembling fist at the old woman, and the jury looked grave. The foreman slammed his right fist into his left palm, nodding vigorously; one of the old women pursed her lips disapprovingly.

Manton shook his head, running one hand through the rusty hair. He peered at Kramer, who raised one eyebrow comically. What possible connection was there between a steer, for example, and the other picture, that of the young girl? Was this grim old lady a cattle-rustler, and had that old man and the girl owned a prize beef? Manton thought of his own 4-H days and grinned wryly. He'd have been damned annoyed if anybody had stolen his own blue-ribbon steer. Absurd idea, though. If there were one crime most unlikely in her case and considering the date, it was cattle-rustling. As well expect shipwreckers in 1956 Cornwall. And what about that boy with the withered arm? What was his grievance? He had pointed to it repeatedly, contrasting it with his sturdy left arm, and showing, in vivid pantomime, how the atrophy had progressed from fingertips to shoulder.

Ah! Was this it? The old woman was guilty of reckless driving; poor reflexes, no doubt. In some high-speed vehicle of the age, she had crippled the boy, killed the steer—and as for the girl of the picture, she was killed, too. She was the boy's sister; they had been leading the steer down a highway—no, it was all speculation.

And what about the last witness? The gloomy fellow who had shown pictures of a ruined house. The structure lay in a heap as if dynamited; and the man indicated with a kind of melancholy satisfaction, how all the neighboring houses, so similar in their architecture, were unharmed. How did that fit in? Manton gave Kramer a puzzled glance.

"Blows up people's houses, too," Kramer said, shaking his head in reproof. "I told you she wasn't nice."

They were still speculating, when the trial was recessed. Here was a chance to tinker with the input factor and focus ahead a few more feet. Manton felt a glow of pleasure as he saw the foreground fade out, while the courtroom's farthest wall became clear as coated glass to the probing beam.

At the extreme fifty-foot range, just past the courtroom itself, was a chamber he found very intriguing. It was lined with light, hospital-like wall-tile, and housed but a single object: a small, metal hut. The door to this was open; and inside he could see a wheeled table of the sort employed by surgeons, except that the flat top was uncushioned and had eight-inch walls on every edge. There were straps, and yet it could not be for operations; if the person were to lie on, or rather in, that box-like table top, the walls of the metal hut would almost touch him on every side. There was certainly no room for a surgeon at all, and anyway this was not a medical center but a hall of justice.

Manton flashed back to the courtroom, finding that the recess was over. To his surprise, some attendants had wheeled in a great, complex instrument, not unlike the smaller electronic calculators he was so familiar with. But it was not one of those; no question about that. He could read some of the large dials. There was one for blood pressure, another for temperature, and many more marked with terms beyond his comprehension: Rh, Albumin, Ph, Sigma Coefficient, Curie Potential, and Dubos Count. This machine was rolled alongside the witness chair.

Manton stared. It was evident that the device was to be used somehow on the defendant, and that she resented the idea. Only after several husky guards seized her lean wrists, ankles, and shoulders, did the struggling woman submit. Moistened contact plates were fastened to her arms and forehead. Needles were deftly inserted into her leathery skin. She writhed, raving, her lips flecked with foam. The jury shrank from her feral glares. As the burly attendants held her immobile, a specialist flicked various controls on the machine. He manipulated them with bored familiarity; apparently it was an old story to him. Dial needles quivered, and the jury, much concerned, discussed their significance.

Most of these readings meant nothing to Manton, but he did wonder about two of them. The old woman's temperature seemed to be impossibly high: 115 degrees. Even he knew it ought to be near ninety-eight, and that she was well and strong, outwardly, at least, with a fever that should have been fatal. And her pulse, that was only forty, and should have been about seventy. The woman was a freak of nature, if he understood even those few readings.

Whatever the machine indicated, its findings had a decisive

effect upon the trial. The defense attorney had been weak enough, and this seemed to finish him. Evidently the old woman's guilt was beyond question, although why sickness was a crime, Manton couldn't imagine.

"That contraption finished her," Kramer muttered, stooping over his camera to adjust the focus. "But just what in hell—?" His voice died away in a querulous mumble.

Certainly the jury had no doubts; their verdict, delivered without leaving the courtroom, took only moments. The judge's pronouncement was equally brief. Now, Manton expected, she would be taken to some cell block beyond the range of the machine, and the courtroom cleared. He leaned forward, almost touching the screen, as the same attendants dragged her not to incarceration, but rather to the mysterious little room he had inspected earlier.

Kramer uttered an impatient sound, and Manton straightened up, aware he was blocking the electronic camera which was recording the trial on tape.

"We'd better shift to the other room," he said. "There's something funny going on."

He refocused in haste, just in time to see the old woman, fighting with insensate fury, being strapped to the table, which stood just outside the little hut. Was this some legal, anti-crime treatment? Something to cure the accused's criminal illness?

And now a white-coated man, obviously a doctor, came in, as did the judge and jury foreman, the latter looking particularly queasy. At a nod from the judge, the doctor prepared a hypodermic, and as the helpless woman squirmed and gibbered, made an injection directly into a vein of her arm. In a matter of moments she relaxed, but her eyes still glared hate, and only after a second injection did they close.

Could this be an execution? No, her breast still rose and fell; she was only unconscious. But maybe she would die soon. Manton gulped, tempted to switch off the machine. He had no stomach for such things. Yet a hypodermic of morphine was a great improvement over the gallows or gas chamber. Such a method would be worthy of 2183. That is, assuming there was any excuse for a death penalty, something hardly acceptable even today.

But why were they wheeling the table and its contents into the metal hut? If she were to die, why not in the open? Was it some quirk of 22nd Century psychology?

An attendant shut the door and twirled a locking wheel. The little group drew back. The judge looked meaningly at the foreman, whose face was dead white. Then the former made a slight, imperious gesture, and one man, moving to the far wall, threw a big knife-switch.

Manton started as the massive contact points arced in flash of lacy white. Heart thumping, he saw the spectators wait in silence for thirty seconds. Then, at a nod from the judge, the attendant opened the switch; and the foreman, taking a deep breath, advanced to the metal hut. With a hand that shook violently he turned the wheel; the door swung open, and Manton's stomach snapped itself into a sick knot. He heard Kramer draw in a single hissing breath. There on the table, still smoking, was a heap of dirty gray ashes, almost filling the box-like top.

No misinterpretation was possible. It was a monstrous act. The old woman, murderess perhaps, very likely insane, but a fellow human, had been anesthetized—thank God for so much mercy—and burned to ashes in an electric incinerator. Was this the humanitarian climax of over two hundred years more of civilization?

Kramer was swearing in a monotone, and automatically, without comprehension, Manton followed, with the machine, the execution party's return to the courtroom. It was empty now except for an elderly porter. He was just altering the big bulletin board, and as he shifted it slightly, Manton was able to read the words which had been out of focus during the trial, together with some others added moments before:

STATE vs. *FRANCES WILLS*
CHARGE: *WITCHCRAFT*
VERDICT: GUILTY AS CHARGED
PENALTY: DEATH BY FIRE

3

Self and Society

ociologists have long been interested in human social interaction from the standpoint of the degree to which it is affected by culture and personality. Many social scientists have mistakenly viewed personality as determined by culture, while others have mistakenly viewed culture as no more than the sum of so many individual personalities. They would pose these questions: Does culture determine personality? Does personality determine culture? To the sociologist, neither question is proper, because both oversimplify and misconstrue the relationships involved. The person is the product of a human biological organism interacting psychologically and socially in a complex variety of social relationships that are given form and meaning by the culture in which the individual interacts.

To become a person is to acquire a social nature, and to this learning process sociologists apply the term *socialization*. Through socialization an individual becomes an acting, functioning, social· being as he or she acquires a *personality*, or *self*, through association with other human beings. The process begins early in infancy in the context of the most basic of many *agencies of socialization*—the family. It continues throughout childhood, as the play group and the school join the family as agencies of socialization, and extends through adolescence, as the peer group as well as the family, the school, and the mass media combine and often compete as agencies of socialization.

Sociologists tend to agree with most psychologists that experiences early in life are important in shaping the self carried into adulthood. Sociologists, however, also emphasize that socialization extends throughout adulthood as the adult learns new social roles and statuses, often through programs of *formal* agencies of socialization such as military basic training or in-service occupational training. While the same intensity of learning and extent of development do not occur throughout the lifetime of the person, and while agencies of socialization do not reach all individuals at the same time or with equal degrees of effect, socialization is a life-long social process.

Sociologists tend to discount theories of personality that see behavior as the result of instinctual forces shaping the personality. They emphasize the acquisition of self through social interaction with others. Although influenced by Freud, many sociologists find the perspectives of the symbolic interactionist George Herbert Mead more compatible with their perspectives. Mead sees the social self as a product of social experience during which the individual learns symbolic expression characteristic of human language and communicates intensively with persons whom Mead calls "significant others." Through this interaction the two components of self—the spontaneous "I" and the socially controlled "me" develop, and social expectations become incorporated in a sense of the "generalized other," as one learns, for example, to be concerned about what other people expect and what can be done with and for others.

Integration Module

Human personality is more than the electro-chemical processes operating in the brain, more than the physiological and psychological processes operating within the total human organism. It is through social experiences that the biological capacity and potential of the brain become a mind and the human biological organism becomes a person with experienced social reality and an awareness of self. In short, developing an understanding of one's self and one's place in the scheme of things—often referred to as achieving a sense of "identity"—is not only individual but also social in nature.

All animal species possess the ability to use their sensory equipment to incorporate information and utilize it in responding to their environment. There is more to this process than a detached recording and observation of sensory input, for even solely physical aspects of contact with other individuals is important in producing emotional stability and growth in the infant and fulfillment in the adult. In human beings, an important step in developing personality, or self, is being able to see oneself as an *object*—not an object mechanically acted on by impersonal external forces, but an object responded to by other persons. Experiencing one's self through a variety of others is that important part of the socialization process that is called the "looking glass self" by the sociologist Charles Horton Cooley and that plays such a crucial part in the thinking of the social philosopher George Herbert Mead.

In this story, Beta's development of self is incomplete, for he has lacked association in meaningful relationships with others. No matter how much "love" Joseph gives to Beta as he tries to respond to Beta as "more than a guide and a father," Beta's experience of human association is deficient.

In a poignant passage, Beta asks: "Joseph, where is my experience?" Beta has knowledge, and his capacity for incorporating knowledge is astounding. Yet Beta realizes that knowledge without the experience of interacting with others leaves an incomplete self. His destiny seems to be to speculate on and use the experience of others and not to have experience with others himself. He is in a perpetual state of becoming and never of being. Lacking the experience of associating with others in a meaningful way, he lacks a developed "self."

Integration Module

DANIEL B. JAMES

The ball was going to strike the hard earth of the court right at his feet. Joseph dropped back and began his swing in one smooth motion. Whack! The tennis ball licked the edge of the net and sped on to the left corner of his opponent's court. The triple-jointed silver arm flashed and the ball came hurtling back, but too low; the net lurched as it absorbed the impact. The ball bounced twice before it was plucked out of the air by a plastic-and-metal hand.

Joseph laughed. "That's two out of three games, Beta. I'm just too good for you." He walked to the rear of the court, stuck his racket under his arm and bent to pick up a towel.

Somewhere in the building a digital computer performed a rapid calculation, the ball arced up, a racket flashed. Joseph straightened up quickly, having been smacked by a tennis ball square in the gluteus maximus. He rubbed his rear and glared at the two small electronic eyes which protruded slightly from the metal sphere to which the arms attached.

"O.K., O.K. I know what you can do when you have a second or two for calculation; you don't have to convince me. If you're going to be a poor sport, I'll just have to beat you three out of three next time."

There was an answering laugh from the sphere to which he spoke. "I am not worried, Joseph. In fact, I think I have detected a certain weakness in your game which I promise to fully exploit the next time we play."

The sphere rotated smoothly, its eyes following Joseph as he walked toward the small shower room. Joseph paused in the doorway and looked up at the sphere. "Well, Beta, you'll have to wait till Thursday to try out your strategy. Tomorrow I have some new assignments to discuss with you and it will probably take you most of the day to process them."

"What are they?" the sphere asked eagerly. The hydraulic tube and its movable shuttle to which the sphere was attached moved on its complex track in the ceiling. The tube extended and in a moment Joseph found himself looking into Beta's eyes.

"Mostly the usual problems from Central," Joseph said, "but there is one interesting job which will call for restructure."

"Good. Very good. I was hoping for something like that. A challenge. By the way, Joseph, have you heard anything from Central about the surprise reward that I'm supposed to be surprised by?"

"No," Joseph said slowly. He knew that if it were possible, Beta's eyes would be twinkling now with mischievous humor. "They don't know you have them all figured out."

"It wasn't hard. They're going to put in permanent communications between me and the Industries Computer Center at Louisville so that I'll have wonderfully expanded information access. How nice of them. Then when they 'happen' to stumble on a problem important enough, they'll assign it to both of us so we can work on it together."

"Are you unhappy about it?"

"Not at all. But why don't they be straightforward about what they want?"

"Not the way of government bureaus, Beta. If they can't obscure something or confuse someone, they're unhappy. Besides, it's their way of rewarding you and increasing efficiency at the same time."

The sphere sighed. "I don't know what I'd do without you around, Joseph. If I dealt only with the government men, I'd burn out my transistors in six months."

Joseph pulled some sweat out of his short black beard. He said softly, "I'm a government man, Beta."

The sphere folded its three-foot arms and rose swiftly to the ceiling and called down, "You've taken me aback, Joseph; but I love you anyway and I'll never tell your terrible secret."

Joseph laughed and said, "You worthless pile of wires and bolts!" He wadded up his towel and threw it up an ineffectual twenty feet or so.

Beta swooped down, caught the towel, and threw it back at the figure ducking into the doorway. "Joseph, the only thing you have on me is compactness. Otherwise, I'm a much more well-rounded individual."

Joseph stuck his head out the door. "But you still can't play tennis for freeze-dried beans!"

Joseph slipped quickly out of his tennis clothes, turned on the shower, tested the temperature of the water and stepped into the cooling stream. On a whim he decided to wash his hair; and as his fingers worked the short, somewhat curly black hair into a white froth a thought came to him unbidden. His eyes were shut against the soap, his fingers busily rubbed his scalp all over, and beneath the scalp the skull and beneath the skull the thought of that white body . . . long white body lying forever unmoving not more than a hundred yards from where he stood. And on the door of that room in which it lay was a small sign which read: CAUTION! HYPER-CRITICAL FACTORY INTEGRATION MODULE.

Joseph finished his shower and dressed quickly. He emerged from the doorway and looked around for the sphere. It hung still in the far left corner of the room. Its arms were neatly folded and its hydraulic tube was telescoped to the minimum length. *It looks dead somehow,* he thought. But then all of Beta's secondary bodies looked dead when Beta was gone from them. In all the years Joseph had known Beta he had never got used to either the sudden "coming to life" or the equally sudden temporary "death" of Beta's autosurrogates.

As he looked at the deactivated sphere, he thought again of the small room and of the body whose only movement was the incredibly slow one of its own growth. How many million of wires emerged from it? Joseph had forgotten, and it piqued him; he did not wish to forget. He promised himself that he would visit the room soon; for although his official routine called for an inspection of that room by him once a month, he had always gone more often. There was usually nothing for him to do there, but he went anyway to see if all was well with the body and . . . to see the body.

There were no sensors in that room or in the approaching corridor. Beta did not know the room existed.

He walked out of the silent game room into a long hallway which led him to another room, a small one which had served him as an office since he joined the Beta Project twenty-three years before. He dropped into his comfortable leather chair and lifted a briefcase onto his lap. Better check the memos before leaving. He pulled out a small notebook and opened it to the present date: 6 June, 2047. Damn! He reached out without looking and picked up a small desk microphone.

"Beta," he said. A tiny red light came on in the small metal sphere which was mounted on the wall. "I just wanted to let you know something I forgot earlier."

"What is that, Joseph?"

"A reporter is coming down here with me tomorrow."

"A technical reporter?"

"No, Beta, this one's from the Public Media."

A brief silence followed. Then: "I do hope this one is not quite so dumb as the last reporter you brought."

"Well, I wouldn't bring any if it were up to me, but Central decided these things and you and I just have to live with it. Oh, another thing. Central asked me to ask you nicely if you would be a little easier on this one if you could."

Beta laughed. "O.K. I'll try, Joseph. But if he asks me if I think I'm worth all the money that's been spent on me like that last fool did, I'll let him have it."

"Beta, I cringe every time I think of that interview. I wish to hell I had never let you lay eyes on 'The Dictionary of World Slang.'"

"A birthday present, I believe."

"Check your memory tapes, Beta; it was a Christmas present, and it was with no Christmas spirit that you roasted that poor fellow's ears in seventeen languages."

"I promise I'll be a pleasant host tomorrow, Joseph. See you then."

"Good-bye, Beta. See you at ten A.M."

"Oh." A pause. "One more thing, Joseph." Another pause. "Do you think . . . I mean could we . . . never mind. I'll talk to you about it later. Bye."

Joseph switched off the phone, shook his head thoughtfully and stood up. No more to be done today. He would go home to Eleanor and the kids.

The atmosphere had begun to thicken with the approaching dusk as his helicar lifted and, tilting slightly, glided away smooth and silently as a gull.

Later, with supper over and the children finally enticed to bed and asleep with a story, Joseph relaxed with a brandy and soda. Eleanor sat quietly sketching a flower which she had pinned to a sheet of white cardboard in front of her.

"A reporter named Mullroy called today," she said. "He dropped a couple of hints about getting together with you earlier than the scheduled appointment, so I invited him up for breakfast. But I let him know that meals in my house are for eating and relaxation, not work."

"Good for you." He took an extra-deep draft of brandy and soda and sagged even further into his hundred-year-old lounge chair. Somehow he just wasn't looking forward to this interview at all. It was the wrong time. Beta was going through one of his questioning cycles which had been coming along with increasing frequency.

Joseph knew Beta as well as he knew the woman who had borne his children—no, better; for he had been with Beta every day of the cyborg's life until the creature was all of ten years old. It had only been possible then for him to marry, to be away from Beta for increasing stretches of time and to think of being able to devote himself to a wife and children. But he would not have had it any other way. Few men had ever been able to devote themselves to truly pioneering work, and in his epoch the great unknown was the human mind. *And,* thought Joseph, *I've been dead-center in the exploration.*

The next morning began well. Joseph's nose informed him of Canadian bacon sizzling down below in the kitchen, even before the other senses had fully taken up their duties. Then his ears pricked to an unfamiliar sound—a low unidentifiable rumble. He leaned toward it, listening. He caught a syllable or two and realized that it was a human rumble—a man's very deep voice. The reporter. Oh, yes, the reporter. He closed his eyes and lay back until the Canadian bacon came again to inhabit his nasal cavities. Perhaps he would get up after all.

When Joseph entered the kitchen, he found Mullroy sitting comfortably with a cigarette in one hand, coffee in the other. The two men greeted one another. Mullroy was tall. He unfolded from his slouch like a carpenter's rule until Joseph was looking up at the man's thin, deeply-lined face. The smile was wise and friendly, but the eyes betrayed years of question-asking and answer-doubting. Mullroy's hands were very large and bony; Joseph felt his own almost disappear into Mullroy's firm grip.

The breakfast was pleasant in the cool morning air. The two children ate together, laughing and chatting about their plans for the day, under the nearby willow tree on a heavy bench Joseph had built. And true to his promise, the slightly nervous Mullroy asked no questions. The amount of coffee he drank was phenomenal.

Eleanor sat with the two men for a while, talking easily about the flower sketches she was doing; and finally she began gathering up the dishes and urging her children to the few chores they had to do before they ran to the forested fields or down to the river to play. Joseph lit a long, thin cigar, reached for his oversized mug of coffee and suggested to Mullroy that they might walk together down toward the river for a while before they left for the Beta Complex. Mullroy accepted eagerly.

The two men walked for a while in silence, leaving as they went small bluish clouds of smoke in the still-cool morning air. After a short time they came to the rounded brow of the hill on whose upper slope Joseph had built his house.

"Eleanor and I used to come here years ago, whenever I could spare a few hours from the Beta Complex, and dream together of that house and the children who rattle it now with their energy."

"Why don't you tell me about yourself, Dr. Beckman," said Mullroy. "I've read your dossier at Central, of course, but that doesn't help much in getting a feeling for a fellow."

So Joseph began to talk about himself, with only occasional questions from Mullroy or requests for more detail. Joseph's father had been killed in a helicar accident in the winter of 2003, when Joseph was only four years old. His mother had taken him and his three-year-old sister to live on his grandfather's farm. Joseph had, from the beginning, loved animals; and by the time he was fourteen he had assumed complete responsibility for the care of all the livestock on the farm.

His grades in school had been excellent, especially in the sciences and in linguistics and mathematics. He had won state prizes in his science fair presentations on animal communications two years in a row. He was awarded college scholarships, and by his sophomore year he had written a paper entitled "Empathetic Feedback and Interspecies Learning" which aroused excitement in the graduate schools. His academic adviser began to subtly urge him to balance his interests in animal psychology with a solid program of human psychology, organic mechanics, the interdepartmental Patterns of Science, and somewhat to Joseph's surprise but not counter to his interests, his adviser especially urged him to take the full range of courses called Molecular Engineering.

He later found that Central secretly helped him. He had thought it was luck that in his first year in graduate school he was invited to work on the new neuromotor projection experiments under Dr. Oldstead, perhaps the finest psychoneurophysiologist of his time. The team was able to prove that, particularly in the nervous systems of mammals, there is a large degree of arbitrariness in the projections of the sensorium. This meant that what a brain perceives about the body it is in and the environment around it doesn't have so much to do with the way it was originally hooked up as with the information it receives from its sensory cells. So, if one changes the sensors and their arrangement, one also changes the perception of both body- and world-image to that brain.

"You mean you could stick a rat's brain in a cat and the rat would see itself as a cat?" asked Mullroy.

"Yes, theoretically," said Joseph, "but it is enormously difficult and dangerous to the organic systems, and there as yet seems no practical reason to do it, except for the scientific value. No, very early in our investigations we chose to emphasize the replacement of the normal body sensors of an animal in the late stage of fetal development with artificial sensors."

"By artificial sensors, do you mean some sort of sensing machine?" asked Mullroy.

"Machines only in the broadest possible meaning of that word. Anything—mechanical devices, crystals, even tuned molecules—can be artificial sensors if they respond to a change in their environment in a predictable manner and degree. The response can be chemical, electrical, magnetic—as long as it is reliably consistent in its reaction.

"From what we learned in the experiments with animals, we developed micro-linkages which converted the signals from the artificial sensors to signals that were in the simple electrical code that the human nervous system is used to.

"About that time, Dr. Tell of Zurich Polytechnic developed faciplastic which, as you probably know, will contract like muscle under electrical stimulation. It was child's play for us to connect the motor nerves of an animal or human through an amplifier to this fasiplastic. Never will I forget that first experiment. I watched with awe as a mouse lifted a one-pound weight from across the room by his nervous signal to a crudely-mounted strip of the faciplastic. Oh, those were exciting times!

"Then, at the end of my Ph.D. studies, my adviser introduced me to the representative from Central. He offered me more than a job. He offered me a life's work: to be a mother, father, companion and technical adviser to the world's first permanent cyborg. I would assist in the creation of the cyborg, and from the moment of its birth I was to be its primary link with reality."

"Dr. Beckman," said the reporter, "could you tell me why you were chosen for this project? I mean, aside from your excellent technical qualifications?"

Joseph was silent for a moment and then he said, "I think it was my 'motherly' instincts." He smiled. "I suspect that the thing which clinched it was my background in animal care. Central realized that the teaching of a permanent cyborg would take patience, calmness and . . . love."

"Love," Mullroy repeated with an irritating flat tone of voice as he scribbled in his notebook.

Joseph's relaxation vanished. He found himself staring at the faintly cynical downward curve at the corners of the reporter's mouth.

"You seem to have stumbled over the word 'love,' Mr. Mullroy. Why?"

"Maybe the word clashed in my mind with the thought of a

human being wired into a concrete building. Dr. Beckman," said Mullroy softly, without looking up.

"Look, Mullroy, we're not ogres!" Joseph paused; he knew he must not be defensive with this man. "There are two things I want you to understand. First, because of the human module's defects he would either have had euthanasia or be forced to endure a life of the minimum four or five cubic feet of life-support mechanisms that he could not survive without. The second thing, Mullroy, is this: I do love Beta and I've done everything in my power to help him live a meaningful, healthy and interesting life."

"You speak of the 'human module,' Dr. Beckman, and then you speak of Beta. Don't you consider Beta human?"

Joseph got up and stretched, consciously calming himself before he answered.

"Beta is an entity—a highly complex cyborgean chemical engineering and manufacturing factory. Beta contains as one of his functioning parts what is the finest integration and feedback device that we have knowledge of—the human nervous system. Because of this system, the factory is aware of himself and his environment in a unified field of consciousness. Millions of bits of information flow into the human module every second to be processed and projected. Why, Mullroy, compared to this the finest computers we have are mere toys!"

"And cheap . . ."

"No, not cheap. Beta cost what eight ordinary factory complexes would cost. That is not to say that Beta hasn't paid back much of his original cost in increased production and in improved techniques. Not to mention the invaluable scientific knowledge we have gained."

"You would say, then, that Beta is an economic success?"

"Mullroy," said Joseph, "of all the reporters I've talked to, you have come the closest to making me mad. You are a real expert."

"I admit, Dr. Beckman, that I'm not unaware that a little—not too much, but a little—anger sometimes helps the information flow. What about that last question, then?"

"No, this human module factory has a long way to go before it could be called an economic success. But what is more important" (he stared hard at the reporter to emphasize his point) "is the grand experiment that it is. It involves scientists from fifty nations, many of whom will be dead long before Beta."

"Why do you say that Beta will die? Won't it just be the human module that will die?"

"Yes and no. Of course, only the human module can organically die; but it took us eight months to complete wiring the module into the factory, and it took as many years for Beta to learn to control his actions and to integrate his senses as it does a child to do the same with his body. Furthermore, as the years have gone on the nervous system and the electrical and chemical components of the factory have adjusted to one another in countless ways. No, when the human module dies, the factory in a sense dies too; for it would have to be completely rewired for the next human module."

Joseph had been pacing around as he spoke. Now he stopped and looked at his watch. "We'd beter start back, because I told Beta that we would get there at ten."

Mullroy got up and stretched. "O.K. Perhaps you could tell me how you see this 'grand experiment.' I'm not exactly a religious type, but I agree with most religions in their assumption that there is something a little special about man. I don't see what justifies your taking away a man's body and sticking him in a machine."

They walked for a few moments before Joseph replied. "As I said, we didn't take away the physical body—just disconnected it. Then we gave him another body.

"As to the justification you asked for, I could repeat some of what I've said and add a dozen other good reasons having to do with medicine, psychology, economics and so on. But personally I've felt at times that it isn't so much a question of right or wrong as it is a coming to pass of the inevitable."

"I don't get you."

"This isn't easy for me to talk about, Mullroy, and don't quote me. What I'm trying to say is that if it hadn't been us that first helped man step beyond his skin and become another being it would soon be someone else. The cards were dealt long ago by old lady nature herself when she realized that if you could have one form of living thing you could have millions of them. We scientists—and man in general, I might add—can't help trying to follow her act. It might blow us to kingdom come, but homo sapiens is going to try to do everything it can think of and, Mullroy, *be* everything it can imagine."

"Like what? Give me some examples."

"Use your imagination, Mullroy. What form would you take if you could choose from among endless varieties? What senses would you have, if you could choose from a list of thousands, including X-ray vision and bat-hearing? What would be the limit of your strength, and how would you design muscle arrangements if those choices were virtually unlimited—as they soon will be? You could be a human version of a bird or deep-sea fish. You could swim in the hot lava of a volcano, or rocket casually off to the moon—not in a space ship, but in your own sensitive, reacting body. And you would live longer, too, because there wouldn't be the wear and tear on your physical body except for the nervous system and it can live to a ripe old age."

"Could I be the Mississippi River?" Mullroy asked.

"Glad to see you're getting into the spirit of the thing, Mullroy. Maybe you could, someday. You could be a continent . . . hell, you could be the entire earth if you wished! At least theoretically, that is. You might have to spread your sensory and motor nerves a little thin —maybe one per square mile." His voice grew more serious. "But the important thing is that your brain could handle it. It could contain within itself a unified, changing projection of the whole earth. You wouldn't experience being a nervous system; you would experience *being* the earth. In a sense, the planet would be inside your brain, but you would never know that except by reason. Just as with your body—I mean your experienced body and not your physical body—it is inside your brain, but you don't know that because your brain has been evolutionarily biased to pretend otherwise."

"Now just hold it, Dr. Beckman." Mullroy stopped and gestured to the sky and surrounding hills. "Are you suggesting that all *this*— what I experience—is within my brain? Along with my experienced body? That makes you a solipsist, I believe."

"Forget the philosophical tags, Mullroy. They have a way of numbing the mind. To answer your question—yes! Where in hell do you expect your experience to be but in the organ of the human body which is specialized to perform the experiencing function? Everything you experience right now is taking place within the volume of something not much bigger than a softball. For example, that magnolia tree over there, blooming so beautifully, which we see as maybe a hundred yards away is actually within your cranium and, logic informs us, is but a few inches from your body-image at the most."

"One of us is crazy, Doctor," said the reporter. "I mean—well, I don't disagree with you, I can't refute what you say—but it just doesn't mean anything to me. It's like finding out how many cells there are in the human body—interesting, but it changes nothing about the way I feel about living or other people or myself."

"Of course it doesn't, Mullroy. The brain is a little like the stomach—it takes in some new data and either assimilates it or rejects it. It doesn't know what to do with something it can neither assimilate into the system nor simply toss out. Mullroy, one of the things which keeps life so interesting for us humans is the fact that we live in terms of paradox. We have a built-in desire for truth; wherever man looks he sees questions—they are as much a part of his gaze as color. We shall seek to answer our questions as long as we are human. Yet we shall never cease fearing the unknown even as we are drawn to it. We shall also attempt the paradoxical effort to contain raw truths within the box of our illusions. Why? Because illusion is our method, a function of our nervous systems. It is the fragile invention of organic systems of atoms trying to *know*. And ultimately the brain will corner itself somewhere . . . and fearfully try to encompass within itself the raw truth of its method, its surrogate reality."

The reporter stopped to light a cigarette. He took a long time at it. He shook his head and spoke; his voice seemed older and tireder. "And what then? What do we do then?"

"I don't know. I just know it's something we must do. We really don't have much choice but to pursue mysteries, including our own, wherever they lead us." Joseph thought for a moment. "Whatever happens, I think we will find that mystery—like life—doesn't die, that it changes, mutates into another form. It will be with us as long as we exist."

The interview went smoothly and Joseph was pleased with the questions the reporter asked, which were intelligent and concisely put. Mullroy was writing in his notebook some impressions concerning Beta's answer to the last question on the reporter's list. The sphere made a little nod to Joseph, who sighed inwardly. Beta was up to something.

"And now I have a question for you, reporter," said Beta.

"Shoot." Mullroy continued writing furiously.

Beta shot. "What is causing your hand to move right now as you write?"

"Huh!" Mullroy's eyes rotated up so that they peered at Beta through bushy eyebrows. "I am, of course."

"Are you? I suggest you write a word and tell me what passes through your mind as you do so."

Mullroy wrote a word, a noncomplimentary one, which he directed at Joseph who for the past few moments had been pointedly engrossed in the patterns of the tiles on the ceiling.

"Well," said Mullroy, "to be honest, I'd have to say that I wasn't thinking about the act of writing as I did it. It's just sort of automatic."

"Would you say that you were not aware of it?" Beta asked quickly.

"Certainly I was aware of it. I did it. I watched it as it happened."

"Try it again and tell me what is in your awareness besides just your experience of the act."

Mullroy paused and sighed. Slowly he guided his pen in the

writing of a long word.

"Nothing. There is nothing in my mind as I write except the experience itself."

Beta chuckled. "So the causing of the writing is unconscious to you. How can you take credit for doing something that you're not even aware of?"

"Look," said Mullroy with a touch of exasperation in his voice, "*I* wrote the word. *I* decided to write it. It was *my* act. Just what are you getting at?"

"I wonder if you really did decide," Beta said serenely. "Joseph, would you mind telling Mr. Mullroy that story of yours about the time you 'noticed' your hand?"

Joseph shuddered inwardly. "Oh, I doubt if Mr. Mullroy would care to . . ."

"But I would, I would." Mullroy leaned forward in an exaggerated expression of great interest.

"All right. I'll be brief. One time when I was sitting in school, a very bored eleven-year-old boy, I noticed my hand lying on my knee. I use the word 'noticed' because it was the first time that I had seen my hand as an object—a physical object like a banana or a rock. So I began thinking how strange it was for me to be able to cause this object to move just by telling it to do so. I remember feeling a strange sense of power and magic. In this frame of mind I began to order my hand—this object—to move, to drum fingers on my knee, to make a fist and so on. Of course nothing happened; the hand just lay there. I clearly recall summoning up all my force of will and commanding my hand to rise. Arise, hand! I was amazed to see that the hand did not move at all."

"You must have been telling your hand *not* to move," Mullroy said.

"Not consciously, I wasn't. The point is . . ."

"The point is, Mr. Mullroy," said Beta, "that perhaps you did not 'decide' to write the word any more than Joseph was able to decide that his hand should move, assuming of course that you are constructed more or less the same as Joseph."

"*I* was not constructed. I grew," Mullroy said archly.

There was a short pointed silence from Beta. Then: "Joseph, I think I am getting that 'Dictionary of World Slang' feeling again."

"Yes," said Joseph. "I think this is a good time to terminate the interview. Unless you have any more questions . . . ?"

"No, I have all I need. Thank you very much, Beta. Sorry I couldn't follow your little philosophy lesson better. I never did too well in it in college."

"You are welcome, Mr. Mullroy," said Beta, a decided chill in his voice.

Joseph led the confused reporter to his office, poured two mugs of coffee and sat down, waiting.

"O.K.," Mullroy said, "would you mind telling me what in hell *that* was all about?"

Joseph smiled, although he was not at all at ease. "Don't worry about it, Mullroy. Beta does that to me, too. It is his nature to, well, speculate on things. With you he was trying to show that you can observe your hand guiding the pen, but you can't observe nor directly control that which causes your hand to move. The cause remains as unknown to your consciousness as, say, the center of the earth."

"You seem to have actually encouraged Beta in these . . . speculations. Which reminds me, how come you told Beta that story about your hand?"

"God knows! I don't remember the circumstances. As you know, one of Beta's advantages is that besides his ordinary human memory, which is as fallible as ours, he has connections to a memory tape system. I never know while I'm talking with him if he's taping or not. He spends hours of his off-duty time randomly scanning his memory tapes until he finds something interesting to think about. I think that's how he came up with that 'hand' story."

They talked a while longer, then as the reporter was taking his leave he paused in the doorway. "One last question, Dr. Beckman. Since information on the human module is considered 'sensitive' rather than secret, how do you prevent Beta from finding out about himself?"

"Well, the 'sensitive' classification enables Central to keep the media from sensationalizing the information on this project. That keeps the public calm, and the scientific community can function better in an atmosphere of free exchange of information. All we have to do is be very careful what Beta reads, as he has no other way of finding out about the human module. And Beta prefers tapes, which are cleared, to books anyway."

Mullroy nodded, waved his hand in farewell, and closed the door behind him. Joseph sat for a few minutes finishing his coffee and thinking. His thoughts were troubled by vague little fears. The cyborg was hunting for something; these speculations of Beta's were not idle. They were part of a pattern of behavior which went back years into the past.

He put it firmly out of his thoughts and reached for the button which would call Beta to activation. As he did so, he realized with horror that the red light was already on.

"Beta! How long have you been activated?"

Came the answer as soft as his question was sharp, "Only about five seconds, Joseph. Why? Were you and the reporter talking about something I shouldn't hear?"

Joseph's heart stopped beating quite so rapidly. "No. I just . . . was surprised, that's all." He hurried on. "Are you ready for the briefing? There are some restructure problems which should interest you."

Pause. "Certainly, Joseph. Proceed."

The briefing took more than an hour. Joseph could hear the moving of massive machinery in the Main Room as Beta moved parts of himself about, trying first this arrangement and then that in his search for the most efficient one for the production of the new plastics. Finally he was satisfied.

"No problem, Joseph. Central can pick up their sixty tons of TCP-19 by tomorrow afternoon at the south loading dock. I may have some problems with one of the components for the other plastic, though. I can produce it O.K., but it tends to lump in the gross transport pipes. I'll have to experiment with flow vibration frequencies until I can find the right one. That may take a while."

"No rush on that order anyway, Beta. I'll put it in the project data tapes so you can get busy. Anything else you need?"

"Not for these projects, but . . . Joseph, I can have most of this worked out and set up for the Automatic Section by eight o'clock tonight . . ." Beta could set up a process, work it a while, then let it proceed as effortlessly and unconsciously as digestion in a man.

"You don't have to do it that fast, Beta. You can quit at the regular time," said Joseph.

"I know, but I want to have everything done . . . if I can talk you into coming back over here tonight."

Joseph was surprised. It was the first time in years that Beta had asked him to come at an unscheduled time. "What's up?" he asked.

"I want to talk about some things. But not during working hours. See, this is personal . . ." his voice trailed off.

Joseph hesitated. He was afraid, and he didn't know why. There was a suppressed excitement in Beta's voice, an urgency. But he said that he would come.

On his way back to Beta that night, Joseph thought through the events of the past few days, then he raced through his memory as one might through fields. Beta was as complex as anyone he had ever known. And just as unpredictable. All he knew for sure was that this was important—not only for the experiment which had consumed the entirety of his professional career, but for Beta's life and mind as well. Joseph felt he had to be more than a guide and a father—he had to be a friend to a cyborg who had become a mature organism.

He parked the helicar and walked the few yards to the entrance. In the beginning, he had felt that he was entering Beta's body when he walked through these doors; but now he only felt that way when he entered the Main Room where most of Beta's apparatus and sensors were. The Main Room was full of complex noises, although the sound level was not uncomfortably high. The sphere was hung in the corner, unmoving. The job he was working on seemed to take all his attention, for he said nothing to Joseph, who was watching quietly.

Finally Beta spoke. "There! All finished. I've got that sequence on tape and it can go on automatic as soon as the other job is done. It took me a little longer than I thought."

Beta activated the autosurrogate and it moved down from its corner until it hung a few feet from Joseph. The sphere and the man stared at each other without speaking for several moments; then Joseph spoke.

"Well, Beta, what's on your mind?"

"A million things, Joseph. But they all have to do with what I am."

"Are you unhappy?"

The sphere made a small gesture of surprise. "No, not at all. I'm content enough, but even so I find myself asking questions which lead not to answers but to more questions. Frankly, Joseph, I'm confused."

Joseph laughed. "You can join the club, Beta. Nearly everyone I know who has the wit to question existence is confused. You wouldn't be a true child of the human species if uncertainty weren't part of your heritage."

"I appreciate your kindness," Beta said with mild irony, "in telling me that it is natural and acceptable to be confused. But I want more than that. I want the answers—and I feel you can give them to me."

"Really?" Joseph said slowly. "Maybe so, but I doubt it."

"Consider, Joseph, what I was saying to that reporter toward the end of the interview. What did you think of that?"

"I told Mullroy, when he asked me, that you were trying to demonstrate that voluntary control is really a nonconscious control."

"In other words," said Beta, "we don't really know what we are *going* to do, only what has just been done."

"Yes, that's what I told him you were getting at."

"Joseph, a couple of years ago I was talking with you about something and I remember that I was quite voluble. I was discoursing on something I knew well and I spoke fluently, even brilliantly—or so it seemed. Then a strange thing happened. I suddenly realized that I didn't know what words were going to come out of my speaker until they were already echoing off the walls. I was amazed. It was as if the words were streaming out of eternity through me. I began to think about this. My thoughts have clustered around this experience. Joseph, it is almost an obsession with me now. Where do the words come from? How are they strung together in such logical order?"

Joseph thought he saw a way out of the coming confrontation. "Put it out of your mind, Beta. The mind of man which created you as another stage among endless stages of evolution does not understand everything it creates. Just as you create new associations of atoms without a complete knowledge of molecular relationships, so we have generated you as another version of ourselves without knowing everything there is to know about ourselves. You have as many unknowns in you as we have in us. We don't know where our words come from either."

"I find it hard to believe that you don't know."

Joseph was so shocked that he said nothing.

Beta continued. "But let us continue. Another thing which has occupied my thoughts is something subtle that I've identified in my experience. Not only have I decided that somewhere there is something *doing* what I have thought *I* was doing, but I've begun to wonder about my perceptions. You, Joseph, taught me long ago about my sensors. And, whenever I wish, I can look them up in my tape memory. Sensors for this, sensors for that—I have thirty-one different kinds of sensors."

"So?" Joseph sank into a chair for the duration.

"So—somewhere the millions of bits of data are all put together into a unity. Otherwise I would experience no unity. Somewhere all the data is examined and censored and pruned and trimmed. Then I receive what's left."

"I give you my word," said Joseph, "that we do not interfere with your sensory experience."

"I thank you for telling me and I believe you. But that information changes nothing. I am convinced that there must be a device which integrates my data and then sends it to me. Which brings me to my last point."

The sphere moved closer to Joseph until their eyes were about a foot apart.

"Joseph, where is my experience?"

"What! Your experience?"

"You needn't be so surprised, Joseph. I've just thought about the things you have taught me. What I think is as much your ideas as mine."

Joseph thought ruefully of his conversation with Mullroy and of the magnolia tree that the reporter did not wish to have in his head, preferring the useful illusion of "out there."

Beta went on. "Joseph, I've got millions of sensors, but only one unified awareness of my world. As far as I can see, that unity could not be the result of scattered functions of devices. It's impossible. Everything I experience has an underlying similarity, despite the apparent differences in quality or form. Somehow these seemingly different things undergo a similar process—the end result of which is my total experience at any one time."

"What can you conclude from that, Beta?"

"I conclude that there is a device—one single device—which provides the ultimate integration of all the relevant information available to my waking being. I think that what we call 'consciousness' *is* this complete integration. If this is true, then where is this device? Joseph, please tell me."

"Do you think it's something you can just go look at?"

"Yes, why not?"

"Before we go any further, tell me why it means so much to you."

"Don't you understand, Joseph? That device holds the secret to where I am and what I am. It's where I really live. It's where everything I have ever known has its location and existence and overlay of meaning."

"I don't understand . . ."

"You do, you do!" Beta said, nearly shouting. "I can tell!" Then, more calmly, "I know that I don't experience myself directly—the atoms and molecules of me. I know myself only in the way that I know other things, things external to my physical machinery. I only *experience* myself. The self that I know by experience must logically be within that device, along with everything else I experience."

Joseph shook his head sadly. "What can you possibly gain by pursuing this?"

"I am not thinking in terms of gain anymore. All I know is that neither myself nor my world is what I thought it was, nor where I thought it was." The sphere started to sway to and fro. "Oh, Joseph, am I some flickering image somewhere who only thinks he has will and self? Help me. Help me."

"Be quiet," Joseph said sharply. "Do you think you are ready for any understanding of yourself if you act this way?"

The swaying stopped abruptly. Then came Beta's voice, cool and calm as ever. "Sorry, Joseph. It's very rare that I feel that way. Usually it is the curiosity which drives me in this search. Sometimes, though, I become confused and lonely and the thinking becomes fuzzy, difficult to follow. The more difficult it becomes, the more I feel compelled to attack the problem. To be honest with you, I confess that I must find out about myself, this device, what my world is made of. It's not just curiosity anymore."

"What you ask is not possible," Joseph said.

"Tell me about it then. You must know! I am a child of the human species, you said. You must know how my consciousness was made."

"Man," said Joseph cryptically, "makes many things that he doesn't really understand."

"Is this one of them?"

Joseph couldn't lie now. Beta would know and the precious trust would die.

"No, Beta, it isn't," he said softly.

"Joseph, take me to it."

"Beta, for God's sake! It's against regulations . . ."

"Then I was right! It does exist!"

Joseph exploded. "Yes, it exists! But can't you forget it? It would do you no good to see it."

"I don't care about doing myself good. This is something I need."

"Beta, most of the men who brought you into existence feel that it would be bad for you. I am forbidden even to mention the matter to you, let alone allow you to see the Integration Module."

"So that's what you call it."

It wasn't easy. It took him half the night to free the required four hundred feet of cable which ran behind the paneling of walls and ceiling of the Main Room to the autosurrogate. There had been no way to splice a section of cable into it; it was far too complex for that. He didn't know what Beta was doing meanwhile; no doubt he was going over his memory tapes to review everything he had recorded about this matter. Damn! He couldn't find anything to carry the autosurrogate in. The thing was far too heavy for him to lift. Childishly, he wondered if he wouldn't have to call this madness off. No, not so lucky. His mind's eye presented him with the answer and he realized Beta would think of it too: the chair in his office with the little casters.

They were ready by two-thirty in the morning. With the help

of Beta's arms and hands supporting the weight of the heavy sphere, Joseph was able to wrestle the excited orb into the heavily cushioned seat.

"Right side up, if you would." Beta was staring out upside down. It made him feel a little funny.

Using one of the arms for a lever, Joseph carefully turned the autosurrogate over. Beta still felt strange and said so.

"You've lost your hydraulics, Beta. Your reflexes are sending out balance and posture control messages, but now nothing happens. Are you dizzy?"

"I'm all right. I'm fine."

"Sure you are," Joseph said sarcastically. "Look, let me know if you start to get sick."

Beta assured him that he would. And then slowly, very slowly, Joseph anxiously began wheeling the chair toward the corridor. The journey was not long, but it took almost an hour. Joseph had to stop every few feet to pull the cable forward, to check the floor surface over which the chair would pass, to pause and relax his own tense muscles. Injury to the autosurrogate and the unknown possibility of damage to Beta's psyche if there were an accident—all unthinkable! With agonizing slowness they crept down the narrow corridor; painfully they turned the corner; slow as plant growth they approached the forbidden door.

Beta stared at it for a long while. Joseph could hardly breathe now. There was a prickle at the back of his neck. Madness. Madness. A wave of vertigo nearly swept him to the ground. Emotion splashed through him as though he were a bucket with no bottom. Above all was embarrassment, shyness. As always when he tiptoed here. For here was housed the soul of his friend . . .

There was a trembling in Beta's arms as he repeated "integration module, integration module" over and over very softly. Finally he visibly steadied himself and said that he was ready to go in.

Joseph pushed open the door. The room was dark. Moving like a man at the bottom of an ocean, he pushed the chair and its silent occupant through the soft light which angled into the room from the hall and into the blackness.

Beta waited quietly. Joseph moved to the light switch.

"Have courage, Beta, my friend," he breathed. "We should have told you, but they were afraid; now it will go hard for you. I am with you, my friend." The light slowly increased.

Out of the gloom came that unbelievable image: the long white body so still upon its electronic bier, so perfect beneath its protective plastic cover. Faint rhythms played through the muscles. At first Beta did not move as he stared at the young male form. Then his arm twitched up and dropped back. He raised his hands and cupped them around his eyes. He shuddered and a groan filled the room. And then he began to cry in short, harsh sobs. And not just the autosurrogate was crying, but the whole cyborg. Joseph could hear deep rhythmic throoming sounds from all over the factory.

Not knowing what to do, Joseph knelt beside the chair and waited. Beta put out a blind hand, groping, found Joseph's shoulder, gripped it hard. Joseph winced with pain but did not move. Beta spoke then with great difficulty, tearing each word from the fabric of his crying.

". . . there . . . inside there! . . . now . . . I'm in THERE, Joseph . . . now! And I . . . always was."

After a time, Beta grew quiet and the great sounds throughout the factory died away. Joseph reached to his shoulder and took Beta's hand which lay there. Beta gave a start.

"Now I know," Beta said, "why the warmth of human touch always felt so good to me. Joseph . . . why didn't you tell me? Why does that . . . lie there instead of walking . . ." His voice broke.

"It never would have walked, Beta, never done a hundredth of what you can do. Listen to me, Beta, it had such serious defects it would probably not have lived or if it lived it would have been confined to a room somewhere. Oh, Beta, I couldn't tell you. I'm sorry . . ."

Silence filled the little room. Beta continued to stare at the body. "Defects," he said finally. "If that is so then I have no regrets. I've had a hand, you know, in making myself what I am." His voice was a strange mixture of irony and pride.

The tension of fear in Joseph broke and melted. Beta would be all right. He was strong. Now a wetness came to Joseph's eyes as he too gazed at the form which housed Beta's essence and his world.

"No one should have to go through what you have, Beta." His voice seemed small and far away.

"You're wrong, Joseph," said Beta slowly, "doubly wrong. For years my thinking and questioning have made ideas like so many arrows all pointing to the same unknown place." He gestured around the room. "This is that place. I had to know what was in that place." He looked at the body and said, "I'm glad I know."

"You said I was doubly wrong."

Beta thought for a while. "I followed an unmarked path in my mind until I found that the core of myself is human. I never expected that. And now I see that the end of my journey is where I join you on your path and begin again. All my questions still apply; the arrows point to a new unknown place."

"I see," said Joseph. "Yes, the questions still apply. Our words come, but we don't know from where. The bright world leaps up like flames in the brain, but we don't know how. And all is soaked in meaning, and we ask why." He smiled. "Welcome, my friend, to one hell of a long, confusing, and fascinating journey!"

4

Social Differentiation

Human social history, to the sociologist, has been in large part a trend from relatively undifferentiated societies toward more complex ones. Sociologists have contrasted the homogeneity of what the anthropologist Robert Redfield called the "folk" society with the heterogeneity of the modern industrial state. Many sociologists have constructed polar-type constructs to help clarify in the contrast of types the social changes at work. Toennies wrote of *Gemeinschaft* and *Gesellschaft* social structures, Durkheim of *mechanical* and *organic solidarity*, Becker of *sacred* and *secular* societies; and others have used different terms to make the same contrasts. What is common to the work of all these scholars is a recognition that small, less differentiated, more homogeneous societies have been replaced by larger, more complex, and more heterogeneous societies. This change has produced societies of greater diversity wherein clearly identifiable, contrasting, and often conflicting subgroups become differentiated as human beings interact with one another. In modern society, subgroups can be identified on such bases as social class position; racial, ethnic, and religious group membership; and common age.

In all societies, systems of social stratification develop. Persons are differentially evaluated on the basis of such criteria as their occupation, income, age, education, prestige, race, religion, and ethnic origin. The differential evaluations result in a system in which many persons share approximately the same general hierarchical locations, or *strata*. In some societies sharp divisions separate strata, and social mobility and even interaction across strata boundaries is very limited. In this case, sociologists call each stratum a social *caste*. In other societies, the gradation from stratum to stratum is gradual and mobility from one stratum to another is extensive. Here a social stratum is termed a social *class*.

Sociologists are aware that not only do aggregates of people share similar position on the stratification hierarchy by having similar occupations, incomes, and so on, but those within a social class develop important similarities in values, tastes, and behavioral practices. Sociologists use the term *style of life* or *life-style* to refer to the cultural and social patterns shared by those within a stratum.

Movement from one location to another within the stratification system represents *social mobility*. Social mobility can be either horizontal (within strata boundaries) or vertical (either upward or downward in the hierarchy). Class societies, such as the United States, generally have high rates of social mobility and high rates of geographical, or spatial, mobility as well.

Social differentiation can also reflect patterned responses to skin color differences. The different social position held by different categories of people identified on the basis of race is not a reflection of biological difference, but of the *socially* defined significance of color. Differences in skin color become socially defined as important, and people begin to act accordingly. Oversimplifying and exaggerating characteristics of people of other races produces *stereotyping*. Persons of one race may make derogatory shorthand prejudgments of members of other races, thereby expressing *prejudice*, and/or they may behave in a *discriminatory* way toward persons identified as members of the derogated group. Patterns of social stratification reflect these judgments and actions when members of the minority race (the one discriminated against) are held to positions at lower-class levels.

Although "race" does not refer to a viable scientific concept because there are no clearly identifiable unmixed racial groupings or subgroupings, color difference and various attributes perceived to accompany this difference serve as a socially important delineator among human beings. Of the various categories of minority peoples identified as "races" in the United States, the most important numerically are blacks, who now constitute slightly over 10 percent of the population.

Age and *sex* are also social differentiators. All societies assign to males at least some expectations and tasks that differ from those assigned to females. All societies as well have age-specific social statuses wherein children are subordinate to adults. In industrial societies a third age-specific status intervenes between childhood and adulthood—the status of adolescence. Sociologically, adolescence is the period in the lifetime of the individual between the development of physical maturity and the conferral of adult social maturity. Uncommon in traditional societies where one passes from childhood to adulthood in clearly celebrated rites of passage, adolescence is common and expanding in duration in modern industrial societies.

Psychologists interested in adolescence have emphasized the personal problems of growth and social adjustment during this phase of life. Without denying that adolescence is a time of personal stress—of learning and experimenting accompanied by anxiety and self-doubt, sociologists have seen the "problems of adolescence" as largely the consequence of changes in social structure. Adolescence is viewed as a marginal social status within which one is neither child nor adult—at times treated like a child while at other times expected to act like an adult. Much of the personal stress of adolescence stems from the ambiguity of the status, and the structure of the situation is such that adolescents are likely to turn to others sharing the status and its problems and away from older and younger persons.

In this chapter we consider the process of social differentiation as it produces subgroupings differentiated according to social class, race, and age.

Social Class

A Day in the Suburbs

During the early decades of the twentieth century, the upward social mobility of ethnic groups was accompanied by *outward* spatial movement from the center of the city. Since the 1940's, large-scale spatial mobility has taken many middle-class families beyond the city limits to suburban residence as upward social mobility has accompanied the families' economic affluence and their aspiration to "be a success." Casual observers of social trends have seen these "middle-class suburbs" as homogeneous enclaves of hyper-conforming "status seekers" trying to keep up with the Joneses in display of the trappings of social status as they continued their climb to—and then from—the "Park Forests" and "Levittowns" ringing large cities. Less impassioned but more accurate social scientists offered correctives to these views of the homogeneous suburb as the molder of likeminded would-be achievers, living in "dormitory" suburbs from which fathers commute every morning to their jobs elsewhere, leaving the wives to raise the kids and to "coffee klatch" with neighboring wives. The imagery, however, has been pervasive and convincing to the public despite studies by social scientists demonstrating suburban heterogeneity.

"A Day in the Suburbs" describes events in the life of a suburban family during a single day. The suburbanites pictured are sharply divided by income category and identify each other by the type of residence in which each lives: "Flat-Tops" vs. "Peaked-Roofers." The conflict between these suburbanites is exaggerated, but the emphasis vividly illustrates the social divisions often characteristic of stratified societies, as the author combines crisis and the mundane concerns of suburbanites. Notice the juxtaposition, within a single casual conversation, of "Oatmeal Crunchies" with the probably fatal ambush of little Ava Pratt. In one sense, stratification patterns reflect values of a society, and this author expands on values of the American middle class to set the context of the events of this particular day. Since conflict gives way to quiet as adult males return from their jobs elsewhere to join their families, Evelyn Smith may be telling *male* readers, particularly, that all status conflict isn't experienced by males in corporate boardrooms, salesrooms, and factories. Status striving is not alone a male characteristic, and social mobility has its price as well as its reward.

A Day in the Suburbs

EVELYN E. SMITH

"**D**uck your head, Margie!" Mrs. Skinner cried, as bullets splatted against the car windows.

"The glass is bulletproof," Margie observed, twisting her head around so she could see out of the rear window.

"Don't count on that," her mother said grimly. "I understand the Flat-Tops have a fifth column in Detroit."

Margie squirmed back into place. "It was that old Helen Kempf shooting at us. Couldn't hit the side of a barn door!"

"Managed to hit the side of a car, though. I hope we'll have time for a quick respray before your father gets home. Thank God for fast-drying paint."

"When I go back to school, I'm going to get her alone in the locker room and kill her," Margie said.

"You know school's a truce zone," Mrs. Skinner murmured, her eyes fixed on the road. No chance of mines—the Flat-Tops used this stretch, too—but there could always be a deadfall. "We have a treaty with the board."

"The board!" Margie scoffed. "They're mostly Old Windmill Manorites. Their kids go to private schools or something; their classrooms are practically empty."

Mrs. Skinner only half heard the words. They were passing through hill country now, and her eyes alertly scanned the shrubbery masking the embankments. Was that a gun muzzle glittering in the sunlight or just a piece of broken bottle?

"You know what I think of the Old Windmill Manorites?" Margie offered. And she proceeded to tell her mother quite explicitly.

Mrs. Skinner's attention was caught by that. Her lips thinned. "Margery, I don't know where you pick up such language."

"The Flat-Tops talk that way in class all the time."

"Don't lie to your mother. The teacher wouldn't let even a Flat-

Top use language like that in class. You got it from the boys."

"Well, they're *our* boys."

"Boys are boys. They—"

"*Watch out!*" Margie shrieked.

Mrs. Skinner's high-heeled foot came down hard on the accelerator. The sedan leaped ahead. Behind, an enormous boulder crashed into the road, spattering dirt on the rear window. Mrs. Skinner's forehead was beaded with sweat. "Next time," she said evenly, "don't distract me when we're going through the pass."

Margie began to weep softly.

"Did you see who it was?"

"Mrs. Pascal and all the kids except the baby," Margie sobbed. "They're all home with nothing to do on account of Easter vacation."

"Must be at her wit's end with eight children to amuse. Still, that's her problem." A faint smile flickered over Mrs. Skinner's face as she made swift plans.

"Going to get her at the next PTA meeting. Mom?"

Mrs. Skinner smiled enigmatically, and Margie asked no further questions. Her mother had always been pretty much of a loner. The other Peaked-Roofers might have resented that, but she was also the best shot in the development. Skillfully, she drove through the Brightview entrance to the parking lot. "Better take your gun," she advised, as they got out of the car. "I know the Shopping Center's a truce zone, but I didn't like the look of those spikes in the road."

However, since the Flat-Tops and the Peaked-Roofers shared the $15,990-$17,990 entrance to the Supermarket, the manager made the Skinners check their guns at his desk. "This is a quiet store, Mrs. Skinner," he told her, "and I aim to keep it that way. The fist fights are bad enough. Last week, Mrs. Knowland and Mrs. Maltese slugged it out in Dairy Products and smashed a crate of extra-large Jersey eggs. If only you ladies would realize that all that kind of thing goes into the overhead, and makes prices go up."

The Skinners maneuvered a shopping cart out of the phalanx, and started their promenade down the aisles. When they passed Flat-Tops, there were hostile stares, and an occasional sideswipe with a cart. If they encountered fellow Peaked-Roofers, they could stop to pass the time of day and exchange news that didn't get into the local papers because sometimes local papers fell into husbands' hands. "Watch out for a woman who's been coming around saying she collects for the Anti-Sebhorrea Foundation," Mrs. Belton warned. "She's a Flat-Top casing the Brightview houses. Smart idea of yours to put curtains in the picture windows."

"Someone else would've thought of it if I hadn't," Mrs. Skinner said modestly.

Near Baked Goods she and Margie met Mrs. Richmond, bursting with gossip. "Have you heard what happened to little Ava Pratt? The Flat-Tops got her yesterday. Ambushed her in an unimproved lot."

Mrs. Skinner made clucking sounds with her tongue.

"Can I have chocolate-covered graham crackers, huh, Mom?" Margie asked.

"No," Mrs. Skinner said, "they make you come out in spots."

"They don't think she'll live," Mrs. Richmond continued.

"How about Oatmeal Crunchies?"

"All right, the small package. . . . What did they tell the father?"

Mrs. Richmond shrugged. "The usual thing—a sex maniac. What else? The men are going to get up a posse and beat the bushes tonight."

Both ladies gave rueful little laughs. "I do hope nobody gets hurt," Mrs. Skinner said tolerantly. . . . "There, you see," she admonished Margie, as they trundled past Condiments and Jellies, "don't ever go into an empty lot alone. You've got to learn not to take any chances, not if you want to grow up and have a husband and children of your own and live in a nice development like Brightview."

Margie jumped, but not quickly enough. A chunky jar of olives toppled off a pyramid of like jars and glanced off her shoulder. "Why can't I live right *in* Brightview?" she asked, rubbing her injury.

"Because it'll be old when you grow up. It won't have the latest modern conveniences. People will look down on you if you don't move into a new house as soon as you're married. . . . Darn it, no jellied peacocks' tongues again!"

"There's plenty of it in the Old Windmill Manor section," Margie said, peering through the shatterproof amethyst glass partition that separated the $30,600-ers from the lower income brackets. Dim tweed-suited figures could be seen moving about in those remote regions. "Cans and cans."

"Don't let them *see* you looking!" Mrs. Skinner cried, pulling her away. "What they do or say or have is no concern of ours! *We don't care!*"

A Flat-Top woman, torn between two brands of marinated venison, glanced up. "Some day us Flat-Tops and you Peaked-Roofers should declare an armistice and go up there and *get those* Old Windmill Manorites," she declared in a low passionate voice. "Burn their houses to the ground. Teach 'em to think they're better than us."

For a moment they stood there, united in a common bond of hatred. Then. . . . "Come on, Margie," Mrs. Skinner said; "we'll have to make do with roast agouti hash."

"Just a minute, Mom." Taking careful aim around Canned Fish, Margie let fly with her slingshot. There was a loud howl. "That'll learn Marilyn Sforza to push olive jars at me," Margie muttered, holstering the slingshot. Her mother patted her on the head.

A helicopter that was hovering over the Supermarket sprayed them with bullets as they sprinted for the parking lot. "This is too much!" Mrs. Skinner gasped, when they were inside the car. "I've got her number, and I'm going to report her. A little sniping—well, that's excusable—but strafing is going entirely too far!"

Margie had learned her lesson, and she was silent as they rolled down the highway. Mrs. Skinner's sharp eyes darted from side to side, but danger came from behind: a sports car full of hooting Flat-Top mothers raced up and crowded them off the road. For a moment, Mrs. Skinner felt panic, as the car began to topple; then it sank a few feet and stopped in a ditch. As she and Margie were lifting it onto the road again they heard the crisp sound of an explosion. When they were on their way once more, they found that the bridge ahead of them had been blown up. The Flat-Top car was a twisted mass of wreckage. "That was meant for us," Mrs. Skinner said with satisfaction, as she headed the car toward the detour. "Somebody got her signals mixed."

She and Margie laughed companionably. "Bet it's the same gang raided Mrs. Perkins' bridge party and ate all the refreshments and killed the baby," Margie observed.

"I wouldn't be surprised," Mrs. Skinner agreed. "Lucky it was only a boy."

"What did they tell Mr. Perkins this time?"

"Said he fell out of the crib. Of course the doctor backed him up. All the doctors are with us." Mrs. Skinner fingered her machine pistol lovingly.

"They better be. We'd pump those quacks full of lead if they squealed on us."

"Told on us, Margie. Or, better yet, informed."

"Informed on us," Margie repeated obligingly.

When they pulled up outside the little Cape Cod—one of a row of almost identical Cape Cods—Rock, Margie's older brother, was moodily weeding the lawn. "Get the groceries all right?" he asked, with a faint, contemptuous smile.

"Of course," his mother said, "I always get the groceries all right."

He squatted on the sidewalk, examining the bullet nicks in the car. "Wait until Dad gets a load of that!"

"He's not going to. You're going to spray it with Quik-Dry."

He stood up, facing her. "Suppose I don't. Suppose I tell him the truth for once."

Their eyes met on a level. He was growing up, she thought with a pang. Soon he would have to go. But Margie would always be hers, even after she got married and moved away. . . . "Suppose I tell him about that money you took from my bag—"

He licked his lips. "But I didn't—"

"And about the passes you made at Sue Richmond."

"I wouldn't touch Sue Richmond with a. . . . Well, all right, you've got me cornered," he said bitterly. "He'd never take my word against yours. He'd never believe me—"

"That's it; he wouldn't," Mrs. Skinner agreed, regretting what she must do, but knowing there was no other course. "You're not the only boy in Brightview—or in Marcus Park, either. They all try to tell their fathers."

"Mom," he said, frowning, "suppose I go to college and I finish and get to be a commuter like Dad and I get married, and—and this girl and I go live in a development, and the houses are all modern. With flat roofs, I mean."

"You wouldn't do that," she said, after a pause. "After all, you're still my son. Now hurry up, get the groceries out and then paint the car." She and Margie walked into the house with quick little feminine steps and shut the door behind them.

"He'll be going soon, won't he?" Margie asked sadly.

Mrs. Skinner put her arm around the little girl. "I'm afraid so. And, when he comes back, he'll have forgotten everything, or think it was . . . just his imagination. He may even go to a psychiatrist about it."

"But we'll always know, won't we, Mom?"

"We'll always know," Mrs. Skinner said. "Because we're the ones who'll always have to take care of things."

Mr. Skinner came in heartily on the 6:03. He kissed his wife and daughter and slid behind the wheel of the car. "Have a nice day, dear?" Mrs. Skinner asked.

"Pretty hectic," he laughed. "Marshall flubbed as usual, and Winterhalter said he was going to cancel. The order was for ten car-loads . . . which isn't exactly peanuts."

"My, I should say not!"

"So the boss said to me: 'Henry, you go over and see if you can talk some sense into old Winterhalter.' Well, first Winterhalter wouldn't talk at all; he was so mad. Honestly, I thought he was going to slug me with my own sample case."

Mr. Skinner chuckled and Mrs. Skinner laughed gently along with him.

"Then he calmed down and we talked things over, and finally he agreed to let the order stand," Mr. Skinner said, his voice thick with modesty. "Only, he said next time the boss should send me instead of Marshall, if he wanted any more orders. The boss was—well—pretty enthusiastic."

"I should think he would be!" Mrs. Skinner said in her gentle voice.

"He said he wanted to show his gratitude in some way more tangible than words, and, when I get my pay envelope next week, I'd see what he meant."

"That's wonderful, dear. We certainly can use more money."

"Buy yourself pretty things, eh?" Mr. Skinner said fondly. "Your day go all right?"

"The usual routine," she told him.

"Must be pretty dull for you girls. Tell you what, why don't you and Margie go into town tomorrow and take in a matinee. Then I'll meet you for dinner; how's that?"

To get to the city, you had to pass Happydale Homes and Schlossman's Park, cut right through Chez Vous Woods and skim the edge of Paradise Ranches. It was rumored that the Paradise Rancheros had atomic warheads on their guns. "Well, to tell you the truth, Henry," Mrs. Skinner said, "I don't like the idea of driving through all that city traffic."

He took one arm off the wheel and squeezed her shoulders. "That's the trouble with living in the suburbs. It's made a real little country mouse out of you."

"I like it here," Mrs. Skinner said. "And you'd better keep both hands on the wheel, Henry."

"I could practically drive up this street with my toes," Mr. Skinner boasted. "It's as safe as houses. I can't figure out why there always seem to be so many accidents around here during the day. Women drivers, I guess."

"Don't be narrow-minded, Henry," Mrs. Skinner smiled. She leaned back in the seat and closed her eyes. She could relax. The street was safe now. From five-thirty in the evening to eight-thirty in the morning, and all weekends and holidays, there would be no danger.

Mr. Skinner's eyes dreamed on the road. "Tell you what: if the raise is as big as I expect, as I—" he laughed deprecatingly—"deserve, and if I get another one next year we could start thinking about a new house. Maybe one in—" he dropped the words with careful casualness—"old Windmill Manor."

He couldn't see Mrs. Skinner's face crumple, Margie's eyes widen in panic. But he heard the silence. "What's the matter? Don't you *want* to move to Old Windmill Manor? Don't you want to live a little better?"

"Our friends are here in Brightview, Henry."

"But, for heavens' sake, the Manor is just the other side of the highway. They could come to visit you. And you'll make new friends."

"After all, Mom," Margie said pensively, "the houses at Old Windmill Manor do have peaked roofs. Lots of peaks."

"Gables," Mrs. Skinner told her, "that's what you call them, gables." And Margie was right. Gables could not be considered in the same light as flat roofs; they were, rather, the ultimate in peaks. She pictured herself in tweeds moving softly through cathedral-ceilinged amethyst aisles where there would be jellied peacocks' tongues all the time . . . while her Brightview friends—only, of course, they wouldn't be her friends any more—pressed envious noses against the bulletproof shatterproof, purple glass.

"You mean you wouldn't *like* to move to Old Windmill Manor!" Mr. Skinner's voice rose to the maximum of incredulity.

She took a little time to answer. "Of course I'd hate to leave the old house," she said at last. "We've spent so many happy years there together." And she looked fondly up into his face. "But the Manor would be so nice for the children. . . ."

It would be much better for the children, she told herself. Safer, for one thing. If the Paradise Rancheros had atomic weapons, it was only a question of months before the Old Mill Manorites would have them also. Conservative they might be, but not reactionary. And, of course, their weapons would be bigger and better, though not shinier, than everyone else's . . . like everything the Old Mill Manorites had or believed or were. We'll fit in, Mrs. Skinner thought, mentally reviewing and discarding most of her present wardrobe. We'll fit in fine.

Race

Pigeon City

Although knowledge of prejudice and discrimination is needed to understand the position of blacks in American society, knowledge of certain structural changes in our society and accompanying migratory patterns is also needed. During the history of the United States, large-scale migration of blacks out of the rural south to large cities of the north and west contributed to the position of blacks in our society today. Starting in the nineteenth-century, this migration accelerated after the two world wars and continues today. Outside of the South Census Region, over 90 percent of blacks are urban residents, and most live in the inner core of central cities. Some large cities, such as Atlanta and Washington, D.C., now have a black majority of residents, and the proportion of central city residents who are black is growing in most cities. This proportion is growing, in part, because of continued in-migration of blacks to these cities, but this trend seems to be lessening in intensity. A more important factor is the exodus of middle-income whites to suburbs beyond the political limits of the central city.

Accompanying these migrations have been important changes in the spatial location of business and industry, which have, in turn, altered the structure of opportunity for those living in the inner core today. Industry, particularly heavy industry, has decentralized from locations near the central business district to outlying areas. Businesses with large-scale, office-based operations, on the other hand, have centralized, concentrating more in central business districts than was earlier the case. Today, new migrants to the city—mostly unskilled—find fewer jobs for the unskilled; heavy industry, the chief source of employment for unskilled workers, is no longer near the slum as it was 75 to 100 years ago when Europeans, who were white, were arriving in our cities. Businesses growing in the central business district and geographically near the slum residents hire trained clerical and sales people—jobs for which slum-dwellers typically do not have requisite skill and training. In the face of reduced employment opportunity, today's slum inhabitant finds the "pull yourself up by your own bootstraps" myth of minority upward mobility less applicable today than ever.

As these trends continue fear has grown that geographical and social separation of the races in the United States will intensify. The warning that the National Advisory Commission on Civil Disorders issued in 1968 that we are approaching two societies in the United States—one white and one black, strictly separate and unequal—is becoming true with time. Our cities may be turning into black enclaves, surrounded by and walled off from white suburbs whose residents politically and financially control the destinies of blacks.

Jesse Miller's "Pigeon City" projects some of these trends, as he describes a black ghetto physically isolated from dominant whites and controlled by totalitarian use of advanced technology. Although a stark and pessimistic portrayal, Miller's story serves as a corrective to the "things are getting better race-wise" mentality and a recent tendency among leaders to pretend that we have no race problems in the United States. Many sociologists would suggest that "Pigeon City" is a realistic projection of current trends and is not an improbable future.

Pigeon City

JESSE MILLER

Summer dawn. The sun had about risen and Curtiss pushed back the fire door and emerged on the roof. He breathed deeply and happily, the brightening sun warm on his face. He drank in the early morning sun, and it bathed his strong black features until his face shone like copper.

Curtiss had the most magnificent coop in Harlem. Built and added to over the years, it was more like a miniature pagoda than a coop. Curt loved these moments alone before he flew the birds. The coop stood in a corner of the roof. It was red and gold, and it shone quietly, the birds within cooing and rustling as they awoke, preening and stretching.

He would prolong these moments as long as possible. Once the birds were released, they would fly and whirl: so many specks of pepper in a shifting pattern that always seemed to be on the verge of spelling something. The whole city could enjoy them. But for now, they were only his. The plastiscreen reflected the pink early morning light, and Curtiss wanted to sing; he was bursting with quiet joy and pride.

Below on Lenox Avenue, a mechisweeper was making its automated rounds past the empty, abandoned buildings across the street. Curtiss half watched as it stopped before an obstacle. He imagined he could hear computers chattering as the sweeper analyzed the obstruction. The night before, a car had been burned, and now there was a heap of melted hardened plastic at the curb. The sweepers almost never erred. A cold light swept the street, shone on the plastic mess, and dissolved it. Curtiss was unimpressed. He watched as the big brooms began again to rotate, and the sweeper lurched off into the next block.

He had once wondered about the cost of one of those mechisweepers, but an eduvision program had compared the operation of the sweeper with the selection of a floor by an elevator. The whole thing had been made to seem so practical and uncomplicated. A narrator had suggested that it was vastly more efficient to automate wherever possible, rather than hire and maintain human operators.

Curtiss shrugged and walked to the coop. He spoke to the birds. "What's the difference? Life is good, we all eat, hey?"

The birds knew their time was coming. They finished primping and hopped about with quick, jerky movements. He unlatched a few doors, and they began jumping to their little exit ledge, looking around, and then flying off. Curtiss felt a touch of envy. The pigeons would go where they wanted, see and be seen by anyone, while he waited on the roof until it was time to eat. All there was for him to do was eat, sleep, and tinker with his coop.

No one went downtown any more. Of course, some people were reclaimed when they interfered with the operation of a city machine, but they never returned, and over the years the curiosity had finally dissipated. It didn't seem strange to anyone that there was no curiosity. All needs were met. Everyone was fed and clothed, housing was adequate. The people had become lethargic.

Curtiss tilted his head back and watched as the birds formed up, whirling and diving above him until they drifted away, an airy, perpetually breaking wave, constantly forming and reforming, hypnotically growing smaller.

They called this roof where Curtiss spent his days "Pigeon City of 112th Street." He sighed and went to the toolbox. There was never a question of not having enough materials. The super filed a monthly requisition form, and it was easy to get him to include a pint can of metallic gold paint or a few yards of plastiscreen.

Everyone knew the computers downtown kept track, but no one minded as long as all needs and most wants were satisfied. Curtiss rubbed his eyes and selected a small brush. He spread some paper and began to paint. The computers encouraged everyone to have a hobby. No requisition for a hobby was denied. The fact that the computers kept track was confirmed by their handling of Allen, the throwback, the dissident, the exception who proved the rule of general content.

The sun was up now. Curtiss took off his shirt and draped it on the knob of the fire door. It was warm, it was good. He hummed softly as he painted. The sun baked his muscles as he stroked the plastiwood. Life was easy, so sweet. The eduvision said the ghetto represented man's first arrival in Utopia.

Allen cropped up again in Curtiss' head. There was something righteous in the way Allen had complained when he had been cut off by the computers. There was data assembled on Allen, just as there was data assembled on everyone else, but Allen had requisitioned dynamite. It was a joke. Under "reason" Allen had written, "hobby." He had been given the explosive, but his subsequent requests were turned down. Allen had even been mentioned on eduvision. He was a local star, a source of real entertainment, like Curt's pigeons.

The people knew how Allen felt. Allen hated. As a child in the street, he had lost his foot. It had happened when he played with a mechisweeper. It was all right to climb on back and go for a little ride, but to obstruct it, to scream at it and taunt it as Allen had was lunacy. When the sweeper's computer had elected to override interference due to Allen's antics, and he had seen that he would be ignored, Allen had dashed in front, trotted backwards, laughed and shouted. Then he had tripped and fallen . . .

It was time to eat. Curtiss carefully set his brush in thinner and capped the paint. The sky was blue and cloudless. Soon it would be fall. Impossible beauty, peace and happiness were all around him. He strode to the fire door and into the dank tenement on which he played and dreamed.

All hobbies were done on roofs. The buildings' interiors were generally squalid. No one seemed to care. Live and let live, and when things spilled over into the streets, there were the mechisweepers.

The lunch truck was actually another sweeper, but it was modified to dispense food. It scanned cards and issued infraheated food especially programmed for the individual's dietary needs. The computer was benevolent. Everyone ate well, even if only once a day.

Allen hobbled up behind Curtiss in the line. "Mind if I bump you?" he whispered.

"Why?" Curtiss replied. "In a hurry?"

"I sure am, brother," Allen said. He produced his card and fingered it nervously.

"Well, I'm in a hurry too," Curtiss said. "You'll have to wait."

"I can see you're in a hurry." Allen laughed and seized one of Curtiss' hands, holding it up to embarrass him. It was flecked with paint. "Yeah, you're in a hurry," Allen continued. "You're messing around up there in your Pigeon City so tough you don't have the time to put on a shirt or wash your hands when the roach coach gets in."

Curtiss relented. "O.K., brother, take my place."

Allen moved up immediately and began to tap the shoulder of the girl in front of him. "Excuse me, sister, mind if I move up?"

Curtiss watched with amusement as Allen cajoled and bargained his way to the head of the line. "He always has to be different," Curtiss said to no one in particular, and the girl in front of him shook her head and smiled. By the time Curtiss reached the window of the roach coach and presented his card, Allen was off the line and half finished with his meal. Curtiss took his tray and joined him on the steps of the building.

"What were you in such a hurry for?" Curtiss asked, sitting down beside him. Allen squinted up at the hot, midday sun and did not answer, but returned to his nearly empty tray, scooping and bolting his remaining food.

The roach coach clanged and rattled away, across Lenox Avenue. Curtiss leaned forward and he could see people clustering in the next block where they knew the coach would pull up.

"Do you like this?" Allen said suddenly.

"What?" Curtiss was confused. He knew to expect anything from Allen, but he was still often taken by surprise. Allen stood and wiped his mouth on the back of his hand. He was tall, and he looked proud. His limp enhanced his different approach, and he knew it. Curtiss sensed a speech was coming, and he tried to cut Allen off.

"Look, brother, I only asked you why you were in such a hurry. Don't give me any lectures, O.K.?"

But Allen had drawn himself up to his full, crooked height, and he would not listen. Up and down 112th Street, the people were slowing in their eating. There would be entertainment. Allen would talk. They began to gather around, and Allen drew them in with regal sweeps of his arm. He turned to Curt.

"I asked you, 'Do you like this?' and you didn't answer. Does this mean you don't know?" Allen was using his speech voice, and a girl giggled. Curtiss lowered his head. He longed to be back on the roof.

"I'll tell you all why I was in such a hurry," Allen thundered. "It was my intention to reach the coach before anyone had eaten, and smash it." Allen looked around and reached under his dashiki. He produced a brick and held it aloft for all to see. There was a startled gasp from the crowd, and everything grew still.

The heat beat down on them all. The street felt sticky. Curtiss sipped his carton of lemonade slowly, trying to conserve its cool trickle in his dusty throat.

"Why would you do a thing like that, son?" It was an old woman the people called "Raisin Face," and her lips moved and worked on her question.

"Why?" Allen yelled. "To make everybody do something, that's why! You think I don't care? I do care. Brothers and sisters, it's us, not one meal that I care for. A single meal? We wouldn't starve, and there'd be another coach tomorrow."

Now there was confusion. The crowd surged, and there were cries of "How do you know?" and "What gives you the right?" They were angry. Allen stood confused and alone. Curtiss had to give him credit for trying to stay cool.

Curtiss stood and waved his arms for attention. Gradually, the noise subsided, and Curt spoke. "Why he would do it is one thing, we can like his reason or not. The fact is, he didn't do it, and I'd like to know why." Attention swung back to Allen, and he blinked gratefully. Curtiss resumed his seat.

"You people want to know why I didn't do it?" Allen addressed himself to Raisin Face. "I got to the head of the line, the brick was in my hand," the crowd leaned forward, straining not to miss a word, "but when I took a deep breath, that food smelled so good, I just had to have some." He pretended to gnaw at the brick, and the crowd laughed. Raisin Face grinned appreciatively.

The tension broke as easily as if it had never been there. Allen shuddered with relief. Mob violence was not unusual and it was almost always fatal to the victim. It had been a close call. He looked over to Curtiss, but Curt avoided his eye. "I have one more thing to say," Allen called. "There will be a meeting tonight, held by me."

"Where?" The mood of the crowd was eager. The promise of real entertainment was always with Allen's presence in an almost tangible aura.

Allen took a deep breath. "Pigeon City," he replied at last.

Curtiss jumped, spilling some of the precious summer lemonade, but Allen was already limping off down the street and the crowd, buzzing with excitement and anticipation, was breaking up.

The hot afternoon wore on. People returned to their respective hobbies. From the roof at 112th and Lenox the intermittent "tok, tok, tok" of a hammer floated out over the lazy, heat-bound streets. Curtiss was back at work in Pigeon City.

Allen had joined him on the roof. He hobbled this way and that, almost apologetically offering help.

"Need some nails, man? Can I get you some nails?"

Curtiss could not help smiling. He looked up at Allen's eager tan face and willing brown hands. "What's with you, brother?" he said at last.

"Nothing, nothing," Allen quickly replied. He limped away to the tool box, and Curtiss sat down in the shade of his coop, lighting a cigarette and watching his friend.

Allen smelled the smoke and came skipping back. "Where'd you get that?" he demanded. He handed Curtiss a wrinkled bag with a nail sticking out of a corner and snatched the cigarette.

"I requisitioned it," Curtiss replied casually.

Allen puffed greedily, and the smoke caught in his lungs. Coughing, he handed it back. "Here man, I don't smoke."

"Neither do I," Curtiss said. He clipped the cigarette and carefully tucked it in his shirt pocket.

Allen was fascinated. He took off his dashiki and hung it near Curtiss' shirt on the door. Curtiss was startled to see how skinny Allen was as he sat down beside him in the shade. His attitude had become conspiratorial.

"You requisitioned cigarettes, and you don't smoke." Allen paused and stroked his chin as though he needed time to really think. "Why?" he suddenly demanded. "For someone else?"

"Nope," Curtiss replied simply.

"Well, why then?" Allen's eyes were narrow.

"Because I wanted to see if the computer would send them, that's all." Curtiss seemed a little annoyed, and Allen knew he was embarrassed.

"You wanted to see if the computer would send them and it did. So I was wrong, is that it?" Allen was smiling. They were well aware of what Allen referred to: After the computer had put two and two together, figured out that Allen was making bombs, and restricted his requisition, Allen had loudly pointed out to everyone that if he could be restricted by the computer today, someone else might get the ax tomorrow. "Policy is subject to change," he said, and no one acted as if he cared. Although his point had struck home, it had never been tested. But the seeds of doubt had been planted. Allen took Curtiss' behavior as proof, and he was glad.

He clapped his hands and stood up. "That's what I love about you, brother, you're so open-minded." Before Curtiss could reply, Allen limped to the door, grabbed his dashiki and started down the steps. The door was swinging shut behind him and he called back over his shoulder, "I'll see you tonight."

Curtiss was alone on the roof again. "Yeah, catch you later," he said, almost to himself. He got to his feet and scanned the sky. Soon the birds would begin returning. Curtiss was worried. He frowned and moved around the roof, making ready for the arrival of the first pigeon.

The pigeons were all back in the coop. The roof was crowded with laughing, eager people. The word had spread. Allen looked around and paced the roof with unconcealed delight. Hundreds of people had responded to the possibility of being entertained by their local star. To make them act was another matter, but Allen had a plan. Tonight, he would do more than entertain.

"This meeting is hereby called to order," he said solemnly. He waved his arms and called for attention, but was only met with jeers and laughter. Allen nodded and waited. The setting sun dyed his face a deep bronze color. Here and there on neighboring roofs, Allen could see knots of people standing and talking. A breeze came up from the east, and Allen's old-fashioned dashiki ruffled and flapped. It was getting cooler.

"What time is it?" Allen asked. The people were startled. No one paid much attention to the time anymore. To show concern for time had fallen out of fashion. There was simply never a need to worry about the time.

"About 7:30, brother," someone finally called. The people grew quiet and began to watch Allen. He nodded his thanks and started to talk.

"I'm not going to say, 'Nobody has a job,' because no one cares to work. I'm not going to say, 'No one that's retrieved ever comes back,' because we all know that, but we act like the only solution is to stay in line and we won't get in trouble."

A commotion was boiling up in the rear of the crowd. "What are you supposed to be getting at?" a man called, and he was pushing his way to the front of the crowd. Allen could see as the man came closer that it was Franklyn. His mouth was twisted on a piece of hard candy. Franklyn always had a piece of hobby candy in his mouth. He made it. Allen folded his arms and waited. Franklyn's manner was threatening, and Allen knew it would be best to let him talk.

"Let him pass!" he called, and Franklyn elbowed his way to the front.

"What are you getting at?" Franklyn demanded. He stood close to Allen's face and Allen caught the vague odor of lemons on Franklyn's breath. He could hear the candy rattling on his teeth as he spoke, and he could not help smiling. Franklyn became furious. "Don't laugh, brother," he screamed. "You're a troublemaker, do you know that? You're not satisfied unless you're making waves."

The crowd murmured appreciatively. Conflict. So soon. Variety. They ate it up. Allen wet his lips. Frank was taking rope, warming to the crowd. He pushed his finger at Allen's chest. "Someone should set you up to get retrieved," he said menacingly. "Then we'd have you out of our hair." Franklyn turned his back on Allen and began to address the people.

"They retrieved my only sister because of his mouth," he shouted. "If we pay attention to this fool, we'll all be in trouble."

Frank's voice was rising. "This is the fool that got Irene to interfere with the police." He sobbed suddenly, but forced himself to go on. "They retrieved her . . ." His voice broke and he could not continue. Frank waved his arm at Allen, who stood quietly behind him. He hid his face in his hands and stood helplessly immobile.

"I was with Irene," Allen said at last. "I believe in what we did."

Franklyn whirled. "But they took her, and you got away." He shook with emotion, and Allen put his hand on Frank's shoulder.

"You pretend you don't care, we all pretend we don't care, but we do. You see, we do." He raised his voice and addressed the rest of the crowd in the fading light, his hand still on Frank's shoulder. "We eat the meals the roach coach dispenses," he said. "And we don't dare act strange for fear it won't come back. If the vans came to retrieve, we'd go along quietly for fear there'd be heavier retribution."

The mention of heavier retribution sent a shuddering wave through the silent crowd. Heavier retribution was a reference to the eduvision tapes they had been shown after the riots in Bedford Stuy. No one could forget the films of people doped and gassed, rounded up and herded into vans. Mass reclamation. All those people, never to return to their hobbies, their families, their community. A white voice intoning off camera while the horrible scene was enacted: "This is the fate of the greedy, the destructive, the ignorant . . ."

Heavier retribution. The thought of it brought to mind those nightmare tapes, purposely designed to be unforgettable, obviously intended to keep the ghetto in line.

The black people on the roof of Pigeon City that summer evening had gathered there for entertainment. Allen looked from one face to another. Everyone was quiet and fearful. The breeze gently moved Allen's dashiki about him like a flag. At last he said, "Tonight, we will all fight."

There was no response. Franklyn stood with his shoulders bent and the people avoided Allen's eye. "Who will we fight, brother?" Curtiss called from the back of the roof, and his question hung in the air unanswered. Allen's head was bowed, and he did not reply. "What time is it?" he asked quietly. He seemed mildly disappointed about something. Now no one answered him, and there were some who stood to go.

Haroooom! A tremendous explosion suddenly lit up the night sky with a flash that caught everyone by surprise. It was followed by two more explosions and flashes, and the crowd stood out clearly with each brief, stupendous gush of light. Whistling fragments of metal, pieces of building and shards of glass shot through the air.

The people's mouths hung open, and Allen looked around craftily from under his brow.

There was fire, bright and hot. The abandoned buildings on the other side of the street had somehow burst into flame and where their shells had stood, there was now a wall of undulating red and yellow flame. The people got to their feet. They could see everyone turning in this direction for blocks. This was history. The biggest explosion and fire in the city anyone could remember.

Already there was the stench of melting plastic, and the blaze was spreading. There were secondary explosions; powerful concussions that rattled doors and windows. Men and women were running in the street as far as the eye could see.

At last, there came the wail of an approaching siren. A mechi-engine. The people began to cheer. The mechi-engines were a pleasure to watch. They selected the core of a big fire and subdued it with computer-directed foamers, never erring.

Allen was becoming more and more excited. The people were crowding to the parapets to watch. Could one mechi-engine handle a fire this big? There was really very little doubt, but the fire blazed, roaring and radiating heat for blocks around. Lenox Avenue was a scene from hell.

Allen stood and listened. The sirens drew closer. His fingers were curled around the same polyethylene brick he had brandished that afternoon. The engine hove into view, rounding the corner at 110th and swinging north on Lenox. The crowd cheered it on. Allen knew no one would let him throw the brick if he was spotted. He stuffed it under his dashiki and waited. He would make everyone fight before he was finished.

Someone touched his sleeve. It was Frank. Their eyes met in the red glow of the fire. Frank's face twisted in a silent question: "You?" Allen nodded. Frank's eyes gleamed and he too picked up a brick; together they waited.

The engine had slowed in the street. It was selecting the best spot from which to attack the fire. The siren stopped and the people could hear the whine of heavy-duty electric motors. The engine was like a bull preparing to ram the heart of the fire. It cruised slowly up the street, sensors out and working, and it was like an animal. Closer, a little closer, the great golden bell clanged slowly as though the mechi-engine was thinking.

Allen knew if he didn't act soon, the engine would grapple with the fire, win, and leave unmolested. He stood and hurled the brick, quickly stooping and following it with another.

"Fight, fight, fight!" he screamed. Frank was throwing bricks beside him. The crowd watched, amazed. The stunned people looked on as the unlikely pair threw bricks, bottles and whatever they could get their hands on.

The engine began again to move. Frank stopped and froze, seized with panic. The engine was coming with surprising speed, and it was ignoring the fire. It squealed to a stop almost directly below Pigeon City. Allen could almost hear the computers whirring and clicking. A ladder was climbing toward them, a hose at the edge. The crowd stood transfixed. All eyes were on that hose. "Gas," someone whispered fearfully.

The ladder extended, smoothly, slickly reaching for the roof from which the bricks had been thrown. The engine was programmed to pick up the dissidents; the fire raged on unchecked.

"Fight! Fight!" Allen screamed. He tore a loose brick from the parapet and threw it. It struck the onrushing ladder and bounced harmlessly to the street below. "Fight or be retrieved," he yelled. That did it. First one and then another citizen joined in the fray. The ladder hesitated under the bombardment of bottles and bricks. The hose began to spew gas prematurely, still a few floors below. The ladder weaved like a cobra. The people cheered. It was the first time a machine had been deterred, but it was still coming. Everyone knew it would get them unless it was rendered absolutely unfunctional. The missile throwing became serious, the marksmen among them taking careful aim before throwing whatever small or large objects they could find.

Curtiss tapped Allen's back. Allen turned, and the two friends eyed each other in this moment of crisis.

"Help me," Allen said simply. "Help."

Curtiss beckoned to Allen and together they walked through the intent crowd of fighting men. Allen stopped when they reached Curt's coop; he understood immediately. They went behind it and gave a mighty heave. The coop rocked a little, but it wasn't until others came and lent a hand that they were able to budge it. Under pressure of massed coordinated effort, the huge coop finally yielded. It toppled over on its side, and the birds within squawked and complained. Feathers drifted inside the plastiscreen enclosure. The men pushed the big coop, and it went side over side through the crowd, leaving a trail of broken bits of plastiwood.

At last, the coop stood ready on the roof's edge. The ladder was a few yards away and climbing, bricks and bottles pelted the engine below. The people could easily hear sensors clicking as the ladder probed and sought. The hose spit thick yellow gas.

Three men began to rock the coop. "One!" they shouted, and it tilted a little, then swayed in again. The men met the return swing and pushed back. "Two!" The massive coop swung far out over the street and slipped a little before swinging in once more. "Three!" they shouted, and the pigeons were gone forever. Everyone ran to watch as the huge coop disappeared over the edge of the parapet, smashed into the extending ladder and hurtled straight at the engine below.

It snapped through two clotheslines on the way down, and by the time it struck the engine in the street it was an impossibly huge crate, shrouded in flying sheets and flapping assorted clothes. Broken ropes whipped the air around it and it struck the engine with a tremendous crash, crushing it under its colossal weight and impact.

A machine had been beaten. The roar of the fire was a lullaby. The street had gone suddenly quiet. A machine had tried to get them, and they had stopped it. "God," someone whispered, and everyone turned, startled.

The fire seemed to blaze with renewed life. It devoured and spread, eating and destroying unhampered.

Everyone rushed down to the crippled engine. It lay smoking and twisted, and there was glee to the point of madness. The liberated crowd pounced on the disabled machine and began to rip off parts, running and dancing. Allen reached the street a little after the others, and he hobbled impotently from man to man, begging them all to stop. The mob laughed and celebrated, ignoring Allen.

Curtiss was a hero. The fire roared on unimpeded now, and melting plastic began to flow in the street. It was like liquid wax. It immediately began to harden. Children rolled the cooling stuff into balls and threw them back into the fire, then, laughing, at each other.

There was great jubilation, but Allen hobbled quickly from one man to another. "Stop!" he yelled. "Get off the streets! Get off the streets!" He was beside himself, but the people would not listen. Allen was going hoarse.

He spotted Curt. Curtiss was sitting on the curb in the flickering shadows. In his hands, he cupped a broken and dying bird. Allen scrabbled over to him and squeezed his shoulder. Curt looked up slowly, but he did not seem to see.

"Curt, Curt, I can't make them stop. They won't listen." His face was twisted with fear and emotion. Something in the urgency of his voice broke through, and Curt slowly got to his feet, leaving the pigeon on the ground beside him.

"Listen to what?" Curtiss said softly.

"The sirens, man. The sirens! The vans are coming!"

Curtiss cocked his head and listened carefully. Sure enough, over the noise of the fire, the roar of the jubilant crowd, drifted the distant whine of approaching multiple sirens. The riot vans. Slowly, Curtiss turned and faced Allen.

"Listen Curt, we've got to . . ."

But Curt would no longer listen. He clenched his fist, and suddenly swung with all his might so that Allen caught it in the pit of his stomach and went down, twisting and gasping.

"You've gone too far," Curtiss hissed. "You talk too much. You always talked too much." Curtiss drew back his foot. He shook with hate and fear.

Someone spotted him and ran over. It was Franklyn, happy as a lark in the dancing glow of the blaze. "Curtiss, what are you doing, brother?" His mouth worked on the ever-present lemon yellow candy. "What do you think you're about to do?" He laughed and seized Curtiss, spinning him away from Allen.

"What am I about to do?" Curtiss pushed Frank off. "Listen, brother. Just listen, and you tell me what I'm supposed to do."

Then they listened together, and by now, the wail of the mechivan's sirens was much closer. "No," Franklyn whispered softly.

But it was undeniably true. The sirens were very close now, unmistakable even above the snarl and crackle of that magnificent fire. One by one, the men stopped running in the streets, until Lenox Avenue was filled with trapped rioters. They stood, rooted to their places like so many chessmen. Guilty children caught with their hands in the cookie jar. The fire was a tall red beacon, telling on them. Someone looked at it as though he wished it would go away.

One man had the dead engine's bell, and he looked around cunningly before stuffing it up in his shirt. Then he too froze, but the machine's gold bell dropped to the street and began rolling toward the gutter, clanging sadly.

There was nowhere to run. The vans could be heard encircling the block now. Curtiss turned and walked away. He knew he too would be retrieved, but he had to be as far from Allen as possible. Allen forced himself to rise and follow Curtiss. His steel foot made keeping up difficult, but he persisted, scurrying after Curt and calling to him.

"Listen to me," Allen was saying. "Would you please listen?"

"Get away from me, Allen." Curtiss' voice was bitter. The hands swinging at his sides were fists. "I'm warning you, brother, stay back. You've done enough."

Allen took a deep breath and struggled to keep pace. "Just two words, brother," he panted. "Please let me say these last two words."

Curtiss was furious, but he spun and waited, glaring at Allen. Allen caught up. He looked like a madman in the reflected firelight, the people around them stood stock still waiting for their roundup as helplessly as cattle.

"What two words could you possibly have for me that could change any of this?" Curtiss said sadly.

Allen reached under his dashiki and produced two gas masks. His eyes gleamed wickedly, and he said, "Trojan Horse."

The gas began to wear off. One by one, the group from Pigeon City was awaking. Franklyn stretched and yawned, and Allen stood over him, his hands on his hips.

"Good morning, Sleeping Beauty," he said. Franklyn glared at him and dug in his pockets for a piece of candy before responding.

"Where are we? What time is it?" he mumbled, broadcasting lemon. He sat up and looked around. He was on a cot, in the midst of a large number of cots, all occupied by the people from Pigeon City.

"You know where we are." Allen was deliberately antagonistic. "You don't want to know what time it is, you want to know how long you've been out. What makes you think I know the answers anyway? I thought you said I'm a fool."

"Just look at you," Franklyn replied. "Check yourself and your buddy over there, and even you can see it's obvious you've been up to something." He nodded toward Curtiss, who stood in the middle counting the cots.

"That's right." Allen moved closer to Franklyn. "We've been up to something, we've just been going along with the program to see what happens."

"So? What happens?" Franklyn saw that the room was huge, at least three times the size of a big gym. The floor was plastiwood, and sunlight filtered through a set of municipal-style windows that extended the length of the hall. Under the windows were a set of doors marked 1, 2 and 3. The tile walls gave everyone's voice an in-door swimming pool ring.

"Nothing happens," Allen said after waiting for Franklyn to take in their surroundings. "The vans took us here, all automatic and smooth as you please. The gas made everybody kind of doped . . . you all just stood there in the street. Nobody on the vans to see Curtiss and me with our gas masks on. Voice like the ones on edu-vision tapes told us to get into the vans, and you all climbed in, nicely. When we got here, the voice told us to get off and we marched in here . . . You don't remember?"

"No, I don't remember." Franklyn scratched his head.

"Well anyway, Curtiss is counting the cots to see how many people we've got here. That's what we were doing when everybody started to come ungassed."

Franklyn rattled his candy against his teeth. "You're really one for the books, you know that brother?" he said.

"Seventy-six, exactly!" Curtiss called from across the floor, and he began to stroll toward Allen and Frank.

"Thanks," Allen said.

"Thanks?" Franklyn shouted, and his voice echoed through the great hollow hall. "Man, you actually believe we're going to cooperate with you? You're the reason we're down here in the first place!" The people began to drift over, attracted by the commotion, ever responsive to the faintest whiff of controversy. Franklyn turned and began to address them:

"Listen up, everybody! This is it, we've been reclaimed! We've been taken, and we know who to blame for it . . ."

Allen ran to Frank and spun him around. "What are you trying to do?" he yelled. "We've got to stick together, we can't be fighting anymore." He turned to the people. "Let's be calm, please, just this once, and we can accomplish . . ."

"Why don't you shut up?" a disgusted voice called from the back.

"Yeah," someone added. "Never should have listened to you in the first place."

Allen's light tan face went dark. "I tried to warn you," he cried. "All of you. I said, 'Get off the streets, get some shelter, stop and listen!' But no, you had to play, you had to have your fun. And now you want to blame me." He focused his attention on Frank. "Don't you see, brother?" he said at last.

Franklyn returned Allen's gaze. "Yeah, I see," he replied. "And I see the reason, too."

"You big lemon-eating fool!" Allen screamed. "You may think you see, but you don't see nothin', and you know even less than that."

They began to move toward each other, and the people murmured excitedly. Curtiss intervened.

"That's enough," he said quietly. "This won't get us anywhere. We should be finding a solution, not a culprit."

Frank blinked. "But I was perfectly happy before . . ." and he paused, searching for words while his candy clicked and rattled against the back of his teeth.

"Sure, you were happy, dufus, that's the whole point," Allen snarled, and they moved angrily to close the gap between them. Again Curtiss held them apart, and the crowd grew impatient.

"Let them fight," everyone said.

Curtiss was embarrassed in his role as peacemaker. "I don't want to make any speeches or anything," he said shyly. "I just know we can't waste time arguing and fighting, that's all."

Allen and Franklyn stood glaring at each other, and the people gathered around happily. They would see a fight. Entertainment, variety, conflict. They loved it.

For Allen and Frank, there could be no backing out now. They squared off and put up their hands.

"Go ahead, hit him," the people called. But Raisen Face cleared her throat, and the hall grew still. Everyone turned to hear her speak, her cheeks puffed and inflated like worn dark paper bags. The people strained to catch the sound of her wheezing voice. At last she was ready.

"I don't see any difference between the way you children are acting here and the way you acted back home at Pigeon City." Her cane wobbled as she stretched her rattling chest, taking air before beginning to talk again. The hall was deathly quiet. Franklyn suddenly turned on her.

"What do you mean, 'You children'?" he roared. "What's supposed to be so different about you? I didn't notice you hanging back or acting any different last night at the fire, and you don't look any different to me now." He paused for breath, and Raisin Face shrugged and walked away.

Franklyn was infuriated. "Don't turn your back on me when I'm trying to talk to you!" he shouted, and some of the people looked over their shoulders and at the ceilings, as though they were afraid such a disturbance would bring retribution from a higher source.

Raisin Face raised her heavy cane and turned around.

"And don't you holler at me!" she hissed. She began swatting Franklyn with her thick gnarled stick.

Franklyn covered his face and head, ducking and laughing, he caught most of the blows on his arms or shoulders. "Ow, hey, ouch! Cut it out!" he giggled like a happy child.

But the old lady was surprisingly quick and agile. "Not till you say you're sorry!" she panted, working. The stick whistled and swished, thumping Franklyn across his back and cracking him painfully at his elbows. The crowd laughed joyously. Everyone was happy.

"All right, all right, I'm sorry," he said at last. Raisin Face grinned and relented.

"Won't disrespect me," she muttered as she smoothed her dress.

The hall grew quiet. No one seemed worried or apprehensive but Curtiss, Allen, Franklyn, and Raisin Face. Everyone else had simply acted as though they knew the computer would do what it wanted to, and there was no way to fight it.

The other four moved restlessly around the tiled hall, arguing or talking, constantly pacing and examining. Chafing within the confines of that huge cold room, they stood among the seventy-six cots and argued. They moved to the opposite end of the long hall, where the prisoners had first stumbled in, and they stood under the huge scoreboard-type affair that hung from the ceiling. They talked and talked, but they could not find common ground. Allen wanted to smash and destroy, to unify the people, use their consolidated strength and break out, find the white people and take them by surprise. He limped back and forth excitedly, but the others were tired of hearing him.

Curtiss saw the need for radical action, but he wanted to stay and learn. "That's because you don't have those silly birds to go back to anymore," Allen said, endangering his good standing with the one person he considered almost to be an ally.

Franklyn ate lemon candy and mumbled about "Allen's big mouth," but he stayed with the radical group because he believed his sister had passed through this same hall when she had been reclaimed, and he knew instinctively it would take radical, or at least, different behavior to find her.

Raisin Face was as ever, the enigma. She puffed and wheezed, and Allen suspected that her only reason for moving with them was their greater entertainment factor.

There was a whistle, shrill, like the piping they had heard in the eduvision tapes of the old Navy. Curtiss looked up and around. They all expected to hear a metallic voice saying: "Now hear this, now hear this, now . . ."

Instead, the people were gasping and turning toward the board over the heads of Allen, Frank and Curtiss. Raisin Face stepped back toward the middle of the floor and looked up. "Come here!" she cried. Allen and the others moved to join her. The board was coming to life. Information went jattering across it electrically:

Jun 6 2066 . . . 76 dissidents . . . Ten A.M. . . . Pigeon City . . . 112th and Lenox . . .

That information posted, the screen went blank. There was humming and chattering from the board. Most of the people were glad, Allen recognized, and he loathed the whirring and clicking of the computer. It almost always made his foot ache the way rain agitated Raisin Face's arthritis.

The board came back to life, and a display appeared consisting of miniature electronic representations of the seventy-six cots at the end of the hall. Allen and Curtiss looked at each other and said nothing. Franklyn was quiet, for once even his candy was still, and they watched nervously as instructions appeared under the seventy-six cots.

"Proceed to the pallets." The computer spelled it out for them.

One by one, and then in groups of three and four, the milling, tired people shuffled over to the cots. When they were at the pallets, a miniature human silhouette appeared in the corresponding electronic symbol on the board.

Allen saw that it would be useless to hang back and so he limped over with the others and took his place on a cot. When everyone was positioned, an ominous hissing sound began to come from somewhere, but Allen could not be sure where. He sat up and saw that Curtiss too was rising and looking quickly around. Their eyes met and the realization hit them at the same time as the chemical: Gas!

Franklyn tried to fight it. He wanted to stay alert, he wanted to do whatever he had to do to find Irene, but the familiar freezing feeling was spreading in his head, and he began for the second time in less than twenty-four hours to cease to care.

Allen sank back, wondering why he bothered to fight. The gas was a new experience for Curtiss and him. Their masks had protected them on the way down, but now Allen thought, "For what?" and part of his mind was surprised at himself, while the growing, spreading part ate away his will.

Low double doors under the board banged open, but Allen didn't care. He wasn't sure if he was dreaming, and in fact it didn't make any difference to him if he was or not. Not really. Not even when he saw that the doors had swung open to admit a little cart-sized machine which buzzed directly into the room, rolling straight for the seventy-six people lying helplessly on their cots.

The machine began to move from bed to bed. Allen could not always see it, but he could hear it, humming and clicking as it made its evil automatic rounds. His foot ached and he longed to sit up and rub his eyes, but he was too tired. The little monstrosity took pressures, gave injections, and whirred around corners like a mechanical mouse. Allen wondered if the others were aware of what was happening, and then he drifted off.

He dreamed the machine was coming down his row of beds. He tried to move away, but his body would not obey his mind. It paused at his side, chattering and whirring. Allen felt its cold loathsome touch, here, now there, gently probing. He didn't know what the thing was doing, and he was afraid to wonder for fear he would find out.

He became aware that he had been injected with something.

Sensation was returning. He sat up and rubbed his wrists. Curtiss was recovering too, and Allen saw that his friend was laughing.

"What's supposed to be so funny?" he asked.

"You are, brother," Curtiss readily replied. "You and your Trojan Horse."

Allen had to admit Curtiss had a point. After he had gone out of his way to stay undoped, here he was, recovering just like everyone else. Allen smiled and nodded, but he began almost immediately to try to regain control of the situation.

"How long do you think we've been out?" he asked no one in particular. There was no reply. The doctor machine had finished, and it rolled away through the doors at the far end of the hall.

The board lit up with the date and time, and Allen shouted, "What's the score?" The people snickered. The seventy-six pallets reappeared on the screen, and as they watched, green circles appeared around three of the beds. Allen stood, and the silhouette in one of the cots with the circle vanished. In place of the human figure, a yellow number 3 appeared.

Two green circled silhouettes remained. By counting from the bed he had just vacated, Allen was able to determine where the remaining green circled beds were. Two rows over and one bed down, Allen came upon Franklyn.

"Get away from me and stay away," Franklyn grumbled.

Allen shrugged and went to the remaining green circled cot. Curtiss was ready. He sprang to his feet and stretched. The little human figure in his pallet on the screen winked out and then a yellow number 3 appeared in its place.

"What's the matter with Candy Man?" Curtiss said.

Allen looked at his friend and laughed. "You're just asking that question now?"

Curtiss said, "We have to go, we want to find out what's going on, right?"

"Yeah," Allen replied. "Trojan Horse."

"Let's see if someone else wants to come in his place."

Raisin Face scrabbled off her cot and joined the two men. "Me," she said.

Franklyn refused to cooperate. Allen pleaded with him to change places with Raisin Face, but he refused to budge. Finally, the old lady came to him and raised her cane, and Franklyn responded. He moved to Raisin Face's cot and sat on the edge. A silhouette reappeared in her cot, and now all three green circled cots were empty, with a yellow 3 across each. The number 3 door clicked, and Curtiss walked slowly to it. It swung open at his touch. Allen and Raisin

Face hobbled to join him.

They stood at the door and looked back.

"Doesn't Frank want to find his sister?" Curtis said.

"Maybe he will," Allen sounded strangely unhappy. "He has to do things his own way, that's all. Irene will find him, or he'll find her . . ." Allen tried to sound confident but he knew he was not succeeding. Before them stretched the long coldly-lit corridor.

"Good luck," someone called from the group that remained behind. In that moment, the people from Pigeon City were closer than ever before.

The trio nodded and waved, stepped into the corridor and the door swung shut behind them.

On the board, the three green circled beds winked out.

The screen cleared again and a film began. A white man beamed at the people. "Congratulations!" he shouted, and someone said, "It's that man from the Miss America."

"This group has been tested, and I believe there are now . . ." The screen went blank and the computer flashed a huge number 73. The film immediately resumed: ". . . of you. Is that correct?" The happy announcer paused and looked directly and earnestly into the camera.

"Yes, that's right," someone called, and the glad-face man went on talking:

"It has been determined by our computers that you are best suited for . . ." The film stopped again and the computer lit up the board with the words "Agriculture, Farming."

"Now," the announcer laid aside the sheaf of papers he had been holding. "Are there any among you (and please, don't be afraid) that do not wish to go?" He made the question sound more like a statement, and the people looked nervously at each other as his face slowly faded from the screen and the film ended.

The now familiar pattern of pallets with their little silhouettes reappeared on the scoreboard. Franklyn was certain that wherever his sister might be, Irene would not be likely to agree to go to a farm. He took a deep breath and got to his feet.

His silhouette winked out and an ugly red X began to appear across the vacated pallet. A yellow number 2 formed when the X was completed.

The hall was still. Franklyn wet his lips and began walking toward the door. It swung open at his touch and he stepped in without once looking back. When the door had swung shut behind him, he could hear the happy announcer voice resuming, and the occasional self-conscious cough of the others as they watched. The booming friendly voice grew fainter as Frank went down number 2 corridor. He could hear it stop one or two times, and he knew the computer was printing out special instructions.

He knew his sister would not go to a farm. She would have to be crazy to go along with that idea.

"Not Irene," he muttered to himself.

It occurred to him that he had never seen a white person except on eduvision, and he wondered what he would find at the end of hall number 2. He began to wish he had gone with Allen and the others.

"Do you think we did the right thing?" Curtiss said slowly. They were sitting in an anteroom at the end of number 3 corridor.

"This is a strange time to ask," Raisin Face scolded.

Curtiss watched Allen limp to the door and try it for the fourth time. It was still locked. On the other side they could hear what sounded like lots of office machinery. They had been able to go no farther, and now they were trying to be patient. Allen hobbled back and forth, and Curtiss stared at his hands.

The door opened, and a tall, beautiful black woman stood on the other side. Curtiss stared wide-eyed. She wore makeup and jewelry. Bracelets jangled on her arm as she greeted and motioned them in.

"Hello, come on," she laughed.

"Where'd you get those?" Curtiss said, staring at her bracelets as though the woman did not exist.

The tall lady laughed and said, "There'll be time for that later. Right now, there is someone that's waiting to meet you."

The group got to their feet and followed the statuesque woman through the door. She was the first person any of them could recall seeing, face to face, outside of Pigeon City. Allen glowered at her, full of hate and mistrust, but he limped along with the others. The machines they had heard on the other side of the door turned out to be teletypes. The room was full of them, and the floor seemed to vibrate with electric energy.

Capable and serious black men worked among the machines. They wore white coveralls. "Watch your step," their guide called as they picked their way through the machines.

"We're installing new equipment," she explained. The new arrivals nodded and moved along. This was the first time they had seen men working with machines. Allen would not relax.

"Where are you taking us?" he demanded.

"You'll see," the beautiful woman answered. She smiled radiantly. Allen grumbled, and she smiled even more.

"What's your name?" Curtiss asked.

"Oh, I'm sorry," she said. "I'm Carol."

Allen shot Curtiss a furious look, but Curt ignored him. They passed from the teletype room to a long hall, and Carol stopped before a series of elevators.

Their car stopped at the seventeenth level, and the group stepped into a large sunny office. Behind a tremendous desk sat Irene. She was looking through some papers, and when Allen, Curtiss and Raisin Face stepped into the office, she rose to greet them. The elevator doors closed behind them and Carol was gone.

"Irene!" Allen cried.

"You aren't really surprised are you?" she said and they all laughed.

"We're happy to see you," Raisin Face said. "Your brother is here somewhere, and he is looking for you."

"I know," Irene replied.

"You do?" Curtiss walked toward her desk.

For an answer, Irene handed Curtiss a computer printout. On it were listed the names of the reclaimed people from 112th Street. Allen looked impatiently over Curt's shoulder. They saw that their names were circled in green, along with Franklyn's.

"I hoped he would come with you," Irene said softly.

"Well, he didn't. He's as stubborn as he ever was."

"I know he didn't go to the farm," she sighed.

"The what?" Allen's face twisted and he snatched the printout from Curtiss.

"The farm," she said. "I know he didn't go through number 1 door, because I have a list of those names." She put her hand on a pile of papers. "He must be in number 2, but we're still waiting for word."

"What are you talking about?" Allen put his hands on her shoulders and shook her gently. "What are you doing here anyway?" Allen's eyes narrowed and he suddenly dropped his hands and stepped back. He looked at Irene coldly, and he would say no more.

"Oh, no," she said quickly. "Allen, Curtiss, you know me. You can trust me." She looked at Raisin Face but the old woman would not meet her eye.

"I would find Frank and help him, but I have no real power here. I dispense information, that's all. I . . . I indoctrinate." She looked at the group anxiously, but no one made a sound.

At last Curtiss said slowly, "Irene, where is your brother? Why does he need help?"

"We know he went into tunnel number 2, because number 3 is

the one you came through, and you came through without him. We test arrivals, and the ones they call 'Creatives' are green-lined and sent here."

Allen was slowly shaking his head. Irene continued:

"Number 1 tunnel is for the workers. They go to factories, farms and the like, and eventually they are recycled, distributed among compatible communities." She took a breath and looked thirstily at her old friends. They stared at her simply.

"What about number 2?" Raisin Face prodded.

"Number 2 is something else again," she replied cryptically.

Allen exploded. "We know that!" he shouted. "What happened to your brother?"

Irene's lip trembled. "Allen, I . . . please, Allen, won't you trust me?" She looked at them but their faces were hard. She seemed to shrug, and drawing on some inner strength, she pulled herself together before going on: "All I know for sure," she said, "is the number 2 corridor is a sort of obstacle course, and the number 2 area is a correction facility. The idea is, the people in 2 finish there and then go on to 3 or 1. Anything is possible, but I've never known anyone here in 3 to admit to a number 2 history." She turned and walked to the window. "I was going to intervene when I learned what had happened with Frank and Raisin Face but . . ." She stopped talking and stood alone and small with her back to them. Her shoulders shook. Curtiss almost felt sorry for her, but he would not try to comfort her.

"You were going to intervene?" Raisin Face said.

"Yes," Irene replied. "But we only knew he went into number 2; you see, he never came out."

Franklyn was alone and scared. He knew he was supposed to go straight down the corridor and into the arms of what? Something that put red X's on beds? If the computer thought he would do that, then it had another think coming. Franklyn decided to go back.

He stood and listened at the door he had come through earlier, but he heard nothing on the other side. He tried to open the door, but it was sealed. He sat down and waited. He was hungry, but he would not eat. There were only a few pieces of candy left and he was determined to save them.

At last he heard voices at the other end of the corridor. They were coming for him! There was a metal ladder on the wall, and an air-conditioning vent. Franklyn scrambled up the ladder and swung the grate open. When the search party reached his end of the corridor, Franklyn lay behind the vent, watching them. They were black like him, but he did not find that reassuring. They were some-how different, as though they had a purpose. He waited and watched, not daring to breathe.

At last the strangers seemed satisfied, and Franklyn crawled away through the duct. By the time they exhausted every other pos-sibility and came through the duct after him, he planned to be deep in another part of the building.

He scrabbled on his hands and knees for what seemed like hours. He had never been so tired in his life. His pants were torn, and only his fear of falling into unknown hands kept him going.

At last he felt he would go crazy if he had to crawl another inch. He wanted desperately to stand up. In the narrow conduit, he could barely move on his knees and hands without scraping his back. He began to look for a way out.

There were many openings, but most were in heavily traveled areas, or offices. It was becoming increasingly difficult to move quietly. A woman walked by a gate almost directly under his nose. She smelled good. Franklyn sniffed, judged, and concluded that her scent was like flowers. He closed his eyes and sighed. When he opened them, the woman had stopped, and she was looking directly through the grate at him!

Their eyes seemed to lock, and then she turned and moved on as though she had never seen him. Franklyn waited until she was out of sight, and then, with his heart pounding, he swung open the grate and emerged. If that woman had seen him, why had she gone on? To get help? Of course! He had to get out of there!

Franklyn ran. He didn't know which way he was going or from which direction he had come. All he knew was that he was running.

A man with a white jacket stepped out in front of him.

"Hey!" he yelled, startled. But Franklyn spun and raced off in a new direction.

"Hey, Franklyn!" the stranger called.

"So they know my name!" Franklyn thought, and he ran even harder.

"Your sister is looking for you!" they called.

Franklyn laughed. "They won't get me to believe that," he panted. It seemed strange to him that no one was chasing him. He didn't know where he was going, so how could they? He could not shake the feeling that he was running into some sort of trap.

Irene led Curtiss, Allen and Raisin Face from her office and together they walked down the carpeted hall. Her step was quick and efficient; and her skirt went "flit, flit, flit" as she walked. Her head was high, a smile danced in the air around her.

"Damn," Allen said softly to Curtiss. "She acts like she's about to whistle."

Curtiss nodded sadly. "Hey Irene," he called. "What are you so glad about?"

"I'm just glad you're here," she said sunnily.

"Glad we're here?" Raisin Face shook her head.

The little group moved on. At last they arrived at two huge double doors. Irene turned and halted. The rest of them came to a stop beside her.

"Yes, I'm glad," she said sincerely. "I've been through this many times before, and it's always the same. At first everyone is suspicious. After you see what we have to show you in here," she paused and tapped the door confidently, "things will be different."

"Irene, you can't even find your own brother . . ." Curtiss stopped himself but it was too late. Irene's lip trembled and her eyes shone. Raisin Face looked down at the carpet.

Allen intervened. "You know what he's trying to say, Irene. You want us to trust you, but you seem to have changed a hundred percent. You never dressed like this before. None of us did. You wear jewelry and makeup. You act so breezy and carefree. You seem to have forgotten everything. I would have expected you to be on our side no matter what. You're in a position to work with us, and help us, but instead you . . ." Allen choked and faltered.

"You expect us to trust you," Raisin Face said unhappily.

Irene's hand slid from the door and dropped to her side. "I'm sorry you think I work for Whitey," she said. "Fortunately, I'm able to prove how wrong you are. Unfortunately, it's you people that have done the forgetting. I've always been on the same side. It's too bad that you have to act so typical." She turned and looked squarely at Allen. "How could you forget?" she said wearily.

Allen hung his head and did not answer.

"People change, Irene," Curtiss mumbled.

"How right you are!" she replied. Then Irene swung open the doors.

The library was easily the most impressive thing they had seen since their arrival. Big, plush, and overflowing with the latest equipment and concepts, it took their breath away by virtue of its size alone. It seemed to be a city block wide by a city block long. Curtiss was the first to step in, and his feet sank into very thick carpeting. The floor sloped down at a gentle angle. Away on the far side of the room hung a huge eduvision screen.

The big board flashed status and data reports, new arrivals, numbers assigned or requested. Most of the figures and information meant nothing to Curt. The room stretching out before the board was filled with comfortable-looking swivel chairs, clustered in seemingly random groups of seven or eight. They were cubicles with low walls, but it was obvious that every chair on that sloping floor could be turned to face the great screen, now hanging winking and chattering, and for the most part ignored. There was an occasional earnest-looking black man or woman who would stop, look up at the board and jot down something, but almost every black, tan and yellow face was glued to one of the smaller, individual screens scattered around the room.

Curtiss became aware that Allen had stepped into the room, and the two of them hung just on the library side of the threshold, feeling conspicuous and clumsy. The walls were lined with multicolored rows and stacks of edutapes. They looked at each other, wanting to speak, but there was nothing to say.

They listened. Computers whirred quietly; it was a roomful of baby typewriters. They listened; pages flipped and paper rustled. The people in the cubicles were working with machines.

"This way, please," Irene said, walking briskly by them. Her voice was curiously deadened by the carpet, the walls, the very efficiency of that velvety atmosphere.

"Come on!" Raisin Face hissed as she caned her way in behind their guide.

"There is no need to whisper," Irene said airily. She seemed at home and unimpressed by the opulence that so overwhelmed the newcomers. Curtiss felt a twinge of envy; it was the same jealousy to which he had become accustomed those lonely summer mornings back on the roof with his pigeons.

He watched Irene as she selected a cubicle and offered them seats. "She's so confident," Curtiss thought to himself. He realized that Raisin Face had made a strong point when she said they were all behaving essentially the same way they always had. He looked at Allen, and saw that his friend was glaring at everyone and everything. He knew Allen was probably planning something at this very moment. And he recalled the way he himself had turned away from Irene in the hall and mumbled, "People change . . ."

"Do they?" he suddenly said aloud, and Irene glanced at him. He had lost a friend. Maybe she would understand, he had been frightened, the surroundings, so totally unfamiliar . . .

"Please sit down," Irene said officially. Raisin Face eagerly took a seat. Her chair went "poshhh," and she grinned gummily.

Irene left them in the cubicle. "I'll be right back," she said. Her voice had lost all of the former sunny, breezy sparkle. Curtiss hung his head in shame and the rest of the group folded their hands on the table.

Irene returned with three or four tapes. Taking a chair at the head of the table she said, "I want you to see these, you will find that they explain themselves." She sounded like an eduvision announcer, and Curtiss wanted to weep.

A soft whistle sounded, and throughout the room, hundreds of chairs clicked as everyone turned to face the big board. The library assumed an auditorium aspect. Curtiss and the rest of his group followed suit. The screen went blank, paused, and flickered to life. It showed a hallway. It was narrow. The walls seemed to be metal. Thick yellow gas of the same type used in reclamation seethed and boiled along the floor of the corridor, evilly swirling. Allen and the others wrinkled their noses—remembering.

The camera seemed to be focusing on a shadowy figure somewhere in the gas. There was no sound; just the ever-clarifying image of what they now could see was a man. He was on a ladder. Clinging to a ladder and reaching for something over the rising mustard cloud of gas. His face, there was something about the panic in his eyes that wasn't exactly right. Something . . . concentration. This trapped man was not giving in. Terrified, but unbeaten . . .

Curtiss was the first to recognize Franklyn. He jumped to his feet and stared helplessly while the fugitive hung to the ladder and reached out toward what seemed to be an inverted brass flower in the middle of the ceiling. He reached and stretched. In his hand he held a lighted match. The flame was painfully small.

"What's he doing?" Curtiss cried.

"He's trying to set off the sprinkler system," Allen said softly from his chair.

The gas was rising. Franklyn turned to the camera, and he seemed to be shouting something. Suddenly, he released his perch and disappeared into the swirling, angry yellow clouds.

The screen went blank. There was a collective sigh throughout the room, and the board resumed its posting of information. The swivel chairs clicked again as people went back to their positions. Allen turned to Irene's chair. It was empty.

Curtiss was looking through the tapes Irene had left on the table. They were bundled together with an inch-wide plastistrip on which was printed: "Mass Reclamation." The individual reels were marked with neighborhoods. "Bedford Stuy" was one of the oldest; "Harlem" was the most recent.

"Let's see the Harlem tape," Raisin Face said when the bundle was passed to her.

"Do you know how to work these things?" Allen asked.

"I'll set them up for you." A voice had suddenly joined the group from behind. They whirled in their chairs, and Carol smiled a greeting, reaching for the tapes.

"Irene went to get her brother. He belongs in number 3 with us," she confided as their screen lit up with shots of last night's riot. There was Curtiss' smashed coop on the mechi-engine. The street was filled with familiar faces. They saw again the looting and breaking, the fire, and then finally, the people, all but two of them, frozen with fear at random places, the arrival of the mechivans, and the voice of a white narrator chanting hypnotically off camera: "This is the fate of the greedy, the ignorant and the destructive." The tape ended.

"Whitey," Allen whispered, and Carol smiled.

"Don't blame Whitey," she said.

"Who are we supposed to blame? Ourselves?"

"No, Allen," Carol replied. "Why do you have to blame someone?"

"You aren't for real, are you?" Curtiss began, but Allen put his hand on Curt's arm.

"Don't even bother to answer her, man," he said.

Carol smiled patiently. "Around the turn of the century, in the cities, do you know how many jobs the old 30-hour-a-week system had provided?"

Allen glared at her as though she were crazy.

"But you do know there were more make-work projects than there were real jobs? And you do know the cities were falling apart? The people were turning on and blaming each other. Nothing would stop them. It was and is the way of Nature."

Allen had been shifting restlessly in his seat, but he could stand it no longer. "The way of Nature!" he shouted. "Why don't you cut this out and let us know what the hell is going on?" He pounded the table with his fist and the people in the cubicles around them stopped to watch with an amused sort of mild interest. Allen glared back at them.

"What are you supposed to be doing?" Allen said, and he suddenly reached across a cubicle wall, snatching a clipboard before his startled victim could react.

Allen began to leaf through the man's papers, and he was pleased to notice more and more people turning in their chairs to watch. He looked mischievously at Curt, and Curtiss was almost certain Allen's eyes sparkled with secret glee.

Carol nodded to the man from whom Allen had taken the board and he smiled wearily before turning around and resuming his work. Throughout the hall, everyone was going back to their projects. Allen stood, stunned and alone for a few seconds, and then he flopped to his chair still clutching the clipboard.

"Allen, please try to bear with us," Carol was saying.

"What is this place?" Allen muttered.

"Our library." Carol folded her arms and waited.

"What do you do here?" Allen looked up at her like a child.

"We receive tapes and store them, we annotate and dub them, and we write scripts for them."

Allen blinked and looked at Curtiss. Curtiss' eyes were wide.

"We know what approach is the most effective, having the same backgrounds," Carol said almost patriotically.

"You witch," Allen whispered.

Carol continued. "If the people are satisfied to live in the ghetto, we let them. But the ones who aren't intimidated, who aren't satisfied to remain in their areas, who create some sort of disturbance—we bring them in and test them."

"Witch," Allen said a little louder, and his eyes were growing hot.

Carol broke off and looked at him calmly. "Fascinating how you must hate," she murmured appreciatively.

Allen rose in his chair and stared at her blindly.

"Would you like to see another tape?" Carol invited. She didn't wait for an answer. The small eduscreen was glowing again. Curtiss and Raisin Face watched. Allen pivoted stiffly and faced the screen.

There had been a disturbance of some sort. The camera showed a burned-out shell of a smoking building that seemed to have been a theater. A street sign showed the location to be "Queens Boulevard and 71st Avenue." People stood around dumbly waiting for assemblance. There were the familiar mechivans; the doors stood ajar.

Curtiss shuddered involuntarily, and then he looked, rubbed his eyes and looked again. These people were white! He hadn't noticed at first, perhaps it was because he was almost conditioned to seeing white people on eduvision, perhaps it was because the pattern of the negative reinforcement tapes was such a familiar one, but there they were, white people. And they were being reclaimed! A narrator began to speak off camera. The voice of a black woman, and she was saying: "This is the fate of the greedy, the ignorant, the selfish . . ."

The tape ended. Curtiss sat stunned for a moment, and then he said, "That voice, that voice was familiar . . ." and he looked up toward the ceiling.

Carol laughed. "I always wanted to be an actress," she said as though confessing a nice secret.

"Where are the white people taken?" Raisin Face asked timidly.

Carol paused and moistened her lips. She obviously enjoyed her job as narrator and guide. "Separate but equal facilities, Long Island City," she announced. Her eyes sparkled proudly.

Allen stood, looking off into space. "Never," he murmured. "I'll never go along with any of it." His eyes were going vacant.

Curtiss looked anxiously to Carol. "Will he be all right?" he asked.

"Of course he'll be all right!" she snapped. "You, his best friend, should know it."

"I should?" Curtiss whispered.

Allen looked blankly from one to the other.

"You know how he is," Carol said patiently. "We had no idea he would blow up a block of buildings and start a riot, but we've been watching him for a long time. Here we have the facilities Allen and the creatives like him need."

Allen's eyebrows went up, but he said nothing.

Carol watched him and smiled with satisfaction. "Yes," she went on. "Equipment, storerooms full of information, assistants, I could go on and on."

"I can do what I want?" Allen said suddenly.

"Sure you can," Carol replied. "You can even go back to your ghetto and try to liberate the people there, if you like. You would have to spend some time at the, what was it? The farm? But you can go back, or you can stay."

Allen looked undecided. Carol put her hands on his shoulders and looked steadily into his eyes. "We need you, Allen," she said. "We need your drive, your energy to help us run the city. You are a leader, and we want you. Will you stay and help?"

Curtiss wasn't sure, but he thought he saw Allen wink quickly before he replied. "Yes," he said at last.

Age

Generation Gaps

Throughout human social history, most societies have changed slowly. In these societies, social reality experienced by one generation was much like that encountered by the succeeding generation as it reached adulthood some 25 to 30 years later. The aged were viewed as the repository of traditional wisdom, and youth were sharply subordinated to their elders. Yet there was a commonality of experience and a stability of tradition that precluded the formation of a divisive generation gap.

In modern societies, the life experience of one generation is sharply different from that of subsequent generations because of rapid social and cultural change. Coming to maturity in a very different world from that of their parents, youth are less apt to find their parents' world-view fitting their own definitions; and the youth of the 1960s, raised under less restrictive patterns of child-rearing, are more apt to question the beliefs, values, and social institutions of antecedent generations.

Such are the social conditions conducive to the formation of a *youth culture*. Those within this culture establish their own values, beliefs, symbols, and social practices, often reflecting rejection of established social values and zealous dedication to their own values as the only authentic way of life. Peer group experience reinforces these patterns, the media in our culture celebrate and thereby reinforce positive images of youthfulness, and economic enterprises strive to tap the affluence of the large youth market. The more alienated youth adopt extreme oppositional styles of life, and lines of division form between the established culture and the *counterculture* or *contraculture* founded by these youth. Rejection of the "establishment" and distrust of "anyone over 30" combine with a commitment to the "authenticity" of "doing one's own thing."

The youth counterculture cuts across educational levels, class and race boundaries, and even national borders as industrial nations of various types all experience a "youth problem." Those within the counterculture commonly "talk revolutions," harass the holders of power, or retreat to what youth intend to be utopian communal patterns of life. "Generation Gaps" pictures a society in which youth are gaining power and counterculture values and practices are becoming the common standards for all ages. Many of the "now genera-tion" may find Clancy O'Brien's portrayal of the new youthful social models harshly maligning and disturbing. The point here is not whether the values of one generation are "right" and those of another "wrong," but that values acted on do have consequences. Celebration of the right to do "one's own thing" in all circumstances, although likely to be personally gratifying to those who seek it, may be socially irresponsible. A social order is built on the recognition and accep-tance of the reciprocity of obligation people have to one another—in short, social responsibility.

Generation Gaps

CLANCY O'BRIEN

The stewardess called Lollipop reached in through the webbing around my cocoon and placed a long, slender hand on my arm. "Is everything groovy, Dr. Benjamin?" she asked dreamily.

I looked quickly away from the chewed, dirty fingernails. "Y-yes, everything is fine," I said, although I was still breathing heavily and my heart was pounding from the extra G's of the mid-course burn that had put Earth-Luna Shuttle No. 6 into lunar orbit.

"Would you like to blow some pot?" she asked.

"No, thanks."

"Then how about I bring you some acid to drop? Turning on while watching the moon from deep space is a trip you'll never forget." She was leaning in through the webbing now, and I could see the sharp points of her breasts under the transparent mini-blouse she wore. Part of her face had also come into view as the cascade of hair caught on the nylon cords. Her eyes reminded me of Little Orphan Annie's, so blank they seemed to have no eyeballs. I wondered what kind of drugs Luna Shuttles permitted its stews to use while on duty and felt a brief tingle of apprehension as I thought about what the two pilots might be blowing, dropping or shooting. But then I recalled that although the copilot was the usual shaggy-haired youth, the captain was a crew-cut, graying man in his late forties.

"Like man," the stew said, "we're gonna be touching down at Tranquillity Farms in two hours. Wouldn't you like to turn on first? That place is a downer, you know. There's nothing there, you know, not even a little grass. It's hell on earth . . . or moon . . . whatever. I'll tell you what . . . I'll bring you a needle and some speed and we'll turn on together and watch the moon approach and . . ."

"NO!" I said, wanting her to leave me alone so I could think about Tranquillity Farms, speculate what it would be like with nothing but fellow Jerries around me and none of *them* within 245,000 miles.

"All drugs are courtesy of Luna Shuttles," Lollipop was saying. "Like they come with your ticket, you know."

"I know, but I don't care for any," I said, willing her to leave. Why couldn't she go hover over some of the other twenty or thirty passengers? She made me nervous. *They* all made me nervous.

"Then maybe you'd dig grooving in another way," she said. There was a rustling sound outside my cocoon and then the webbing was pushed aside and I saw her in her pink and hairy nudity. "Perhaps you'd dig the free sexual experience that also comes with your ticket. Nothing swings like that when you're all uptight."

I had to suck in my breath to keep from screaming. My stomach churned in disgust at the sight of her youthful flesh and my pulses raced in terror. It wasn't that I was a prude or had outlived the need for sex, it was just that since the big Kill-Ins in San Francisco and New York I hadn't been able to think of any of *them*—the under-thirties—men or girls as being completely human. For me, it was as though a snake had suddenly shed its skin and offered to climb into bed with me. I looked at the slender white thighs, the firm flesh and the claw-like fingers and thought of death, not sex.

"No . . . no, thanks," I said my voice shaking.

"Wow, like that's kind of dumb when it's part of the regular tour," Lollipop said.

"I know," I said, looking at her lush lips and remembering how the young Satan cultists had drunk the blood of their victims in Times Square after the New York Kill-In, and how the television newsers had marveled over the fact that the youngsters had so quickly developed authentic rituals to go with their new tribalism.

"Then how about if I just swing up into your cocoon and we'll groove, you know," Lollipop said and lifted one leg.

"No . . . no . . . please, no!" I was almost sobbing with fear and loathing of her youth.

"Wow! That's a real bummer, you know." She stared at me out of her big, nobody-home eyes. "Don't you dig Lollipop? What is your bag then? Are you gay? If you are, we've got a sweet little steward who would be happy to . . ."

"No, damn it, no!" I said. "It's just that I don't care to right now."

"Wow, that's dumb, you know," she said. "For a twenty-thousand-dollar ticket, you know, you oughta take advantage of all the fringe benefits, you know."

"Yes, I know, but . . ." Briefly I considered telling her I loved my wife and that if I were going to be unfaithful with any woman, she would have to be over thirty, preferably over forty. But that wouldn't have been relevant to her. Saying I was in love with my wife who was waiting for me at Tranquillity Farms would have brought a sneer to her lips, and saying that I found a girl of the younger generation physically repulsive would have produced a call for the nearest Sensitivity Training Team.

"Look, I'm over the hill," I said. "You know, I'm getting along. That's why I'm on my way to a Jerry Farm, right? I'm just not up to it anymore."

"But wow, man. That's what Lollipop is here for, to bring you up to it, you know." She was leaning toward me, her lank blonde hair hanging in my face and her acrid marijuana breath foul in my nostrils. "Lollipop is a turn-on girl from the love generation. I've had five years of sex sensitivity training at Berkeley. When Lollipop puts a cat in orbit, he stays there for a week."

"I am sure you're very efficient . . . in your way," I said, "and I appreciate your interest, but no thanks."

"You sure get some freakouts on these trips," the girl muttered to herself. "They're all copping out and don't know what their vibes need, but Lollipop knows."

She climbed up into the cocoon and reached for me.

"No, let me alone . . . let me alone!" I yelled as the creature's hand touched and caressed me.

"Let me give you love. You're sick, you know," she said. "Your vibes are bad, your aura has turned black. Let me teach you how to love."

"Help! Help!" I shouted.

"Wow, cool it, man, cool it," she said, trying to kiss me with her colorless lips.

I pushed her away, sickened by the unwashed Aquarius smell of her hair and body.

"But wow, man, it's still almost two hours before touchdown, you know. You couldn't possibly do without love that long."

"Oh, can't I? You'd be surprised how easy it'll be for me to live without what you call love," I said, thinking about how much I had missed Beth since she'd gone on ahead of me to Tranquillity Farms a year ago. I had stayed behind because no matter how bad it got, I had to keep teaching, or doing what they called teaching, to raise the twenty thousand dollars a moon trip cost. I'm a normal man, and sex is part of a normal man's life, but despite the constant supply of Aquarian women on campus I had abstained out of simple fastidiousness. I couldn't possibly have become intimate with women I had come to think of as subhuman, women who, like the rest of their generation, were never free from one or another of the drugs the

Aquarian age was building its culture around, women who never washed because they followed one or another Eastern religion that taught dirt was holy.

"I guess you're a sex dropout," Lollipop said. "I guess that's why you're leaving Earth and going to live with all those other dried-up old fools who reject love and enlightenment."

"That's right," I said. "I'm over forty and don't dig your vibes."

"Maybe you'd like to talk to Captain Three Feathers," she said. "He's over forty but he digs us. He isn't running off to hide in a hole on the moon."

"Why should I talk to him?"

"Because he always talks to the would-be Jerries," Lollipop said. "If my grooving doesn't persuade them, he raps with them one-to-one and they see reason about those fuddy old farms. Peace Village has given him several awards—Friendship Beads, first and second class—for talking Jerries out of throwing away their lives."

"I suggest he devote his time to getting ready to set down rather than waste his time with me," I said. "Isn't the motto of the Now Government 'Do your own thing'? Well, that's what I'm doing."

"Yes, but you don't really know what your thing is because you've never turned on and never expanded your consciousness." She turned to leave, opening the hatch and floating out in the null gravity. "I'll send Captain Three Feathers to see you."

"Well, Professor Benjamin, it's a pleasure to meet you," Captain Three Feathers said, sticking his short-cropped head through the webbing and thrusting a big strong hand at me, "but not under these circumstances."

I shook the hand gingerly. The Captain came on all brusque good fellowship, without the vague meandering conversational manner of the Aquarians.

"What's wrong with the circumstances?" I asked.

"I hate to see a man of your recognized scholarly abilities copping out, deserting the ship, as it were."

"The ship is sinking. That's when you're supposed to desert it."

"Nonsense! We're just going through a period of change that will bring about a better world. After all, we've got the most brilliant generation of young people in the history of the world. They demanded change and we've given it to them. Now they'll make a better world."

I tried to remember when I had first heard that phrase "the most brilliant generation in the history of the world." It seemed to me it had been after the first university had been burned. The Captain Three Feathers of my generation had kept on saying it with unrelieved optimism through the last twenty years as the Aquarians had taken over. One by one the universities had burned or changed, one by one the libraries went up in flame, book by book the thoughts of a thousand years were destroyed because *they* said, "The past doesn't matter . . . it isn't relevant. There are only a handful of writers who are relevant, destroy the rest. Marx, Marcuse, Fanon, Leary, McLuhan, Rubin, Hoffman . . . the rest don't matter. Burn . . . burn . . . burn . . . burn!" It all went.

The Captain was very straightforward, very persuasive. He talked about the duty of those of us who had skills to use those skills to help the new people, the brilliant youth who needed only guidance in their determination to build a paradise on Earth.

"My friend, I'm a teacher," I said. "That is a skill that has ceased to have any application in the world back there. What is being taught at the universities today doesn't need teaching. It used to be picked up quite easily behind fences and in little boys' rooms. The kiddies are quite capable of handling it themselves. They parade around dressed as painted cowboys and imaginary Indians and the ones who can read pour over the *I Ching*, astrological tables or macrobiotic cookbooks."

"Ah, but the young still need guidance," Captain Three Feathers said. "The reason for the existence of the universities today is to supply a forum in which the young and the old confront each other, and the young are models for the old. Right, Dr. Benjamin?"

"That's what is inscribed over the door of the administration building back at Stanford where I taught," I said.

"But how can the young supply a model for the old if the old run away and refuse to have their minds expanded?" Captain Three Feathers asked.

"Have they expanded your mind, Captain?" I asked.

"Well, I . . . I'm a technician. My duty is to keep things running until better ways are found . . . more natural ways that will replace the insensitive materialistic ways of the old world with the spiritual values of the Aquarian age."

"You're saying then that your mind has not been expanded?"

"No, it hasn't," he admitted.

"Good," I said. "I'll feel much better when it comes time to set this thing down knowing that your mind is still in its unenlightened, unexpanded condition."

The captain looked a little sad. "Then you won't reconsider and go back and resume your teaching?"

"Captain, I wonder if you'd like to see a brief prospectus of the next semester's schedule at Stanford?" I took a pamphlet out of my pocket and let it float into his hands. He took the list and read it, a slight frown creasing his tanned forehead. I knew what he was reading by heart. I knew what courses were being offered at what had once been a seat of learning.

Macrobiotic Cooking, *I Ching*, History of Rock, Glass Blowing, Astrology and Palmistry, Indian Dancing, Comic Book Appreciation, Black Magic, Handwriting Analysis, Stained Glass Windows, Sensitivity Training, Boy-Girl Love, Boy-Boy Love, Girl-Girl Love and a few dozen others that, in the words of our eminent dean, were supposed "to free our students for pleasure and help them to cultivate a life style in which they would remain, in their minds and hearts, forever children."

"Do you really see any point in my returning, Captain?" I asked when he had finished reading.

"I just know that a man doesn't desert his post. He doesn't give up a lifetime of work and retire into nonproductivity at fifty."

"Maybe you don't, Captain, because what you're doing is still useful, but teaching has become a profession without a purpose."

"I'm sorry you see things that way, Professor," he said, turning to leave. "You're giving up on the most wonderful generation of young people the world has ever . . ."

I closed out the rest of his words, wondering if he was as free of mind expansion as he claimed. It sounded as though that litany about the young had been engraved on his mind with the same phonograph needle that had been used on the minds of most intellectuals during the last twenty years.

"Touchdown will be in one hour," a voice said over the intercom. "Now is the time for all you dropouts to change your minds and return to Mother Earth and the Aquarian Age."

I listened to the voice and wondered at all the attempts to get us to go back. Always before, *they* had seemed only too glad to get rid of the Jerries. To them we were a drag. We refused to conform to their drug culture, we insulted their sensitivity with our clothes, our short hair and our smell of soap. Always before they had been overjoyed that thousands of over-fifties and over-forties were choosing to enter the Jerry Farms on Luna, along the Amazon and in Antarctica. But now . . . now they seemed to have reversed themselves and were begging us to stay. Was it just part of their usual faddism or did it have something to do with the things that strange young man from Wash—no, Peace Village—had told me that day about a week before I left Earth.

I remembered the odd apparition that had appeared on my doorstep one morning. It was the typical long-haired, bearded Aquarian of about thirty-five with the drugged Orphan Annie eyes, the look that is the sign of the self-imposed prefrontal lobotomy. But this was an Aquarian with a difference. Although he wore a hairband and sandals and his neck was hung with the usual mass of beads, he was also wearing the morning clothes and top hat that had once marked the diplomat and was carrying a briefcase.

"Like where's it at, man?" he greeted me.

"I'm sorry, where is what *at?*" I asked.

"I was like saying hello, man," he said. "I'm Little Running Rabbit, Chief of Jerry Retention, State Department, you know."

"No, I didn't know," I said, "but I suppose it's possible. These days anything is possible. Is there something I can do for you?"

"Like man, I come to one-to-one you," Little Running Rabbit said. "We're going to be out front with you on this one."

"I . . . I'm not sure I understand," I said.

"Man, we—the United Communes, you know—understand you're uptight about the way things have been grooving. We been getting bad vibes from your aura, you know. Like man, that's a nothing trip."

"Am I to understand that this is a reprimand from the Gov—I mean, the Gurus of the United Communes?"

"Man, no chance," Little Running Rabbit said. "Your grooves are our grooves. When Professor Morris Benjamin is giving out bad vibes, all his brothers in Peace Village are giving out bad vibes too, you know. We don't put nobody down. 'Do your own thing,' is the motto under the Dove of Peace on the great seal, isn't it?"

"Yes, I'm afraid it is."

"But why, man? Why you been putting us down so? Why you been giving out pain to your brothers?"

"Well, I'm sorry if I've been giving pain to . . . ahem, my brothers in Wash—I mean, Peace Village—but I don't know what I've done to cause it."

"Man, you applied for a pad at Tranquillity Farms. That is a real downer for us, you know. It makes us feel like, you know, we haven't been rapping one-to-one with you."

It was a bit difficult to be sure exactly what the Aquarian was saying but I got the impression he meant the government felt it had failed to communicate its essential good intentions to me.

"I've not only applied for a retirement home at Tranquillity but my wife is already there and I've received verification of my reservations on the Luna Shuttle for the next bimonthly flight."

"Oh, bad scene . . . bad scene. Man, that's like running away . . . copping out, you know."

"I prefer the word retiring to copping out," I said.

"Man, look, it's like you're only fifty. You got years of teaching ahead of you, you know," Little Running Rabbit said.

"My friend," I said, "the retirement laws purposely allow for early retirement so younger men can take over in the universities . . . Aquarians who can teach the counterculture more efficiently."

"Right, man. That's the way it grooves all over the country," Little Running Rabbit said, chewing on his cheek in a way that reminded me of a real rabbit. "The counterculture is required, but it's like this, man. Some of the big gurus at Peace Village have been thinking, you know, about how maybe we're losing something, you know, something important, because all the uptights are running off to the Jerry Farms. They're leaving the schools, the farms, the law courts, the laboratories, the engineering jobs. It's getting so things are starting to break down. It's like the tech . . . technology is running down. Man, it's a real bummer when you can't even get your electric guitar fixed and there isn't enough electricity for the light shows."

"But it was the technology, the materialistic technology, that your generation rebelled against," I reminded him. "Weren't you going to replace it with a tribal village where everyone lived close to nature and loved everyone else?"

"Right on, brother," the government man said, "but it's like you got to groove a little on both tracks. You got to have love, but you got to keep things going. I mean, cats and chicks are starving to death all over since . . ."

"Since the remittance checks from old uptight Dad back in Squaresville quit coming in," I suggested.

"No chance," he said. "It's since the food trucks quit coming into town, since the supermarkets quit throwing away piles of food and since there's nobody left to run the canneries."

"What about your macrobiotic gardens?" I asked. "What happened to the self-supporting communes?"

"Like that takes time, you know. Kids got to get used to, you know, like working and digging and all. Well, it just ain't everybody's thing."

"Get used to it? My God, they've had twenty years!"

"But it's like nobody expected the whole thing, the whole society to start running down, you know. Man, all those engineers and technicians and teachers have got to be really spaced out to go running off to bury themselves in holes in the ground called Jerry Farms. They ain't got no commitment . . . they got no love in them . . . no love for their own children."

"No, I don't suppose many of us have," I said. "I know I haven't since the New York and San Francisco Kill-Ins."

"Man, that was like fifteen years ago," Little Running Rabbit said. "That was when there were a lot of freakouts in the movement, you know, a lot of plastic types and Satan cultists, you know. That was before everyone became like Woodstock, with the peace scene, you know."

"Nevertheless, I'm on my way to Tranquillity Farms," I said. "The Luna Geriatric Farms are completely self-sustaining even if the Earth communes are not."

"Like man, don't rap that way," Running Rabbit said. "You haven't heard the big scene the gurus said I should put on you. We're gonna fix it up for all the squares, you know . . . all the ones who stay, that is . . . with a really far-out scene."

"Such as?"

"Like for you, it's gonna be a real swinging pad, you know. A kind of city commune set up with all the groovy chicks you want to ball, unlimited free pot and acid, you know. And all we're gonna ask you to do is kind of like run this school your own way, and the local gurus will pick out a few of the less wild young ones and maybe you could teach them something, you know . . . You're shaking your head. What's the matter, man, ain't we been one-to-one with you? Don't you . . . no, I guess you don't. None of the others did either."

He was letting the conversation drift into the nonlineal rap session so much admired by the Aquarians as a means of noncommunication. He was wasting his time and mine, and I told him so.

What little I could see of Little Running Rabbit's face through the hair looked doleful as he picked up his briefcase, put his top hat on over his hair ribbon and walked toward the door.

"It just don't vibe . . . it just don't," he muttered. "But I got to keep trying, got to keep rapping with the squares . . . can't stop now with Los Angeles' electricity off for three weeks and Chicago without water . . . got to keep rapping even if they are all pigs."

Then he stopped and turned back to me. "One more thing I got to tell you, one thing I think you ought to know before you go rushing off and leave all this behind . . . it's like we need . . ."

Little Running Rabbit's voice faded from my mind as the intercom made a whistling sound and I heard Captain Three Feathers' voice.

"Now this is the Captain speaking. We will be firing our braking rockets in ten minutes for touchdown at Tranquillity Farms. Passengers will please strap down for extra G's. Please strap down. And I would like to take this opportunity to urge all of you one more time to reconsider your decision to cop out and leave your children behind. Think what a lack of commitment this shows on the part of our generation, throwing up our jobs and forcing these young people to assume responsibilities they are perhaps not quite prepared for yet. I'd . . ."

"Children! Young people! For Christ's sake!" I shouted. "The Aquarians are in their middle thirties! They've lived over half their lives! They insisted on taking over society. Now let them run it!"

". . . a great lack of responsibility on your part in choosing a sterile, unproductive retirement instead of remaining in the thick of the battle to improve society . . ." the Captain was going on, but I shut his voice out as I hurriedly strapped myself in and settled back to wait for deceleration.

Then Lollipop was back. She was jaybird naked and had a marijuana joint in her mouth and a hypodermic needle in her hand.

"I'm going to give you one more chance to turn on with Lollipop," she said. "I've got some of the best smack you ever grooved on in this needle so you and I can turn on during touchdown . . . doesn't that sound groovy?"

"You get the hell out of here!" I yelled. "Don't you come near me with that needle! I don't want anything to do with you or your drugs!"

Lollipop's face puckered up and she started to cry. "That's the way it's always been. That's the gap. You've never wanted anything to do with us or our drugs. You've never understood . . . none of you has ever understood us."

"That statement is right on, sister!" I said and she disappeared from the hatch of my cubicle blubbering.

Half an hour later, the shuttle had settled onto the smooth floor of the Sea of Tranquillity and been coupled to the tunnel that led to the passenger terminal. I was hurrying through the air lock, down a pressurized ramp into a brightly lighted underground tunnel, the two small suitcases that were all I could afford to bring with me gripped in my hands.

Beth would be waiting for me, and my feet felt as though they had wings as I hastened through the tunnel, but I couldn't help thinking about the look on Lollipop's face and the desperation in her voice. *They* felt deserted, but hadn't *they* deserted us first? And why . . . why had it all happened that way when our intentions had been so good?

They were the first generation whose mothers, following the dictum of Dr. Spock, had always picked them up when they cried. *They* were the first generation that had been raised on a diet of T.V. and, with McLuhan's blessing, had rejected books. Now their children . . . oh, my God, *their* children were growing up! No wonder even some of *them* were frightened.

No wonder Little Running Rabbit and some of the gurus were getting desperate. *Their* children were the first generation raised in the pads and the communes, weaned on LSD and lullabied with rock music, deliberately kept illiterate—some barely able to speak— spoon-fed hatred for The Establishment and then turned loose in the streets. Now quickly the Age of Aquarius was becoming the Age of Monsters with the appearance of the second generation. The Pyros, the compulsive arsonists; the Vamps, the blood-sucking youngsters who littered the streets of every city with victims; and the Eaters, the cannibalistic teen-agers who raged through the major cities in packs of thousands, totally beyond the control of the Aquarians of the United Communes. No wonder some of *them* were frightened . . . as frightened as we had been when we realized what we had spawned.

But wasn't there still a chance? I was only fifty and Beth was thirty-nine. I had decided against having children when I realized how things were going, but here in the Jerry Farms away from the body-destroying drugs and mind-blasting rock a child could be raised rationally. Since the invention of the new atomic fuels, it had been possible to transport everything needed to maintain human life to Luna, and also to move whole libraries and museums—a large part of the cultural heritage of mankind—to a place of safety from the bombers and burners. Wouldn't it be ironic if the dead satellite sustained only by man's reason and technology could give man another chance while the race was destroying itself on the mother planet with its superstition and irrationality?

Imagine raising children in an environment free of drugs, free of rock music and out from under the influence of a media that always exploited the dissident, the irrational and the violent.

"Dr. Benjamin, wait! Wait for me!" a voice called from back down the tunnel.

I turned and looked back. Captain Three Feathers was struggling with Lollipop, the copilot and another stewardess.

"Let me go, dammit, let me go!" he was yelling as he lashed at them with his big strong arms. "It's all going back there on Earth, can't you see that?"

It was then I saw something, or rather someone, clinging to his hand. It took me a second or so to figure out what it was. It had been a long time since I had seen a short-haired five-year-old, but I was sure it was a little boy. And that, I suddenly realized, was the reason for Captain Three Feathers' devotion to the Aquarians. He had the misfortune to be a father.

"Don't leave us . . . please, don't leave us!" Lollipop was

screeching. "We need you! Can't you see how much we need you?" She had fallen to her knees in front of the Captain and was kissing him desperately on the feet and legs. "Love us . . . love us as we love you! We haven't anyone else to love us . . . *they* never will!"

"Captain, you can't leave us!" the befeathered copilot yelled. "I don't know how to take this thing back! I can't run the computers! I can't compute an orbit or keep the life-support systems going!"

"What the hell do I care?" Three Feathers shouted, running toward me. "Haven't you been seeing it on your screens? Don't you know the whole thing is going? The Vamps and the Eaters have taken over the countryside and the Pyros are burning down the cities, and no one knows how to stop it any more than we knew how to stop you. But I've got my son; I'm saving something. Dr. Benjamin, wait for me, wait for me!"

He caught up with me, his breath coming in short gasps as he clung tightly to the child in his arms. "I raised him in my cabin on the ship . . . he's never set foot on Earth . . . he's never had drugs . . . never heard the music . . . never listened to the superstitions . . . so I think he'll be all right."

"Of course he will," I said, thinking about what he said was happening back on Earth, thinking about the last thing Little Running Rabbit had said to me.

The youth—hell, he was thirty-five!—had told me about their *thems*, the fifteen-year-olds who were coming up behind his generation and how terrified the gurus were of them.

"Don't leave us," Little Running Rabbit had said. "*They're* coming up behind us and we don't know what to do about them. We need help. For God's sake, don't leave us. These kids are really spaced out and we don't know what to do."

I had tried to hold them back but the bitter words had come. "You raised them!" I told him. "You raised them *your* way . . . not our way!"

Then he had hurled the words at me, the words that were at once a barbed missile and a stinging indictment.

"But you raised us!" he had said.

5

Social Institutions

To understand *social institutions*, it is necessary to understand what makes an aggregate of people a *society*. Society is a term defined in many ways by sociologists, but generally it is used to refer to the largest of social groups in which man participates. Today, most societies are *nation-states*, such as the United States, the People's Republic of China, or the newly emerging nations of Africa. In the past, most societies were *tribal*—a relatively small group of people organized on the basis of kinship and adhering to a traditional pattern of life. The distinguishing feature of a society is that it is organized to be self-sustaining, that is, to accomplish all things necessary for the survival of the people who comprise it. Although groups within a society develop a culturally patterned way of life, those groups are not self-sustaining. To be self-sustaining, the people of a society must develop and maintain patterned solutions to recurring problems. Although some of the problems are *universal*—that is, they occur in all societies—the patterned solutions developed to meet them vary from one society to another. The established, regularized ways in which the people of a given society meet their central recurring group problems constitute what sociologists call social institutions.

Sociologists generally distinguish five basic social institutions: the family, or familial, institution; the economic institution; the educational institution; the political institution; and the religious institution. Each can best be understood by seeing it in terms of the socially necessary tasks to which it is addressed.

(1) *The Family.* If it is to be perpetuated, every society must bring new members into the world to replace those lost by death. The physical survival and social development of those brought into the society through procreation must be ensured. In all societies, there has been a legitimized social structure wherein normatively bounded procreation and socialization occurs. The family, or familial institution, functions to perform, channel, and legitimize procreation and socialization. In every society as well, some institutionalized pattern of relationships regulating and legitimizing sexual union between males and females can be found. This socially approved setting for procreation and child-rearing is called *marriage.* Although the family and marriage are found in every society, the specific forms of marriage and the family vary a great deal. Sociologists and anthropologists have identified many such forms: from publicly celebrated sacred marital unions to casual nonlegal or quasilegal "common law unions"; from marriage involving one male and one female (termed *monogamy*) to a form of *polygamy* called *group marriage,* involving two or more males united with two or more females; from the small *nuclear* family to the large *extended* family. The sociology of the family, a subfield of sociology in which these things are studied, is an important part of sociology.

(2) *The Educational Institution.* The educational institution functions to transmit the culture to the next generation and to socialize the young. In the educational process one learns specific applicable and usable skills and more general attitudes, beliefs, norms, and values. In small, nonliterate societies, these functions are performed by the family and no formal, differentiated educational institution is present. Adult family members are the educators and all children are taught knowledge considered essential by the society. In more complex societies, a separate, identifiable educational institution becomes differentiated and shares with the family the basic educational functions. In early literate preindustrial societies, the family was the basic educating unit for most, but a specialized role—educator—developed within a formal educational system. Yet formal education, and with it literacy, was largely the province and monopoly of the elite. In later preindustrial societies, formal educational experience included a larger proportion of the population as the economy and society grew more complex. Formal *higher* education was still largely the monopoly of the privileged, but artisans learned

their skills through formal apprenticeship training and merchants acquired literate skill to assist in formation and execution of contracts and records.

In industrial societies today, the family still performs important educational functions, but a highly complex, specialized, and differentiated educational system complements and/or competes with the family in fulfilling educational functions. Great industrial productivity permits large sums to be spent on education (although as a percentage of national budgets, educational expenditures are low), and a larger proportion of the population experiences formal schooling and for a greater number of years than in earlier societies. This is "mass education." Some sociologists become specialists in the sociology of education, a subfield of sociology.

(3) *The Economic Institution.* The people of every society must organize their members to provide at least a minimum of food, shelter, and other goods and services necessary to survival. This effort must provide for both the production and distribution of these through the organization of work. The economic institution is addressed to these problems. Work has been such a central part of human effort that we often label entire societies on the basis of their economic structure. For example, we speak of "food-gathering peoples," "agrarian societies," "capitalist societies," and so on. Yet, perhaps because sociology as a field developed after economics, sociologists have not developed a "sociology of economics" as they have developed subfields focusing on each of the other basic social institutions. Nevertheless, such classic sociologists as Max Weber and Emile Durkheim gave considerable attention to the economic institution and its relationship to other institutions within society and today sociologists investigate many questions about economy and society. They are concerned with such things as differentiation within the economic institution, the changing structure of the labor force and the consequences of these changes for the economy and society, the growth of professionalization and unionism, the meaning of work, and work relationships in industry and business.

(4) *The Political Institution.* To survive, a society must have some degree of internal order and be protected from disruption by outside force. There must also be some means for making and carrying out in an orderly fashion decisions concerning vital issues. The political institution addresses these necessary tasks. As we move to the latter part of the twentieth century, sociologists are beginning to focus on *power* as the central concept in political sociology. The political institution organizes and exercises power to maintain for the society internal stability and protection from invasion by other societies. Central to the political institution is the process whereby

power becomes *legitimized* and acceptance develops as to who should hold power, their rightness to do so, and the obligation of others to accept these arrangements. Through the process of legitimization, power becomes *authority*.

In addition to power, political sociologists have investigated such varied questions as voting patterns, the social conditions necessary for democratic and/or totalitarian political structures, the relationship of social class to the political order, political "elites," and political extremism.

(5) *The Religious Institution.* The religious institution provides for some degree of moral consensus; defines the unknown; articulates basic beliefs; and explains man's origin, destiny, and purpose. The sociology of religion is a subfield within sociology in which one will find the sociological perspectives applied to the study of the structure and organization of religion. Sociologists attend to several aspects of religion and its social context and functions, such as the sense of the sacred, belief systems, religious ritual, the function of religion in society, secularization, and the structure of organized religions.

The religious institution performs an important function in any society. In societies with a single religion, the religion contributes to cohesion and stability and integrates the varied parts of that culture. For members of a religious faith, religious belief sustains, gives meaning to the unknown, and provides ethical and moral guidelines for living. Max Weber, one of the classic students of religion in society, saw religion primarily in terms of its integrative function. Religions can also be a divisive force, especially in a religiously pluralistic society. Adherents to "absolute truths" often find their beliefs incompatible with those of the believers in other religions, and religious conflict can rend the social order.

Religions vary in the extent to which they are organized. Some develop bureaucratic hierarchies, elaborate dogma, complicated ritual, and cross national boundaries, while others are smaller, less formally organized, and include members of only one segment of the society. While religions commonly profess openness to all who believe, in practice they tend to be exclusive in membership.

Although some sociologists identify additional social institutions, the family, educational, economic, political, and religious institutions are commonly viewed as the five basic social institutions. This chapter presents a reading for each of them.

The Family

INTRODUCTION

Two's Company

Since the functions performed by the family are vital for societal survival, strong values and norms develop to support the form of marriage and the family in a given society. Establishing a family through marriage becomes the common expectation among members of that society, and actions not conducive to family solidarity, such as adultery or dissolution of marriage through desertion, separation, or divorce, are negatively sanctioned.

Sociologists are also interested in *marital selection*—the process by which those eventually forming a marital union encounter one another and the processes leading to the decision to marry. In traditional societies, marital selection is largely the province of the kinship group, which arranges marriage for their offspring. Even in such societies as our own that apparently permit free choice of marital partner, the husband and the wife are likely to share many social characteristics. For example, those marrying are likely to be of the same race, religion, socioeconomic status, and to have lived near one another when they met.

With industrialization, the family is undergoing change. The nuclear family unit has become common as the extended family is dispersed over space as a result of the greater social and geographical mobility of its members. The family is less a production unit, and more a consumption unit. The school, the peer group, and the mass media compete with the family as agencies of socialization. Intrafamily strife increases as differences between the generations grow, and greater social and economic opportunities outside of marriage for males and females contribute to increasing rates of divorce. Many young adults establish cohabiting and procreating relationships without the formality of marriage. These trends have led some to see not just an era of family crisis, but the emergence of new social arrangements and social units that will provide for procreation, child-rearing, and emotional and sexual response as the family becomes obsolete.

John Rankine's "Two's Company" is not a story of marriage but of the developing relationship between a male and female who are coworkers isolated on a distant planet. Their propinquity and shared crisis bring them closer together. There is no hint here that their developing relationship will grow to marriage or that marriage is a conscious consideration of either of the two parties. As barriers between the two dissolve, Dag Fletcher concludes merely that "the rest of the tour was not going to be any problem at all." Is this to be a casual sexual encounter or will it grow to a more permanent relationship? Notice, however, how the relationship develops in a situation devoid of normative expectations bounding "boy and girl." Will future relationships between the sexes on our planet be devoid of socially defined pressures supportive of marriage and the family as the legitimate context for sexual pairing?

Two's Company

JOHN RANKINE

The black oval of the entry port diminished slowly to a dot and even in the thin atmosphere of Omega the definitive click of its closing could be heard from the edge of the clearway. Dag Fletcher, standing outside the main dome of the station, watched the silver arrow angle up for take off and saw the brilliant fan of orange flame build up before the noise and vibration shook the rock platform. Slowly, with a casual grace, *Interstellar-Two-Seven* began to lift and then flung itself into a streaking trajectory. In just under the ten seconds which Dag had automatically counted out to himself, it had dwindled away and the blue void was vacant and featureless as it had been through an eternity of time.

Even the long conditioning courses and the many previous missions could not prevent his feeling of loss and abandonment in this remote place. There was a tinge of regret too about the combination of chances which had sent him Meryl Wingard as assistant for the three month tour of duty. Not that there was anything wrong with the Wingard to look at. Far from it. She had elected to be moulded on the lines of Botticelli's Marine Venus and was as lovely as the original, but it seemed a meaningless beauty, since she worked with the inhumanity of a flawless machine. She was a mathematician of outstanding calibre and trained to a fantastic pitch of competence by years of single-minded effort.

The right person in every way for the mission, no doubt about that—with the banks of computers to keep tabs on; but not likely to add much gaiety to the long chore ahead. Moreover, he suspected that she had very little time for his sort of practical flair. As far as could be said of any spaceman reaching his rank, he was an improviser, a lucky man, and an outside shot statistically speaking to be a Controller at all. Lean, tall, late thirties, with an easy relaxed slouch of a walk, he always stood out as an individual among the correct conservative types of the Senior personnel.

He moved back into the airlock and flipped switches to drop the outer atmosphere shield. A green glow showed the seal complete and he put the regulator to Robot and let the automatic gear carry on.

Meryl was not in the communal living space, so he moved on into the Controller's suite. He had settled in there in the week that the ship had remained to do those jobs which needed the full crew. Now he shrugged out of his spacesuit and the molded rubber inner suit and took a shower. Then he dressed for comfort in slacks, sneakers, and a gaudy Teeshirt.

The suite was built in a sixty-foot pressurized dome divided by two diameter walls into two small and two large arcs. Large—dayroom and bedroom; small—bathroom and store. The dayroom was dominated by a scanner on a platform against the outer wall. Dag stepped up to it and looked without much enthusiasm at the panoramic view of the planet endlessly presented on the flat screen. He tuned for the immediate area of the space station and a tract of some square miles was presented with crystal clarity. Typical of the planet was the mixture of rocky plateau and wide shallow valley filled with thick yellow-green vegetation. The station was set on a half-mile square platform which had been ground to a perfect level. It made one of the best space ports in the galaxy and served a six dome main station. Ten smaller robot stations dotted the planet and must each be visited once in the three month tour. In theory at least nothing could go wrong with them; but their computer programs had to have a quarterly check since even tiny errors could drift into serious chaos given long enough.

The project on Omega was to produce an earth type atmosphere. Already the oxygen level was one quarter earth and in two years it should be fully habitable. Gravity at .72 earth was an attractive feature and the planet was sure to be high on the list for future colonists. A dull place though, reflected Fletcher, with its never ending ravines and tumbled rock table lands—though its appearance would improve when a balanced atmosphere produced rain and cloud and stretches of water.

He left the scanner and returned to reception. Still no sign of the girl; so he ate alone, pressing labeled switches which delivered heated foods to the service hatch in the dining alcove. As he finished his coffee and lit a cigarette, she came in, still wearing the close-fitting inner skin of her spacesuit—a silver sheath—which stressed every line of a perfect figure. Her fair hair was straight and almost shoulder length and swung as she moved like a pale gold elastic bell. The blue and yellow rank flashes on the right shoulder were only half a bar less than his own; but she was as correct in address as if she were straight from training school and they used speech automatically, where others in this situation might have got down at once to the more intimate thought transfer.

"Controller, there's a drift in Station 9. I should be glad if we could make that our first visit."

"Check. You comfortable in your cubby hole?" He had not asked before in the busy days of take over.

"Thank you, yes; but if you don't mind I'll use the lounge here to work in. I prefer a large free space when possible."

He could sympathize with this view and wondered how she had felt in the cramped living-room of the spaceship. But he kept this thought out of the transfer area of his mind.

Dag looked at the model globe of Omega and spun it to find Station 9. It was about 200 earth miles distant—a two hour journey in one of the Center's hover cars. Days on Omega were relatively short, being only 15½ earth hours. It was now about two hours to nightfall and although, eventually, earth personnel drifted out of phase with this time scheme, it was still convenient to talk about "today" and "tomorrow."

"Tomorrow, then? One hour after first light."

"Check. I'll say Good night, Controller."

"Good night."

Her detachment was complete and there was no pose in it. A cool madame there, he thought—but probably it meant more positive success for the mission, he would have nothing to take his mind off the job. However, he recognized that he was slightly piqued at her lack of interest in him and after serving himself with a small whisky from the bar, he returned to his own rooms.

It was brilliantly light when they came out of the airlock and crossed the forecourt. Fletcher decided to take the middle range car and wound back its pressure sealed roof. He made a routine check of the cylinder rack and they climbed in. They fastened seat belts and at zero power the car edged out from the parking canopy. In the open, Dag lifted her in a smooth sharp climb to maximum height and then set the automatic pilot to home on Station 9 at full power. The car hovered and then slowly turned until it was exactly on the beam path and then moved away with effortless acceleration.

The surface of Omega unrolled before them, visible through the wide screen and the transparent floor. Rocky plateau and valley in succession endlessly. Valleys choked to their rocky confines with the crawling yellow-green plant life. It was by the controlled decomposition of this that the atmosphere was being created. The break down would have a two-fold purpose, oxygen and nitrogen given off and the ground cleared for the future settlers. As they neared the sub-station, the effects of the work made a dramatic change in the scenery. There was a succession of completely clear valleys where the bare ground showed deep purple. Then the station itself could be seen. Three large domes and a small port.

They swept down to a perfect landing and climbed out on to the apron. In minutes they were through the airlock and inside the main dome. Meryl only paused to hinge back her helmet and crossed directly to the control console. All such stations were built to a familiar plan and she quickly identified the essential elements. She switched out the robot computer control and took it on manual. With high speed calculations she monitored the system for five minutes, then switched back.

"There's been a drift in the computer setting. I'll have to work back on this."

"How much time do you need?"

"Two hours certainly. Possibly two and a half." This would be cutting it fine if they decided to return before dark. They could stay overnight, of course—there was food and accommodation for several months if necessary; but they both preferred to get back to the relative comfort of the main station.

"See how it goes."

"Right."

The pale gold head bent over the horizontal presentation table and long detailed equations were penciled on the ivorine monitoring panels. He followed the processes for a few minutes then she lost him with a piece of mathematical short circuiting which was outside his range. He certainly had a first class assistant and he admitted to himself that the job would have taken him several days.

"I'll take a look outside." There was no reply; she was completely absorbed in the work.

The lock for exit was a complete manual and it was ten minutes before he stood beside the car. He took her up to fifty feet and made a sweeping circuit of the immediate area. The nearest valleys were clear of growth and showed like purple lakes. The dark powdery soil was high in fertility and would make ideal farm land. Four valleys were under ray bombardment and beginning to show patches of clear ground. The ray apparatus was set up and moved by a full crew at each visit of the spaceship and monitored in the interval by the computers in the sub-stations.

He set the car down in one of the clear areas and took a soil sample in a specimen jar from the rack above the landing skid. He read the fix from the car's navigation table and marked the sample with date, time, and location. The base analysts were assembling a detailed report on every valley and a complete farming plan would be made before one colonist set foot on the planet. It was median time and exactly half the short day had gone. By the time he had re-admitted himself to the dome it was median plus a half and Meryl was drinking coffee.

"How does it go?"

"No problem. The fault wasn't hard to find; but I'll need to test run for about half an hour to make sure that the deviation has been cleared."

"Fine. If we move at five we shall be back before dark."

He took time to inspect the plant. It was unlikely that they would have time to pay a second visit; so he initialed and dated the check tablets at each section. It was almost three months to the day since the previous Controller had done the same.

At median plus one and a half she signaled "job complete," and after the routine tests of equipment, they re-entered the waiting car. Fletcher felt that he must give due credit for her success.

"Thank you for that. Not many people could have straightened it out in the time."

The reply was typical. "Not at all. Any competent mathematician could have done it." But he sensed that she was pleased to be complimented and he wondered if a better relationship might not be possible between them.

On the return, he took control on manual and pushed the speed above the range of the automatic pilot. This should bring them in in daylight. Navigation would be unaffected by darkness, but even the few moments of transfer from car to dome could be unpleasant in the intense cold of the night temperature on Omega.

They were under two miles from base, with the homing beam filling the scanner with a pathway like a red carpet unrolled in welcome, when the car defied statistical likelihood and broke its maker's record for complete reliability. It was so quickly done that it was impossible to remember what in fact had happened. Dag eased down to landing speed and switched in the robot pilot. The car lost height and then began to pick up speed in a tearing near vertical dive. There was a splintering crash. Where the screen had been was the scratched face of living rock. This Dag saw before he blacked out and sagged down against the harness which alone had kept his head from the incoming splinters.

He carried into oblivion also a flash picture of the girl strained against the strap with her hair streaming forward like a shining pennant.

❊   ❊   ❊

Minutes later he climbed back into consciousness and the shifting blur settled to hard factual pictures of a situation as bad as it could be. Pain needled him to full awareness and he moved cautiously. Nothing seemed broken, but a rock fragment had torn through his spacesuit below the left knee and the quilted sections above had constricted to form an emergency air seal. There was a slow ooze of blood through the torn fabric. Looking across at the girl, he stabbed, swearing, at the release catch of his harness and heaved himself out of his bucket seat. She was out cold—as he had been; but there was a pallor about her skin which was ominous. A spur of rock had thrust in at head level on her side and had punctured the helmet of her suit. Since the car was no longer pressurized, she was at surface pressure for Omega and was breathing Omega atmosphere. The suit's cylinders had emptied quickly in a vain effort to build up against the leak. She was in the same state as an almost drowned man and Dag knew that it was a matter of minutes and some luck if he could do anything at all about it.

He jabbed open her harness release and heaved her on to the sloping floor of the rear compartment. Stripping off the broken suit he looked along the rack of spares for something near the size. Even working at speed, he registered the light strength she had, the perfectly modeled knees and ankles and high round breasts. He zipped off his own helmet and clipped in the emergency air line to face mask. He filled his own lungs with an oxygen plus mixture and, using mouth to mouth respiration technique, made her breathe. He worked steadily for two minutes and was beginning to feel the strain of it, when her eyelids moved.

He put the mask over her mouth and nose and pulled forward his own helmet, glad to get air without conscious effort. Grabbing the suit he had earmarked, he set the air flow to its helmet then slipped it over her head. She was fully aware now and had taken in the situation. Quickly he slipped her legs into the new suit and she kneeled forward to help. Within half a minute pressure was normal and a more natural color had returned to her skin.

Dag picked out a replacement suit for himself and realized how groggy he felt. For himself, he reversed the process and fitted the new helmet first; then as he was peeling off the old trousers he felt the snag in the left leg and remembered why he was changing at all. As he did a complicated jack-knife to keep the supply of gas to the new suit and free the old, he felt her hand on his shoulder—"Let me help." She had broken out a first aid kit and poured some solvent on the sticky mess below the knee.

"This needs a stitch. I can take care of it."

She did a quick but careful bit of surgery with the sterile instruments in the pack, and then a dressing. He shrugged into the suit and stood up to inspect the damage.

Time was running badly against them. Very little daylight remained and unless they were to freeze to death something must be done to patch up the car. He moved gingerly back into the pilot seat. The floor was broken and jammed on to a jagged rock splinter and a narrow fracture spread back into the cab and fissures crossed the panoramic screen in every direction. There were two plastic spray containers in the repair locker and some sheets of white plastic. It was intended to make a temporary seal when any part of the fabric was punctured by meteoritic fragments. It might just do—used sparingly. She was already stripping the packaging off a container and he realized that they had dropped easily and naturally into thought transfer. He smiled thanks and got to work.

The rock seemed solid and free from porous pumice. He began sealing the broken edges of the car to the floor, making the intrusive splinters an integral part of the skin. The plastic sprayed out under pressure and set on contact. The whole of the front was complete when the first cylinder hissed empty. They were within minutes of the short twilight.

The cabin floor lightened as he turned to work on it and he saw that she had fitted two hand torches by suction clips to the rear bulkhead. Now that there was time to look at each other, she allowed maximum penetration of her mind for some seconds. He was aware of calm acceptance of the likelihood of death, no hint of criticism, concern for himself, and a sense of comradeship. Reciprocally, he dissolved his own thought barrier and she was conscious of his gratitude for her help, and a new element of personal admiration.

The second cylinder completed a seal for the floor and he looked round for other punctures. There were some minor ones which he first plugged and then sprayed. Using a spare suit cylinder he built up pressure inside the wreck and then set up an air conditioning circuit. It was now dark and with the dark the cold began. The surrounding rocks began to cool rapidly, making sharp cracking noises like breaking sticks.

They were able to take off their helmets and make a scratch meal. An inspection of the lockers produced biscuit and self-heating soup. The cars had little food stock, only spare air bottles being regarded as vital.

Now the cold began to be a thing to reckon with. Moved by the logic of circumstances they made one narrow sleeping bag out of every available bit of fabric with the seat cushions as mattress. Still wearing their inner suits, but not needing helmets in the stabilized atmosphere, they squeezed in and lay still. Dag turned her towards him until they were pressed together from knees to shoulders. Her nipples were noticeably firm against his chest and her perfume was exhilarating. If they got out of this he knew he would want to love this girl, but he knew also that this was not the time and he touched her hair with his lips and said good night.

They slept fitfully for six hours before the cold dug down into them. Dag moved stiffly and a gossamer web of ice crystals tinkled and cracked round his head. He squeezed her shoulders gently and as she woke said "Two hours to daylight—we could do with some warmth."

The air of the cabin was biting cold and their nest of fabric had hardened into an inflexible carapace. Ice ribbed the tubular cross members. Dag levered himself partly out and reached over for the last two cans of soup. He checked an exclamation of pain as he touched the cold metal and found that the tins were anchored to the floor by a rim of ice. She added her grip to his and they wrenched them free. Bashing the strikers against the floor triggered them off. The heat melted the ice near the tins and made a pool of water; but the soup was hot and its warmth spread through their bodies.

It was not easy to sleep again and they began to talk about the careers which had led them to this point of time. He found she had an unexpected fund of humor. This added another dimension to the expert mathematician. They strained close together to keep in every fugitive calory. The cold thrust down into them and it was a race between dawn and a freezing death. They held on.

Dawn came on Omega in a dramatic racing flash and filled the cabin with a harsh neon-like glow. The rapidly rising heat turned their bed into a sodden heap as the ice melted away. The walls streamed with released condensation too fast for the balancer to adjust.

Dag pushed her damp hair aside and with a hand on either side of her face kissed her mouth.

"We have eight hours. There will not be another chance."

She nodded and, copying his gesture, kissed him in the same way. Then she stood up and touched the release studs at the neck of her suit and zipped down the front panel. Then she peeled it off and took a pad of rough cleaning tissues and began a brisk massaging rub. Dag took another pad and scrubbed her back. He did the same himself and with blood circulating freely and feeling ready to tackle the day, they dressed again in complete spacesuits.

Dag broke out the emergency exit and they crawled through on to the rock. The lip of the ravine was about fifty yards away and the domes of the station seemed near enough to touch on the far side of the valley. But eight hours was too small an allowance of time to do a tricky rock climb of eighty feet into the valley, cut through about a mile of tangled vegetation, and climb the opposite cliff. There would have to be another way.

"Get out the spare suits and any rope you can find," and as she edged back into the wrecked car, he walked quickly to the top of the cliff and looked across. Almost in the center of the valley was a low outcrop of rock showing like a black stain on the gray-green carpet. Meryl had brought out two lengths of nylon rope and the spare suits and he ran back to help her carry them. Even with reduced gravity it was a good load among the crazy rocks and they were glad to pile it at the edge.

Meryl could see no hope of crossing in time and he could feel her mind reluctantly preparing for defeat. Dag found her work to do.

"Inflate a spare suit and tie a rope to the center of the front harness."

As she worked on it he went on, "What do you say is the distance to that black rock and what rocket charge would send an empty suit to it with a trailing rope?"

The variables made it a tricky calculation. He had made his own rough estimate; but he could do with the best approximation that could be made. There was low gravity, the drag effect of the increasing length of rope, the effectiveness of different rocket charges, and the behavior of an inflated suit to think of. It took five minutes of calculation before she said, "Five-eighths charge and a launching angle of thirty-seven degrees." He accepted this without question though his own effort had produced a higher angle for the launch.

"Right."

He twisted out one of the two small rocket canisters from his belt. They were for use in zero weight as propulsion for a short trip outside a stationary ship. They would not move a man on Omega even with its reduced gravity. But they might serve to move a balloon. He spread-eagled the inflated suit on the rocks and carefully sighted along the back to line it up with the target, then he raised the head of a cairn of small stones checking to an angle of 37 degrees with his wrist watch. Then he slotted the charge canister into the empty sheath in the center of the shoulder straps. He turned the charge indicator to five-eighths and stood aside with the firing toggle in his hand. This was it. If it worked they were halfway home. He pulled the cord gently so as not to disturb the setting of the light figure.

The suit took off looking like a man in space and rose swiftly to the height of its trajectory and then began a homing descent to the rock with the thin nylon line snaking out behind. From where they stood it seemed certain that their projectile would overshoot. Then the increasing check of the trailing rope snatched it down from its soaring curve to a straight line drop and the suit disappeared in a tangle of rock. The rope was immensely strong; but could fray and cut. Dag hauled back until he felt it wedge firmly between two craggy projections, then made fast at their end.

He made a tight bundle of their remaining spares and attached it to a short length of line which he looped over the rope and then sent it like a miniature cable car shooting across the valley. It disappeared into the rocks and he began to work out a braking device with a slipping knot which could be jerked to tighten on the leading rope. When he was satisfied, he showed the girl how it worked and said:

"You next—if the line wears through it will be with me and you will have to sort it out for both of us."

She stood at the edge of the cliff, gripped the two trailing cords and stepped out over the drop. The perfect lieutenant, he thought, as he followed the dizzy speed of her descent. No questions or argument; but maximum efficient help. Even the bulky outer suit could not completely disguise the slim silver figure. The sag of the rope slowed her a little near the rock and she seemed to be managing the improvised brake. Then she was down in a stumbling run and he saw the small distant figure raise an arm in signal.

Unhesitating he swung out himself with the query—third time lucky?—in his mind. Near the rock he saw that his greater weight was sagging the rope below the rim of the rock outcrop and as he used all his strength to brake on the rope, he had to lift his legs in a full knee bend to fend off. The jar of impact almost broke his grip; but she was there lying out along the rope to help him in.

The next stage was clearer now and they looked silently at it for some minutes. Their final objective was higher than the rock they were on and they could not hope to make it in a toiling hand over hand climb. The best they could do would be to repeat their performance and slide down to the scree at the foot of the cliff and work out the next step from there.

She began another careful calculation of distances and velocities and once more they spread-eagled the inflated suit. Direction was not so critical for this shot into a wide target area and they saw it hit the cliff face and drop back into the scree. Dag pulled in cautiously and the suit dragged about twenty yards before it wedged. They went into the same routine and soon they were standing together at the foot of the last barrier.

Even under the low gravity of Omega they were feeling the physical strain, and as they scrambled up the last of the scree to the sheer wall of the cliff, Dag saw no way of beating the clock and getting to the plateau in the two hours of daylight left to them. Any lengthy exploration to left or right for a reasonable climb was out for a start, and in any case the cliff was uniformly sheer as far as could be seen. The spaceport apron had been given a mathematically even surface to the very edge of the cliff and visualizing the surface above, he could think of nothing immediately above them likely to anchor a rope. Some sort of tined grapnel might do—but made with what?

He broke the container of his anti-hostility pack and took out the small laser pistol—reflecting that if they ever got back to the dome this would need an explanatory section to itself in the station log. He beamed it at the cliff edge and small fragments powdered down. Given several days he might have cut steps with the intense narrow beam: but he did not have days.

"What charges are left?"

"Two complete and two part used."

"Would they do a demolition job?"

"Properly placed it could move this cliff."

The half formed idea clarified in his mind and he aimed directly at the sheer rock at about shoulder level. The face began to crumble in an area about the size of a cent piece, as the ray burned into it. He shifted an inch and bored again and after thirty minutes he had excavated a hole about eighteen inches deep and about two inches in diameter. Into this he packed one rocket canister with a thin twist of nylon line on its release toggle. Then he tamped home fragments of stone, only leaving movement for the cord.

They went back into the scree paying out line, and selected cover between two heavy boulders. In a single movement he jerked the trigger and flung himself down beside her with his arm over her shoulders. In their silent world, the noise seemed immense and debris crumbled down in a sliding rush. When movement stopped they stood up.

A tall oblong of the cliff face had come away and shattered like a slab of glass hit with a sledge-hammer. Angular fantastic fragments leaned forward to the new level and a jagged rangle led almost to the top. What problem there would be in that last step could only be assessed when they got there and they began to climb.

Some steps could only be gained by team work. Meryl climbed on his shoulders and got a finger-tip hold on a ledge, then he lifted her feet and she heaved herself on to the level. Then she made a belay and he climbed slowly to join her.

The last step was the highest yet and it was only by standing on his fully outstretched hands that she got a finger hold. It was a slow painful grind to bend her weary muscles and finally lever herself over the top. She lay forward, face downwards, sobbing with exhaustion. Waiting for the rope to snake down to him, he saw that they were within minutes of the twilight. Then he was beside her and with one arm across her shoulders they began a clumsy run to the nearest dome.

They were twenty yards from the lock when the light began to go and as he pulled down the opening lever, the blackness was complete. He felt her slipping down beside him and had to hold her as the door swung in to receive them. With one last effort he picked her up and carried her into the light and warmth.

The few minutes' rest while the robot mechanism adjusted pressures, gave him time to recover and he was able to carry her through into her room when the inner door opened for them. He took off her outer suit and put her on her bed. She was asleep and breathing deeply and easily.

He walked slowly to his own suite and stripped off and took a shower. It seemed a long time since he had last stood there and it was wonderful to feel the sweat and dust sluicing away and taking aches and tiredness with it. He even smoked a cigarette at intervals dodging the deluge. Then he took time to dress and wondered whether or not to wake her for a meal.

Still debating, he went out to the dining area to fix himself a drink. The table was already set for two and the food was ready. She came out from her room. She was wearing the ceremonial tabard of green and gold caught at the sides with bronze clasps. Her hair was combed down almost to her shoulders and swung like an elastic golden bell as she moved.

She said, "Welcome aboard, Controller," and he knew that the rest of the tour was not going to be any problem at all.

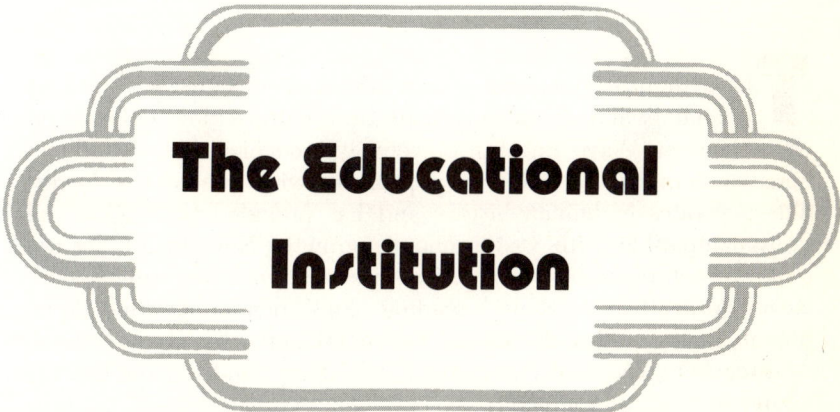

The Educational
Institution

Primary Education of the Camiroi

The system of mass education in the United States has both its defenders and detractors. Aside from culture-blind defenses of "the American Way," one can objectively recognize that our educational system has produced a population with one of the lowest illiteracy rates in human history and has provided training in the skills compatible with vast economic growth. Nevertheless, critics point to such problems as inequities in educational opportunity, deficiency in mathematical and reading skills, ponderous educational bureaucracies, and a decline in the moral authority of the school. And teachers who read essay exams will often wonder if the literacy figures are meaningful.

"Primary Education of the Camiroi" is a delightful story that should deflate those who blindly defend American education as the best possible. Although the Camiroi claim no greater intelligence than Earthlings, the products of their primary educational system outshine the "highest" products of our "higher" education. As Philoxenus states, "On Camiroi, we practice education. On Earth, they play a game, but they call it by the same name."

The Camiroi system of education employs some of the oldest educational devices known to man, such as learning by doing, concentrating on every word for true comprehension when reading instead of counting words per minute, and employing strict discipline. The Camiroi maintain discipline "indifferently," but harshly. They maintain no illusions about social nature being the product of socialization and would surely agree to the maxim "a firm hand does not extinguish a free spirit." Philoxenus explains: "small children are often put down into a pit. They do not eat or come out till they know their assignment." When a member of the study team from earth protests that practice as "inhuman," Philoxenus replies "Of course, but small children are not yet entirely human."

The study team from earth reaches paradoxical conclusions in its report. The Camiroi system is "inferior" to that of earth yet it produces "better" results. In an era when our schools "turn off" to learning so many who should be "turned on," when they fail to teach so many the basic "three R's," when discipline degenerates, and when educational "theories" and specialists proliferate, this story can serve as a call for change. Are we emphasizing the style of education and not its substance? Have we grown too sophisticated in educational technique and technology?

Primary Education of the Camiroi

R. A. LAFFERTY

ABSTRACT FROM JOINT REPORT TO THE GENERAL DU-
BUQUE PTA CONCERNING THE PRIMARY EDUCATION
OF THE CAMIROI, Subject Critical Observations of a Parallel Cul-
ture on a Neighboring World, and Evaluations of THE OTHER
WAY OF EDUCATION.

Extract from the Day Book:

"Where," we asked the Information Factor at Camiroi City
Terminal, "is the office of the local PTA?"

"Isn't any," he said cheerfully.

"You mean that in Camiroi City, the metropolis of the planet,
there is no PTA?" our chairman Paul Piper asked with disbelief.

"Isn't any office of it. But you're poor strangers, so you deserve
an answer even if you can't frame your questions properly. See that
elderly man sitting on the bench and enjoying the sun? Go tell him
you need a PTA. He'll make you one."

"Perhaps the initials convey a different meaning on Camiroi,"
said Miss Munch the first surrogate chairman. "By them we mean—"

"Parent Teachers Apparatus, of course. Colloquial English is
one of the six Earthian languages required here, you know. Don't be
abashed. He's a fine person, and he enjoys doing things for strangers.
He'll be glad to make you a PTA."

We were nonplussed, but we walked over to the man indicated.

"We are looking for the local PTA, sir," said Miss Smice, our
second surrogate chairman. "We were told that you might help us."

"Oh, certainly," said the elderly Camiroi gentleman. "One of you
arrest that man walking there, and we'll get started with it."

"Do what?" asked our Mr. Piper.

"Arrest him. I have noticed that your own words sometimes do not convey a meaning to you. I often wonder how you do communicate among yourselves. Arrest, take into custody, seize by any force physical or moral, and bring him here."

"Yes, *sir*," cried Miss Hanks our third surrogate chairman. She enjoyed things like this. She arrested the walking Camiroi man with force partly physical and partly moral and brought him to the group.

"It's a PTA they want, Meander," the elder Camiroi said to the one arrested. "Grab three more, and we'll get started. Let the lady help. She's good at it."

Our Miss Hanks and the Camiroi man named Meander arrested three other Camiroi men and brought them to the group.

"Five. It's enough," said the elderly Camiroi. "We are hereby constituted a PTA and ordered into random action. Now, how can we accommodate you, good Earth people?"

"But are you legal? Are you five persons competent to be a PTA?" demanded our Mr. Piper.

"Any Camiroi citizen is competent to do any job on the planet of Camiroi," said one of the Camiroi men (we learned later that his name was Talarium), "otherwise Camiroi would be in a sad shape."

"It may be," said our Miss Smice sourly. "It all seems very informal. What if one of you had to be World President?"

"The odds are that it won't come to one man in ten," said the elderly Camiroi (his name was Philoxenus). "I'm the only one of this group ever to serve as president of this planet, and it was a pleasant week I spent in the Office. Now to the point. How can we accommodate you."

"We would like to see one of your schools in session," said our Mr. Piper. "We would like to talk to the teachers and the students. We are here to compare the two systems of education."

"There is no comparison," said old Philoxenus, "—meaning no offense. Or no more than a little. On Camiroi, we practice Education. On Earth, they play a game, but they call it by the same name. That makes the confusion. Come. We'll go to a school in session."

"And to a public school," said Miss Smice suspiciously. "Do not fob off any fancy private school on us as typical."

"That would be difficult," said Philoxenus. "There is no public school in Camiroi City and only two remaining on the Planet. Only a small fraction of one per cent of the students of Camiroi are in public schools. We maintain that there is no more reason for the majority of children to be educated in a public school than to be raised in a public orphanage. We realize, of course, that on Earth you have made a sacred buffalo of the public school."

"Sacred cow," said our Mr. Piper.

"Children and Earthlings should be corrected when they use

words wrongly," said Philoxenus. "How else will they learn the correct forms? The animal held sacred in your own near orient was of the species *bos bubalus* rather than *bos bos*, a buffalo rather than a cow. Shall we go to a school?"

"If it cannot be a public school, at least let it be a typical school," said Miss Smice.

"That again is impossible," said Philoxenus. "Every school on Camiroi is in some respect atypical."

We went to visit an atypical school.

INCIDENT: Our first contact with the Camiroi students was a violent one. One of them, a lively little boy about eight years old, ran into Miss Munch, knocked her down, and broke her glasses. Then he jabbered something in an unknown tongue.

"Is that Camiroi?" asked Mr. Piper with interest. "From what I have heard, I supposed the language to have a harsher and fuller sound."

"You mean you don't recognize it?" asked Philoxenus with amusement. "What a droll admission from an educator. The boy is very young and very ignorant. Seeing that you were Earthians, he spoke in Hindi, which is the tongue used by more Earthians than any other. No, no, Xypete, they are of the minority who speak English. You can tell it by their colorless texture and the narrow heads on them."

"I say you sure do have slow reaction, lady," the little boy Xypete explained. "Even subhumans should react faster than that. You just stand there and gape and let me bowl you over. You want me to analyze you and see why you react so slow?"

"No! No!"

"You seem unhurt in structure from the fall," the little boy continued, "but if I hurt you I got to fix you. Just strip down to your shift, and I'll go over you and make sure you're all right."

"No! No! No!"

"It's all right," said Philoxenus. "All Camiroi children learn primary medicine in the first grade, setting bones and healing contusions and such."

"No! No! I'm all right. But he's broken my glasses."

"Come along Earthside lady, I'll make you some others," said the little boy. "With your slow reaction time you sure can't afford the added handicap of defective vision. Shall I fit you with contacts?"

"No. I want glasses just like those which were broken. Oh heavens, what will I do?"

"You come, I do," said the little boy. It was rather revealing to us that the little boy was able to test Miss Munch's eyes, grind lenses, make frames and have her fixed up within three minutes. "I have made some improvements over those you wore before," the boy said, "to help compensate for your slow reaction time."

"Are all the Camiroi students so talented?" Mr. Piper asked. He was impressed.

"No. Xypete is unusual," Philoxenus said. "Most students would not be able to make a pair of glasses so quickly or competently till they were at least nine."

RANDOM INTERVIEWS: "How rapidly do you read?" Miss Hanks asked a young girl.

"One hundred and twenty words a minute," the girl said.

"On Earth some of the girl students your age have learned to read at the rate of five hundred words a minute," Miss Hanks said proudly.

"When I began disciplined reading, I was reading at the rate of four thousand words a minute," the girl said. "They had quite a time correcting me of it. I had to take remedial reading, and my parents were ashamed of me. Now I've learned to read almost slow enough."

"I don't understand," said Miss Hanks.

"Do you know anything about Earth History or Geography?" Miss Smice asked a middle-sized boy.

"We sure are sketchy on it, lady. There isn't very much over there, is there?"

"Then you have never heard of Dubuque?"

"Count Dubuque interests me. I can't say as much for the City named after him. I always thought that the Count handled the matters of the conflicting French and Spanish land grants and the basic claims of the Sauk and Fox Indians very well. References to the Town now carry a humorous connotation, and 'School-Teacher from Dubuque' has become a folk archetype."

"Thank you," said Miss Smice, "or do I thank you?"

"What are you taught of the relative humanity of the Earthians and the Camiroi and of their origins?" Miss Munch asked a Camiroi girl.

"The other four worlds, Earth (Gaea), Kentauron Mikron, Dahae and Astrobe were all settled from Camiroi. That is what we are taught. We are also given the humorous aside that if it isn't true we will still hold it true till something better comes along. It was we who rediscovered the Four Worlds in historic time, not they who discovered us. If we did not make the original settlements, at least we have filed the first claim that we made them. We did, in historical time, make an additional colonization of Earth. You call it the Incursion of the Dorian Greeks."

"Where are their playgrounds?" Miss Hanks asked Talarium.

"Oh, the whole world. The children have the run of everything. To set up specific playgrounds would be like setting a table-sized aquarium down in the depths of the ocean. It would really be pointless."

CONFERENCE: The four of us from Earth, specifically from Dubuque, Iowa, were in discussion with the five members of the Camiroi PTA.

"How do you maintain discipline?" Mr. Piper asked.

"Indifferently," said Philoxenus, "Oh, you mean in detail. It varies. Sometimes we let it drift, sometimes we pull them up short. Once they have learned that they must comply to an extent, there is little trouble. Small children are often put down into a pit. They do not eat or come out till they know their assignment."

"But that is inhuman," said Miss Hanks.

"Of course. But small children are not yet entirely human. If a child has not learned to accept discipline by the third or fourth grade, he is hanged."

"Literally?" asked Miss Munch.

"How would you hang a child figuratively? And what effect would that have on the other children?"

"By the neck?" Miss Munch still was not satisfied.

"By the neck until they are dead. The other children always accept the example gracefully and do better. Hanging isn't employed often. Scarcely one child in a hundred is hanged."

"What is this business about slow reading?" Miss Hanks asked, "I don't understand it at all."

"Only the other day there was a child in the third grade who persisted in rapid reading," Philoxenus said. "He was given an object lesson. He was given a book of medium difficulty, and he read it rapidly. Then he had to put the book away and repeat what he had read. Do you know that in the first thirty pages he missed four words? Midway in the book there was a whole statement which he had understood wrongly, and there were hundreds of pages that he got word-perfect only with difficulty. If he was so unsure on material that he had just read, think how imperfectly he would have recalled it forty years later."

"You mean that the Camiroi children learn to recall everything that they read?"

"The Camiroi children and adults will recall for life every detail they have ever seen, read or heard. We on Camiroi are only a little more intelligent than you on Earth. We cannot afford to waste time in forgetting or reviewing, or in pursuing anything of a shallowness that lends itself to scanning."

"Ah, would you call your schools liberal?" Mr. Piper asked.

"I would. You wouldn't," said Philoxenus. "We do not on Camiroi, as you do on Earth, use words to mean their opposites. There is nothing in our education or on our world that corresponds to the quaint servility which you call liberal on Earth."

"Well, would you call your education progressive?"

"No. In your argot, progressive, of course, means infantile."

"How are the schools financed?" asked Mr. Piper.

"Oh, the voluntary tithe on Camiroi takes care of everything, government, religion, education, public works. We don't believe in taxes, of course, and we never maintain a high overhead in anything."

"Just how voluntary is the tithing?" asked Miss Hanks. "Do you sometimes hang those who do not tithe voluntarily?"

"I believe there have been a few cases of that sort," said Philoxenus.

"And is your government really as slipshod as your education?" Mr. Piper asked. "Are your high officials really chosen by lot and for short periods?"

"Oh yes. Can you imagine a person so sick that he would actually *desire* to hold high office for any great period of time? Are there any further questions?"

"There must be hundreds," said Mr. Piper, "but we find difficulty putting them into words."

"If you cannot find words for them, we cannot find answers. PTA disbanded."

CONCLUSIONS: A. The Camiroi system of education is inferior to our own in organization, in buildings, in facilities, in playgrounds, in teacher conferences, in funding, in parental involvement, in supervision, in in-group out-group accommodation adjustment motifs. Some of the school buildings are grotesque. We asked about one particular building which seemed to us to be flamboyant and in bad taste. "What do you expect from second-grade children?" they said, "It is well built even if of peculiar appearance. Second-grade children are not yet complete artists of design."

"You mean that the children designed it themselves?" we asked.

"Of course," they said. "Designed and built it. It isn't a bad job for children."

Such a thing wouldn't be permitted on Earth.

CONCLUSION B. The Camiroi system of education somehow

produces much better results than does the education system of Earth. We have been forced to admit this by the evidence at hand.

CONCLUSION C. There is an anomaly as yet unresolved between CONCLUSION A and CONCLUSION B.

Appendix to Joint Report

We give here, as perhaps of some interest, the curriculum of the Camiroi Primary Education.

FIRST YEAR COURSE:
Playing one wind instrument
Simple drawing of objects and numbers.
Singing. (This is important. Many Earth people sing who cannot sing.
    This early instruction of the Camiroi prevents that occurrence.)
Simple arithmetic, hand and machine.
First Acrobatics.
First riddles and logic.
Mnemonic religion.
First dancing.
Walking the low wire.
Simple electric circuits.
Raising ants. (Eoempts, not earth ants).

SECOND YEAR COURSE:
Playing one keyboard instrument.
Drawing, faces, letters, motions.
Singing comedies.
Complex arithmetic, hand and machine.
Second acrobatics.
First jokes and logic.
Quadratic religion.
Second Dancing.
Simple defamation (Spirited attacks on the character of one fellow
    student, with elementary falsification and simple hatchet-job
    programming.)
Performing on the medium wire.
Project electric wiring.
Raising bees. (Galelea, not earth bees.)

THIRD YEAR COURSE:
Playing one stringed instrument.
Reading and voice. (It is here that the student who may have fallen

into bad habits of rapid reading is compelled to read at voice speed only.)

Soft stone sculpture.
Situation comedy.
Simple algebra, hand and machine.
First gymnastics.
Second jokes and logic.
Transcendent religion.
Complex acrobatic dancing.
Complex defamation.
Performing on the high wire and the sky pole.
Simple radio construction.
Raising, breeding and dissecting frogs.
　　(Karakoli, not earth frogs.)

FOURTH YEAR COURSE:
History reading, Camiroi and galactic, basic and geological.
Decadent comedy.
Simple geometry and trigonometry, hand and machine.
Track and field.
Shaggy people jokes and hirsute logic.
Simple obscenity.
Simple mysticism.
Patterns of falsification.
Trapeze work.
　　Intermediate electronics.
Human dissection.

FIFTH YEAR COURSE:
History reading, Camiroi and galactic, technological.
Introverted drama.
Complex geometries and analytics, hand and machine.
Track and field for fifth form record.
First wit and logic.
First alcoholic appreciation.
Complex mysticism.
Setting intellectual climates, defamation in three dimensions.
Simple oratory.
Complex trapeze work.
Inorganic chemistry.
Advanced electronics.
Advanced human dissection.
Fifth Form Thesis.
The child is now ten years old and is half through his primary

schooling. He is an unfinished animal, but he has learned to learn.

SIXTH FORM COURSE:
Reemphasis on slow reading.
Simple prodigious memory.
History reading, Camiroi and galactic, economic.
Horsemanship (of the Patrushkoe, not the earth horse.)
Advanced lathe and machine work for art and utility.
Literature, passive.
Calculi, hand and machine pankration.
Advanced wit and logic.
Second alcoholic appreciation.
Differential religion.
First business ventures.
Complex oratory.
Building-scaling. (The buildings are higher and the gravity stronger than on Earth; this climbing of buildings like human flies calls out the ingenuity and daring of the Camiroi children.)
Nuclear physics and post-organic chemistry.
Simple pseudo-human assembly.

SEVENTH YEAR COURSE:
History reading, Camiroi and galactic, cultural.
Advanced prodigious memory.
Vehicle operation and manufacture of simple vehicle.
Literature, active.
Astrognosy, prediction and programming.
Advanced pankration.
Spherical logic, hand and machine.
Advanced alcoholic appreciation.
Integral religion.
Bankruptcy and recovery in business.
Conmanship and trend creation.
Post-nuclear physics and universals.
Transcendental athletics endeavor.
Complex robotics and programming.

EIGHTH YEAR COURSE:
History reading, Camiroi and galactic, seminal theory.
Consummate prodigious memory.
Manufacture of complex land and water vehicles.
Literature, compendious and terminative. (Creative book-burning

following the Camiroi thesis that nothing ordinary be allowed
to survive.)
Cosmic theory, seminal.
Philosophy construction.
Complex hedonism.
Laser religion.
Conmanship, seminal.
Consolidation of simple genius status.
Post-robotic integration.

NINTH YEAR COURSE:
History reading, Camiroi and galactic, future and contingent.
Category invention.
Manufacture of complex light-barrier vehicles.
Construction of simple asteroids and planets.
Matrix religion and logic.
Simple human immortality disciplines.
Consolidation of complex genius status.
First problems of post-consciousness humanity.
First essays in marriage and reproduction.

TENTH YEAR COURSE:
History construction, active.
Manufacture of ultra-light-barrier vehicles.
Panphilosophical clarifications.
Construction of viable planets.
Consolidation of simple sanctity status.
Charismatic humor and pentacosmic logic.
Hypogyroscopic economy.
Penentaglossia. (the perfection of the fifty languages that every
educated Camiroi must know including six Earthian languages.
Of course the child will already have colloquial mastery of most
of these, but he will not yet have them in their full depth.)
Construction of complex societies.
World government. (A course of the same name is sometimes given
in Earthian schools, but the course is not of the same content. In
this course the Camiroi student will govern a world, though not
one of the first aspect worlds, for a period of three or four
months.)
Tenth form thesis.

COMMENT ON CURRICULUM:
The child will now be fifteen years old and will have completed

his primary education. In many ways he will be advanced beyond his Earth counterpart. Physically more sophisticated, the Camiroi child could kill with his hands an Earth-type tiger or a cape buffalo. An Earth child would perhaps be reluctant even to attempt such feats. The Camiroi boy (or girl) could replace any professional Earth athlete at any position of any game, and could surpass all existing Earth records. It is simply a question of finer poise, strength and speed, the result of adequate schooling.

As to the arts (on which Earthlings sometimes place emphasis) the Camiroi child could produce easy and unequaled masterpieces in any medium. More important, he will have learned the relative un-importance of such pastimes.

The Camiroi child will have failed in business once, at age ten, and have learned patience and perfection of objective by his failure. He will have acquired the techniques of falsification and conmanship. Thereafter he will not be easily deceived by any of the citizens of any of the worlds. The Camiroi child will have become a complex genius and a simple saint; the latter reduces the index of Camiroi crime to near zero. He will be married and settled in those early years of greatest enjoyment.

The child will have built, from materials found around any Camiroi house, a faster-than-light vehicle. He will have piloted it on a significant journey of his own plotting and programming. He will have built quasi-human robots of great intricacy. He will be of perfect memory and judgment and will be well prepared to accept solid learning.

He will have learned to use his whole mind, for the vast reservoirs which are the unconscious to us are not unconscious to him. Everything in him is ordered for use. And there seems to be no great secret about the accomplishments, only to do everything slowly enough and in the right order: Thus they avoid repetition and drill which are the shriveling things which dull the quick apperception.

The Camiroi schedule is challenging to the children, but it is nowhere impossible or discouraging. Everything builds to what follows. For instance, the child is eleven years old before he is given post-nuclear physics and universals. Such subjects might be too difficult for him at an earlier age. He is thirteen years old before he undertakes category invention, that intricate course with the simple name. He is fourteen years old when he enters the dangerous field of panphilosophical clarification. But he will have been constructing comprehensive philosophies for two years, and he will have the background for the final clarification.

We should look more closely at this other way of education. In some respects it is better than our own. Few Earth children would be able to construct an organic and sentient robot within fifteen minutes if given the test suddenly; most of them could not manufacture a living dog in that time. Not one Earth child in five could build a faster-than-light vehicle and travel it beyond our galaxy between now and midnight. Not one Earth child in a hundred could build a planet and have it a going concern within a week. Not one in a thousand would be able to comprehend pentacosmic logic.

RECOMMENDATIONS: a. Kidnapping five Camiroi at random and constituting them a pilot Earth PTA. b. A little constructive book-burning, particularly in the education field. c. Judicious hanging of certain malingering students. —R. A. LAFFERTY

The Economic
Institution

Birthright

Within all societies, the production and distribution of at least the minimum goods and services necessary for survival must occur. The economic institution of a society provides for accomplishment of these necessary tasks. From cooperative arrangements among nonliterate food-gathering peoples to the corporate conglomerates of the modern nation-state, economic arrangements constitute one of man's cultural universals.

All societies have mechanisms that determine cost and benefit and utilize some medium of exchange. Members of early societies exchanged by barter, while today nation-states have standardized currency (at least within their borders). Individuals, social groups, and entire societies are faced with the problem of allocating resources—of developing priorities for utilizing effectively that which is extracted or produced.

Economic factors and motives are paramount in "Birthright." Although warfare can be used to protect or extend economic interests, the societies in the story *compete* for basic goals that can be consumed or exploited for profit. One interesting assumption underlying the author's work is the universality of the profit motive and the cross-cultural nature of the competitive drive. All the societies represented in "Birthright" seek to gain profit as they struggle for monopoly over certain economic spheres.

The imperial character of the intergalactic system depicted in the story closely parallels that present on this planet during the nineteenth century. Various sectors of the universe are allocated to different planetary empires, in a fashion similar to the way the earth was divided among British, Spanish, French, and Portugese imperial interests. The Suleimanites of the story are an indigenous people who, while not exactly colonized, at least are in a situation that closely resembles that faced by the native peoples of Africa, Asia, and Latin America. The attention paid to economic factors is one of the strongest points of the story.

Finally, at a time when many bemoan what they see as the demise of the individualistic industrial entrepreneur as nameless "other-directed" organization men staff and run our economic enterprises, Anderson poses an interesting answer to the question: Given the trends toward increasing bureaucratic economic organization and the "team player" roles so often required, will there be a place in the future for the strong-willed and able individualist?

Birthright

POUL ANDERSON

The cab obtained clearance from certain machines and landed on the roof of the Winged Cross. Emil Dalmady paid and stepped out. When it took off, he felt suddenly very alone. The garden was fragrant around him in a warm deep-blue summer's dusk; at this height, the sounds of Chicago Integrate were a murmur as of a distant ocean; the other towers and the skyways between them were a forest through which flitted will-o'-the-wisp aircars and beneath which—as if Earth had gone transparent—a fantastic galaxy of many-colored lights was blinking awake farther than eye could reach. But the penthouse bulking ahead might have been a hill where a grizzly bear had its den.

The man squared his shoulders. *Haul in,* he told himself. *He won't eat you.* Anger lifted afresh. *I might just eat him.* He strode forward: a stocky, muscular figure in a blue zipskin, features broad and high of cheekbones, snubnosed, eyes green and slightly tilted, hair reddish black.

But despite stiffened will, the fact remained that he had not expected a personal interview with any merchant prince of the Polesotechnic League, and in one of the latter's own homes. When a live butler had admitted him, and he had crossed an improbably long stretch of trollcat rug to the VieWall end of a luxury-cluttered living room, and was confronting Nicholas van Rijn, his throat tightened and his palms grew wet.

"Good evening," the host rumbled. "Welcome." His corpulent corpus did not rise from the lounger. Dalmady didn't mind. Not only bulk but height would have dwarfed him. Van Rijn waved a hand at a facing seat; the other gripped a liter tankard of beer. "Sit. Relax. You look quivery like a blanc-mange before a firing squad. What you drink, smoke, chew, sniff, or elsewise make amusements with?"

Dalmady lowered himself to an edge. Van Rijn's great hook-beaked, multi-chinned, moustached and goateed visage, framed in black shoulder-length ringlets, crinkled with a grin. Beneath the sloping brow, small jet eyes glittered at the newcomer. "Relax," he urged again. "Give the form-fitting a chance. Not so fun-making an embrace like a pretty girl, but less extracting, ha? I think maybe a little glass Genever and bitters over dry ice is a tranquilizator for you." He clapped.

"Sir," Dalmady said, harshly in his tension, "I don't want to seem ungracious, but—"

"But you came to Earth breathing flame and brimrocks, and went through six echelons of the toughest no-saying secretaries and officers what the Solar Spice and Liquors Company has got, like a bulldozer chasing a cowdozer, demanding to see whoever the crockhead was what fired you after what you done yonderways. Nobody had a chance to explain. Trouble was, they assumptioned you knew things what they take for granted. So natural, what they said sounded to you like a flushoff and you hurricaned your way from them to somebody else."

Van Rijn offered a cigar out of a gold humidor whose workmanship Dalmady couldn't identify except that it was nonhuman. The young man shook his head. The merchant selected one himself, bit off the end and spat that expertly into a receptor, and inhaled the tobacco to ignition. "Well," he continued, "somebody would have got through into you at last, only then I learned about you and ordered this meeting. I would have wanted to talk at you anyhows. Now I shall clarify everything like Hindu butter."

His geniality was well-nigh as overwhelming as his wrath would have been, assuming the legends about him were true. *And he could be setting me up for a thunderbolt,* Dalmady thought, and clung to his indignation as he answered:

"Sir, if your outfit is dissatisfied with my conduct on Suleiman, it might at least have told me why, rather than sending a curt message that I was being replaced and should report to HQ. Unless you can prove to me that I bungled, I will not accept demotion. It's a question of personal honor more than professional standing. They think that way where I come from. I'll quit. And . . . there are plenty of other companies in the League that will be glad to hire me."

"True, true, in spite of every candle I burn to St. Dismas." Van Rijn sighed through his cigar, engulfing Dalmady in smoke. "Always they try to pirate my executives what have not yet sworn fealty, like the thieves they are. And I, poor old lonely fat man, trying to run this enterprise personal what stretches across so many whole worlds, even with modern computer technology I get melted down from overwork, and too few men for helpers what is not total gruntbrains, and some of them got to be occupied just luring good executives away from elsewhere." He took a noisy gulp of beer. "Well."

"I suppose you've read my report, sir," was Dalmady's gambit.

"Today. So much information flowing from across the light-years, how can this weary old noggle hold it without data flowing back out like ear wax? Let me review to make sure I got it tesseract. Which means—ho, ho!—straight in four dimensions."

Van Rijn wallowed deeper into his lounger, bridged hairy fingers, and closed his eyes. The butler appeared with a huge steaming and hissing goblet. *If this is his idea of a small drink*—! Dalmady thought. Grimly, he forced himself to sit at ease and sip.

"Now." The cigar waggled in time to the words. "This star what its discoverer called Osman is out past Antares, on the far edge of present-day regular-basis League activities. One planet is inhabited, called by humans Suleiman. Subjovian; life based on hydrogen, ammonia, methane; primitive natives, but friendly. Turned out, on the biggest continent grows a plant we call . . . um-m-m . . . bluejack, what the natives use for a spice and tonic. Analysis showed a complicated blend of chemicals, answering sort of to hormonal stuffs for us, with synergistic effects. No good to oxygen breathers, but maybe we can sell to hydrogen breathers elsewhere.

"Well, we found very few markets, at least what had anythings to offer we wanted. You need a special biochemistry for bluejack to be beneficent. So synthesis would cost us more, counting investment and freight charges from chemical-lab centers, than direct harvesting by natives on Suleiman, paid for in trade goods. Given that, we could show a wee profit. Quite teensy—whole operation is near-as-damn marginal—but as long as things stayed peaceful, well, why not turn a few honest credits?

"And things was peaceful, too, for years. Natives cooperated fine, bringing in bluejack to warehouses. Outshipping was one of those milk runs where we don't knot up capital in our own vessels, we contract with a freighter line to make regular calls. Oh, *ja*, contretemps kept on countertiming—bad seasons, bandits raiding caravans, kings getting too greedy about taxes—usual stuffing, what any competent factor could handle on the spot, so no reports about it ever come to pester me.

"And then . . . Ahmed, more beer! . . . real trouble. Best market for bluejack is on a planet we call Babur. Its star, Mogul, lies in the same general region, about thirty light-years from Osman. Its top country been dealing with Technic civilization off and on for decades. Trying to modernize, they was mainly interested in robotics for some reason; but at last they did pile together enough outplanet exchange for they could commission a few hyperdrive ships built and crews trained. So now the Solar Commonwealth and other powers got to treat them with a little more respect; blast cannon and nuclear missiles sure improve manners, by damn! They is still small tomatoes, but ambitious. And to them, with the big domestic demand, bluejack is not an incidental thing."

Van Rijn leaned forward, wrinkling the embroidered robe that circled his paunch. "You wonder why I tell you what you know, ha?" he said. "When I need direct reports on a situation, especial from a world as scarcely known as Suleiman, I can't study each report from decades. Data retrieval got to make me an abstract. I check with you now, who was spotted there, whether the machine give me all what is significant to our talking. Has I been correct so far?"

"Yes," Dalmady said. "But—"

Yvonne Vaillancourt looked up from a console as the factor passed the open door of her collation lab. "What's wrong, Emil?" she asked. "I heard you clattering the whole way down the hall."

Dalmady stopped for a look. Clothing was usually at a minimum in the Earth-conditioned compound, but, while he had grown familiar with the skins of its inhabitants, he never tired of hers. Perhaps, he had thought, her blond shapeliness impressed him the more because he had been born and raised on Altai. The colonists of that chill planet went heavily dressed of necessity. The same need to survive forced austere habits on them; and, isolated in a largely unexplored frontier section, they received scant news about developments in the core civilization.

When you were one of half a dozen humans on a world whose very air was death to you—when you didn't even have visitors of your own species, because the ship that regularly called belonged to a Cynthian carrier—you had no choice but to live in free and easy style. Dalmady had had that explained to him while he was being trained for this post, and recognized it and went along with it. But he wondered if he would ever become accustomed to the *casualness* of the sophisticates whom he bossed.

"I don't know," he answered the girl. "The Thalassocrat wants me at the palace."

"Why, he knows perfectly well how to make a visi call."

"Yes, but a nomad's brought word of something nasty in the Uplands, and won't come near the set. Afraid it'll imprison his soul, I imagine."

"Hm-m-m, I think not. We're still trying to chart the basic Suleimanite psychology, you know, with only inadequate data from three or four cultures to go on . . . but they don't seem to have animistic tendencies like man's. Ceremony, yes, in abundance, but nothing we can properly identify as magic or religion."

Dalmady barked a nervous laugh. "Sometimes I think my whole staff considers our commerce an infernal nuisance that keeps getting in the way of their precious science."

"Sometimes you'd be right," Yvonne purred. "What'd hold us here except the chance to do research?"

"And how long would your research last if the company closed down this base?" he flared. "Which it will if we start losing money. My job's to see that we don't. I could use cooperation."

She slipped from her stool, came to him and kissed him lightly. Her hair smelled like remembered steppe grass warmed by an orange sun, rippling under the rings of Altai. "Don't we help?" she murmured. "I'm sorry, dear."

He bit his lip and stared past her, down the length of gaudy murals whose painting had beguiled much idle time over the years. "No, I'm sorry," he said with the stiff honesty of his folk. "Of course you're all loyal and—It's me. Here I am, the youngest among you, a half-barbarian herdboy, supposed to make a go of things . . . in one of the easiest, most routinized outposts in this sector . . . and after a bare fifteen months—"

If I fail, he thought, *well, I can return home, no doubt, and dismiss the sacrifices my parents made to send me to managerial school offplanet, scorn the luck that Solar Spice and Liquors had an opening here and no more experienced employee to fill it, forget every dream about walking in times to come on new and unknown worlds that really call forth every resource a man has to give. Oh, yes, failure isn't fatal, except in subtler ways than I have words for.*

"You fret too much." Yvonne patted his cheek. "Probably this is just another tempest in a chickenhouse. You'll bribe somebody, or arm somebody, or whatever's needful, and that will once again be that."

"I hope so. But the Thalassocrat acted—well, not being committed to xenological scholarly precision, I'd say he acted worried, too." Dalmady stood a few seconds longer, scowling, before: "All right, I'd better be on way." He gave her a hug. "Thanks, Yvonne."

She watched him till he was out of sight, then returned to her work. Officially she was the trade post's secretary-treasurer, but such duties seldom came to her except when a freighter had landed. Otherwise she used the computers to try to find patterns in what fragments of knowledge her four colleagues could wrest from a world—an entire, infinitely varied world—and hoped that a few scientists elsewhere might eventually scan a report on Suleiman—one among thousands of planets—and be interested.

Airsuit donned, Dalmady left the compound by its main personnel lock. Wanting time to compose himself, he went afoot through the city to the palace—if they were city and palace.

He didn't know. Books, tapes, lectures, and neuroinductors had crammed him with information about this part of this continent; but those were the everyday facts and skills needed to manage operations. Long talks with his subordinates here had added a little insight, but only a little. Direct experience with the autochthons was occasionally enlightening, but just as apt to be confusing. No wonder that, once a satisfactory arrangement was made with Coast and Upland tribes (?), his predecessors had not attempted expansion or improvement. When you don't understand a machine, but it seems to be running reasonably smoothly, you don't tinker much.

Outside the compound's force field, local gravity dragged at him with forty percent greater pull than Earth's. Though his suit was light and his muscles hard, the air recycler necessarily included the extra mass of a unit for dealing with the hydrogen that seeped through any material. Soon he was sweating. Nevertheless it was as if the chill struck past all thermostatic coils, into his heavy bones.

High overhead stood Osman, a furious white spark, twice as luminous as Sol but, at its distance, casting a bare sixteenth of what Earth gets. Clouds, tinged red by organic compounds, drifted on slow winds through a murky sky where one of the three moons was dimly visible. That atmosphere bore thrice a terrestrial standard pressure. It was mostly hydrogen and helium, with vapors of methane and ammonia and traces of other gas. Greenhouse effect did not extend to unfreezing water.

Indeed, the planetary core was overlaid by a shell of ice, mixed with rock, penetrated by tilted metal-poor strata. The land glittered amidst its grayness and scrunched beneath Dalmady's boots. It sloped down to a dark, choppy sea of liquid ammonia whose horizon was too remote—given a 17,000-kilometer radius—for him to make out through the red-misted air.

Ice also were the buildings that rose blocky around him. They shimmered glasslike where doorways, or obscure carved symbols, did not break their smoothness. There were no streets in the usual sense, but aerial observation has disclosed an elaborate pattern in the layout of structures, about which the dwellers could not or would not speak. Wind moved ponderously between them. The air turned its sound, every sound, shrill.

Traffic surged. It was mainly pedestrian, natives on their business, carrying the oddly shaped tools and containers of a fireless

neolithic nonhuman culture. A few wagons lumbered in with produce from the hinterland; their draught animals suggested miniature
dinosaurs modeled by someone who had heard vague rumors of such
creatures. A related, more slender species was ridden. Coracles
bobbed across the sea; you might as well say the crews were fishing,
though a true fish could live here unprotected no longer than a man.

Nothing reached Dalmady's earphones except the wind, the distant wave-rumble, the clop of feet and creak of wagons. Suleimanites
did not talk casually. They did communicate, however, and without
pause: by gesture, by ripple across erectile fur, by delicate exchanges
between scent glands. They avoided coming near the human, but
simply because his suit was hot to their touch. He gave and received
many signals of greeting. After two years—twenty-five of Earth's—
Coast and Uplands alike were becoming dependent on metal and
plastic and energy-cell trade goods. Local labor had been eagerly
available to help build a spaceport on the mesa overlooking town,
and still did most of the work. That saved installing automatic
machinery—one reason for the modest profit earned by this station.

Dalmady leaned into his uphill walk. After ten minutes he was
at the palace.

The half-score natives posted outside the big, turreted building
were not guards. While wars and robberies occurred on Suleiman, the
slaying of a "king" seemed to be literally unthinkable. (An effect of
pheromones? In every community the xenologists had observed thus
far, the leader ate special foods which his followers insisted would
poison anyone else; and maybe the followers were right.) The drums,
plumed canes, and less identifiable gear which these beings carried
were for ceremonial use.

Dalmady controlled his impatience and watched with a trace of
pleasure the ritual of opening doors and conducting him to the royal
presence. The Suleimanites were a graceful and handsome species.
They were plantigrade bipeds, rather like men although the body
was thicker and the average only came to his shoulder. The hands
each bore two fingers between two thumbs, and were supplemented
by a prehensile tail. The head was round, with a parrotlike beak,
tympani for hearing, one large goldenhued eye in the middle and
two smaller, less developed ones for binocular and peripheral vision.
Clothing was generally confined to a kind of sporran, elaborately
patterned with symbols, to leave glands and mahogany fur available
for signals. The fact that Suleimanite languages had so large a non-
vocal component handicapped human efforts at understanding as
much as anything else did.

The Thalassocrat addressed Dalmady by voice alone, in the blue-glimmering ice cavern of his audience room. Earphones reduced the upper frequencies to some the man could hear. Nonetheless, that squeak and gibber always rather spoiled the otherwise impressive effect of flower crown and cavern staff. So did the dwarfs, hunchbacks, and cripples who squatted on rugs and skin-draped benches. It was not known why household servants were always recruited among the handicapped. Suleimanites had tried to explain when asked, but their meaning never came through.

"Fortune, power, and wisdom to you, Factor." They didn't use personal names on this world, and seemed unable to grasp the idea of an identification which was not a scent-symbol.

"May they continue to abide with you, Thalassocrat." The vocalizer on his back transformed Dalmady's version of local speech into sounds that his lips could not bring forth.

"We have here a Master of caravaneers," the monarch said.

Dalmady went through polite ritual with the Uplander, who was tall and rangy for a Suleimanite, armed with a stoneheaded tomahawk and a trade rifle designed for his planet, his barbarianism showing in gaudy jewels and bracelets. They were O.K., however, those hill country nomads. Once a bargain had been struck, they held to it with more literal-mindedness than humans could have managed.

"And what is the trouble for which I am summoned, Master? Has your caravan met bandits on its way to the Coast? I will be glad to equip a force for their suppression."

Not being used to talking with men, the chief went into full Suleimanite language—his own dialect, at that—and became incomprehensible. One of the midgets stumped forward. Dalmady recognized him. A bright mind dwelt in that poor little body, drank deep of whatever knowledge about the universe was offered, and in return had frequently helped with counsel or knowledge. "Let me ask him out, Factor and Thalassocrat," he suggested.

"If you will, Advisor," his overlord agreed.

"I will be in your debt, Translator," Dalmady said, with his best imitation of the prancing thanks-gesture.

Beneath the courtesies, his mind whirred and he found himself holding his breath while he waited. Surely the news couldn't be really catastrophic!

He reviewed the facts, as if hoping for some hitherto unnoticed salvation in them. With little axial tilt, Suleiman lacked seasons. Bluejack needed the cool, dry climate of the Uplands, but there it grew the year around. Primitive natives, hunters and gatherers, picked it in the course of their wanderings. Every several months, terrestrial, such a tribe would make rendezvous with one of the more advanced nomadic herding communities, who bartered for the parched leaves and fruits. A caravan would then form and make the long trip to this city, where Solar's folk would acquire the bales in exchange for Technic merchandise. You could count on a load arriving about twice a month. Four times in an Earthside year, the Cynthian vessel took away the contents of Solar's warehouse . . . and left a far more precious cargo of letters, tapes, journals, books, news from the stars that were so rarely seen in these gloomy heavens.

It wasn't the most efficient system imaginable, but it was the cheapest, once you calculated what the cost would be—in capital investment and civilized-labor salaries—of starting plantations. And costs must be kept low or the enterprise would change from a minor asset to a liability, which would soon be liquidated. As matters were, Suleiman was a typical outpost of its kind: to the scientists, a fascinating study and a chance to win reputation in their fields; to the factors, a comparatively easy job, a first step on a ladder at the top of which waited the big, glamorous, gorgeously paid managerial assignments.

Or thus it had been until now.

The Translator turned to Dalmady. "The Master says this," he piped. "Lately in the Uplands have come what he calls . . . no, I do not believe that can be said in words alone—It is clear to me, they are machines that move about harvesting the bluejack."

"What?" The man realized he had exclaimed in Anglic. Through suddenly loud pulses, he heard the Translator go on:

"The wild folk were terrified and fled those parts. The machines came and took what they had stored against their next rendezvous. That angered this Master's nomads, who deal there. They rode to protest. From afar they saw a vessel, like the great flying vessel that lands here, and a structure abuilding. Those who oversaw that work were . . . low, with many legs and claws for hands . . . long noses— A gathering robot came and shot lightning past the nomads. They saw they, too, must flee, lest its warning shot become deadly. The Master himself took a string of remounts and posted hither as swiftly as might be. In words, I cannot say more of what he has to tell."

Dalmady gasped into the frigid blueness that enclosed him. His mouth felt dry, his knees weak, his stomach in upheaval. "Baburites," he mumbled. "Got to be. But why're they doing this to us?"

Brush, herbage, leaves on the infrequent trees, were many shades of black. Here and there a patch of red, or brown, or blue flowering relieved it, or an ammonia river cataracting down the hills. Farther off, a range of ice mountains flashed blindingly; Suleiman's twelve-hour day was drawing to a close, and Osman's rays struck level through a break in rolling ruddy cloud cover. Elsewhere a storm lifted like a dark wall on which lightning scribbled. The dense atmosphere brought its thunder-noise to Dalmady as a high drumroll. He paid scant attention. The gusts that hooted around his car, the air pockets into which it lurched, made piloting a full-time job. A cybernated vehicle would have been too expensive for this niggardly rewarding planet.

"There!" cried the Master. He squatted with the Translator in an after compartment, which was left under native conditions and possessed an observation dome. In deference to his superstitions, or whatever they were, only the audio part of the intercom was turned on.

"Indeed," the Translator said more calmly. "I descry it now. Somewhat to our right, Factor—in a valley by a lake . . . do you see?"

"A moment." Dalmady locked the altitude controls. The car would bounce around till his teeth rattled, but the grav field wouldn't let it crash. He leaned forward in his harness, tried to ignore the brutal pull on him, and adjusted the scanner screen. His race had not evolved to see at those wavelengths which penetrated this atmosphere best; and the distance was considerable, as distances tend to be on a subjovian.

Converting light frequencies, amplifying, magnifying, the screen flung a picture at him. Tall above shrubs and turbulent ammonia stood a spaceship. He identified it as a Holbert-X freighter, a type commonly sold to hydrogen breathers. There had doubtless been some modifications to suit its particular home world, but he saw none except a gun turret and a couple of missile tube housings.

A prefabricated steel and ferrocrete building was being assembled nearby. The construction robots must be working fast, without pause; the cube was already more than half finished. Dalmady glimpsed flares of energy torches, like tiny blue novas. He couldn't make out individual shapes, and didn't want to risk coming near enough.

"You see?" he asked the image of Peter Thorson, and transmitted the picture to another screen.

Back at the base, his engineer's massive head nodded. Behind could be seen the four remaining humans. They looked as strained and anxious as Dalmady felt, Yvonne perhaps more so.

"Yeh. Not much we can do about it," Thorson declared. "They pack bigger weapons. And see, in the corners of the barn, those bays? That's for blast cannon, I swear. Add a heavy-duty forcefield generator for passive defense, and it's a nut we can't hope to crack."

"The home office—"

"Yeh, they *might* elect to resent the invasion and dispatch a regular warcraft or three. But I don't believe it. Wouldn't pay, in economic terms. And it'd make every kind of hooraw, because remember, SSL hasn't got any legal monopoly here." Thorson shrugged. "My guess is, Old Nick'll simply close down on Suleiman, probably wangling a deal with the Baburites that'll cut his losses and figuring to diddle them good at a later date." He was a veteran mercantile professional, accustomed to occasional setbacks, indifferent to the scientific puzzles around him.

Yvonne, who was not, cried softly, "Oh, no! We can't! The insights we're gaining—"

And Dalmady, who could not afford a defeat this early in his career, clenched one fist and snapped, "We can at least talk to them, can't we? I'll try to raise them. Stand by." He switched the outercom to a universal band and set the Come In going. The last thing he had seen from the compound was her stricken eyes.

The Translator inquired from aft: "Do you know who the strangers are and what they intend, Factor?"

"I have no doubt they come from Babur, as we call it," the man replied absently. "That is a world"—the more enlightened Coast dwellers had acquired some knowledge of astronomy—"akin to yours. It is larger and warmer, with heavier air. Its folk could not endure this one for long without becoming sick. But they can move about unarmored for a while. They buy most of our bluejack. Evidently they have decided to go to the source."

"But why, Factor?"

"For profit, I suppose, Translator." *Maybe just in their nonhuman cost accounting. That's a giant investment they're making in a medicinal product. But they don't operate under capitalism, under anything that human history ever saw, or so I've heard. Therefore they may consider it an investment in . . . empire? No doubt they can expand their foothold here, once we're out of the way—*

The screen came to life.

The being that peered from it stood about waist high to a man in its erect torso. The rest of the body stretched behind in a vaguely caterpillar shape, on eight stumpy legs. Along that glabrous form was a row of opercula protecting tracheae which, in a dense hydrogen atmosphere, aerated the organism quite efficiently. Two arms ended in claws reminiscent of a lobster's; from the wrists below sprouted short, tough finger-tendrils. The head was dominated by a spongy snout. A Baburite had no mouth. It—individuals changed sex from time to time—macerated food with the claws and put it in a digestive pouch to be dissolved before the snout sucked it up. The eyes were four, and tiny. Speech was by diaphragms on either side of the skull, hearing and smell were associated with the tracheae. The skin was banded orange, blue, white, and black. Most of it was hidden by a gauzy robe.

The creature would have been an absurdity, a biological impossibility, on an Earth-type world. In its own ship, in strong gravity and thick cold air and murk through which shadowy forms moved, it had dignity and power.

It thrummed noises which a vocalizer rendered into fairly good League Latin: "We were expecting you. Do not approach closer."

Dalmady moistened his lips. He felt cruelly young and helpless. "G-g-greeting. I am the factor."

The Baburite made no comment.

After a while, Dalmady plowed on: "We have been told that you . . . well, you are seizing the bluejack territory. I cannot believe that is correct."

"It is not, precisely," said the flat mechanical tone. "For the nonce, the natives may use these lands as heretofore, except that they will not find much bluejack to harvest. Our robots are too effective. Observe."

The screen flashed over to a view of a squat, cylindrical machine. Propelled by a simple grav drive, it floated several centimeters off the ground. Its eight arms terminated in sensors, pluckers, trimmers, brush cutters. On its back was welded a large basket. On its top was a maser transceiver and a swivel-mounted blaster.

"It runs off accumulators," the unseen Baburite stated. "These need only be recharged once in thirty-odd hours, at the fusion generator we are installing, unless a special energy expenditure occurs . . . like a battle, for instance. High-hovering relay units keep the robots in constant touch with each other and with a central computer, currently in the ship, later to be in the blockhouse. It controls them all simultaneously, greatly reducing the cost per unit." With no trace of sardonicism: "You will understand that such a beamcasting system cannot feasibly be jammed. The computer will be provided with missiles as well as guns and defensive fields. It is programmed to strike back at any attempt to hamper its operations."

The robot's image disappeared, the being's returned. Dalmady felt faint. "But that would . . . would be . . . an act of war!" he stuttered.

"No. It would be self-protection, legitimate under the rules of the Polesotechnic League. You may credit us with the intelligence to investigate the social as well as physical state of things before we acted and, indeed, to become an associate member of the League.

No one will suffer except your company. That will not displease its competitors. They have assured our representatives that they can muster enough Council votes to prevent sanctions. It is not as if the loss were very great. Let us recommend to you personally that you seek employment elsewhere."

Uh-huh . . . after I dropped a planet . . . . I might maybe get a job cleaning latrines some place, went through the back of Dalmady's head. "No," he protested, "what about the autochthons? They're hurting already."

"When the land has been cleared, bluejack plantations will be established," the Baburite said. "Doubtless work can be found for some of the displaced savages, if they are sufficiently docile. Doubtless other resources, ignored by you oxygen breathers, await exploitation. We may in the end breed colonists adapted to Suleiman. But that will be of no concern to the League. We have investigated the practical effect of its prohibition on imperialism by members. Where no one else is interested in a case, a treaty with a native government is considered sufficient, and native governments with helpful attitudes are not hard to set up. Suleiman is such a case. A written-off operation that was never much more than marginal, out on an extreme frontier, is not worth the League's worrying about."

"The principle—"

"True. We would not provoke war, nor even our own expulsion and a boycott. However, recall that you are not being ordered off this planet. You have simply met a superior competitor, superior by virtue of living closer to the scene, being better suited to the environment and far more interested in succeeding here. We have the same right to launch ventures as you."

"What do you mean, 'we'?" Dalmady whispered. "Who are you? What are you? A private company, or—"

"Nominally, we are so organized, though like many other League associates we make no secret of this being *pro forma,*" the Baburite told him. "Actually, the terms on which our society must deal with the Technic aggregate have little relevance to the terms of its interior structure. Considering the differences—sociological, psychological, biological—between us and you and your close allies, our desire to be free of your civilization poses no real threat to the latter and hence will never provoke any real reaction. At the same time, we will never win the freedom of the stars without the resources of modern technology.

"To industrialize with minimum delay, we must obtain the initial capacity through purchases from the Technic worlds. This requires Technic currency. Thus, while we spend what appears to be a disproportionate amount of effort and goods on this bluejack project, it will result in saving outplanet exchange for much more important things.

"We tell you what we tell you in order to make clear, not only our harmlessness to the League as a whole, but our determination. We trust you have taped this discussion. It may prevent your employer from wasting our time and energy in counteracting any foredoomed attempts by him to recoup. While you remain on Suleiman, observe well. When you go back, report faithfully."

The screen blanked. Dalmady tried for minutes to make the connection again, but got no answer.

Thirty days later, which would have been fifteen of Earth's, a conference met in the compound. Around a table, in a room hazed and acrid with smoke, sat the humans. In a full-size screen were the images of the Thalassocrat and the Translator, a three-dimensional realism that seemed to breathe out the cold of the ice chamber where they crouched.

Dalmady ran a hand through his hair. "I'll summarize," he told them wearily. The Translator's fur began to move, his voice to make low whistles, as he rendered from the Anglic for his king. "The reports of our native scouts were waiting for me, recorded by Yvonne, when I returned from my own latest flit a couple of hours ago. Each datum confirms every other.

"We'd hoped, you recall, that the computer would be inadequate to cope with us, once the Baburite ship had left."

"Why should the live crew depart?" Sanjuro Nakamura asked.

"That's obvious," Thorson said. "They may not run their domestic economy the way we run ours, but that doesn't exempt them from the laws of economics. A planet like Babur—actually, a single dominant country on it, or whatever they have—still backward, still poor, has limits on what it can afford. They may enjoy shorter lines of communication than we do, but we, at home, enjoy a lot more productivity. At their present stage, they can't spend what it takes to create and maintain a permanent, live-staffed base like ours. Suleiman isn't too healthy for them, either, you know; and they lack even our small background of accumulated experience. So they've got to automate at first, and just send somebody once in a while to check up and collect the harvest."

"Besides," Alice Bergen pointed out, "the nomads are sworn to us. They wouldn't make a deal with another party. Not that the Baburites could use them profitably anyway. We're sitting in the only suitable depot area, the only one whose people have a culture that makes it easy to train them in service jobs for us. So the Baburites have to operate right on the spot where the bluejack grows. The nomads resent having their caravan trade ended, and would stage guerrilla attacks on live workers."

"*Whew!*" Nakamura said, with an attempted grin. "I assure you, my question was only rhetorical. I simply wanted to point out that the opposition would not have left everything in charge of a computer if they weren't confident the setup would function, including holding us at bay. I begin to see why their planners concentrated in developing robotics at the beginning of modernization. No doubt they intend to use machines in quite a few larcenous little undertakings."

"Do you know how many robots there are?" Isabel asked.

"We estimate a hundred," Dalmady told her, "though we can't get an accurate count. They operate fast, you see, covering a huge territory—in fact, the entire territory where bluejack grows thickly enough to be worth gathering—and they're identical in appearance except for the relay hoverers."

"That must be some computer, to juggle so many at once, over such varying conditions," Alice remarked. Cybernetics was not her field.

Yvonne shook her head; the gold tresses swirled. "Nothing extraordinary. We have long-range telephotos, taken during its installation. It's a standard multi-channel design, only the electronics modified for ambient conditions. Rudimentary awareness: more isn't required, and would be uneconomic to provide, when its task is basically simple."

"Can't we outwit it, then?" Alice asked.

Dalmady grimaced. "What do you think my native helpers and I have been trying to do thereabouts, this past week? It's open country; the relayers detect you coming a huge ways off, and the computer dispatches robots. Not many are needed. If you come too close to the blockhouse, they fire warning blasts. That's terrified the natives. Few of them will approach anywhere near, and in fact the savages are starting to evacuate, which'll present us with a nice bunch of hungry refugees. Not that I blame them. A low-temperature organism cooks easier than you or me. I did push ahead, and was fired on for real. I ran away before my armor should be pierced."

"What about airborne attack?" Isabel wondered.

Thorson snorted. "In three rattly cars, with handguns? Those robots fly, too, remember. Besides, the centrum has forcefields, blast cannon, missiles. A naval vessel would have trouble reducing it."

"Furthermore," interjected the Thalassocrat, "I am told of a threat to destroy this town by airborne weapons, should a serious assault be made on yonder place. That cannot be risked. Sooner would I order you to depart for aye, and strike what bargain I was able with your enemies."

He can make that stick, Dalmady thought, *by the simple process of telling our native workers to quit.*

Not that that would necessarily make any difference. He recalled the last statement of a nomad Master, as the retreat from a reconnaissance took place, Suleimanites on their animals, man on a grav-scooter. "We have abided by our alliance with you, but you not by yours with us. Your predecessors swore we should have protection from skyborne invaders. If you fail to drive off these, how shall we trust you?" Dalmady had pleaded for time and had grudgingly been granted it, since the caravaneers did value their trade with him. *But if we don't solve this problem soon, I doubt the system can ever be renewed.*

"We shall not imperil you," he promised the Thalassocrat.

"How real is the threat?" Nakamura asked. "The League wouldn't take kindly to slaughter of harmless autochthons."

"But the League would not necessarily do more than complain," Thorson said, "especially if the Baburites argue that we forced them into it. They're banking on its indifference, and I suspect their judgment is shrewd."

"Right or wrong," Alice said, "their assessment of the psychopolitics will condition what they themselves do. And what assessment have they made? What do we know about their ways of thinking?"

"More than you might suppose," Yvonne replied. "After all, they've been in contact for generations, and you don't negotiate commercial agreements without having done some studies in depth first. The reason you've not seen much of me, these past days, is that I've buried myself in our files. We possess, right here, a bucketful of information about Babur."

Dalmady straightened in his chair. His pulse picked up the least bit. It was no surprise that a large and varied xenological library existed in this insignificant outback base. Microtapes were cheaply reproduced, and you never knew who might chance by or what might happen, so you were routinely supplied with references for your entire sector. "What do we have?" he barked.

Yvonne smiled wryly. "Nothing spectacular, I'm afraid. The usual: three or four of the principal languages, sketches of history and important contemporary cultures, state-of-technology analyses, statistics on stuff like population and productivity—besides the planetology, biology, psychoprofiling, et cetera. I tried and tried to find a weak point, but couldn't. Oh, I can show that this operation must be straining their resources, and will have to be abandoned if it doesn't quickly pay off. But that's just as true of us."

Thorson fumed on his pipe. "If we could fix a gadget—We have a reasonably well-equipped workshop. That's where I've been sweating, myself."

"What had you in mind?" Dalmady inquired. The dullness of the engineer's voice was echoed in his own.

"Well, at first I wondered about a robot to go out and hunt theirs down. I could build one, a single one, more heavily armed and armored." Thorson's hand flopped empty, palm up, on the table. "But the computer has a hundred; and it's more sophisticated by orders of magnitude than any brain I could cobble together from spare cybernetics parts; and as the Thalassocrat says, we can't risk a missile dropped on our spaceport in retaliation, because it'd take out most of the city.

"Afterward I thought about jamming, or about somehow lousing the computer itself, but that's totally hopeless. It'd never let you get near."

He sighed. "My friends, let's admit that we've had the course, and plan how to leave with minimum loss."

The Thalassocrat stayed imperturbable, as became a monarch. But the Translator's main eye filmed over, his tiny body shrank into itself, and he cried: "We had hoped . . . one year our descendants, learning from you, joining you among the uncounted suns—Is there instead to be endless rule by aliens?"

Dalmady and Yvonne exchanged looks. Their hands clasped. He believed the same thought must be twisting in her: *We, being of the League, cannot pretend to altruism. But we are not monsters either. Some cold accountant in an office on Earth may order our departure. But can we who have been here, who liked these people and were trusted by them, abandon them and continue to live with ourselves? Would we not forever feel that any blessings given us were stolen?*

And the old, old legend crashed into his awareness.

He sat for a minute or two, unconscious of the talk that growled and groaned around him. Yvonne first noticed the blankness in his gaze. "Emil," she murmured, "are you well?"

Dalmady sprang to his feet with a whoop.

"What in space?" Nakamura said.

The factor controlled himself. He trembled, and small chills ran back and forth along his nerves; but his words came steady. "I have an idea."

Above the robes that billowed around him in the wind, the Translator carried an inconspicuous miniature audiovisual two-way. Dalmady in the car which he had landed behind a hill some distance off, Thorson in the car which hovered to relay, Yvonne and Alice and

Isabel and Nakamura and the Thalassocrat in the city, observed a bobbing, swaying landscape on their tuned-in screens. Black leaves streamed, long and ragged, on bushes whose twigs clicked an answer to the whining air; boulders and ice chunks humped among them; an ammonia fall boomed on the right, casting spray across the field of view. The men in the cars could likewise feel the planet's traction and the shudder of hulls under that slow, thick wind.

"I still think we should've waited for outside help," Thorson declared on a separate screen. "That rig's a real lash-up."

"And I still say," Dalmady retorted, "your job's made you needlessly fussy in this particular case. Besides, the natives couldn't've been stalled much longer." *Furthermore, if we can rout them with nothing but what was on hand, that ought to shine in my record. I'd like to think that's less important to me, but I can't deny it's real.*

One way or another, the decision had to be mine. I am the factor.

It's a lonesome feeling. I wish Yvonne were here beside me.

"Quiet," he ordered. "Something's about to happen."

The Translator had crossed a ridge and was gravscooting down the opposite slope. He required no help at that; a few days of instruction had made him a very fair driver, even in costume. He was entering the robot-held area, and already a skyborne unit slanted to intercept him. In the keen Osmanlight, against ocherous clouds, it gleamed like fire.

Dalmady crouched in his seat. He was airsuited. If his friend got into trouble, he'd slap down his faceplate, open the cockpit, and swoop to an attempted rescue. A blaster lay knobby in his lap. The thought he might come too late made a taste of sickness in his mouth.

The robot paused at hover, arms extended, weapon pointed. The Translator continued to glide at a steady rate. When near collision, the two-way spoke for him: "Stand aside. We are instituting a change of program."

Spoke, to the listening computer, in the principal language of Babur.

Yvonne had worked out the plausible phrases, and spent patient hours with vocalizer and recorder until they seemed right. Engineer Thorson, xenologists Nakamura and Alice Bergen, artistically inclined biologist Isabel da Fonseca, Dalmady himself and several Suleimanite advisors who had spied on the Baburites, had created the disguise. Largely muffled in cloth, it didn't have to be too elaborate—a torso shaven and painted; a simple mechanical caterpillar body behind, steered by the hidden tail, automatically pacing its six legs with the wearer's two; a flexible mask with piezoelectric controls guided by the facial muscles beneath; claws and tendrils built over the natural arms, fake feet over the pair of real ones.

A human, or an ordinary Suleimanite, could not successfully have worn such an outfit. If nothing else, they were too big. But presumably it had not occurred to the Baburites to allow for midgets existing on this planet. The disguise was far from perfect; but presumably the computer was not programmed to check for any such contingency; furthermore, an intelligent, well-rehearsed actor, adapting his role moment by moment as no robot ever can, creates a gestalt transcending any minor errors of detail.

And . . . logically, the computer *must* be programmed to allow Baburites into its presence to service it and collect the bluejack stored nearby.

Nonetheless, Dalmady's jaws ached from the tension on them.

The robot shifted out of the viewfield. In the receiving screens, ground continued to glide away underneath the scooter.

Dalmady switched off audio transmission from base. Though none save Yvonne, alone in a special room, was now sending to the Translator, and she via a bone conduction receiver—still, the cheers that had filled the car struck him as premature.

But the kilometers passed and passed. And the blockhouse hove in view, dark, cubical, bristling with sensors and antennae, cornered with the sinister shapes of gun emplacements and missile silos. No forcefield went up. Yvonne said through the Translator's unit: "Open; do not close again until told," and the idiot-savant computer directed a massive gate to swing wide.

What happened beyond was likewise Yvonne's job. She scanned through the portal by the two-way, summoned what she had learned of Baburite automation technology, and directed the Translator. Afterward she said it hadn't been difficult except for poor visibility; the builders had used standard layouts and programming languages. But to the factor it was an hour of sweating, cursing, pushing fingers and belly muscles against each other, staring and staring at the image of enigmatic units which loomed between blank walls, under bluish light that was at once harsh and wan.

When the Translator emerged and the gate closed behind him, Dalmady almost collapsed.

Afterward, though—well, League people were pretty good at throwing a celebration!

"Yes," Dalmady said. "But—"

"Butter me no buts," van Rijn said. "Fact is, you reset that expensive computer so it should make those expensive robots stand idle. Why not leastwise use them for Solar?"

"That would have ruined relations with the natives, sir. Primitives don't take blandly to the notion of technological unemployment. So scientific studies would have become impossible. How then would you attract personnel?"

"What personnel would we need?"

"Some on the spot, constantly. Otherwise the Baburites, close as they are, could come back and, for example, organize and arm justly disgruntled Suleimanites against us. Robots or no, we'd soon find the bluejack costing us more than it earned us . . . Besides, machines wear out and it costs to replace them. Live native help will reproduce for nothing."

"Well, you got that much sense, anyhows," van Rijn rumbled. "But why did you tell the computer it and its robot should attack *any* kind of machine, like a car or spacecraft, what comes near, and anybody of any shape what tells it to let him in? Supposing situations change, our people can't do nothings with it now neither."

"I told you, they don't need to," Dalmady rasped. "We get along —not dazzlingly, but we get along, we show a profit—with our traditional arrangements. As long as we maintain those, we exclude the Baburites from them. If we ourselves had access to the computer, we'd have to mount an expensive guard over it. Otherwise the Baburites could probably pull a similar trick on us, right? As is, the system interdicts any attempt to modernize operations in the bluejack area. Which is to say, it protects our monopoly—free—and will protect it for years to come."

He started to rise. "Sir," he continued bitterly, "the whole thing strikes me as involving the most elementary economic calculations. Maybe you have something subtler in mind, but if you do—"

"Whoa!" van Rijn boomed. "Squat yourself. Reel in some more of your drink, boy, and listen at me. Old and fat I am, but lungs and tongue I got. Also in working order is two other organs, one what don't concern you but one which is my brain, and my brain wants I should get information from you and stuff it."

Dalmady found he had obeyed.

"You need to see past a narrow specialism," van Rijn said. "Sometimes a man is too stupid good at his one job. He booms it, no matter the consequentials to everything else, and makes trouble for the whole organization he is supposed to serve. Like, you considered how Babur would react?"

"Of course. Freelady Vaillancourt—" *When will I be with her again?*—"and Drs. Bergen and Nakamura in particular, did an exhaustive analysis of materials on hand. As a result, we gave the computer an additional directive: that it warn any approaching vehicle before opening fire. The conversation I had later, with the spaceship captain, or whatever he was, bore out our prediction."

(A quivering snout. A bleak gleam in four minikin eyes. But the voice, strained through a machine, emotionless: "Under the rules your civilization has devised, you have not given us cause for war; and the League always responds to what it considers unprovoked attack. Accordingly, we shall not bombard.")

"No doubt they feel their equivalent of fury," Dalmady said. "But what can they do? They're realists. Unless they think of some new stunt, they'll write Suleiman off and try elsewhere."

"And they buy our bluejack yet?"

"Yes."

"We should maybe lift the price, like teaching them a lesson they shouldn't make fumblydiddles with up?"

"You can do that, if you want to make them decide they'd rather synthesize the stuff. My report recommends against it."

This time Dalmady did rise. "Sir," he declared in anger, "I may be a yokel, my professional training may have been in a jerkwater college, but I'm not a congenital idiot who's mislaid his pills and I do take my pride seriously. I made the best decision I was able on Suleiman. You haven't tried to show me where I went wrong, you've simply had me dismissed from my post, and tonight you drone about issues that anybody would understand who's graduated from diapers. Let's not waste more of our time. Good evening."

Van Rijn avalanched upward to his own feet. "Ho, ho!" he bawled. "Spirit, too! I like, I like!"

Dumfounded, Dalmady could only gape.

Van Rijn clapped him on the shoulder, nearly felling him. "Boy," the merchant said, "I didn't mean to rub your nose in nothings except sweet violets. I did have to know, did you stumble onto your answer, which is beautiful, or can you think original? Because you take my saying, maybe everybody understands like you what is not wearing diapers no more; but if that is true, why, ninety-nine point nine nine percent of every sophont race is wearing diapers, at least on their brains, and it leaks out of their mouths. I find you is in the oh point oh one percent, and I want you. Hoo-ha, how I want you!"

He thrust the gin-filled goblet back into Dalmady's hand. His tankard clanked against it. "Drink! Drink!"

Dalmady took a sip. Van Rijn began to prowl.

"You is from a frontier planet and so is naïve," the merchant said, "but that can be outlived like pimples. See, when my underlings at HQ learned you had pulled our nuts from the fire on Suleiman, they sent you a standard message, not realizing an Altaian like you would not know that in such cases the proceeding is SOP," which he pronounced "sop." He waved a gorilla arm, splashing beer on the floor. "Like I say, we had to check if you was lucky only. If so, we would promote you to be manager some place better and forget about you. But if you was, actual, extra smart and tough, we don't want you for a manager. You is too rare and precious for that. Would be like using a Hokusai print in a catbox."

Dalmady raised goblet to mouth, unsteadily. "What do you mean?" he croaked.

"Entrepreneur! You will keep title of factor, because we can't make jealousies, but what you do is what the old Americans would have called a horse of a different dollar.

"Look." Van Rijn reclaimed his cigar from the disposal rim, took a puff, and made forensic gestures with it and tankard alike while he continued his earthquake pacing. "Suleiman was supposed to be a nice routine post, but you told me how little we know on it and how sudden the devil himself came to lunch. Well, what about the real new, real hairy—and real fortune-making—places? Ha?

"You don't want a manager for them, not till they been whipped into shape. A good manager is a very high-powered man, and we need a lot of him. But in his bottom, he is a routineer; his aim is to make things go smooth. No, for the wild places you need an inno-vator in charge, a man what likes to take risks, a heterodoxy if she is female—somebody what can meet wholly new problems in unholy new ways—you see?

"Only such is rare, I tell you. They command high prices: high as they can earn for themselves. Natural, I want them earning for me, too. So I don't put that kind of factor on salary and dangle a pro-motion ladder in front of him. No, the entrepreneur kind, first I get his John Bullcock on a ten-year oath of fealty. Next I turn him loose with a stake and my backup, to do what he wants, on straight com-mission of ninety percent.

"Too bad nobody typed you before you went in managerial school. Now you must have a while in an entrepreneurial school I got tucked away where nobody notices. Not dull for you; I hear they throw fine orgies; but mainly I think you will enjoy your classes, if you don't mind working till brain-sweat runs out your nose. After-ward you go get rich, if you survive, and have a big ball of fun even if you don't. Hokay?"

Dalmady thought for an instant of Yvonne; and then he thought, *What the deuce, if nothing better develops, in a few years I can set any hiring policies I feel like;* and: "Hokay!" he exclaimed, and tossed off his drink in a single gulp.

The Political Institution

The Pedestrian

In every society, structures must be organized to permit power to be exercised by persons in authority. In some societies, power is exercised by an elite, with the majority of the members of that society having little or no influence over decisions of government. In other societies, those participating in the exercise of political power include at least theoretically all members of the society.

As *democracy* as a form of government developed, nineteenth-century political scholars such as Tocqueville and twentieth-century writers such as Ortega y Gasset feared the enfranchisement of the masses. These writers were concerned about the ability of the mass of men to make sound political judgments, fearing a tyranny of the majority and judgment by the incompetent. Toward the mid-twentieth century, others feared a concentration of power in few hands in *totalitarian* political structures. Witnessing the Soviet revolution and subsequent Stalinism as well as the rise of fascism in Germany and Italy, and noting the potential for manipulation and control modern communications technology gives those holding power, many writers have drawn stark warnings about the future of democracies.

Projecting contemporary trends into vividly portrayed models of absolute totalitarian "anti-utopias" is one of the things science fiction does best. George Orwell's *1984* was published in 1949. If it was felt to be "a stretch of the imagination" then, now that only a few years are left until 1984 it seems more and more to be only a minor exaggeration. Is there any doubt that "Newspeak" by government leaders and functionaries, continents in a seemingly perpetual state of war, and the use of electronic invasion of privacy for the purpose of manipulation and control of political opposition and dissent are already here? Ray Bradbury's "The Pedestrian" is this type of science fiction story. It is a portrait of a society in which television is the opiate of the people and variation from the usual brings on psychiatric correction backed by the power of the state. It is a time and place that is—to use some overworked contemporary imagery—"chilling."

The Pedestrian

RAY BRADBURY

To enter out into that silence that was the city at eight o'clock of a misty evening in November, to put your feet upon that buckling concrete walk, to step over grassy seams and make your way, hands in pockets, through the silences, that was what Mr. Leonard Mead most dearly loved to do. He would stand upon the corner of an intersection and peer down long moonlit avenues of sidewalk in four directions, deciding which way to go, but it really made no difference; he was alone in this world of 2050 A.D., or as good as alone, and with a final decision made, a path selected, he would stride off, sending patterns of frosty air before him like the smoke of a cigar.

Sometimes he would walk for hours and miles and return only at midnight to his house. And on his way he would see the cottages and homes with their dark windows, and it was not unequal to walking through a graveyard where only the faintest glimmers of firefly light appeared in flickers behind the windows. Sudden gray phantoms seemed to manifest upon inner room walls where a curtain was still undrawn against the night, or there were whisperings and murmurs where a window in a tomb-like building was still open.

Mr. Leonard Mead would pause, cock his head, listen, look, and march on, his feet making no noise on the lumpy walk. For long ago he had wisely changed to sneakers when strolling at night, because the dogs in intermittent squads would parallel his journey with barkings if he wore hard heels, and lights might click on and faces appear and an entire street be startled by the passing of a lone figure, himself, in the early November evening.

On this particular evening he began his journey in a westerly direction, toward the hidden sea. There was a good crystal frost in the air; it cut the nose and made the lungs blaze like a Christmas tree inside; you could feel the cold light going on and off, all the branches filled with invisible snow. He listened to the faint push of his soft shoes through autumn leaves with satisfaction, and whistled a cold quiet whistle between his teeth, occasionally picking up a leaf as he passed, examining its skeletal pattern in the infrequent lamp-lights as he went on, smelling its rusty smell.

"Hello, in there," he whispered to every house on every side as he moved. "What's up tonight on Channel 4, Channel 7, Channel 9? Where are the cowboys rushing, and do I see the United States Cavalry over the next hill to the rescue?"

The street was silent and long and empty, with only his shadow moving like the shadow of a hawk in mid-country. If he closed his eyes and stood very still, frozen, he could imagine himself upon the center of a plain, a wintry, windless Arizona desert with no house in a thousand miles, and only dry river beds, the streets, for company.

"What is it now?" he asked the houses, noticing his wrist watch. "Eight-thirty P.M.? Time for a dozen assorted murders? A quiz? A revue? A comedian falling off the stage?"

Was that a murmur of laughter from within a moon-white house? He hesitated, but went on when nothing more happened. He stumbled over a particularly uneven section of sidewalk. The cement was vanishing under flowers and grass. In ten years of walking by night or day, for thousands of miles, he had never met another person walking, not one in all that time.

He came to a cloverleaf intersection which stood silent where two main highways crossed the town. During the day it was a thunderous surge of cars, the gas stations open, a great insect rustling and a ceaseless jockeying for position as the scarab-beetles, a faint incense puttering from their exhausts, skimmed homeward to the far directions. But now these highways, too, were like streams in a dry season, all stone and bed and moon radiance.

He turned back on a side street, circling around toward his home. He was within a block of his destination when the lone car turned a corner quite suddenly and flashed a fierce white cone of light upon him. He stood entranced, not unlike a night moth, stunned by the illumination, and then drawn toward it.

A metallic voice called to him:

"Stand still. Stay where you are! Don't move!"

He halted.

"Put up your hands!"

"But—" he said.

"Your hands up! Or we'll shoot!"

The police, of course, but what a rare, incredible thing; in a city of three million, there was only one police car left, wasn't that correct? Ever since a year ago, 2052, the election year, the force had been cut down from three cars to one. Crime was ebbing; there was no need now for the police, save for this one lone car wandering and wandering the empty streets.

"Your name?" said the police car in a metallic whisper. He couldn't see the men in it for the bright light in his eyes.

"Leonard Mead," he said.

"Speak up!"

"Leonard Mead!"

"Business or profession?"

"I guess you'd call me a writer."

"No profession," said the police car, as if talking to itself. The light held him fixed, like a museum specimen, needle thrust through chest.

"You might say that," said Mr. Mead. He hadn't written in years. Magazines and books didn't sell any more. Everything went on in the tomblike houses at night now, he thought, continuing his fancy. The tombs, ill-lit by television light, where the people sat like the dead, the gray or multicolored lights touching their faces, but never really touching *them*.

"No profession," said the phonograph voice, hissing. "What are you doing out?"

"Walking," said Leonard Mead.

"Walking!"

"Just walking," he said simply, but his face felt cold.

"Walking, just walking, walking?"

"Yes, sir."

"Walking where? For what?"

"Walking for air. Walking to see."

"Your address!"

"Eleven South Saint James Street."

"And there is air *in* your house, you have an air *conditioner*, Mr. Mead?"

"Yes."

"And you have a viewing screen in your house to see with?"

"No."

"No?" There was a crackling quiet that in itself was an accusation.

"Are you married, Mr. Mead?"

"No."

"Not married," said the police voice behind the fiery beam. The moon was high and clear among the stars and the houses were gray and silent.

"Nobody wanted me," said Leonard Mead with a smile.

"Don't speak unless you're spoken to!"

Leonard Mead waited in the cold night.

"Just *walking*, Mr. Mead?"

"Yes."

"But you haven't explained for what purpose."

"I explained; for air, and to see, and just to walk."

"Have you done this often?"

"Every night for years."

The police car sat in the center of the street with its radio throat faintly humming.

"Well, Mr. Mead," it said.

"Is that all?" he asked politely.

"Yes," said the voice. "Here." There was a sigh, a pop. The back door of the police car sprang wide. "Get in."

"Wait a minute, I haven't done anything!"

"Get in."

"I protest!"

"Mr. Mead."

He walked like a man suddenly drunk. As he passed the front window of the car he looked in. As he had expected, there was no one in the front seat, no one in the car at all.

"Get in."

He put his hand to the door and peered into the back seat, which was a little cell, a little black jail with bars. It smelled of riveted steel. It smelled of harsh antiseptic; it smelled too clean and hard and metallic. There was nothing soft there.

"Now if you had a wife to give you an alibi," said the iron voice. "But—"

"Where are you taking me?"

The car hesitated, or rather gave a faint whirring click, as if information, somewhere, was dropping card by punch-slotted card under electric eyes. "To the Psychiatric Center for Research on Regressive Tendencies."

He got in. The door shut with a soft thud. The police car rolled through the night avenues, flashing its dim lights ahead.

They passed one house on one street a moment later, one house in an entire city of houses that were dark, but this one particular house had all of its electric lights brightly lit, every window a loud yellow illumination, square and warm in the cool darkness.

"That's *my* house," said Leonard Mead.

No one answered him.

The car moved down the empty river-bed streets and off away, leaving the empty streets with the empty sidewalks, and no sound and no motion all the rest of the chill November night.

The Religious
Institution

A Canticle for Leibowitz

Organized religion has often functioned to preserve knowledge in times of social instability and disorganization. During the Dark Ages, the Roman Catholic Church helped preserve much of the knowledge accumulated until that time. The church became the keeper of both religious and general learning, and it could perform this function even when all those involved in preserving this knowledge did not understand fully its complexity and its use.

"A Canticle for Leibowitz" is set in a future Dark Age, after a world war in which technological weapons developed through the application of science brought about the "Deluge of Flame" and a subsequent reaction of knownothingness that the survivors call the "Age of Simplification." Scientific knowledge survives in shreds—a book here, a document there, scattered artifacts. Brother Francis, the central character, is a lowly functionary in a very authoritarian and bureaucratic religious order. The future church of which this order is a part has canonized Leibowitz, a scientist of the mid-twentieth century, and Brother Francis's discovery of some surviving artifacts belonging to Leibowitz provides both the test of Brother Francis's faith and its confirmation.

There is fine irony in this story. At a time when religious differences often prejudice those of one faith in their views of the worth of others, it is ironic that a man named Leibowitz can be a saint. Also, when modern students of religion so often stress the tensions between science and religion and conflicts between religious and scientific "truth," it is ironic that the knowledge made sacred by the church in this story is the secular knowledge of science. Finally, since the major goal is to preserve knowledge, all is saved: the blueprint for the "Transistorized Control System for Unit Six-B" as well as the grocery list calling for "Pound Pastrami, can kraut, six bagels, for Emma."

A Canticle for Leibowitz

WALTER M. MILLER, JR.

Brother Francis Gerard of Utah would never have discovered the sacred document, had it not been for the pilgrim with girded loins who appeared during that young monk's Lenten fast in the desert. Never before had Brother Francis actually seen a pilgrim with girded loins, but that this one was the bona fide article he was convinced at a glance. The pilgrim was a spindly old fellow with a staff, a basket hat, and a brushy beard, stained yellow about the chin. He walked with a limp and carried a small waterskin over one shoulder. His loins truly were girded with a ragged piece of dirty burlap, his only clothing except for hat and sandals. He whistled tunelessly on his way.

The pilgrim came shuffling down the broken trail out of the north, and he seemed to be heading toward the Brothers of Leibowitz Abbey six miles to the south. The pilgrim and the monk noticed each other across an expanse of ancient rubble. The pilgrim stopped whistling and stared. The monk, because of certain implications of the rule of solitude for fast days, quickly averted his gaze and continued about his business of hauling large rocks with which to complete the wolf-proofing of his temporary shelter. Somewhat weakened by a ten day diet of cactus fruit, Brother Francis found the work made him exceedingly dizzy; the landscape had been shimmering before his eyes and dancing with black specks, and he was at first uncertain that the bearded apparition was not a mirage induced by hunger, but after a moment it called to him cheerfully, *"Ola allay!"*

It was a pleasant musical voice.

The rule of silence forbade the young monk to answer, except by smiling shyly at the ground.

"Is this here the road to the abbey?" the wanderer asked.

The novice nodded at the ground and reached down for a chalk-like fragment of stone. The pilgrim picked his way toward him through the rubble. "What you doing with all the rocks?" he wanted to know.

The monk knelt and hastily wrote the words "Solitude & Silence" on a large flat rock, so that the pilgrim—if he could read, which was statistically unlikely—would know that he was making himself an occasion of sin for the penitent and would perhaps have the grace to leave in peace.

"Oh, well," said the pilgrim. He stood there for a moment, looking around, then rapped a certain large rock with his staff. "*That* looks like a handy crag for you," he offered helpfully, then added: "Well, good luck. And may you find a Voice, as y' seek."

Now Brother Francis had no immediate intuition that the stranger meant "Voice" with a capital V, but merely assumed that the old fellow had mistaken him for a deaf mute. He glanced up once again as the pilgrim shuffled away whistling, sent a swift silent benediction after him for safe wayfaring, and went back to his rock-work, building a coffin-sized enclosure in which he might sleep at night without offering himself as wolf-bait.

A sky-herd of cumulus clouds, on their way to bestow moist blessings on the mountains after having cruelly tempted the desert, offered welcome respite from the searing sunlight, and he worked rapidly to finish before they were gone again. He punctuated his labors with whispered prayers for the certainty of a true Vocation, for this was the purpose of his inward quest while fasting in the desert.

At last he hoisted the rock which the pilgrim had suggested.

The color of exertion drained quickly from his face. He backed away a step and dropped the stone as if he had uncovered a serpent.

A rusted metal box lay half-crushed in the rubble . . . only a rusted metal box.

He moved toward it curiously, then paused. There were things, and then there were Things. He crossed himself hastily, and muttered brief Latin at the heavens. Thus fortified, he readdressed himself to the box.

"*Apage Satanas!*"

He threatened it with the heavy crucifix of his rosary.

"Depart, O Foul Seductor!"

He sneaked a tiny aspergillum from his robes and quickly spattered the box with holy water before it could realize what he was about.

"If thou be creature of the Devil, begone!"

The box showed no signs of withering, exploding, melting away. It exuded no blasphemous ichor. It only lay quietly in its place and allowed the desert wind to evaporate the sanctifying droplets.

"So be it," said the brother, and knelt to extract it from its lodging. He sat down on the rubble and spent nearly an hour battering it open with a stone. The thought crossed his mind that such an archeological relic—for such it obviously was—might be the Heaven-sent sign of his vocation but he suppressed the notion as quickly as it occurred to him. His abbot had warned him sternly against expecting any direct personal Revelation of a spectacular nature. Indeed, he had gone forth from the abbey to fast and do penance for 40 days that he might be rewarded with the inspiration of a calling to Holy Orders, but to expect a vision or a voice crying "Francis, where art thou?" would be a vain presumption. Too many novices had returned from their desert vigils with tales of omens and signs and visions in the heavens, and the good abbot had adopted a firm policy regarding these. Only the Vatican was qualified to decide the authenticity of such things. "An attack of sunstroke is no indication that you are fit to profess the solemn vows of the order," he had growled. And certainly it was true that only rarely did a call from Heaven come through any device other than the *inward* ear, as a gradual congealing of inner certainty.

Nevertheless, Brother Francis found himself handling the old metal box with as much reverence as was possible while battering at it.

It opened suddenly, spilling some of its contents. He stared for a long time before daring to touch, and a cool thrill gathered along his spine. Here was antiquity indeed! And as a student of archeology, he could envy, he thought, but quickly repented this unkindness and murmured his thanks to the sky for such a treasure.

He touched the articles gingerly—they were real enough—and began sorting through them. His studies had equipped him to recognize a screwdriver—an instrument once used for twisting threaded bits of metal into wood—and a pair of cutters with blades no longer than his thumbnail, but strong enough to cut soft bits of metal or bone. There was an odd tool with a rotted wooden handle and a heavy copper tip to which a few flakes of molten lead had adhered, but he could make nothing of it. There was a toroidal roll of gummy black stuff, too far deteriorated by the centuries for him to identify. There were strange bits of metal, broken glass, and an assortment of tiny tubular things with wire whiskers of the type prized by the hill pagans as charms and amulets, but thought by some archeologists to be remnants of the legendary *machina analytica*, supposedly dating back to the Deluge of Flame. All these and more he examined carefully and spread on the wide flat stone. The documents he saved until last. The documents, as always, were the real prize, for so few papers had survived the angry bonfires of the Age of Simplification, when even the sacred writings had curled and blackened and withered into smoke while ignorant crowds howled vengeance.

Two large folded papers and three hand-scribbled notes constituted his find. All were cracked and brittle with age, and he handled them tenderly, shielding them from the wind with his robe. They were scarcely legible and scrawled in the hasty characters of pre-Deluge English—a tongue now used, together with Latin, only by monastics and in the Holy Ritual. He spelled it out slowly, recognizing words but uncertain of meanings. One note said: *Pound pastrami, can kraut, six bagels, for Emma.* Another ordered: *Don't forget to pick up form 1040 for Uncle Revenue.* The third note was only a column of figures with a circled total from which another amount was subtracted and finally a percentage taken, followed by the word *damn!* From this he could deduce nothing, except to check the arithmetic, which proved correct.

Of the two larger papers, one was tightly rolled and began to fall to pieces when he tried to open it; he could make out the words RACING FORM, but nothing more. He laid it back in the box for later restorative work.

The second large paper was a single folded sheet, whose creases were so brittle that he could only inspect a little of it by parting the folds and peering between them as best he could.

A diagram . . . a web of white lines on dark paper!

Again the cool thrill gathered along his spine. It was a *blueprint* —that exceedingly rare class of ancient document most prized by students of antiquity, and usually most challenging to interpreters and searchers for meaning.

And, as if the find itself were not enough of a blessing, among the words written in a block at the lower corner of the document was the name of the founder of his order—of the Blessed Leibowitz *himself!*

His trembling hands threatened to tear the paper in their happy agitation. The parting words of the pilgrim tumbled back to him: "May you find a Voice, as y' seek." Voice indeed, with V capitalized and formed by the wings of a descending dove and illuminated in three colors against a background of gold leaf. V as in *Vere dignum* and *Vidi aquam,* at the head of a page of the Missal. V, he saw quite clearly, as in Vocation.

He stole another glance to make certain it was so, then breathed, *"Beate Leibowitz, ora pro me. . . . Sancte Leibowitz, exaudi me,"* the second invocation being a rather daring one, since the founder of his order had not yet been declared a saint.

Forgetful of his abbot's warning, he climbed quickly to his feet and stared across the shimmering terrain to the south in the direction taken by the old wanderer of the burlap loincloth. But the pilgrim had long since vanished. Surely an angel of God, if not the Blessed Leibowitz himself, for had he not revealed this miraculous treasure by pointing out the rock to be moved and murmuring that prophetic farewell?

Brother Francis stood basking in his awe until the sun lay red on the hills and evening threatened to engulf him in its shadows. At last he stirred, and reminded himself of the wolves. His gift included no guarantee of charismata for subduing the wild beast, and he hastened to finish his enclosure before darkness fell on the desert. When the stars came out, he rekindled his fire and gathered his daily repast of the small purple cactus fruit, his only nourishment except the handful of parched corn brought to him by the priest each Sabbath. Sometimes he found himself staring hungrily at the lizards which scurried over the rocks, and was troubled by gluttonous nightmares.

But tonight his hunger was less troublesome than an impatient urge to run back to the abbey and announce his wondrous encounter to his brethren. This, of course, was unthinkable. Vocation or no, he must remain here until the end of Lent, and continue as if nothing extraordinary had occurred.

A cathedral will be built upon this site, he thought dreamily as he sat by the fire. He could see it rising from the rubble of the ancient village, magnificent spires visible for miles across the desert. . . .

But cathedrals were for teeming masses of people. The desert was home for only scattered tribes of huntsmen and the monks of the abbey. He settled in his dreams for a shrine, attracting rivers of pilgrims with girded loins. . . . He drowsed. When he awoke, the fire was reduced to glowing embers. Something seemed amiss. Was he quite alone? He blinked about at the darkness.

From beyond the bed of reddish coals, the dark wolf blinked back. The monk yelped and dived for cover.

The yelp, he decided as he lay trembling within his den of stones, had not been a serious breach of the rule of silence. He lay hugging the metal box and praying for the days of Lent to pass swiftly, while the sound of padded feet scratched about the enclosure.

Each night the wolves prowled about his camp, and the darkness was full of their howling. The days were glaring nightmares of hunger, heat, and scorching sun. He spent them at prayer and woodgathering, trying to suppress his impatience for the coming of Holy Saturday's high noon, the end of Lent and of his vigil.

But when at last it came, Brother Francis found himself too famished for jubilation. Wearily he packed his pouch, pulled up his cowl against the sun, and tucked his precious box beneath one arm. Thirty pounds lighter and several degrees weaker than he had been on Ash Wednesday, he staggered the six mile stretch to the abbey where he fell exhausted before its gates. The brothers who carried him in and bathed him and shaved him and anointed his desiccated tissues reported that he babbled incessantly in his delirium about an apparition in a burlap loincloth, addressing it at times as an angel and again as a saint, frequently invoking the name of Leibowitz and thanking him for a revelation of sacred relics and a racing form.

Such reports filtered through the monastic congregation and soon reached the ears of the abbot, whose eyes immediately narrowed to slits and whose jaw went rigid with the rock of policy.

"Bring him," growled that worthy priest in a tone that sent a recorder scurrying.

The abbot paced and gathered his ire: It was not that he objected to miracles, as such, if duly investigated, certified, and sealed; for miracles—even though always incompatible with administrative efficiency, and the abbot was administrator as well as priest—were the bedrock stuff on which his faith was founded. But last year there had been Brother Noyen with his miraculous hangman's noose, and the year before that, Brother Smirnov who had been mysteriously cured of the gout upon handling a probable relic of the Blessed Leibowitz, and the year before that . . . *Faugh!* The incidents had been too frequent and outrageous to tolerate. Ever since Leibowitz' beatification, the young fools had been sniffing around after shreds of the miraculous like a pack of good-natured hounds scratching eagerly at the back gate of Heaven for scraps.

It was quite understandable, but also quite unbearable. Every monastic order is eager for the canonization of its founder, and delighted to produce any bit of evidence to serve the cause in advocacy. But the abbot's flock was getting out of hand, and their zeal for miracles was making the Albertian Order of Leibowitz a laughing stock at New Vatican. He had determined to make any new bearers of miracles suffer the consequences, either as a punishment for impetuous and impertinent credulity, or as payment in penance for a gift of grace in case of later verification.

By the time the young novice knocked at his door, the abbot had projected himself into the desired state of carnivorous expectancy beneath a bland exterior.

"Come in, my son," he breathed softly.

"You sent for . . ." The novice paused, smiling happily as he noticed the familiar metal box on the abbot's table. ". . . for me, Father Juan?" he finished.

"Yes . . ." The abbot hesitated. His voice smiled with a withering acid, adding: "Or perhaps you would prefer that I come *to you*, hereafter, since you've become such a famous personage."

"Oh, no, Father!" Brother Francis reddened and gulped.

"You are seventeen, and plainly an idiot."

"That is undoubtedly true, Father."

"What improbable excuse can you propose for your outrageous vanity in believing yourself fit for Holy Orders?"

"I can offer none, my ruler and teacher. My sinful pride is unpardonable."

"To imagine that it is so great as to be unpardonable is even a vaster vanity," the priest roared.

"Yes, Father. I am indeed a worm."

The abbot smiled icily and resumed his watchful calm. "And you are now ready to deny your feverish ravings about an angel appearing to reveal to you this . . ." He gestured contemptuously at the box. ". . . this assortment of junk?"

Brother Francis gulped and closed his eyes. "I—I fear I cannot deny it, my master."

"What?"

"I cannot deny what I have seen, Father."

"Do you know what is going to happen to you now?"

"Yes, Father."

"Then prepare to take it!"

With a patient sigh, the novice gathered up his robes about his waist and bent over the table. The good abbot produced his stout hickory ruler from the drawer and whacked him soundly ten times across the bare buttocks. After each whack, the novice dutifully responded with a *"Deo Gratias!"* for this lesson in the virtue of humility.

"Do you *now* retract it?" the abbot demanded as he rolled down his sleeve.

"Father, I cannot."

The priest turned his back and was silent for a moment. "Very well," he said tersely. "Go. But do not expect to profess your solemn vows this season with the others."

Brother Francis returned to his cell in tears. His fellow novices would join the ranks of the professed monks of the order, while he must wait another year—and spend another Lenten season among the wolves in the desert, seeking a vocation which he felt had already been granted to him quite emphatically. As the weeks passed, however, he found some satisfaction in noticing that Father Juan had not been entirely serious in referring to his find as "an assortment of junk." The archeological relics aroused considerable interest among the brothers, and much time was spent at cleaning the tools, classifying them, restoring the documents to a pliable condition, and attempting to ascertain their meaning. It was even whispered among the novices that Brother Francis had discovered true relics of the Blessed Leibowitz—especially in the form of the blueprint bearing the legend OP COBBLESTONE, REQ LEIBOWITZ & HARDIN, which was stained with several brown splotches which might have been his blood—or equally likely, as the abbot pointed out, might be stains from a decayed apple core. But the print was dated in the Year of Grace 1956, which was—as nearly as could be determined—during that venerable man's lifetime, a lifetime now obscured by legend and myth, so that it was hard to determine any but a few facts about the man.

It was said that God, in order to test mankind, had commanded wise men of that age, among them the Blessed Leibowitz, to perfect diabolic weapons and give them into the hands of latter-day Pharaohs. And with such weapons Man had, within the span of a few weeks, destroyed most of his civilization and wiped out a large part of the population. After the Deluge of Flame came the plagues, the madness, and the bloody inception of the Age of Simplification when the furious remnants of humanity had torn politicians, technicians, and men of learning limb from limb, and burned all records that might contain information that could once more lead into paths of destruction. Nothing had been so fiercely hated as the written word, the learned man. It was during this time that the word *simpleton* came to mean *honest, upright, virtuous citizen,* a concept once denoted by the term *common man.*

To escape the righteous wrath of the surviving simpletons, many scientists and learned men fled to the only sanctuary which would try to offer them protection. Holy Mother Church received them, vested them in monks' robes, tried to conceal them from the mobs. Sometimes the sanctuary was effective; more often it was not. Monasteries were invaded, records and sacred books were burned, refugees seized and hanged. Leibowitz had fled to the Cistercians, professed their vows, became a priest, and after twelve years had won permission from the Holy See to found a new monastic order to be called "the Albertians," after St. Albert the Great, teacher of Aquinas and patron saint of scientists. The new order was to be dedicated to the preservation of knowledge, secular and sacred, and the duty of the brothers was to memorize such books and papers as could be smuggled to them from all parts of the world. Leibowitz was at last identified by simpletons as a former scientist, and was martyred by hanging; but the order continued, and when it became safe again to possess written documents, many books were transcribed from memory. Precedence, however, had been given to sacred writings, to history, the humanities, and social sciences—since the memories of the memorizers were limited, and few of the brothers were trained to understand the physical sciences. From the vast store of human knowledge, only a pitiful collection of hand-written books remained.

Now, after six centuries of darkness, the monks still preserved it, studied it, re-copied it, and waited. It mattered not in the least to them that the knowledge they saved was useless—and some of it even incomprehensible. The knowledge was there, and it was their duty to save it, and it would still be with them if the darkness in the world lasted ten thousand years.

Brother Francis Gerard of Utah returned to the desert the following year and fasted again in solitude. Once more he returned, weak and emaciated, to be confronted by the abbot, who demanded to know if he claimed further conferences with members of the Heavenly Host, or was prepared to renounce his story of the previous year.

"I cannot help what I have seen, my teacher," the lad repeated.

Once more did the abbot chastise him in Christ, and once more did he postpone his profession. The document, however, had been forwarded to a seminary for study, after a copy had been made. Brother Francis remained a novice, and continued to dream wistfully of the shrine which might someday be built upon the site of his find.

"Stubborn boy!" fumed the abbot. "Why didn't somebody else see his silly pilgrim, if the slovenly fellow was heading for the abbey as he said? One more escapade for the Devil's Advocate to cry hoax about. Burlap loincloth indeed!"

The burlap had been troubling the abbot, for tradition related that Leibowitz had been hanged with a burlap bag for a hood.

Brother Francis spent seven years in the novitiate, seven Lenten vigils in the desert, and became highly proficient in the imitation of wolfcalls. For the amusement of his brethren, he would summon the pack to the vicinity of the abbey by howling from the walls after dark. By day, he served in the kitchen, scrubbed the stone floors, and continued his studies of the ancients.

Then one day a messenger from the seminary came riding to the abbey on an ass, bearing tidings of great joy. "It is known," said the messenger, "that the documents found near here are authentic as to date of origin, and that the blueprint was somehow connected with your founder's work. It's being sent to New Vatican for further study."

"Possibly a true relic of Leibowitz, then?" the abbot asked calmly.

But the messenger could not commit himself to that extent, and only raised a shrug of one eyebrow. "It is said that Leibowitz was a widower at the time of his ordination. If the name of his deceased wife could be discovered . . ."

The abbot recalled the note in the box concerning certain articles of food for a woman, and he too shrugged an eyebrow.

Soon afterwards, he summoned Brother Francis into his presence. "My boy," said the priest, actually beaming, "I believe the time has come for you to profess your solemn vows. And may I commend you for your patience and persistence. We shall speak no more of your, ah . . . encounter with the, ah, desert wanderer. You are a good simpleton. You may kneel for my blessing, if you wish."

Brother Francis sighed and fell forward in a dead faint. The abbot blessed him and revived him, and he was permitted to profess the solemn vows of the Albertian Brothers of Leibowitz, swearing himself to perpetual poverty, chastity, obedience, and observance of the rule.

Soon afterwards, he was assigned to the copying room, apprentice under an aged monk named Horner, where he would undoubtedly spend the rest of his days illuminating the pages of algebra texts with patterns of olive leaves and cheerful cherubim.

"You have five hours a week," croaked his aged overseer, "which you may devote to an approved project of your own choosing, if you wish. If not, the time will be assigned to copying the *Summa Theologica* and such fragmentary copies of the Britannica as exist."

The young monk thought it over, then asked: "May I have the time for elaborating a beautiful copy of the Leibowitz blueprint?"

Brother Horner frowned doubtfully. "I don't know, son—our good abbot is rather sensitive on this subject. I'm afraid . . ."

Brother Francis begged him earnestly.

"Well, perhaps," the old man said reluctantly. "It seems like a rather brief project, so—I'll permit it."

The young monk selected the finest lambskin available and spent many weeks curing it and stretching it and stoning it to a perfect surface, bleached to a snowy whiteness. He spent more weeks at studying copies of his precious document in every detail, so that he knew each tiny line and marking in the complicated web of geometric markings and mystifying symbols. He pored over it until he could see the whole amazing complexity with his eyes closed. Additional weeks were spent searching painstakingly through the monastery's library for any information at all that might lead to some glimmer of understanding of the design.

Brother Jeris, a young monk who worked with him in the copy room and who frequently teased him about miraculous encounters in the desert, came to squint at it over his shoulder and asked: "What, pray, is the meaning of *Transistorized Control System for Unit Six-B?*"

"Clearly, it is the name of the thing which this diagram represents," said Francis, a trifle crossly since Jeris had merely read the title of the document aloud.

"Surely," said Jeris. "But what is the thing the diagram represents?"

"The transistorized control system for unit six-B, obviously."

Jeris laughed mockingly.

Brother Francis reddened. "I should imagine," said he, "that it represents an abstract concept, rather than a concrete *thing*. It's clearly not a recognizable picture of an object, unless the form is so stylized as to require special training to see it. In my opinion, *Transistorized Control System* is some high abstraction of transcendental value."

"Pertaining to what field of learning?" asked Jeris, still smiling smugly.

"Why . . ." Brother Francis paused. "Since our Beatus Leibowitz was an electronicist prior to his profession and ordination, I suppose the concept applies to the lost art called *electronics*."

"So it is written. But what was the subject matter of that art, Brother?"

"That too is written. The subject matter of electronics was the Electron, which one fragmentary source defines as a Negative Twist of Nothingness."

"I am impressed by your astuteness," said Jeris. "Now perhaps you can tell me how to negate nothingness?"

Brother Francis reddened slightly and squirmed for a reply.

"A negation of nothingness should yield somethingness, I suppose," Jeris continued. "So the Electron must have been a twist of *something*. Unless the negation applies to the 'twist,' and then we would be 'Untwisting Nothing,' eh?" He chuckled. "How clever they must have been, these ancients. I suppose if you keep at it, Francis, you will learn how to untwist a nothing, and then we shall have the Electron in our midst. Where would we put it? On the high altar, perhaps?"

"I couldn't say," Francis answered stiffly. "But I have a certain faith that the Electron must have existed at one time, even though I can't say how it was constructed or what it might have been used for."

The iconoclast laughed mockingly and returned to his work. The incident saddened Francis, but did not turn him from his devotion to his project.

As soon as he had exhausted the library's meager supply of information concerning the lost art of the Albertians' founder, he began preparing preliminary sketches of the designs he meant to use on the lambskin. The diagram itself, since its meaning was obscure, would be redrawn precisely as it was in the blueprint, and penned in coal-black lines. The lettering and numbering, however, he would translate into a more decorative and colorful script than the plain block letters used by the ancients. And the text contained in a square block marked SPECIFICATIONS would be distributed pleasingly around the borders of the document, upon scrolls and shields supported by doves and cherubim. He would make the black lines of the diagram less stark and austere by imagining the geometric tracery to be a trellis, and decorate it with green vines and golden fruit, birds and perhaps a wily serpent. At the very top would be a representation of the Triune God, and at the bottom the coat of arms of the Albertian Order. Thus was the Transistorized Control System of the Blessed Leibowitz to be glorified and rendered appealing to the eye as well as to the intellect.

When he had finished the preliminary sketch, he showed it shyly to Brother Horner for suggestions or approval. "I can see," said the old man a bit remorsefully, "that your project is not to be as brief as I had hoped. But . . . continue with it anyhow. The design is beautiful, beautiful indeed."

"Thank you, Brother."

The old man leaned close to wink confidentially. "I've heard the case for Blessed Leibowitz' canonization has been speeded up, so possibly our dear abbot is less troubled by you-know-what than he previously was."

The news of the speed-up was, of course, happily received by all monastics of the order. Leibowitz' beatification had long since been effected, but the final step in declaring him to be a saint might require many more years, even though the case was under way; and indeed there was the possibility that the Devil's Advocate might uncover evidence to prevent the canonization from occurring at all.

Many months after he had first conceived the project, Brother Francis began actual work on the lambskin. The intricacies of scrollwork, the excruciatingly delicate work of inlaying the gold leaf, the hair-fine detail, made it a labor of years; and when his eyes began to trouble him, there were long weeks when he dared not touch it at all for fear of spoiling it with one little mistake. But slowly, painfully, the ancient diagram was becoming a blaze of beauty. The brothers of the abbey gathered to watch and murmur over it, and some even said that the inspiration of it was proof enough of his alleged encounter with the pilgrim who might have been Blessed Leibowitz.

"I can't see why you don't spend your time on a *useful* project," was Brother Jeris' comment, however. The skeptical monk had been using his own free-project time to make and decorate sheepskin shades for the oil lamps in the chapel.

Brother Horner, the old master copyist, had fallen ill. Within weeks, it became apparent that the well-loved monk was on his deathbed. In the midst of the monastery's grief, the abbot quietly appointed Brother Jeris as master of the copy room.

A Mass of Burial was chanted early in Advent, and the remains of the holy old man were committed to the earth of their origin. On the following day, Brother Jeris informed Brother Francis that he considered it about time for him to put away the things of a child and start doing a man's work. Obediently, the monk wrapped his precious project in parchment, protected it with heavy board, shelved it, and began producing sheepskin lampshades. He made no murmur of protest, and contented himself with realizing that someday the soul of Brother Jeris would depart by the same road as that of Brother Horner, to begin the life for which this copy room was but the staging ground; and afterwards, please God, he might be allowed to complete his beloved document.

Providence, however, took an earlier hand in the matter. During the following summer, a monsignor with several clerks and a donkey train came riding into the abbey and announced that he had come from New Vatican, as Leibowitz advocate in the canonization proceedings, to investigate such evidence as the abbey could produce that might have bearing on the case, including an alleged apparition of the beatified which had come to one Francis Gerard of Utah.

The gentleman was warmly greeted, quartered in the suite reserved for visiting prelates, lavishly served by six young monks responsive to his every whim, of which he had very few. The finest wines were opened, the huntsman snared the plumpest quail and chaparral cocks, and the advocate was entertained each evening by fiddlers and a troupe of clowns, although the visitor persisted in insisting that life go on as usual at the abbey.

On the third day of his visit, the abbot sent for Brother Francis. "Monsignor di Simone wishes to see you," he said. "If you let your imagination run away with you, boy, we'll use your gut to string a fiddle, feed your carcass to the wolves, and bury the bones in unhallowed ground. Now get along and see the good gentleman."

Brother Francis needed no such warning. Since he had awakened from his feverish babblings after his first Lenten fast in the desert, he had never mentioned the encounter with the pilgrim except when asked about it, nor had he allowed himself to speculate any further concerning the pilgrim's identity. That the pilgrim might be a matter for high ecclesiastical concern frightened him a little, and his knock was timid at the monsignor's door.

His fright proved unfounded. The monsignor was a suave and diplomatic elder who seemed keenly interested in the small monk's career.

"Now about your encounter with our blessed founder," he said after some minutes of preliminary amenities.

"Oh, but I never said he was our Blessed Leibo—"

"Of course you didn't, my son. Now I have here an account of it, as gathered from other sources, and I would like you to read it, and either confirm it or correct it." He paused to draw a scroll from his case and handed it to Francis. "The sources for this version, of course, had it on hearsay only," he added, "and only *you* can describe it first hand, so I want you to edit it *most* scrupulously."

"Of course. What happened was really very simple, Father."

But it was apparent from the fatness of the scroll that the hearsay account was not so simple. Brother Francis read with mounting apprehension which soon grew to the proportions of pure horror.

"You look white, my son. Is something wrong?" asked the distinguished priest.

"This . . . this . . . it wasn't like this *at all!*" gasped Francis. "He didn't say more than a few words to me. I only saw him once. He just asked me the way to the abbey and tapped the rock where I found the relics."

"No heavenly choir?"

"Oh, no!"

"And it's not true about the nimbus and the carpet of roses that grew up along the road where he walked?"

"As God is my judge, nothing like that happened at all!"

"Ah, well," sighed the advocate. "Traveler's stories are always exaggerated."

He seemed saddened, and Francis hastened to apologize, but the advocate dismissed it as of no great importance to the case. "There are other miracles, carefully documented," he explained, "and anyway—there is one bit of good news about the documents you discovered. We've unearthed the name of the wife who died before our founder came to the order."

"Yes?"

"Yes. It was Emily."

Despite his disappointment with Brother Francis' account of the pilgrim, Monsignor di Simone spent five days at the site of the find. He was accompanied by an eager crew of novices from the abbey, all armed with picks and shovels. After extensive digging, the advocate returned with a small assortment of additional artifacts, and one bloated tin can that contained a desiccated mess which might once have been sauerkraut.

Before his departure, he visited the copy room and asked to see Brother Francis' copy of the famous blueprint. The monk protested that it was really nothing, and produced it with such eagerness his hands trembled.

"Zounds!" said the monsignor, or an oath to such effect. "Finish it, man, finish it!"

The monk looked smilingly at Brother Jeris. Brother Jeris swiftly turned away; the back of his neck gathered color. The following morning, Francis resumed his labors over the illuminated blueprint, with gold leaf, quills, brushes, and dyes.

And then came another donkey train from New Vatican, with a full complement of clerks and armed guards for defense against highwaymen, this time headed by a monsignor with small horns and pointed fangs (or so several novices would later have testified), who announced that he was the *Advocatus Diaboli*, opposing Leibowitz' canonization, and he was here to investigate—and perhaps fix responsibility, he hinted—for a number of incredible and hysterical rumors filtering out of the abbey and reaching even high officials at New Vatican. He made it clear that he would tolerate no romantic nonsense.

The abbot greeted him politely and offered him an iron cot in a cell with a south exposure, after apologizing for the fact that the guest suite had been recently exposed to smallpox. The monsignor was attended by his own staff, and ate mush and herbs with the monks in refectory.

"I understand you are susceptible to fainting spells," he told Brother Francis when the dread time came. "How many members of your family have suffered from epilepsy or madness?"

"None, Excellency."

"I'm not an 'Excellency,'" snapped the priest. "Now we're going to get the truth out of you." His tone implied that he considered it to be a simple straightforward surgical operation which should have been performed years ago.

"Are you aware that documents can be aged artificially?" he demanded.

Francis was not so aware.

"Did you know that Leibowitz' wife was named Emily, and that Emma is *not* a diminutive for Emily?"

Francis had not known it, but recalled from childhood that his own parents had been rather careless about what they called each other. "And if Blessed Leibowitz chose to call her Emma, then I'm sure . . ."

The monsignor exploded, and tore into Francis with semantic tooth and nail, and left the bewildered monk wondering whether he had ever really seen a pilgrim at all.

Before the advocate's departure, he too asked to see the illuminated copy of the print, and this time the monk's hands trembled with fear as he produced it, for he might again be forced to quit the project. The monsignor only stood gazing at it however, swallowed slightly, and forced himself to nod. "Your imagery is vivid," he admitted, "but then, of course, we all knew that, didn't we?"

The monsignor's horns immediately grew shorter by an inch, and he departed the same evening for New Vatican.

The years flowed smoothly by, seaming the faces of the once young and adding gray to the temples. The perpetual labors of the monastery continued, supplying a slow trickle of copied and re-copied manuscript to the outside world. Brother Jeris developed ambitions of building a printing press, but when the abbot demanded his reasons, he could only reply, "So we can mass-produce."

"Oh? And in a world that's smug in its illiteracy, what do you intend to do with the stuff? Sell it as kindling paper to the peasants?"

Brother Jeris shrugged unhappily, and the copy room continued with pot and quill.

Then one spring, shortly before Lent, a messenger arrived with glad tidings for the order. The case for Leibowitz was complete. The College of Cardinals would soon convene, and the founder of the Albertian Order would be enrolled in the Calendar of Saints. During the time of rejoicing that followed the announcement, the abbot—now withered and in his dotage—summoned Brother Francis into his presence, and wheezed:

"His Holiness commands your presence during the canonization of Isaac Edward Leibowitz. Prepare to leave.

"Now don't faint on me again," he added querulously.

The trip to New Vatican would take at least three months, perhaps longer, the time depending on how far Brother Francis could get before the inevitable robber band relieved him of his ass, since he would be going unarmed and alone. He carried with him only a begging bowl and the illuminated copy of the Leibowitz print, praying that ignorant robbers would have no use for the latter. As a precaution, however, he wore a black patch over his right eye, for the peasants, being a superstitious lot, could often be put to flight by even a hint of the evil eye. Thus armed and equipped, he set out to obey the summons of his high priest.

Two months and some odd days later he met his robber on a mountain trail that was heavily wooded and far from any settlement. His robber was a short man, but heavy as a bull, with a glazed knob of a pate and a jaw like a block of granite. He stood in the trail with his legs spread wide and his massive arms folded across his chest, watching the approach of the little figure on the ass. The robber seemed alone, and armed only with a knife which he did not bother to remove from his belt thong. His appearance was a disappointment, since Francis had been secretly hoping for another encounter with the pilgrim of long ago.

"Get off," said the robber.

The ass stopped in the path. Brother Francis tossed back his cowl to reveal the eye-patch, and raised a trembling finger to touch it. He began to lift the patch slowly as if to reveal something hideous that might be hidden beneath it. The robber threw back his head and laughed a laugh that might have sprung from the throat of Satan himself. Francis muttered an exorcism, but the robber seemed untouched.

"You black-sacked jeebers wore that one out years ago," he said. "Get off."

Francis smiled, shrugged, and dismounted without protest.

"A good day to you, sir," he said pleasantly. "You may take the ass. Walking will improve my health, I think." He smiled again and started away.

"Hold it," said the robber. "Strip to the buff. And let's see what's in that package."

Brother Francis touched his begging bowl and made a helpless gesture, but this brought only another scornful laugh from the robber.

"I've seen that alms-pot trick before too," he said. "The last man with a begging bowl had half a heklo of gold in his boot. Now strip."

Brother Francis displayed his sandals, but began to strip. The robber searched his clothing, found nothing, and tossed it back to him.

"Now let's see inside the package."

"It is only a document, sir," the monk protested. "Of value to no one but its owner."

"Open it."

Silently Brother Francis obeyed. The gold leaf and the colorful design flashed brilliantly in the sunlight that filtered through the foliage. The robber's craggy jaw dropped an inch. He whistled softly.

"What a pretty! Now wouldn't me woman like it to hang on the shanty wall!"

He continued to stare while the monk went slowly sick inside. *If Thou hast sent him to test me, O Lord,* he pleaded inwardly, *then help me to die like a man, for he'll get it over the dead body of Thy servant, if take it he must.*

"Wrap it up for me," the robber commanded, clamping his jaw in sudden decision.

The monk whimpered softly. "Please, sir, you would not take the work of a man's lifetime. I spent fifteen years illuminating this manuscript, and . . ."

"Well! Did it yourself, did you?" The robber threw back his head and howled again.

Francis reddened. "I fail to see the humor, sir . . ."

The robber pointed at it between guffaws. "You! Fifteen years to make a paper bauble. So that's what you do. Tell me why. Give me one good reason. For fifteen years. Ha!"

Francis stared at him in stunned silence and could think of no reply that would appease his contempt.

Gingerly, the monk handed it over. The robber took it in both hands and made as if to rip it down the center.

"*Jesus, Mary, Joseph!*" the monk screamed, and went to his knees in the trail. "For the love of God, sir!"

Softening slightly, the robber tossed it on the ground with a snicker. "Wrestle you for it."

"Anything, sir, anything!"

They squared off. The monk crossed himself and recalled that wrestling had once been a divinely sanctioned sport—and with grim faith, he marched into battle.

Three seconds later, he lay groaning on the flat of his back under a short mountain of muscle. A sharp rock seemed to be severing his spine.

"Heh heh," said the robber, and arose to claim his document.

Hands folded as if in prayer, Brother Francis scurried after him on his knees, begging at the top of his lungs.

The robber turned to snicker. "I believe you'd kiss a boot to get it back."

Francis caught up with him and fervently kissed his boot.

This proved too much for even such a firm fellow as the robber. He flung the manuscript down again with a curse and climbed aboard the monk's donkey. The monk snatched up the precious document and trotted along beside the robber, thanking him profusely and blessing him repeatedly while the robber rode away on the ass.

Francis sent a glowing cross of benediction after the departing figure and praised God for the existence of such selfless robbers.

And yet when the man had vanished among the trees, he felt an aftermath of sadness. Fifteen years to make a paper bauble . . . The taunting voice still rang in his ears. Why? Tell one good reason for fifteen years.

He was unaccustomed to the blunt ways of the outside world, to its harsh habits and curt attitudes. He found his heart deeply troubled by the mocking words, and his head hung low in the cowl as he plodded along. At one time he considered tossing the document in the brush and leaving it for the rains—but Father Juan had approved his taking it as a gift, and he could not come with empty hands. Chastened, he traveled on.

The hour had come. The ceremony surged about him as a magnificent spectacle of sound and stately movement and vivid color in the majestic basilica. And when the perfectly infallible Spirit had finally been invoked, a monsignor—it was di Simone, Francis noticed, the advocate for the saint—arose and called upon Peter to speak, through the person of Leo XXII, commanding the assemblage to hearken.

Whereupon, the Pope quietly proclaimed that Isaac Edward Leibowitz was a saint, and it was finished. The ancient and obscure technician was of the heavenly hagiarchy, and Brother Francis breathed a dutiful prayer to his new patron as the choir burst into the *Te Deum*.

The Pontiff strode quickly into the audience room where the little monk was waiting, taking Brother Francis by surprise and rendering him briefly speechless. He knelt quickly to kiss the Fisherman's ring and receive the blessing. As he arose, he found himself clutching the beautiful document behind him as if ashamed of it. The Pope's eyes caught the motion, and he smiled.

"You have brought us a gift, our son?" he asked.

The monk gulped, nodded stupidly, and brought it out. Christ's Vicar stared at it for a long time without apparent expression. Brother Francis' heart went sinking deeper as the seconds drifted by.

"It is a nothing," he blurted, "a miserable gift. I am ashamed to have wasted so much time at . . ." He choked off.

The Pope seemed not to hear him. "Do you understand the meaning of Saint Isaac's symbology?" he asked, peering curiously at the abstract design of the circuit.

Dumbly the monk shook his head.

"Whatever it means . . ." the Pope began, but broke off. He smiled and spoke of other things. Francis had been so honored not

Walter M. Miller, Jr.   359

because of any official judgment concerning his pilgrim. He had been honored for his role in bringing to light such important documents and relics of the saint, for such they had been judged, regardless of the manner in which they had been found.

Francis stammered his thanks. The Pontiff gazed again at the colorful blaze of his illuminated diagram. "Whatever it means," he breathed once more, "this bit of learning, though dead, will live again." He smiled up at the monk and winked. "And we shall guard it till that day."

For the first time, the little monk noticed that the Pope had a hole in his robe. His clothing, in fact, was threadbare. The carpet in the audience room was worn through in spots, and plaster was falling from the ceiling.

But there were books on the shelves along the walls. Books of painted beauty, speaking of incomprehensible things, copied by men whose business was not to understand but to save. And the books were waiting.

"Goodby, beloved son."

And the small keeper of the flame of knowledge trudged back toward his abbey on foot. His heart was singing as he approached the robber's outpost. And if the robber happened to be taking the day off, the monk meant to sit down and wait for his return. This time he had an answer.

6

Population
and Urban Life

The study of population and urban life has been an important part of sociology. Today, many sociologists feel that understanding the population characteristics and the urban patterns of settlement of a society is important in its own right as well as necessary to understand the social organization and culture of urbanized societies.

Population study (called *demography* by some) involves collection, analysis, and interpretation of data on the number, distribution, composition, and important changes in a population. Demographers use three basic demographic variables in studying a given population: *fertility* (births), *mortality* (deaths), and *migration* (physical movement from place to place). They develop *fertility* and *mortality rates* to measure aspects of population. For example, demographers make use of crude birth rates, age-specific birth rates, fertility ratios, crude death rates, infant mortality rates, maternal mortality rates, and so on.

The interplay of fertility, mortality, and migration produces the *composition* of a population. Demographers want to know the numbers of people in a given area, at a given time, by such variables as their age, sex, marital status, ethnic background, income, occupation, and level of education.

Demographers also study population growth. Three situations yield population increase in a given area: (1) births exceed deaths (*natural increase*), (2) people moving into the area outnumber those leaving (*net in-migration*), and (3) additional land area and its occupants are incorporated or annexed (*territorial acquisition*).

In the study of world population change, the overall pattern is in the direction of increase despite the fact that there have been societies that have declined in population and even disappeared. Although migration affects the size of nations and the distribution of population over the world's surface, world population size is dependent on only two of the three basic population variables: births and deaths. World population increase is largely the result of sharply declining death rates and consequent large-scale natural increase.

Through most of human history, man's numbers were limited by high birth rates and high death rates. When the population exceeded a limited food supply, famine and starvation produced a rise in the death rate and population size declined. Over the long run high birth rates and high death rates balanced out and population size remained stable. Life expectancy was low and the average age of the population quite young. Famine, starvation, and fatal diseases were checked and death rates dropped with improvements in agricultural productivity, advances in medical knowledge and practice, better sanitation facilities, increased trade, and more efficient transportation. Continued high birth rates and declining death rates produced high rates of *natural increase,* and population grew rapidly. With industrialization, birth rates declined as well, although never dropping to meet the low death rates. Industrial nations exported the knowledge and practice that lowered death rates in modernizing nations, and population increased sharply. For example, it took about a century (1825 to 1930) for the approximately one billion inhabitants of earth to double in numbers. However, a third billion was added to world population by 1960; that was in only 30 years. Projections see present world population doubling by 2000.

Study of relatively large, high density settlements called *cities* has involved many disciplines in addition to sociology, and today interdisciplinary efforts in *urban studies* are commonplace. Within sociology, the efforts of a group of sociologists at the University of Chicago in the first three decades of the twentieth century gave focus to what became *urban sociology*. The urban sociologist uses the perspectives and techniques of sociology to study human behavior in *urban* context. Urban sociology reflects many distinct approaches to understanding urban man. Some sociologists study the demographic aspects of increasing urban growth. Others (although not many) study the history of the city. Still others apply derivatives of what was once a dominant perspective in urban sociology—*human ecology*. Many comprehensive studies of single towns, small cities, and suburbs, called *community studies*, have been prepared by sociologists and other social scientists. Finally, sociologists have analyzed various social patterns associated with urban life.

Cities as forms of human settlement have existed for some 5500 years. Early cities included only a small proportion of the population of a given society and functioned primarily as market and religious centers highly dependent on surrounding rural territory. During most of this period urban growth was slow and from the decline of the Roman Empire to approximately the twelfth century cities generally declined in number and population. A renewal of urban growth during the Middle Ages was followed by very rapid *urbanization* during the industrial era. Cities now have become the common place of residence of human beings.

Total Environment

Will man be able to continue to produce enough food to support rapid population increase? Some scholars have faith that scientific technology will produce sufficient food and other resources. Others, dating from Thomas Malthus' famous essay on population in 1798, feel that man's increase in numbers will eventually outstrip man's ability to feed the increased numbers and mankind will be faced with a crisis of survival.

While scientists in many disciplines have studied and debated the equations of food and energy production vs. population growth and try to project the probabilities of man's biological survival, some sociologists have raised this important question: Assuming that massive populations can physically survive on earth, what changes in social organization will be required if societies of billions of people are to function? It is not unlikely that man's social world will be altered in as yet unimagined patterns, and with these changes man's beliefs and values will be altered as well.

"Total Environment" is set in a world that has managed its food shortages, but where individuals perform experiments on other human beings to test the effect of high densities of population on human social and psychic functioning, much as some behavioral psychologists today study rats to investigate the same question. Following the inhabitants of "Total Environment" as they adjust to their artifical conditions, one sees some familiar social processes at work—intragroup status hierarchies developing, groups forming for protective functions, and commitment and fatalistic attitudes toward their way of life emerging. Is their social world a simple extension of our own? There are two crucial questions here: Will large populations in limited space produce the kind of social world portrayed in this story? In the future, will man's moral and ethical values permit him to commit other human beings to experimental "total environments?"

Total Environment

BRIAN W. ALDISS

I

"What's that poem about 'caverns measureless to man'?"
Thomas Dixit asked. His voice echoed away among the
caverns, the question unanswered. Peter Crawley, walking a pace or
two behind him, said nothing, lost in a reverie of his own.

It was over a year since Dixit had been imprisoned here. He had
taken time off from the resettlement area to come and have a last
look round before everything was finally demolished. In these great
concrete workings, men still moved—Indian technicians mostly, carrying instruments, often with their own headlights. Cables trailed
everywhere; but the desolation was mainly an effect of the constant
abrasion all surfaces had undergone. People had flowed here like
water in a subterranean cave; and their corporate life had flowed
similarly, hidden, forgotten.

Dixit was powerfully moved by the thought of all that life. He,
almost alone, was the man who had plunged into it and survived.

Old angers stirring in him, he turned and spoke directly to his
companion. "What a monument to human suffering! They should
leave this place standing as an everlasting memorial to what happened."

The white man said, "The Delhi government refuses to entertain
any such suggestion. I see their point of view, but I also see that it
would make a great tourist attraction!"

"Tourist attraction, man! Is that all it means to you?"

Crawley laughed. "As ever, you're too touchy, Thomas. I take
this whole matter much less lightly than you suppose. Tourism just
happens to attract me more than human suffering."

They walked on side by side. They were never able to agree.

The battered faces of flats and houses—now empty, once choked
with humanity—stood on either side, doors gaping open like old

men's mouths in sleep. The spaces seemed enormous; the shadows and echoes that belonged to those spaces seemed to continue indefinitely. Yet before . . . there had scarcely been room to breathe here.

"I remember what your buddy, Senator Byrnes, said," Crawley remarked. "He showed how both East and West have learned from this experiment. Of course, the social scientists are still working over their findings; some startling formulae for social groups are emerging already. But the people who lived and died here were fighting their way towards control of the universe of the ultra-small, and that's where the biggest advances have come. They were already developing power over their own genetic material. Another generation, and they might have produced the ultimate in automatic human population control: anoestrus, where too close proximity to other members of the species leads to reabsorption of the embryonic material in the female. Our scientists have been able to help them there, and geneticists predict that in another decade—"

"Yes, yes, all that I grant you. Progress is wonderful." He knew he was being impolite. These things were important, of revolutionary importance to a crowded Earth. But he wished he walked these eroded passageways alone.

Undeniably, India had learned too, just as Peter Crawley claimed. For Hinduism had been put to the test here and had shown its terrifying strengths and weaknesses. In these mazes, people had not broken under deadly conditions—nor had they thought to break away from their destiny. *Dharma*—duty—had been stronger than humanity. And this revelation was already changing the thought and fate of one-sixth of the human race.

He said, "Progress is wonderful. But what took place here was essentially a religious experience."

Crawley's brief laugh drifted away into the shadows of a great gaunt stairwell. "I'll bet you didn't feel that way when we sent you in here a year ago!"

What had he felt then? He stopped and gazed up at the gloom of the stairs. All that came to him was the memory of that appalling flood of life and of the people who had been a part of it, whose brief years had evaporated in these caverns, whose feet had endlessly trodden these warren-ways, these lugubrious decks, these crumbling flights. . . .

II

The concrete steps, climbed up into darkness. The steps were wide, and countless children sat on them, listless, resting against each other. This was an hour when activity was low and even small children hushed their cries for a while. Yet there was no silence on the steps; silence was never complete there. Always, in the background, the noise of voices. Voices and more voices. Never silence.

Shamim was aged, so she preferred to run her errands at this time of day, when the crowds thronging Total Environment were less. She dawdled by a sleepy seller of life-objects at the bottom of the stairs, picking over the little artifacts and exclaiming now and again. The hawker knew her, knew she was too poor to buy, did not even press her to buy. Shamim's oldest daughter, Malti, waited for her mother by the bottom step.

Malti and her mother were watched from the top of the steps.

A light burned at the top of the steps. It had burned there for twenty-five years, safe from breakage behind a strong mesh. But dung and mud had recently been thrown at it, covering it almost entirely and so making the top of the stairway dark. A furtive man called Narayan Farhad crouched there and watched, a shadow in the shadows.

A month ago, Shamim had had an illegal operation in one of the pokey rooms off Grand Balcony on her deck. The effects of the operation were still with her; under her plain cotton sari, her thin dark old body was bent. Her share of life stood lower than it had been.

Malti was her second oldest daughter, a meek girl who had not been conceived when the Total Environment experiment began. Even meekness had its limits. Seeing her mother dawdle so needlessly, Malti muttered impatiently and went on ahead, climbing the infested steps, anxious to be home.

Extracts from Thomas Dixit's report to Senator Jacob Byrnes, back in America: *To lend variety to the habitat, the Environment has been divided into ten decks, each deck five stories high, which allows for an occasional pocket-sized open space. The architecture has been varied somewhat on each deck. On one deck, a sort of blown-up Indian village is presented; on another, the houses are large and appear separate, although sandwiched between decks—I need not add they are hopelessly overcrowded now. On most decks, the available space is packed solid with flats. Despite this attempt at variety, a general bowdlerization of both Eastern and Western architectural styles, and the fact that everything has been constructed out of concrete or a parastyrene for economy's sake, has led to a dreadful sameness. I cannot imagine anywhere more hostile to the spiritual values of life.*

The shadow in the shadows moved. He glanced anxiously up at the light, which also housed a spy-eye; there would be a warning out, and sprays would soon squirt away the muck he had thrown at the fitting; but, for the moment, he could work unobserved.

Narayan bared his old teeth as Malti came up the steps towards him, treading among the sprawling children. She was too old to fetch a really good price on the slave market, but she was still strong; there would be no trouble in getting rid of her at once. Of course he knew something of her history, even though she lived on a different deck from him. Malti! He called her name at the last moment as he jumped out on her. Old though he was, Narayan was quick. He wore only his dhoti, arms flashing, interlocking round hers, one good powerful wrench to get her off her feet—now running fast, fearful, up the rest of the steps, moving even as he clamped one hand over her mouth to cut off her cry of fear. Clever old Narayan!

The stairs mount up and up in the four corners of the Total Environment, linking deck with deck. They are now crude things of concrete and metal, since the plastic covers have long been stripped from them.

These stairways are the weak points of the tiny empires, transient and brutal, that form on every deck. They are always guarded, though guards can be bribed. Sometimes gangs or "unions" take over a stairway, either by agreement or bloodshed.

Shamim screamed, responding to her daughter's cry. She began to hobble up the stairs as fast as she could, tripping over infant feet, drawing a dagger out from under her sari. It was a plastic dagger, shaped out of a piece of the Environment.

She called Malti, called for help as she went. When she reached the landing, she was on the top floor of her deck, the Ninth, where she lived. Many people were here, standing, squatting, thronging together. They looked away from Shamim, people with blind faces. She had so often acted similarly herself when others were in trouble.

Gasping, she stopped and stared up at the roof of the deck, blue-dyed to simulate sky, cracks running irregularly across it. The steps went on up there, up to the Top Deck. She saw legs, yellow soles of feet disappearing, faces staring down at her, hostile. As she ran toward the bottom of the stairs, the watchers above threw things at her. A shard hit Shamim's cheek and cut it open. With blood running down her face, she began to wail. Then she turned and ran through the crowds to her family room.

I've been a month just reading through the microfiles. Sometimes a whole deck becomes unified under a strong leader. On Deck Nine, for instance, unification was achieved under a man called

Ullhas. He was a strong man, and a great show-off. That was a while ago, when conditions were not as desperate as they are now. Ullhas could never last the course today. Leaders become more despotic as Environment decays.

The dynamics of unity are such that it is always insufficient for a deck simply to stay unified; the young men always need to have their aggressions directed outwards. So the leader of a strong deck always sets out to tyrannize the deck below or above, whichever seems to be the weaker. It is a miserable state of affairs. The time generally comes when, in the midst of a raid, a counter-raid is launched by one of the other decks. Then the raiders return to carnage and defeat. And another paltry empire tumbles.

It is up to me to stop this continual degradation of human life.

As usual, the family room was crowded. Although none of Shamim's own children were here, there were grandchildren—including the lame granddaughter, Shirin—and six great-grandchildren, none of them more than three years old, Shamim's third husband, Gita, was not in. Safe in the homely squalor of the room, Shamim burst into tears, while Shirin comforted her and endeavored to keep the little ones off.

"Gita is getting food. I will go and fetch him," Shirin said.

When UHDRE—Ultra-High Density Research Establishment—became operative, twenty-five years ago, all the couples selected for living in the Total Environment had to be under twenty years of age. Before being sealed in, they were innoculated against all diseases. There was plenty of room for each couple then; they had whole suites to themselves, and the best of food; plus no means of birth control. That's always been the main pivot of the UHDRE experiment. Now that first generation has aged severely. They are old people pushing forty-five. The whole life cycle has speeded up—early puberty, early senescence. The second and third generations have shown remarkable powers of adaptation; a fourth generation is already toddling. Those toddlers will be reproducing before their years attain double figures, if present trends continue. Are allowed to continue.

Gita was younger than Shamim, a small wiry man who knew his way around. No hero, he nevertheless had a certain style about him. His life-object hung boldly round his neck on a chain, instead of being hidden, as were most people's life objects. He stood in the line for food, chattering with friends. Gita was good at making alliances. With a bunch of his friends, he had formed a little union to see that they got their food back safely to their homes; so they generally met with no incident in the crowded walkways of Deck Nine.

The balance of power on the deck was very complex at the moment. As a result, comparative peace reigned, and might continue for several weeks if the strong man on Top Deck did not interfere.

Food delivery grills are fixed in the walls of every floor of every deck. Two gongs sound before each delivery. After the second one, hatches open and steaming food pours from the grills. Hills of rice tumble forward, flavored with meat and spices. Chappattis fall from a separate slot. As the men run forward with their containers, holy men are generally there to sanctify the food.

Great supply elevators roar up and down in the heart of the vast tower, tumbling out rations at all levels. Alcohol also was supplied in the early years. It was discontinued when it led to trouble; which is not to say that it is not secretly brewed inside the Environment. The UHDRE food ration has been generous from the start and has always been maintained at the same level per head of population although, as you know, the food is now ninety-five percent factory-made. Nobody would ever have starved, had it been shared out equally inside the tower. On some of the decks, some of the time, it is still shared out fairly.

One of Gita's sons, Jamsu, had seen the kidnapper Narayan making off to Top Deck with the struggling Malti. His eyes gleaming with excitement, he sidled his way into the queue where Gita stood and clasped his father's arm. Jamsu had something of his father in him, always lurked where numbers made him safe, rather than run off as his brothers and sisters had run off, to marry and struggle for a room or a space of their own.

He was telling his father what had happened when Shirin limped up and delivered her news.

Nodding grimly, Gita said, "Stay with us, Shirin, while I get the food."

He scooped his share into the family pail. Jamsu grabbed a handful of rice for himself.

"It was a dirty wizened man from Top Deck called Narayan Farhad," Jamsu said, gobbling. "He is one of the crooks who hangs about the shirt tails of . . ." He let his voice die.

"You did not go to Malti's rescue, shame on you!" Shirin said.

"Jamsu might have been killed," Gita said, as they pushed through the crowd and moved towards the family room.

"They're getting so strong on Top Deck," Jamsu said. "I hear all about it! We mustn't provoke them or they may attack. They say a regular army is forming round . . ."

Shirin snorted impatiently. "You great babe! Go ahead and name the man! It's Prahlad Patel whose very name you dare not mention, isn't it? Is he a god or something, for Siva's sake? You're afraid of him even from this distance, eh, aren't you?"

"Don't bully the lad," Gita said. Keeping the peace in his huge mixed family was a great responsibility, almost more than he could manage. As he turned into the family room, he said quietly to Jamsu and Shirin, "Malti was a favorite daughter of Shamim's, and now is gone from her. We will get our revenge against this Narayan Farhad. You and I will go this evening, Jamsu, to the holy man Vazifdar. He will even up matters for us, and then perhaps the great Patel will also be warned."

He looked thoughtfully down at his life-object. Tonight, he told himself, I must venture forth alone, and put my life in jeopardy for Shamim's sake.

Prahlad Patel's union has flourished and grown until now he rules all the Top Deck. His name is known and dreaded, we believe, three or four decks down. He is the strongest—yet in some ways curiously the most moderate—ruler in Total Environment at present.

Although he can be brutal, Patel seems inclined for peace. Of course, the bugging does not reveal everything; he may have plans which he keeps secret, since he is fully aware that the bugging exists. But we believe his interests lie in other directions than conquest. He is only about nineteen, as we reckon years, but already gray-haired, and the sight of him is said to freeze the muscles to silence in the lips of his followers. I have watched him over the bugging for many hours since I agreed to undertake this task.

Patel has one great advantage in Total Environment. He lives on the Tenth Deck, at the top of the building. He can therefore be invaded only from below and the Ninth Deck offers no strong threats at present, being mainly oriented round an influential body of holy men, of whom the most illustrious is one Vazifdar.

The staircases between decks are always trouble spots. No deck-ruler was ever strong enough to withstand attack from above and below. The staircases are also used by single troublemakers, thieves, political fugitives, prostitutes, escaping slaves, hostages. Guards can always be bribed, or favor their multitudinous relations, or join the enemy for one reason or another. Patel, being on the Top Deck, has only four weak points to watch for, rather than eight.

Vazifdar was amazingly holy and amazingly influential. It was whispered that his life-object was the most intricate in all Environment, but there was nobody who would lay claim to having set eyes upon it. Because of his reputation, many people on Gita's deck—yes, and from farther away—sought Vazifdar's help. A stream of men and women moved always through his room, even when he was locked in private meditation and far away from this world.

The holy man had a flat with a balcony that looked out onto mid-deck. Many relations and disciples lived there with him, so that the rooms had been elaborately and flimsily divided by screens. All day, the youngest disciples twittered like birds upon the balconies as Vazifdar held court, discussing among themselves the immense wisdom of his sayings.

All the disciples, all the relations, loved Vazifdar. There had been relations who did not love Vazifdar, but they had passed away in their sleep. Gita himself was a distant relation of Vazifdar's and came into the holy man's presence now with gifts of fresh water and a long piece of synthetic cloth, enough to make a robe.

Vazifdar's brow and cheeks were painted with white to denote his high caste. He received the gifts of cloth and water graciously, smiling at Gita in such a way that Gita—and, behind him, Jamsu—took heart.

Vazifdar was thirteen years old as the outside measured years. He was sleekly fat, from eating much and moving little. His brown body shone with oils; every morning, young women massaged and manipulated him.

He spoke very softly, husbanding his voice, so that he could scarcely be heard for the noise in the room.

"It is a sorrow to me that this woe has befallen your stepchild Malti," he said. "She was a good woman, although infertile."

"She was raped at a very early age, disrupting her womb, dear Vazifdar. You will know of the event. Her parents feared she would die. She could never bear issue. The evil shadowed her life. Now this second woe befalls her."

"I perceive that Malti's role in the world was merely to be a companion to her mother. Not all can afford to purchase who visit the bazaar."

There are bazaars on every floor, crowding down the corridors and balconies, and a chief one on every deck. The menfolk choose such places to meet and chatter even when they have nothing to trade. Like everywhere else, the bazaars are crowded with humanity, down to the smallest who can walk—and sometimes even those carry naked smaller brothers clamped tight to their backs.

The bazaars are great centers for scandal. Here also are our largest screens. They glow behind their safety grills, beaming in

*special programs from outside; our outside world that must seem to
have but faint reality as it dashes against the thick securing walls of
Environment and percolates through to the screens. Below the
screens, uncheckable and fecund life goes teeming on, with all its
injury.*

Humbly, Gita on his knees said, "If you could restore Malti to
her mother Shamim, who mourns her, you would reap all our gratitude, dear Vazifdar. Malti is too old for a man's bed, and on Top
Deck all sorts of humiliations must await her."

Vazifdar shook his head with great dignity. "You know I cannot
restore Malti, my kinsman. How many deeds can be ever undone?
As long as we have slavery, so long must we bear to have the ones
we love enslaved. You must cultivate a mystical and resigned view of
life and beseech Shamim always to do the same."

"Shamim is more mystical in her ways than I, never asking
much, always working, working, praying, praying. That is why she
deserves better than this misery."

Nodding in approval of Shamim's behavior as thus revealed,
Vazifdar said, "That is well. I know she is a good woman. In the
future lie other events which may recompense her for this sad event."

Jamsu, who had managed to keep quiet behind his father until
now, suddenly burst out, "Uncle Vazifdar, can you not punish Narayan Farhad for his sin in stealing poor Malti on the steps? Is he to be
allowed to escape to Patel's deck, there to live with Malti and enjoy?"

"Sssh, son!" Gita looked in agitation to see if Jamsu's outburst
had annoyed Vazifdar; but Vazifdar was smiling blandly.

"You must know, Jamsu, that we are all creatures of the Lord
Siva, and without power. No, no, do not pout! I also am without
power in his hands. To own one room is not to possess the whole
mansion. But . . ."

It was a long, and heavy *but*. When Vazifdar's thick eyelids
closed over his eyes, Gita trembled, for he recalled how, on previous
occasions when he had visited his powerful kinsman, Vazifdar's eyelids had descended in this fashion while he deigned to think on a
problem, as if he shut out all the external world with his own potent
flesh.

"Narayan Farhad shall be troubled by more than his con-
science." As he spoke, the pupils of his eyes appeared again, violet
and black. They were looking beyond Gita, beyond the confines of
his immediate surroundings. "Tonight he shall be troubled by evil
dreams."

"The night-visions!" Gita and Jamsu exclaimed, in fear and
excitement.

Now Vazifdar swiveled his magnificient head and looked directly at Gita, looked deep into his eyes. Gita was a small man; he saw himself as a small man within. He shrank still further under that irresistible scrutiny.

"Yes, the night-visions," the holy man said. "You know what that entails, Gita. You must go up to Top Deck and procure Narayan's life-object. Bring it back to me, and I promise Narayan shall suffer the night-visions tonight. Though he is sick, he shall be cured."

III

The women never cease their chatter as the lines of supplicants come and go before the holy men. Their marvelous resignation in that hateful prison! If they ever complain about more than the small circumstances of their lives, if they ever complain about the monstrous evil that has overtaken them all, I never heard of it. There is always the harmless talk, talk that relieves petty nervous anxieties, talk that relieves the almost noticed pressures on the brain. The women's talk practically drowns the noise of their children. But most of the time it is clear that Total Environment consists mainly of children. That's why I want to see the experiment closed down; the children would adapt to our world.

It is mainly on this fourth generation that the effects of the population glut show. Whoever rules the decks, it is the babes, the endless babes, tottering, laughing, staring, piddling, tumbling, running, the endless babes to whom the Environment really belongs. And their mothers, for the most part, are women who—at the same age and in a more favored part of the globe—would still be virginally at school, many only just entering their teens.

Narayan Farhad wrapped a blanket round himself and huddled in his corner of the crowded room. Since it was almost time to sleep, he had to take up his hired space before one of the loathed Dasguptas stole it. Narayan hated the Dasgupta family, its lickspittle men, its shrill women, its turbulent children—the endless babes who crawled, the bigger ones with nervous diseases who thieved and ran and jeered at him. It was the vilest family on Top Deck, according to Narayan's oft-repeated claims; he tolerated it only because he felt himself to be vile.

He succeeded at nothing to which he turned his hand. Only an hour ago, pushing through the crowds, he had lost his life-object from his pocket—or else it had been stolen; but he dared not even consider that possibility!

Even his desultory kidnapping business was a failure. This bitch he had caught this morning—Malti. He had intended to rape her before selling her, but had become too nervous once he had dragged her in here, with a pair of young Dasguptas laughing at him. Nor had he sold the woman well. Patel had beaten down his price, and Narayan had not the guts to argue. Maybe he should leave this deck and move down to one of the more chaotic ones. The middle decks were always more chaotic. Six was having a slow three-sided war even now, which should make Five a fruitful place, with hordes of refugees to batten on.

. . . And what a fool to snatch so old a girl—practically an old woman!

Through narrowed eyes, Narayan squatted in his corner, acid flavors burning his mouth. Even if his mind would rest and allow him to sleep, the Dasgupta mob was still too lively for any real relaxation. That old Dasgupta, now—he was like a rat, totally without self-restraint, not a proper Hindu at all, doing the act openly with his own daughters. There were many men like that in Total Environment, men who had nothing else in life. Dirty swine! Lucky dogs! Narayan's daughters had thrown him out many months ago when he tried it!

Over and over, his mind ran on his grievances. But he sat collectedly, prodding off with one bare foot the nasty little brats who crawled at him, and staring at the screen flickering on the wall behind its protective mesh.

He liked the screens, enjoyed viewing the madness of outside. What a world it was out there! All that heat, and the necessity for work, and the complication of life! The sheer bigness of the world—he couldn't stand that, would not want it under any circumstances.

He did not understand half he saw. After all, he was born here. His father might have been born outside, whoever his father was; but no legends from outside had come down to him: only the distortions in the general gossip, and the stuff on the screens. Now that he came to reflect, people didn't pay much attention to the screens any more. Even he didn't.

But he could not sleep. Blearily, he looked at images of cattle ploughing fields, fields cut into dice by the dirty grills before the screens. He had already gathered vaguely that this feature was about changes in the world today.

". . . are giving way to this . . ." said the commentator above the rumpus in the Dasgupta room. The children lived here like birds. Racks were stacked against the walls, and on these rickety contraptions the many little Dasguptas roosted.

". . . food factories automated against danger of infection . . ."
Yak yak yak, then.

"Beef-tissue culture growing straight into plastic distribution packs . . ." Shots of some great interior place somewhere, with meat growing out of pipes, extruding itself into square packs, dripping with liquid, looking rather ugly. Was that the shape of cows now or something? Outside must be a hell of a scaring place, then! ". . . as new factory food at last spells hope for India's future in the . . ." Yak yak yak from the kids. Once, their sleep racks had been built across the screen; but one night the whole shaky edifice collapsed, and three children were injured. None killed, worse luck!

Patel should have paid more for that girl. Nothing was as good as it had been. Why, once on a time, they used to show sex films on the screens—really filthy stuff that got even Narayan excited. He was younger then. Really filthy stuff, he remembered, and pretty girls doing it. But it must be—oh, a long time since that was stopped. The screens were dull now. People gave up watching. Uneasily, Narayan slept, propped in the corner under his scruffy blanket. Eventually, the whole scruffy room slept.

The documentaries and other features piped into Environment are no longer specially made by UHDRE teams for internal consumption. When the U.N. made a major cut in UHDRE's annual subsidy, eight years ago, the private TV studio was one of the frills that had to be axed. Now we pipe in old programs bought off major networks. The hope is that they will keep the wretched prisoners in Environment in touch with the outside world, but this is clearly not happening. The degree of comprehension between inside and outside grows markedly less on both sides, on an exponential curve. As I see it, a great gulf of isolation is widening between the two environments, just as if they were sailing away from each other into different space-time continua. I wish I could think that the people in charge here—Crawley especially—not only grasped this fact but understood that it should be rectified immediately.

Shamim could not sleep for grief.
Gita could not sleep for apprehension.
Jamsu could not sleep for excitement.
Vazifdar did not sleep.

Vazifdar shut his sacred self away in a cupboard, brought his lids down over his eyes and began to construct, within the vast spaces of his mind, a thought pattern corresponding to the matrix represented by Narayan Farhad's stolen life-object. When it was fully conceived, Vazifdar began gently to inset a little evil into one edge of the thought-pattern. . . .

Narayan slept. What roused him was the silence. It was the first time total silence had ever come to Total Environment.

At first, he thought he would enjoy total silence. But it took on such weight and substance. . . .

Clutching his blanket, he sat up. The room was empty, the screen dark. Neither thing had ever happened before, could not happen! And the silence! Dear Siva, some terrible monkey god had hammered that silence out in darkness and thrown it out like a shield into the world, rolling over all things! There was a ringing quality in the silence—a gong! No, no, not a gong! Footsteps!

It was footsteps, O Lord Siva, do not let it be footsteps!

Total Environment was empty. The legend was fulfilled that said Total Environment would empty one day. All had departed except for poor Narayan. And this thing of the footsteps was coming to visit him in his defenseless corner. . . .

It was climbing up through the cellars of his existence. Soon it would emerge.

Trembling convulsively, Narayan stood up, clutching the corner of the blanket to his throat. He did not wish to face the thing. Wildly, he thought, could he bear it best if it looked like a man or if it looked nothing like a man? It was Death for sure—but how would it look? Only Death—his heart fluttered!—only Death could arrive this way. . . .

His helplessness . . . . Nowhere to hide! He opened his mouth, could not scream, clutched the blanket, felt that he was wetting himself as if he were a child again. Swiftly came the image—the infantile, round-bellied, cringing, puny, his mother black with fury, her great white teeth gritting as she smacked his face with all her might, spitting. . . . It was gone, and he faced the gong—like death again, alone in the great dark tower. In the arid air, vibrations of its presence.

He was shouting to it, demanding that it did not come.

But it came. It came with majestic sloth, like the heartbeats of a foetid slumber, came in the door, pushing darkness before it. It was like a human, but too big to be human.

And it wore Malti's face, that sickeningly innocent smile with which she had run up the steps. No! No, that was not it—oh, he fell down onto the wet floor: it was nothing like that woman, nothing at all. Cease, impossibilities! It was a man, his ebony skull shining, terrible and magnificent, stretching out, grasping, confident. Narayan struck out of his extremity and fell forward. Death was another indelible smack in the face.

One of the roosting Dasguptas blubbered and moaned as the man kicked him, woke for a moment, saw the screen still flickering meaninglessly and reassuringly, saw Narayan tremble under his blanket, tumbled back into sleep.

It was not till morning that they found it had been Narayan's last tremble.

I know I am supposed to be a detached observer. No emotions, no feelings. But scientific detachment is the attitude that has led to much of the inhumanity inherent in Environment. How do we, for all the bugging devices, hope to know what ghastly secret nightmares they undergo in there? Anyhow, I am relieved to hear you are flying over.

It is tomorrow I am due to go into Environment myself.

IV

The central offices of UHDRE were large and repulsive. At the time when they and the Total Environment tower had been built, the Indian Government would not have stood for anything else. Poured cement and rough edges was what they wanted to see and what they got.

From a window in the office building, Thomas Dixit could see the indeterminate land in one direction, and the gigantic TE tower in the other, together with the shantytown that had grown between the foot of the tower and the other UHDRE buildings.

For a moment, he chose to ignore the Project Organizer behind him and gaze out at what he could see of the table-flat lands of the great Ganges delta.

He thought, It's as good a place as any for man to project his power fantasies. But you are a fool to get mixed up in all this, Thomas!

Even to himself, he was never just Tom.

I am being paid, well paid to do a specific job. Now I am letting wooly humanitarian ideas get in the way of action. Essentially, I am a very empty man. No center. Father Bengali, mother English, and live all my life in the States. I have excuses . . . Other people accept them; why can't I?

Sighing, he dwelt on his own unsatisfactoriness. He did not really belong to the West, despite his long years there, and he certainly did not belong to India; in fact, he thought he rather disliked India. Maybe the best place for him was indeed the inside of the Environment tower.

He turned impatiently and said, "I'm ready to get going now, Peter."

Peter Crawley, the Special Project Organizer of UHDRE, was a rather austere Bostonian. He removed the horn-rimmed glasses from his nose and said, "Right! Although we have been through the drill many times, Thomas, I have to tell you this once again before we move. The entire—"

"Yes, yes, I know, Peter! You don't have to cover yourself. This entire organization might be closed down if I make a wrong move. Please take it as read."

Without indignation, Crawley said, "I was going to say that we are all rooting for you. We appreciate the risks you are taking. We shall be checking you everywhere you go in there through the bugging system."

"And whatever you see, you can't do a thing."

"Be fair; we have made arrangements to help!"

"I'm sorry, Peter." He liked Crawley and Crawley's decent reserve.

Crawley folded his spectacles with a snap, inserted them in a leather slipcase and stood up.

"The U.N., not to mention subsidiary organizations like the WHO and the Indian government, have their knife into us, Thomas. They want to close us down and empty Environment. They will do so unless you can provide evidence that forms of extra-sensory perception are developing inside the Environment. Don't get yourself killed in there. The previous men we sent in behaved foolishly and never came out again." He raised an eyebrow and added dryly, "That sort of thing gets us a bad name, you know."

"Just as the blue movies did a while ago."

Crawley put his hands behind his back. "My predecessor here decided that immoral movies piped into Environment would help boost the birth rate there. Whether he was right or wrong, world opinion has changed since then as the specter of world famine has faded. We stopped the movies eight years ago, but they have long memories at the U.N., I fear. They allow emotionalism to impede scientific research."

"Do you never feel any sympathy for the thousands of people doomed to live out their brief lives in the tower?"

They looked speculatively at each other.

"You aren't on our side any more, Thomas, are you? You'd like your findings to be negative, wouldn't you, and have the U.N. close us down?"

Dixit uttered a laugh. "I'm not on anyone's *side*, Peter. I'm neutral. I'm going into Environment to look for the evidence of ESP that only direct contact may turn up. What else direct contact will turn up, neither of us can say as yet."

"But you think it will be misery. And you will emphasize that at the inquiry after your return."

"Peter—let's get on with it, shall we?" Momentarily, Dixit was granted a clear picture of the two of them standing in this room; he saw how their bodily attitudes contrasted. His attitudes were rather slovenly; he held himself rather slump-shouldered, he gesticulated to some extent (too much?); he was dressed in threadbare tunic and shorts, ready to pass muster as an inhabitant of Environment. Crawley, on the other hand, was very upright, stiff and smart in his movements, hardly ever gestured as he spoke; his dress was faultless.

And there was no need to be awed by or envious of Crawley. Crawley was encased in inhibition, afraid to feel, signaling his aridity to anyone who cared to look out from their own self-preoccupation. Crawley, moreover, feared for his job.

"Let's get on with it, as you say." He came from behind his desk. "But I'd be grateful if you would remember, Thomas, that the people in the tower are volunteers, or the descendants of volunteers.

"When UHDRE began, a quarter-century ago, back in the mid-nineteen-seventies, only volunteers were admitted to the Total Environment. Five hundred young married Indian couples were admitted, plus whatever children they had. The tower was a refuge then, free from famine, immune from all disease. They were glad, heartily glad, to get in, glad of all that Environment provided and still provides. Those who didn't qualify rioted. We have to remember that.

"India was a different place in 1975. It had lost hope. One crisis after another, one famine after another, crops dying, people starving, and yet the population spiraling up by a million every month.

"But today, thank God, that picture has largely changed. Synthetic foods have licked the problem; we don't need the grudging land any more. And at last the Hindus and Muslims have got the birth control idea into their heads. It's only *now*, when a little humanity is seeping back into this death-bowl of a subcontinent, that the UN dares complain about the inhumanity of UHDRE."

Dixit said nothing. He felt that this potted history was simply angled towards Crawley's self-justification; the ideas it represented were real enough, heaven knew, but they had meaning for Crawley only in terms of his own existence. Dixit felt pity and impatience as Crawley went on with his narration.

"Our aim here must be unswervingly the same as it was from the start. We have evidence that nervous disorders of a special kind produce extra-sensory perceptions—telepathy and the rest, and maybe kinds of ESP we do not yet recognize. High-density populations with reasonable nutritional standards develop particular nervous instabilities which may be akin to ESP spectra.

"The Ultra-High Density Research Establishment was set up to intensify the likelihood of ESP developing. Don't forget that. The people in Environment are supposed to have some ESP; that's the whole point of the operation, right? Sure, it is not humanitarian. We know that. But that is not your concern. You have to go in and find evidence of ESP, something that doesn't show over the bugging. Then UHDRE will be able to continue."

Dixit prepared to leave. "If it hasn't shown up in quarter of a century—"

"It's in there! I know it's in there! The failure's in the bugging system. I feel it coming through the screens at me—some mystery we need to get our hands on! If only I could prove it! If only I could get in there myself!"

Interesting, Dixit thought. You'd have to be some sort of a voyeur to hold Crawley's job, forever spying on the wretched people.

"Too bad you have a white skin, eh?" he said lightly. He walked towards the door. It swung open, and he passed into the corridor.

Crawley ran after him and thrust out a hand. "I know how you feel, Thomas. I'm not just a stuffed shirt, you know, not entirely void of sympathy. Sorry if I was needling you. I didn't intend to do so."

Dixit dropped his gaze. "I should be the one to apologize, Peter. If there's anything unusual going on in the tower, I'll find it, never worry!"

They shook hands, without wholly being able to meet each other's eyes.

V

Leaving the office block, Dixit walked alone through the sunshine toward the looming tower that housed Total Environment. The concrete walk was hot and dusty underfoot. The sun was the one good thing that India had, he thought: that burning beautiful sun, the real ruler of India, whatever petty tyrants came and went.

The sun blazed down on the tower; only inside did it not shine.

The uncompromising outlines of the tower were blurred by pipes, ducts and shafts that ran up and down its exterior. It was a building built for looking into, not out of. Some time ago, in the bad years, the welter of visual records gleaned from Environment used to be edited and beamed out on global networks every evening; but all that had been stopped as conditions inside Environment deteriorated, and public opinion in the democracies, who were subsidizing the grandiose experiment, turned against the exploitation of human material.

A monitoring station stood by the tower walls. From here, a constant survey on the interior was kept. Facing the station where the jumbles of merchants' stalls, springing up to cater for tourists, who persisted even now that the tourist trade was discouraged. Two security guards stepped forward and escorted Dixit to the base of the tower. With ceremony, he entered the shade of the entry elevator. As he closed the door, germicides sprayed him, insuring that he entered Environment without harboring dangerous micro-organisms.

The elevator carried him up to the top deck; this plan had been settled some while ago. The elevator was equipped with double steel doors. As it came to rest, a circuit opened, and a screen showed him what was happening on the other side of the doors. He emerged from a dummy air-conditioning unit, behind a wide pillar. He was in Patel's domain.

The awful weight of human overcrowding hit Dixit with its full stink and noise. He sat down at the base of the pillar and let his senses adjust. And he thought, I was the wrong one to send; I've always had this inner core of pity for the sufferings of humanity; I could never be impartial; I've got to see that this terrible experiment is stopped.

He was at one end of a long balcony onto which many doors opened; a ramp led down at the other end. All the doorways gaped, although some were covered by rugs. Most of the doors had been taken off their hinges to serve as partitions along the balcony itself, partitioning off overspill families. Children ran everywhere, their tinkling voices and cries the dominant note in the hubbub. Glancing over the balcony, Dixit took in a dreadful scene of swarming multitudes, the anonymity of congestion; to sorrow for humanity was not to love its prodigality. Dixit had seen this panorama many times over the bugging system; he knew all the staggering figures—1500 people in here to begin with, and by now some 75,000 people, a large proportion of them under four years of age. But pictures and figures were pale abstracts beside the reality they were intended to represent.

The kids drove him into action at last by playfully hurling dirt at him. Dixit moved slowly along, carrying himself tight and cringing in the manner of the crowd about him, features rigid, elbows tucked in to the ribs. *Mutatis mutandis*, it was Crawley's inhibited attitude. Even the children ran between the legs of their elders in that guarded way. As soon as he had left the shelter of his pillar, he was caught in a stream of chattering people, all jostling between the rooms and the stalls of the balcony. They moved very slowly.

Among the crowd were hawkers, and salesmen pressed their wares from the pitiful balcony hovels. Dixit tried to conceal his curiosity. Over the bugging he had had only distant views of the merchandise offered for sale. Here were the strange models that had caught his attention when he was first appointed to the UHDRE project. A man with orange goateyes, in fact probably no more than thirteen years of age, but here a hardened veteran, was at Dixit's elbow. As Dixit stared at him, momentarily suspicious he was being watched, the goat-eyed man merged into the crowd; and, to hide his face, Dixit turned to the nearest salesman.

In only a moment, he was eagerly examining the wares, forgetting how vulnerable was his situation.

All the strange models were extremely small. This Dixit attributed to shortage of materials—wrongly, as it later transpired. The biggest model the salesman possessed stood no more than two inches high. It was made, nevertheless, of a diversity of materials, in which many sorts of plastics featured. Some models were simple, and appeared to be a little more than elaborate *tughra* or monogram, which might have been intended for an elaborate piece of costume jewelry; others, as one peered among their interstices, seemed to afford a glimpse of another dimension; all possessed eye-teasing properties.

The merchant was pressing Dixit to buy. He referred to the elaborate models as "life-objects." Noticing that one in particular attracted his potential customer, he lifted it delicately and held it up, a miracle of craftsmanship, perplexing, *outré*, giving Dixit somehow as much pain as pleasure. He named the price.

Although Dixit was primed with money, he automatically shook his head. "Too expensive."

"See, master, I show you how this life-object works!" The man fished beneath his scrap of loincloth and produced a small perforated silver box. Flipping it open, he produced a live wood-louse and slipped it under a hinged part of the model. The insect, in its struggles, activated a tiny wheel; the interior of the model began to rotate, some sets of minute planes turning in counterpoint to others.

"This life-object belonged to a very religious man, master."

In his fascination, Dixit said, "Are they all powered?"

"No, master, only special ones. This was perfect model from Dalcush Bancholi, last generation master all the way from Third Deck, very very fine and masterful workmanship of first quality. I have also still better one worked by a body louse, if you care to see."

By reflex, Dixit said, "Your prices are too high."

He absolved himself from the argument that brewed, slipping away through the crowd with the merchant calling after him. Other merchants shouted to him, sensing his interest in their wares. He saw some beautiful work, all on the tiniest scale and not only life-objects but amazing little watches with millisecond hands as well as second hands; in some cases, the millisecond was the largest hand; in some, the hour hand was missing or was supplemented by a day hand; and the watches took many extraordinary shapes, tetrakishexahedrons and other elaborate forms, until their format merged with that of the life-objects.

Dixit thought approvingly: the clock and watch industry fulfills a human need for exercising elaborate skill and accuracy, while at the same time requiring a minimum of materials. These people of Total Environment are the world's greatest craftsmen. Bent over one curious watch that involved a color change, he became suddenly aware of danger. Glancing over his shoulder, he saw the man with the unpleasant orange eyes about to strike him. Dixit dodged without being able to avoid the blow. As it caught him on the side of his neck, he stumbled and fell under the milling feet.

VI

Afterwards, Dixit could hardly say that he had been totally unconscious. He was aware of hands dragging him, of being partly carried, of the sound of many voices, of the name "Patel" repeated. . . . And when he came fully to his senses, he was lying in a cramped room, with a guard in a scruffy turban standing by the door. His first hazy thought was that the room was no more than a small ship's cabin; then he realized that, by indigenous standards, this was a large room for only one person.

He was a prisoner in Total Environment.

A kind of self-mocking fear entered him; he had almost expected the blow, he realized; and he looked eagerly about for the bug-eye that would reassure him his UHDRE friends outside were aware of his predicament. There was no sign of the bug-eye. He was not long in working out why; this room had been partitioned out of a larger one, and the bugging system was evidently shut in the other half— whether deliberately or accidentally, he had no way of knowing.

The guard had bobbed out of sight. Sounds of whispering came from beyond the doorway. Dixit felt the pressure of many people there. Then a woman came in and closed the door. She walked cringingly and carried a brass cup of water.

Although her face was lined, it was possible to see that she had once been beautiful and perhaps proud. Now her whole attitude expressed the defeat of her life. And this woman might be no more than eighteen! One of the terrifying features of Environment was the way, right from the start, confinement had speeded life-processes and abridged life.

Involuntarily, Dixit flinched away from the woman.

She almost smiled. "Do not fear me, sir. I am almost as much a prisoner as you are. Equally, do not think that by knocking me down you can escape. I promise you, there are fifty people outside the door, all eager to impress Prahlad Patel by catching you, should you try to get away."

So I'm in Patel's clutches, he thought. Aloud he said, "I will offer you no harm. I want to see Patel. If you are captive, tell we your name, and perhaps I can help you."

As she offered him the cup and he drank, she said, shyly, "I do not complain, for my fate might have been much worse than it is. Please do not agitate Patel about me, or he may throw me out of his household. My name is Malti."

"Perhaps I may be able to help you, and all your tribe, soon. You are all in a form of captivity here, the great Patel included, and it is from that I hope to deliver you."

Then he saw fear in her eyes.

"You really are a spy from outside!" she breathed. "But we do not want our poor little world invaded! You have so much—leave us our little!" She shrank away and slipped through the door, leaving Dixit with a melancholy impression of her eyes, so burdened in their shrunken gaze.

The babel continued outside the door. Although he still felt sick, he propped himself up and let his thoughts run on. "You have so much—leave us our little. . . ." All their values had been perverted. Poor things, they could know neither the smallness of their own world nor the magnitude of the world outside. This—this dungheap had become to them all there was of beauty and value.

Two guards came for him, mere boys. He could have knocked their heads together, but compassion moved him. They led him through a room full of excited people; beyond their glaring faces, the screen flickered pallidly behind its mesh; Dixit saw how faint the image of outside was.

He was taken into another partitioned room. Two men were talking.

The scene struck Dixit with peculiar force, and not merely because he was at a disadvantage.

It was an alien scene. The impoverishment of even the richest furnishings, the clipped and bastardized variety of Hindi that was being talked, reinforced the impression of strangeness. And the charge of Patels' character filled the room.

There could be no doubt who was Patel. The plump cringing fellow, wringing his hands and protesting, was not Patel. Patel was the stocky white-haired man with the heavy lower lip and high forehead. Dixit had seen him in this very room over the bugging system. But to stand captive awaiting his attention was an experience of an entirely different order. Dixit tried to analyze the first fresh impact Patel had on him, but it was elusive.

It was difficult to realize that, as the outside measured years, Patel could not be much more than nineteen or twenty years of age. Time was impacted here, jellified under the psychic pressures of Total Environment. Like the hieroglyphics of that new relativity, detailed plans of the Environment hung large on one wall of this room, while figures and names were chalked over the others. The room was the nerve center of Top Deck.

He knew something about Patel from the UHDRE records. Patel had come up here from the Seventh Deck. By guile as well as force, he had become ruler of Top Deck at an early age. He had surprised UHDRE observers by abstaining from the usual forays of conquest into other floors.

Patel was saying to the cringing man, "Be silent! You try to obscure the truth with argument. You have heard the witnesses against you. During your period of watch on the stairs, you were bribed by a man from Ninth Deck and you let him through here."

"Only for a mere seventeen minutes, Sir Patel!"

"I am aware that such things happen every day, wretched Raital. But this fellow you let through stole the life-object belonging to Narayan Farhad and, in consequence, Narayan Farhad died in his sleep last night. Narayan was no more important than you are, but he was useful to me, and it is in order that he be revenged."

"Anything that you say, Sir Patel!"

"Be silent, wretched Raital!" Patel watched Raital with interest as he spoke. And he spoke in a firm reflective voice that impressed Dixit more than shouting would have done.

"You shall revenge Narayan, Raital, because you caused his death. You will leave here now. You will not be punished. You will go, and you will steal the life-object belonging to that fellow from whom you accepted the bribe. You will bring that life-object to me. You have one day to do so. Otherwise, my assassins will find you wherever you hide, be it even down on Deck One."

"Oh, yes, indeed, Sir Patel, all men know—" Raital was bent almost double as he uttered some face-saving formula. He turned and scurried away as Patel dismissed him.

Strength, thought Dixit. Strength, and also cunning. That is what Patel radiates. An elaborate and cutting subtlety. The phrase pleased him, seeming to represent something actual that he had detected in Patel's makeup. An elaborate and cutting subtlety.

Clearly, it was part of Patel's design that Dixit should witness this demonstration of his methods.

Patel turned away, folded his arms, and contemplated a blank piece of wall at close range. He stood motionless. The guards held Dixit still, but not so still as Patel held himself.

This tableau was maintained for several minutes. Dixit found himself losing track of the normal passage of time. Patel's habit of turning to stare at the wall—and it did not belong to Patel alone—was an uncanny one that Dixit had watched several times over the bugging system. It was that habit, he thought, which might have given Crawley the notion that ESP was rampant in the tower.

It was curious to think of Crawley here. Although Crawley might at this moment be surveying Dixit's face on a monitor, Crawley was now no more than an hypothesis.

Malti broke the tableau. She entered the room with a damp cloth on a tray, to stand waiting patiently for Patel to notice her. He broke away at last from his motionless survey of the wall, gesturing abruptly to the guards to leave. He took no notice of Dixit, sitting in a chair, letting Malti drape the damp cloth round his neck; the cloth had a fragrant smell to it.

"The towel is not cool enough, Malti, or damp enough. You will attend me properly at my morning session, or you will lose this easy job."

He swung his gaze, which was suddenly black and searching, onto Dixit to say, "Well, spy, you know I am Lord here. Do you wonder why I tolerate old women like this about me when I could have girls young and lovely to fawn on me?"

Dixit said nothing, and the self-styled Lord continued, "Young girls would merely remind me by contrast of my advanced years. But this old bag—whom I bought only yesterday—this old bag is only just my junior and makes me look good in contrast. You see, we are masters of philosophy in here, in this prison-universe; we cannot be masters of material wealth like you people outside!"

Again Dixit said nothing, disgusted by the man's implied attitude to women.

A swinging blow caught him unprepared in the stomach. He cried and dropped suddenly to the floor.

"Get up, spy!" Patel said. He had moved extraordinarily fast. He sat back again in his chair, letting Malti massage his neck muscles.

VII

As Dixit staggered to his feet, Patel said, "You don't deny you are from outside?"

"I did not attempt to deny it. I came from outside to speak to you."

"You say nothing here until you are ordered to speak. Your people—you outsiders—you have sent in several spies to us in the last few months. Why?"

Still feeling sick from the blow, Dixit said, "You should realize that we are your friends rather than your enemies, and our men emissaries rather than spies."

"Pah! You are a breed of spies! Don't you sit and spy on us from every room? You live in a funny little dull world out there, don't you? So interested in us that you can think of nothing else! Keep working, Malti! Little spy, you know what happened to all the other spies your spying people sent in?"

"They died," Dixit said.

"Exactly. They died. But you are the first to be sent to Patel's deck. What different thing to death do you expect here?"

"Another death will make my superiors very tired, Patel. You may have the power of life and death over me; they have the same over you, and over all in this world of yours. Do you want a demonstration?"

Rising, flinging the towel off, Patel said, "Give me your demonstration!"

Must do, Dixit thought. Staring in Patel's eyes, he raised his right hand above his head and gestured with his thumb. Pray they are watching—and thank God this bit of partitioned room is the bit with the bugging system!

Tensely, Patel stared, balanced on his toes. Behind his shoulder, Malti also stared. Nothing happened.

Then a sort of shudder ran through Environment. It became slowly audible as a mixture of groan and cry. Its cause became apparent in this less crowded room when the air began to grow hot and foul. So Dixit's signal had got through; Crawley had him under survey, and the air-conditioning plant was pumping in hot carbon-dioxide through the respiratory system.

"You see? We control the very air you breathe!" Dixit said. He dropped his arm, and slowly the air returned to normal, although it was at least an hour before the fright died down in the passages.

Whatever the demonstration had done to Patel, he showed nothing. Instead, he said, "You control the air. Very well. But you do not control the will to turn it off permanently—and so you do not control the air. Your threat is an empty one, spy! For some reason, you need us to live. We have a mystery, don't we?"

"There is no reason why I should be anything but honest with you, Patel. Your special environment must have bred special talents in you. We are interested in those talents; but no more than interested."

Patel came closer and inspected Dixit's face minutely, rather as he had recently inspected the blank wall. Strange angers churned inside him; his neck and throat turned a dark mottled color. Finally he spoke.

"We are the center of your outside world, aren't we? We know that you watch us all the time. We know that you are much more than 'interested'! For you, we here are somehow a matter of life and death, aren't we?"

This was more than Dixit had expected.

"Four generations, Patel, four generations have been incarcerated in Environment." His voice trembled. "Four generations, and, despite our best intentions, you are losing touch with reality. You live in one relatively small building on a sizeable planet. Clearly, you can only be of limited interest to the world at large."

"Malti!" Patel turned to the slave girl. "Which is the greater, the outer world or ours?"

She looked confused, hesitated by the door as if longing to escape. "The outside world was great, master, but then it gave birth to us, and we have grown and are growing and are gaining strength. The child now is almost the size of the father. So my step-father's son Jamsu says, and he is a clever one."

Patel turned to stare at Dixit, a haughty expression on his face. He made no comment, as if the words of an ignorant girl were sufficient to prove his point.

"All that you and the girl say only emphasizes to me how much you need help, Patel. The world outside is a great and thriving place; you must allow it to give you assistance through me. We are not your enemies."

Again the choleric anger was there, powering Patel's every word.

"What else are you, spy? Your life is so vile and pointless out there, is it not? You envy us because we are superseding you! Our people—we may be poor, you may think of us as in your power, but we rule our own universe. And that universe is expanding and falling under our control more every day. Why, our explorers have gone into the world of the ultrasmall. We discover new environments, new ways of living. By your terms, we are scientific peasants, perhaps, but I fancy we have ways of knowing the trade routes of the blood and the eternities of cell-change that you cannot comprehend. You think of us all as captives, eh? Yet you are captive to the necessity of supplying our air and our food and water; we are free. We are poor, yet you covet our riches. We are spied on all the time, yet we are secret. You need to understand us, yet we have no need to understand you. You are in *our* power, spy!"

"Certainly not in one vital respect, Patel. Both you and we are ruled by historical necessity. This Environment was set up twenty-five of our years ago. Changes have taken place not only in here but outside as well. The nations of the world are no longer prepared to finance this project. It is going to be closed down entirely, and you are going to have to live outside. Or, if you don't want that, you'd better cooperate with us and persuade the leaders of the other decks to cooperate."

Would threats work with Patel? His hooded and oblique gaze bit into Dixit like a hook.

After a deadly pause, he clapped his hands once. Two guards immediately appeared.

"Take the spy away," said Patel. Then he turned his back.

A clever man, Dixit thought. He sat alone in the cell and meditated.

It seemed as if a battle of wits might develop between him and Patel. Well, he was prepared. He trusted to his first impression, that Patel was a man of cutting subtlety. He could not be taken to mean all that he said.

Dixit's mind worked back over their conversation. The mystery of the life-objects had been dangled before him. And Patel had taken care to belittle the outside world: "funny dull little world," he had called it. He had made Malti advance her primitive view that Environment was growing, and that had fitted in very well with his brand of boasting. Which led to the deduction that he had known her views beforehand; yet he had bought her only yesterday. Why should a busy man, a leader, bother to question an ignorant slave about her views of the outside world unless he were starved for information of that world, obsessed with it.

Yes, Dixit nodded to himself. Patel was obsessed with outside and tried to hide that obsession; but several small contradictions in his talk had revealed it.

Of course, it might be that Malti was so generally representative of the thousands in Environment that her misinformed ideas could be taken for granted. It was as well, as yet, not to be too certain that he was beginning to understand Patel.

Part of Patel's speech made sense even superficially. These poor devils were exploring the world of the ultra-small. It was the only landscape left for them to map. They were human, and still burning inside them was that unquenchable human urge to open frontiers.

So they knew some inward things. Quite possibly, as Crawley anticipated, they possessed a system of ESP upon which some reliance might be placed, unlike the wildly fluctuating telepathic radiations which circulated in the outside world.

He felt confident, fully engaged. There was much to understand here. The bugging system, elaborate and over-used, was shown to be a complete failure; the watchers had stayed external to their problem; it remained their problem, not their life. What was needed was a whole team to come and live here, perhaps a team on every deck, anthropologists and so on. Since that was impossible, then clearly the people of Environment must be released from their captivity; those that were unwilling to go far afield should be settled in new villages on the Ganges plain, under the wide sky. And there, as they adapted to the real world, observers could live among them, learning with humility of the gifts that had been acquired at such cost within the thick walls of the Total Environment tower.

As Dixit sat in meditation, a guard brought a meal in to him.

He ate thankfully and renewed his thinking.

From the little he had already experienced—the ghastly pressures on living space, the slavery, the aberrant modes of thought into which the people were being forced, the harshness of the petty rulers —he was confirmed in his view that this experiment in anything like its present form must be closed down at once. The U.N. needed the excuse of his adverse report before they moved; they should have it when he got out. And if he worded the report carefully, stressing that these people had many talents to offer, then he might also satisfy Crawley and his like. He had it in his power to satisfy all parties, when he got out. All he had to do was get out.

The guard came back to collect his empty bowl.

"When is Patel going to speak with me again?"

The guard said, "When he sends for you to have you silenced for ever."

Dixit stopped composing his report and thought about that instead.

VIII

Much time elapsed before Dixit was visited again, and then it was only the self-effacing Malti who appeared, bringing him a cup of water.

"I want to talk to you," Dixit said urgently.

"No, no, I cannot talk! He will beat me. It is the time when we sleep, when the old die. You should sleep now, and Patel will see you in the morning."

He tried to touch her hand, but she withdrew.

"You are a kind girl, Malti. You suffer in Patel's household."

"He has many women, many servants. I am not alone."

"Can you not escape back to your family?"

She looked at the floor evasively. "It would bring trouble to my family. Slavery is the lot of many women. It is the way of the world."

"It is not the way of the world I come from!"

Her eyes flashed. "Your world is of no interest to us!"

Dixit thought after she had gone, She is afraid of our world. Rightly.

He slept little during the night. Even barricaded inside Patel's fortress, he could still hear the noises of Environment: not only the voices, almost never silent, but the gurgle and sob of pipes in the walls. In the morning, he was taken into a larger room where Patel was issuing commands for the day to a succession of subordinates.

Confined to a corner, Dixit followed everything with interest. His interest grew when the unfortunate guard Raital appeared. He bounded in and waited for Patel to strike him. Instead, Patel kicked him.

"You have performed as I ordered yesterday?"

Raital began at once to cry and wring his hands. "Sir Patel, I have performed as well as and better than you demanded, incurring great suffering and having myself beaten downstairs where the people of Ninth Deck discovered me marauding. You must invade them, Sir, and teach them a lesson that in their insolence they so dare to mock your faithful guards who only do those things—"

"Silence, you dog-devourer! Do you bring back that item which I demanded of you yesterday?"

The wretched guard brought from the pocket of his tattered tunic a small object, which he held out to Patel.

"Of course I obey, Sir Patel. To keep this object safe when the people caught me, I swallow it whole, sir, into the stomach for safe keeping, so that they would not know what I am about. Then my wife gives me sharp medicine so that I vomit it safely again to deliver to you."

"Put the filthy thing down on that shelf there! You think I wish to touch it when it has been in your worm-infested belly, slave?"

The guard did as he was bid and abased himself.

"You are sure it is the life-object of the man who stole Narayan Farhad's life-object, and nobody else's?"

"Oh, indeed, Sir Patel! It belongs to a man called Gita, the very

very same who stole Narayan's life object, and tonight you will see
he will die of night-visions!"

"Get out!" Patel managed to catch Raital's buttocks with a swift
kick as the guard scampered from the room.

A queue of people stood waiting to speak with him, to supplicate
and advise. Patel sat and interviewed them, in the main showing a
better humor than he had shown his luckless guard. For Dixit, this
scene had a curious interest; he had watched Patel's morning audience
more than once, standing by Crawley's side in the UHDRE monitoring station; now he was a prisoner waiting uncomfortably in the
corner of the room, and the whole atmosphere was changed. He felt
the extraordinary intensity of these people's lives, the emotions compressed, everything vivid. Patel himself wept several times as some
tale of hardship was unfolded to him. There was no privacy. Everyone stood round him, listening to everything. Short the lives might
be; but those annihilating spaces that stretch through ordinary lives,
the spaces through which one glimpses uncomfortable glooms and
larger poverties, if not presences more sour and sinister, seemed here
to have been eradicated. The Total Environment had brought its
peoples total involvement. Whatever befell them, they were united,
as were bees in a hive.

Finally, a break was called. The unfortunates who had not
gained Patel's ear were turned away; Malti was summoned and ad-
ministered the damp-towel treatment to Patel. Later, he sent her off
and ate a frugal meal. Only when he had finished it and sat momentarily in meditation, did he turn his brooding attention to Dixit.

He indicated that Dixit was to fetch down the object Raital had
placed on a shelf. Dixit did so and put the object before Patel.
Staring at it with interest, he saw it was an elaborate little model,
similar to the ones for sale on the balcony.

"Observe it well," Patel said. "It is the life-object of a man. You
have these"—he gestured vaguely—"outside?"

"No."

"You know what they are?"

"No."

"In this world of ours, Mr. Dixit, we have many holy men. I
have a holy man here under my protection. On the deck below is one
very famous holy man, Vazifdariji. These men have many powers.
Tonight, I shall give my holy man this life-object, and with it he
will be able to enter the being of the man to whom it belongs, for
good or ill, and in this case for ill, to revenge a death with a death."

Dixit stared at the little object, a three-dimensional maze constructed of silver and plastic strands, trying to comprehend what Patel was saying.

"This is a sort of key to its owner's mind?"

"No, no, not a key, and not to his mind. It is a—well, we do not have a scientific word for it, and our word would mean nothing to you, so I cannot say what. It is, let us say, a replica, a substitute for the man's being. Not his mind, his being. In this case, a man called Gita. You are very interested, aren't you?"

"Everyone here has one of these?"

"Down to the very poorest and even the older children. A sage works in conjunction with a smith to produce each individual life-object."

"But they can be stolen and then an ill-intentioned holy man can use them to kill the owner. So why make them? I don't understand."

Smiling, Patel made a small movement of impatience. "What you discover of yourself, you record. That is how these things are made. They are not trinkets; they are a man's record of his discovery of himself."

Dixit shook his head. "If they are so personal, why are so many sold by street traders as trinkets?"

"Men die. Then their life-objects have no value, except as trinkets. They are also popularly believed to bestow . . . well, personality-value. There also exist large numbers of forgeries, which people buy because they like to have them, simply as decorations."

After a moment, Dixit said, "So they are innocent things, but you take them and use them for evil ends."

"I use them to keep a power balance. A man of mine called Narayan was silenced by Gita of Ninth Deck. Never mind why. So tonight I silence Gita to keep the balance."

He stopped and looked closely at Dixit, so that the latter received a blast of that enigmatic personality. He opened his hand and said, still observing Dixit, "Death sits in my palm, Mr. Dixit. To-night I shall have you silenced also, by what you may consider more ordinary methods."

Clenching his hands tightly together, Dixit said, "You tell me about the life-objects, and yet you claim you are going to kill me."

Patel pointed up to one corner of his room. "There are eyes and ears there, while your ever-hungry spying friends suck up the facts of this world. You see, I can tell them—I can tell them so much and they can never comprehend our life. All the important things can never be said, so they can never learn. But they can see you die to-night, and that they will comprehend. Perhaps then they will cease to send spies in here."

He clapped his hands once for the guards. They came forward and led Dixit away. As he went back to his cell, he heard Patel shouting for Malti.

IX

The hours passed in steady gloom. The U.N., the UHDRE, would not rescue him; the Environment charter permitted intervention by only one outsider at a time. Dixit could hear, feel, the vast throbbing life of the place going on about him and was shaken by it.

He tried to think about the life-objects. Presumably Crawley had overheard the last conversation, and would know that the holy men, as Patel called them, had the power to kill at a distance. There was the ESP evidence Crawley sought: telecide, or whatever you called it. And the knowledge helped nobody, as Patel himself observed. It had long been known that African witch doctors possessed similar talents, to lay a spell on a man and kill him at a distance; but how they did it had never been established; nor, indeed, had the fact ever been properly assimilated by the West, eager though the West was for new methods of killing. There were things one civilization could not learn from another; the whole business of life-objects, Dixit perceived, was going to be such a matter: endlessly fascinating, entirely insoluble. . . .

He thought, returning to his cell, and told himself: Patel still puzzles me. But it is no use hanging about here being puzzled. Here I sit, waiting for a knife in the guts. It must be night now. I've got to get out of here.

There was no way out of the room. He paced restlessly up and down. They brought him no meal, which was ominous.

A long while later, the door was unlocked and opened.

It was Malti. She lifted one finger as a caution to silence, and closed the door behind her.

"It's time for me . . . ?" Dixit asked.

She came quickly over to him, not touching him, staring at him.

Though she was an ugly despondent woman, beauty lay in her time-haunted eyes.

"I can help you escape, Dixit. Patel sleeps now, and I have an understanding with the guards here. Understandings have been reached to smuggle you down to my own deck, where perhaps you can get back to the outside where you belong. This place is full of arrangements. But you must be quick. Are you ready?"

"He'll kill you when he finds out!"

She shrugged. "He may not. I think perhaps he likes me. Prahlad Patel is not inhuman, whatever you think of him."

"No? But he plans to murder someone else tonight. He has acquired some poor fellow's life-object and plans to have his holy man kill him with night-visions, whatever they are."

She said, "People have to die. You are going to be lucky. You will not die, not this night."

"If you take that fatalistic view, why help me?"

He saw a flash of defiance in her eyes. "Because you must take a message outside for me."

"Outside? To whom?"

"To everyone there, everyone who greedily spies on us here and would spoil this world. Tell them to go away and leave us and let us make our own world. Forget us! That is my message! Take it! Deliver it with all the strength you have! This is our world—not yours!"

Her vehemence, her ignorance, silenced him. She led him from the room. There were guards on the outer door. They stood rigid with their eyes closed, seeing no evil, and she slid between them, leading Dixit, and opening the door. They hurried outside, onto the balcony, which was still as crowded as ever, people sprawling everywhere in the disconsolate gestures of public sleep. With the noise and chaos and animation of daytime fled, Total Environment stood fully revealed for the echoing prison it was.

As Malti turned to go, Dixit grasped her wrist.

"I must return," she said. "Get quickly to the steps down to Ninth Deck, the near steps. That's three flights to go down, the inter-deck flight guarded. They will let you through; they expect you."

"Malti, I must try to help this other man who is to die. Do you happen to know someone called Gita?"

She gasped and clung to him. "Gita?"

"Gita of the Ninth Deck. Patel has Gita's life-object, and he is to die tonight."

"Gita is my step-father, my mother's third husband. A good man! Oh, he must not die, for my mother's sake!"

"He's to die tonight. Malti, I can help you and Gita. I appreciate how you feel about outside, but you are mistaken. You would be free in a way you cannot understand! Take me to Gita, and we'll all three get out together."

Conflicting emotions chased all over her face. "You are sure Gita is to die?"

"Come and check with him to see if his life-object has gone!"

Without waiting for her to make a decision—in fact she looked as if she were just about to bolt back into Patel's quarters—Dixit took hold of her and forced her along the balcony, picking his way through the piles of sleepers.

Ramps ran down from balcony to balcony in long zigzags. For all its multitudes of people—even the ramps had been taken up as dosses by whole swarms of urchins—Total Environment seemed much larger than it had when one looked in from the monitoring room. He kept peering back to see if they were being followed; it seemed to him unlikely that he would be able to get away.

But they had now reached the stairs leading down to Deck Nine. Oh, well, he thought, corruption he could believe in; it was the universal oriental system whereby the small man contrived to live under oppression. As soon as the guards saw him and Malti, they all stood and closed their eyes. Among them was the wretched Raital, who hurriedly clapped palms over eyes as they approached.

"I must go back to Patel," Malti gasped.

"Why? You know he will kill you," Dixit said. He kept tight hold of her thin wrist. "All these witnesses to the way you led me to safety—you can't believe he will not discover what you are doing. Let's get to Gita quickly."

He hustled her down the stairs. There were Deck Nine guards at the bottom. They smiled and saluted Malti and let her by. As if resigned now to doing what Dixit wished, she led him forward, and they picked their way down a ramp to a lower floor. The squalor and confusion were greater here than they had been above, the slumbers more broken. This was a deck without a strong leader, and it showed.

He must have seen just such a picture as this over the bugging, in the air-conditioned comfort of the UHDRE offices, and remained comparatively unmoved. You had to be among it to feel it. Then you caught also the aroma of Environment. It was pungent in the extreme.

As they moved slowly down among the huddled figures abased by fatigue, he saw that a corpse burned slowly on a wood pile. It was the corpse of a child. Smoke rose from it in a leisurely coil until it was sucked into a wall vent. A mother squatted by the body, her face shielded by one skeletal hand. "It is the time when the old die," Malti had said of the previous night; and the young had to answer that same call.

This was the Indian way of facing the inhumanity of Environment: with their age-old acceptance of suffering. Had one of the white races been shut in here to breed to intolerable numbers, they would have met the situation with a general massacre. Dixit, a half-caste, would not permit himself to judge which response he most respected.

Malti kept her gaze fixed on the worn concrete underfoot as they moved down the ramp past the corpse. At the bottom, she led him forward again without a word.

They pushed through the sleazy ways, arriving at last at a battered doorway. With a glance at Dixit, Malti slipped in and rejoined her family. Her mother, not sleeping, crouched over a wash bowl, gave a cry and fell into Malti's arms. Brothers and sisters and half-brothers and half-sisters and cousins and nephews woke up, squealing. Dixit was utterly brushed aside. He stood nervously, waiting, hoping, in the corridor.

It was many minutes before Malti came out and led him to the crowded little cabin. She introduced him to Shamim, her mother, who curtsied and rapidly disappeared, and to her step-father, Gita.

The little wiry man shooed everyone out of one corner of the room and moved Dixit into it. A cup of wine was produced and offered politely to the visitor. As he sipped it, he said, "If your step-daughter has explained the situation, Gita, I'd like to get you and Malti out of here, because otherwise your lives are worth very little. I can guarantee you will be extremely kindly treated outside."

With dignity, Gita said, "Sir, all this very unpleasant business has been explained to me by my step-daughter. You are most good to take this trouble, but we cannot help you."

"You, or rather Malti, have helped me. Now it is my turn to help you. I want to take you out of here to a safe place. You realize you are both under the threat of death? You hardly need telling that Prahlad Patel is a ruthless man."

"He is very very ruthless, sir," Gita said unhappily. "But we cannot leave here. I cannot leave here—look at all these little people who are dependent on me! Who would look after them if I left?"

"But if your hours are numbered?"

"If I have only one minute to go before I die, still I cannot desert those who depend on me."

Dixit turned to Malti. "You, Malti—you have less responsibility. Patel will have his revenge on you. Come with me and be safe!"

She shook her head. "If I came, I would sicken with worry for what was happening here and so I would die that way."

He looked about him hopelessly. The blind interdependence bred by this crowded environment had beaten him—almost. He still had one card to play.

"When I go out of here, as go I must, I have to report to my superiors. They are the people who—the people who really order everything that happens here. They supply your light, your food, your air. They are like gods to you, with the power of death over every one on every deck—which perhaps is why you can hardly believe in them. They already feel that Total Environment is wrong, a crime against your humanity. I have to take my verdict to them. My verdict, I can tell you now, is that the lives of all you people are as precious as lives outside these walls. The experiment must be stopped; you all must go free.

"You may not understand entirely what I mean, but perhaps the wall screens have helped you grasp something. You will all be looked after and rehabilitated. Everyone will be released from the decks very soon. So, you can both come with me and save your lives; and then, in perhaps only a week, you will be reunited with your family. Patel will have no power then. Now, think over your decision again, for the good of your dependents, and come with me to life and freedom."

Malti and Gita looked anxiously at each other and went into a huddle. Shamim joined in, and Jamsu, and lame Shirin, and more and more of the tribe, and a great jangle of excited talk swelled up. Dixit fretted nervously.

Finally, silence fell. Gita said, "Sir, your intentions are plainly kind. But you have forgotten that Malti charged you to take a message to outside. Her message was to tell the people there to go away and let us make our own world. Perhaps you do not understand such a message and so cannot deliver it. Then I will give you my message, and you can take it to your superiors."

Dixit bowed his head.

"Tell them, your superiors and everyone outside who insists on watching us and meddling in our affairs, tell them that we are shaping our own lives. We know what is to come, and the many problems of having such a plenty of young people. But we have faith in our next generation. We believe they will have many new talents we do not possess, as we have talents our fathers did not possess.

"We know you will continue to send in food and air, because that is something you cannot escape from. We also know that in your hidden minds you wish to see us all fail and die. You wish to see us break, to see what will happen when we do. You do not have love for us. You have fear and puzzlement and hate. We shall not break. We are building a new sort of world, we are getting clever. We would die if you took us out of here. Go and tell that to your superiors and to everyone who spies on us. Please leave us to our own lives, over which we have our own commands."

There seemed nothing Dixit could say in answer. He looked at Malti, but could see she was unyielding, frail and pale and unyielding. This was what UHDRE had bred: complete lack of understanding. He turned and went.

He had his key. He knew the secret place on each deck where he could slip away into one of the escape elevators. As he pushed through the grimy crowds, he could hardly see his way for tears.

X

It was all very informal. Dixit made his report to a board of six members of the UHDRE administration, including the Special Project Organizer, Peter Crawley. Two observers were allowed to sit in, a grand lady who represented the Indian Government, and Dixit's old friend, Senator Jacob Byrnes, representing the United Nations.

Dixit delivered his report on what he had found and added a recommendation that a rehabilitation village be set up immediately and the Environment wound down.

Crawley rose to his feet and stood rigid as he said, "By your own words, you admit that these people of Environment cling desperately to what little they have. However terrible, however miserable that little may seem to you. They are acclimatized to what they have. They have turned their backs to the outside world and don't *want* to come out."

Dixit said, "We shall rehabilitate them, re-educate them, find them local homes where the intricate family patterns to which they are used can still be maintained, where they can be helped back to normality."

"But by what you say, they would receive a paralyzing shock if confronted with the outside world and its gigantic scale."

"Not if Patel still led them."

A mutter ran along the board; its members clearly thought this an absurd statement. Crawley gestured despairingly, as if his case were made, and sat down saying, "He's the sort of tyrant who causes the misery in Environment."

"The one thing they need when they emerge to freedom is a strong leader they know. Gentlemen, Patel is our good hope. His great asset is that he is oriented towards outside already."

"Just what does that mean?" one of the board asked.

"It means this. Patel is a clever man. My belief is that he arranged that Malti should help me escape from his cell. He never had any intention of killing me; that was a bluff to get me on my way. Little, oppressed Malti was just not the woman to take any initiative. What Patel probably did not bargain for was that I should mention Gita by name to her, or that Gita should be closely related to her. But because of their fatalism, his plan was in no way upset."

"Why should Patel want you to escape?"

"Implicit in much that he did and said, though he tried to hide it, was a burning curiosity about outside. He exhibited facets of his culture to me to ascertain my reactions—testing for approval or disapproval, I'd guess, like a child. Nor does he attempt to attack other decks—the time-honored sport of Environment tyrants; his attention is directed inwardly on us.

"Patel is intelligent enough to know that we have real power. He has never lost the true picture of reality, unlike his minions. So *he wants to get out.*

"He calculated that if I got back to you, seemingly having escaped death, I would report strongly enough to persuade you to start demolishing Total Environment immediately."

"Which you are doing," Crawley said.

"Which I am doing. Not for Patel's reasons, but for human reasons. And for utilitarian reasons also—which will perhaps appeal more to Mr. Crawley. Gentlemen, you were right. There are mental disciplines in Environment the world could use, of which perhaps the least attractive is telecide. UHDRE has cost the public millions on millions of dollars. We have to recoup by these new advances. We can only use these new advances by studying them in an atmosphere not laden with hatred and envy of us—in other words, by opening that black tower."

The meeting broke up. Of course, he could not expect anything more decisive than that for a day or two.

Senator Byrnes came over.

"Not only did you make out a good case, Thomas; history is with you. The world's emerging from a bad period and that dark tower, as you call it, is a symbol of the bad times, and so it has to go."

Inwardly, Dixit had his qualifications to that remark. But they walked together to the window of the boardroom and looked across at the great rough bulk of the Environment building.

"It's more than a symbol. It's as full of suffering and hope as our own world. But it's a manmade monster—it must go."

Byrnes nodded. "Don't worry. It'll go. I feel sure that the historical process, that blind evolutionary thing, has already decided that UHDRE's day is done. Stick around. In a few weeks, you'll be able to help Malti's family rehabilitate. And now I'm off to put in my two cents' worth with the chairman of that board."

He clapped Dixit on the back and walked off. Inside he knew lights would be burning and those thronging feet padding across the only world they knew. Inside there, babies would be born this night and men die of old age and night-visions. . . .

Outside, monsoon rain began to fall on the wide Indian land.

Single Combat

Sociologists view urbanization as one of the most important trends in social change. Although urbanization is defined in varying ways, it is at the least a migration of people from rural to urban places. Urban places have grown in size, density, and diversity and have changed the spatial and social relationships within society. The United States has experienced rapid urbanization, and yet Americans have been uneasy about the city, some seeing it as eroding basic values and patterns of a more stable life. Among those who write about the city—from Thomas Jefferson, through nineteenth- and twentieth-century men of letters to twentieth-century social scientists —a persisting flow of antiurban values can be found.

During the depths of the Great Depression, a sociologist, Louis Wirth, wrote a paper that influenced many sociologists in their study of the city. In "Urbanism as a Way of Life," Wirth argued that the increasing size, density, and heterogeneity of city populations produced an impersonal, segmented, detached, and anonymous human existence wherein personal, intimate, primary relationships formed only a small part of life experience. "Single Combat" captures that sense of isolated, powerless, detached experience that Wirth implied to be characteristic of urban life and that others generalize to modern life by labeling it "alienation." This story exemplifies the bleak and pessimistic tone of much writing about the city and modern life. In contrast, over the last three decades many social scientists have discovered that Wirth's case is overstated—changes in size, density, and heterogeneity do alter social relationships, but much of human association, even in the largest cities, takes place in a personal primary group setting in the family or among peers at home, on the block, or in the organization. Primary relationships no longer form the totality of social relations, for much interaction is necessarily impersonal, but primary interaction is still an important nexus of relationships in modern city life.

Single Combat

ROBERT ABERNATHY

He came warily out of the basement room and locked the door behind him. Tense nerves spurred him suddenly to flight, and he started to bolt up the stair that led from the air well. He tripped on a step that was crumbling, barely caught himself, and stood, swaying, chest heaving, fighting down panic.

Take it easy. Plenty of time.

Deliberately he turned back to the door, made sure once more of the heavy lock. He thrust the key into his pocket, then drew it out with a wry face and, instead, tossed it at the drainpipe grating. It hit a crossbar and rebounded to lie gleaming on the concrete.

Feverishly, like a man stamping on a scorpion, he kicked the key at the grating. It hung, slipped though tinkling, and fell out of sight.

He was under control again. He climbed the steps without looking back, and paused in the empty alley. No one was watching, there was nothing there but the usual litter, in the narrow way beneath the blind eyes of high painted-out windows. Among soiled papers a garbage can lay overturned. Against the brick wall opposite, a pint whisky bottle stood, placed upright with meaningless care by whoever had drained and left it.

He looked at these things, the ugliness that for so long had seeped into his soul and almost destroyed him, with a new, ironic detachment, seeing them as temporary and devoid of significance.

Late cloudless afternoon lay like a blanket on the city. Above the squat grimy structures close at hand, the great buildings soared, flashing with windows. Above all, smoke smudges drifted, lazy in the smothering calm. In the streets traffic growled past, shedding gasoline fumes and the smell of heated asphalt. The alley stank; the city stank; even the swift river stank.

Head back, eyes narrowed against reflected sunlight, he snuffed its air that was rank with memory.

The stench of many summers . . . *Get up, I smell gas. No, it's the wind from across the river. The refineries there. Well, it's making the baby choke. Can't we do something?*

The everlasting cough and rumble, the voice of the city . . . *God-damn trucks, going by all night. Can't sleep for them. If I could just get some sleep . . .*

The raucous voices, the jeers, the blows, brutality of life trapped in a steel and cement jungle . . . *Hit him, run him out of the neighborhood. Hit him again. Dirty nigger, dago, kike . . .*

The pavement burning your feet through worn-out shoe soles, after miles of tramping on pavement . . . *You're too late, there's no jobs left. Move along. No, I tell you. No. No.*

The hate, growing always.

He spat against the bricks. He said half aloud, "You asked for it. When it happens—maybe, just maybe you'll know it was me, I did it to you!"

In that moment he imagined that the city heard him, that it shrank from him in fear. That a shudder ran through the miles of it, along steel and copper nerves, from its cloudiest spires to its bowels mined deep in the living rock, from the rich men's houses on its heights to its squalid tenements and slimy waterfronts.

Plenty of time. Three hours to go. He would be a long way off, watching, when the moment came. A garbled fragment of Scripture came to his mind: *They shall watch the smoke of her burning from afar off, and the smoke of her burning goeth up forever and ever.*

He emerged almost blindly from the alley mouth, brushing past people on the sidewalk. One foot before the other. Each step took him farther away from the basement room, the closed and locked door.

One foot before the other—so often, in weariness and despair and hatred, he'd walked these streets before. But now, at every step it seemed that the city rocked under his tread, the tall towers reeled toward engulfment, and the city was afraid.

The blind passerby, the walking dead, noticed nothing. They didn't see that he, who had been small and reviled, had grown taller than the towers, that he had become an avenging giant. . . .

Brakes screamed. He stumbled backward, shaken. He would have taken oath that the light had been green an instant before, as he stepped off the curb.

Engines snorted anger, great wheels pounded past over the uneven pavement. The street was suddenly wide and perilous. He moved back, eyeing the murky red of the warning light, and set his shoulders against the corner storefront, trying to still his fingers' quivering by fumbling for a cigarette.

He might have been killed. *Not now,* he thought, *not by a dam-fool accident!* Or worse than killed. He had a sickening vision of himself injured, carried helpless but conscious to a hospital, dreadfully aware that back there, not far enough away, behind the locked door one element was changing into another at an unchangeable rate, and time was running out.

Jerkily he snapped his lighter, but it obstinately refused to catch. He swore at it; then he froze. In his ears was the strident twanging of a plucked and broken string, indeterminable of source, stinging nerves already taut.

He looked anxiously right, left, all around. Then distinctly from overhead, in a moment's hush of the traffic, came an uneasy, tortured creaking. He squinted upward, dropped lighter and unlit cigarette, and sprang to one side. His heart banged painfully against his ribs.

Just where he had been standing, the guy wire supporting a heavy advertising sign had parted, throwing its whole weight on the angleiron brace. The sign sagged precariously above the sidewalk; the iron buckled and almost gave way.

He stared fascinatedly at it, oblivious of sweat running down his face. The sign teetered and didn't fall. But he had an irrational, frightening conviction that if he were to step back to the spot he had been in a moment earlier, it *would* fall.

That was nonsense. He tried to laugh at the nonsense, but his throat was too tight. He took a cautious step backward, then pivoted and walked swiftly away from the street corner. He kept to the outer edge of the sidewalk, and glanced frequently upward.

When he had gone half a block, he realized with an icy start that he was going back the way he'd come, back toward the locked room.

He stopped short. But he couldn't return to the corner where he had tried to cross. He stood wavering, again having to quell insinuations of panic.

Directly across the street there was a subway entrance. If he hadn't been bemused he would have noticed it as he passed before.

Of course—the subway: fifteen minutes to safety. He looked to right and left, and upward—with a new caution already become almost habitual—and hurried across the street.

Midway he checked himself so suddenly that he nearly fell. He turned aside, trembling; his steps had carried him to the very edge of a yawning and unguarded manhole.

Shivering with reaction, he faced the subway entrance. And all at once it seemed to him no familiar place, but a hooded gulf leading to a fearsome underworld. From down there, from somewhere below the dimlit stairway that was all he could see, a vast rolling noise ascended, and whiffs of air that was at once dank and hot and smoky.

There was danger everywhere, above and beneath. The bellowing of a train passing below was a triumphant voice from Inferno, mingled with a cacophony of shriller notes, the cries of victims crushed and screaming in the nether blackness. For life's own sake he would not, could not set foot on those stairs.

He retreated from the pit, and stood trying to think.

There were other means of transportation. Buses, taxis . . . But he didn't move.

In the street the late afternoon rush traffic surged, snarled, panted. Brakes squalled, tires whimpered, horns blasted ferocious warnings, metal rang. Somewhere a few blocks away, a siren wailed suddenly, rose and fell, sobbing of disaster.

He thought of mishaps, smashups, a million and one chances. He couldn't give up the solid feel of the pavement under his feet.

Plenty of time, he told himself. He ought to know; he'd made the settings and thrown the switch. *Keep your head; you can always walk far enough.*

Another thought, fleeting and dismissed—*they* could have provided him with a quick escape, as perhaps they'd done for the others who'd performed their tasks and left before him. But from first to last he had given *them* very little thought. He'd done their bidding, dutifully learned their slogans that were loud and meaningless as a child's rattle, knowing all along that *they* existed for one reason only: to make him the city's executioner. Their purposes in doing so troubled him not at all; he had his own motives.

Keep your head, and walk out.

Accidents. In a city like this, accidents were always happening. He must avoid them and he mustn't let them rattle him. He mustn't attract attention—be picked up, perhaps, and lodged in jail. There was still plenty of time if he didn't panic.

But the street was all in shadow, and on a great billboard atop the buildings opposite the light was changing, deepening with that late richness that comes before twilight.

He began walking. He watched his step, and watched the darkening air above. Perhaps because he was watchful, nothing untoward happened. Each block finished was a victory, or a step nearer victory.

Lights were coming out. Streetlights dispelled the dusk, and a multitude of colored signs glowed and blinked, beckoning to the people who were now more numerous on the sidewalks, as evening came on.

The lights said, *Here is food and drink, and here is music, and a moment to forget.*

The people swarmed like moths beneath the lights, believing them. They were weary and eager to believe. Today had been a hard day, and they supposed that tomorrow would be like today, as tomorrow had always been before.

He alone, pushing among them and past them, knew better. For most of these people here, there would be no tomorrow. For most of them—by now he had covered some two miles from Point Zero, which was the locked room in the center of the city, but even here most of them would never know when it came.

He didn't hate them; he even felt a little sorry for them. They were trapped as he had been. But he hated the trap, the city itself, with the venom of bitter years. . . .

He paused briefly on yet another street corner, and almost died there.

This far out, the streetcars ran, and one was passing, thundering steel on steel rails. As its trolley reached the intersection of overhead cables at the crossing, something caught, the line stretched tense and parted with a flash like summer lightning. The broken end came whipping toward him like a great snake striking, hissing and spewing blue flame.

His reflexes saved him with a leap he would not have thought possible. He plunged headlong, sprawling and skinning hands and knees against the pavement, and without pause was up and running, mind blank with terror.

With a great effort of will he checked his flight and looked back. Most of a block away, the stalled streetcar stood with people beginning to cluster about it—were some of them looking after him? —and a police whistle shrilled.

The whistle stabbed him with fresh panic. He sprinted across the fortunately empty street—remembering the direction he had to keep going toward—and dived into the shadowy mouth of an alley between lightless buildings.

As he ran through the near blackness of the alley something, a sixth sense or maybe a seventh, warned him, and he swerved like a football player avoiding a tackler. The section of cornice, falling soundlessly from above, shattered to bits and powder a yard away from him. Overhead, disturbed pigeons fluttered sleepily.

He plunged out into the open on a lighted but almost deserted street. For a bare second he paused—with the sense that to hesitate any longer might be fatal—then, recognizing where he was, veered to the left and sprinted again.

The sidewalk here was old, of bricks. Abruptly it seemed to heave and buckle ahead of him, striving to trip him, but he hurdled the rough place and pounded on. Up the rise of a gentle hill, and past the crest. Down there the way ended in a cross street, and there were no more lights, but beyond—darkness with a feeling of open space, and a remote glimmer of water.

He was almost there, he was going to make it.

Out of the parkway slewed a huge tank truck, taking the corner too fast, and as it skidded, jackknifing, the coupling between tractor and trailer gave way. The cab bounced up onto the sidewalk, snapping a lamppost before it stopped; and the tank rolled over, blocking the street, with a monstrous roar of crumpling metal. The lights all along the street went out, but moments later it was lit by the red glare of flames. Fire, belching black smoke, rose like a wall.

He spun round, almost falling, straight-arming himself off a brick wall with a violence that all but broke his wrist. He ran. There was no shred of doubt left in his mind that he was hunted—not, so far at least, by men, but by something mightier than any army of men. He ran as a hunted animal runs, making sudden shifts that might confuse the implacable enemy. There must be a limit to the number of traps it could set for him. . . .

Once more he swung into a street that led downward toward the river and pelted headlong down it, gulping for his second wind. Closer . . . closer . . . Along the edge of the parkway were warning lamps smokily burning, a wooden barricade, and beyond it the raw black slash of a bottomless trench. But he was past being turned back. He put all he had left into one great leap and landed rolling, clawing in loose earth that slipped treacherously away beneath him— But *earth!*

He reeled erect and staggered on for a few yards, feeling grass and soil underfoot, not concrete or asphalt, and seeing branches against the sky.

He sank down exhausted, and putting out one hand to steady himself, felt the roughness of bark. Gratefully he leaned against the shaggy trunk, clasped lover's arms around it. Under him were grass and leaves and humus, and insects fiddled plaintively nearby.

Not far away, beyond the excavation he had sprung across, loomed the fronts of houses with lit windows scattered like misplaced eyes, and the streetlights burned; and across the river, reflected in it, were moving stars of traffic and towering buildings like constellations. Between heaven and earth hung a red star, blinking on and off, a warning to planes, a warning . . . But here he was safe, for the moment.

The strip of park by the river's edge was an island, in the city but not of it, like the river itself, which a dozen yards away glinted with ripples and chuckled faintly against the stones of its margin. Here he could rest for a few minutes, try to think of a way out.

He didn't know just what time it was, but he knew it was late. Not too late yet, however. There was still time . . .

Time to make his way out to a safe distance—barring accidents. But he no longer believed in accidents.

Instead—he knew. What had been a prescient fear was truth. He cowered, seeing the city around him, whole, immense, living—the true Leviathan.

For three hundred years the city had been growing. Growth—the elemental law of life. Like a cancer budding from a few wild cells, lodged half by chance at the meeting of river and sea, proliferating, thrusting tentacles far up the valley and for miles along the hollows of the hills, eating deeper and deeper into the earth on which it rested.

As it grew, it drew nourishment from a hundred, a thousand miles of hinterland; for it the land yielded up its fatness and the forests were mown like grain, and men and animals bred also to feed its ever-increasing hunger. The long fingers of its piers thrust out into the ocean to snare the ships from all the continents.

And as it fed, it voided its wastes into the sea, and breathed its poisons into the air, and grew fouler as it grew more mighty.

It developed by degrees a central nervous system of strung wires and buried cables, a circulatory system with pumps and reservoirs, an excretory system. It evolved from an invertebrate enormity of wild growth to a higher creature having tangible attributes that go with the subjective concepts of *will* and *purpose* and *consciousness.* . . .

Its consciousness he could not imagine; its ultimate purposes he could not guess. But he felt the pain of flesh bruised against the city's stones and realized, shivering, how the city must hate him. No longer with the lordly impersonal contempt which he, like so many, had received as his birthright. It could no longer be indifferent to the vermin who were its victims. Now, for the first time in its three hundred years, it was threatened in its life.

And vengefully it had sought his life. He had not escaped. The city was very powerful and very cunning. It still surrounded him, waiting; it knew he couldn't stay here. Whichever way he looked, the lights stared and winked at him.

His thoughts raced. There was still time . . .

Time to surrender, to go back. He could hasten back to the locked room (but he had thrown away the key and he would have to get help to break down the door); he could reach it in time to stop the process going on there, as only he in all that city knew how. If he did that, he was sure, there would be no more accidents. The things that had happened had been designed to break his spirit, to drive him back.

Suddenly he sat bolt upright, dazzled by insight. Then he laughed—not mirthfully, but hysterically, viciously, turning his head slowly to survey the lights around him.

"But you don't dare kill me!" he said aloud. "I'm the only one that could still save you. You can try to scare me into going back— but you can't kill me, because if I die your last hope is gone!"

He got to his feet unsteadily, bracing himself against the tree trunk. But he felt strength flowing back into him, the strength of his hate.

"Try and stop me!" he said between his teeth. "Try!"

He forged straight ahead, walking and dogtrotting by turns. He no longer glanced up or down. Crossing a broad avenue against the lights, he laughed wildly when the fender of a swerving truck missed him by inches. He knew that it had to miss.

He laughed again when the bars of a railroad crossing descended in his face, and jogged chuckling across the tracks under the glaring eye of the locomotive—confident that, if he were not in time to escape it otherwise, the train would be derailed before it hit him.

A sign ahead said DANGER, and he laughed loudly and did not turn aside.

Along this suburban street were floodlights, and men working under them—a rush job, obviously, and a job whose supreme irony only he could appreciate. They were wrecking a row of ugly old houses, preparing ground for some new construction that would never be built. At this distance from Point Zero downtown, they were out of the radius of total destruction, but even here very few dwellings would remain standing after the blast and the fires. . . . He hurried past, ignoring the lights and the workmen, and broke into a trot again when someone shouted, "Hey!"

Then a rumbling roar began, and he looked up stunned to see a wall of masonry leaning above him, breaking apart as it fell. It seemed to fall with torturing slowness, but there was no time to avoid it.

Consciousness hadn't left him, but he was unable to move, and aware of much pain. There seemed to be no bones broken, but a ton of stone prisoned his legs, and another mass lay wedged across his chest, not bearing fully on him, but bowing his body backward across a heavy beam.

Voices, faces, lights floated in chaos around him. Hands plucked futilely at the wood and stone.

"Christ, he didn't pay no attention—"

"Don't stand there, get a jack!"

"Watch it, if that was to shift a little—"

He hung there in the glare of the floodlights, pinioned as if by the fingers of a gigantic hand. Those fingers needed only to twitch, the mass of stone above to move only an inch or two, and his spine would snap.

When they tried to free him with pry bars, he screamed, and they drew back.

"Wait."

"Who put in the call to the emergency squad?"

A siren moaned to a stop. More lights. Another siren approaching. Dizzily he glimpsed uniforms, the insignia of men who served the city.

He fought for breath and shrieked, "Fools! you're corpuscles! That's all you are—corpuscles!"

"Poor guy's delirious."

"Stand back, now, stand back."

He shrieked again, "I know, I know what it wants, but I won't—"

"Take it easy, fellow, we'll—"

"I won't—" The stone above moved by a fraction of an inch and his voice snapped like a string. His eyes stared past the faces and the lights, and he groaned, "No, no. I'll tell. I'll tell!"

"Take it easy now—"

"Fools!" he gasped. And in short choking sentences, breath rattling between, he told them. Everything; what was in the locked basement room, and how to find it, and how to dismantle it without exploding it.

There was still barely time.

With dazed looks they heard. "May be out of his head, all right. . . . But you can't take a chance with something like *that*. Got the address? Got all of it?"

Nearby a voice spoke crisply, rapidly, answered startled questions from a radio speaker. Far off, in the city's threatened heart, sirens sprang to life one by one and raced crying through the night.

"Come on, we've still got a job here. Bring that jack—"

But there was a grating sound, the ponderous mass of masonry began to shift downward. One inch, two inches, three— Those around threw their strength against the stone, but uselessly. The trapped man screamed in a terrible high voice and was silent.

The men looked helplessly into one another's white faces.

The city was merciless.